Control

Teir Marks

D1528596

To all of you who want to get lost in a world of sweet romance and sensual eroticism, I wrote this for you. Dive in and enjoy!

• • •

1

Alijah sat in the waiting room a bit impatiently. She'd been there since eight o'clock, and it was now going on eleven. She would have left an hour ago if she hadn't needed a job thirty minutes after her scheduled interview.

For the hundredth time, she found herself looking at her watch. She was tempted to get up and leave. However, after having no luck on the past two days' job search and her other two interviews being a bust, at no fault of her own, she needed this job. So, she had to stay.

Since she moved to Colorado, she seemed to be down on her luck. She'd been staying with her friend Lawrence, and she was more than tired of mooching off of him. Alijah had never considered being someone's assistant, but there she sat, waiting to be called into her interview. Truly a testament to how badly she needed a job.

Though she had been a secretary for a bit while she attended college, this was completely different — something many people didn't often realize.

She had always wanted to be a painter. She'd studied art in college and graduated with her bachelor's degree, but she knew that the road she traveled to fulfill her dreams would not be easy upon taking up that major.

"Ms. Douglas, Mr. Cayman will see you now."

The sound of the voice brought her out of her thoughts. She looked to her right to see a slender, blonde woman looking at her expectantly. Rising from her seat, Alijah followed the woman as she led the way into the office.

The first thing she noticed was brown hair and a voice like velvet that seemed to caress her. That voice she noted, however, was also angry.

The blonde motioned to one of the seats, and Alijah took it as the woman left the room. She was then left to listen to Mr. Cayman, as he had been called, finish his conversation, and, again, she noted he wasn't too happy.

"Resume," he stated, and his voice jolted her. Alijah hadn't known that she had spaced out. Pulling her resume from the manila folder she held, she handed it to him.

She sat in silence as he looked it over, knowing it wouldn't take him long. She'd only worked a handful of jobs. Her longest being the four years she attended college when she worked as a secretary, a position she hadn't been too fond of, yet it kept extra money in her pockets. However, no matter how much she despised it, here she was again, in almost the same position.

"I see you were a secretary for quite a while. What happened with that job?" Alijah looked up at him and his hazel eyes locked with her green ones.

"I moved," she replied simply. He said nothing and glanced back down at her resume.

"It says here that you minored in Culinary Arts." Alijah nodded. "That may come in handy."

Silence befell them again, and Alijah began to nibble on her bottom lip. Something she only ever did when she was nervous. Finally, Mr. Cayman sighed and leaned back in the high-backed chair, his eyes leveling on her.

"You're hired."

Alijah nodded her head slowly. "Okay, when do I start?"

"Tonight," Mr. Cayman began grabbing a card from his top drawer. "All of your belongings can be moved tonight, and what you don't need can be put into storage. I want to get an early start tomorrow and-"

"Wait, wait, wait," Alijah stated, cutting him off. "What do you mean move my belongings?"

"You were aware that this was a personal assistant position, correct?" He questioned, raising a brow.

"Well, yes, but-"

"A twenty-four-hour personal assistant position."

Alijah let out a sigh of her own. That part she was not aware of. She had merely thought it would be like any other office job. She had to admit that she hadn't read the entire job posting. She just knew she needed to go for it. Now she regretted that she hadn't.

She contemplated saying no, forget it, but she knew she shouldn't be so hasty. After all, Lawrence was a nice guy; but he would only let her mooch off of him for so long. To Alijah's way of thinking, if she took the job, she could save the money she made and then begin to look for another one when she had enough saved. Possibly even pursue her art career.

"Alright," she finally answered.

"Call when you're all packed," he stated, handing her the card. Again, she just nodded before standing and exiting his office.

Once outside the building, she hopped into Lawrence's car and headed back to his apartment. She was mentally drained, but she didn't have much repacking to do on the bright side.

Kieran groaned as he thought about the green-eyed beauty again since she'd left him two hours ago. His mind constantly reminded him of how they sparkled — contrasting against her dark brown hair and succulent deep caramel skin. Shaking his head, he cursed under his breath as he felt his slacks become tighter. Getting up, he made his way to the massive set of windows, peering down at the view.

What was wrong with him? As a grown man, the simple thought of a woman shouldn't turn him on so much, but it did. Perhaps it was the fact that he'd never come across a black woman with green eyes or that he had never been so sexually attracted to one.

Yes, he thought they were attractive. Though never to the extent where he wanted to pound them into his desk, but that was precisely what was happening. Maybe it was because it was all new to him. She was merely a novelty. He knew he would be over it soon and back to his typical milky, skinned blondes.

Kieran rechecked his watch. He'd given her a card to call his driver when she was packed; however, that still hadn't happened, and he was getting a bit frustrated. He wanted her to be at his condo by the time he left the office. Granted, that wouldn't be for quite some time.

Deciding to take his mind off of that, he got back to work. The last two weeks had been hard on him. He'd had to fire his previous personal assistant because she hadn't realized their relationship was one that only consisted of business. She'd thrown hints several times, and he'd ignored her. However, when he found her naked, spread eagle in his home office, that was the last straw.

He had commenced his search for a new assistant but hadn't had much luck until today, using his Vice-President of Operations assistant, Chloe. All of the women and the one man he'd seen had all been more interested in the fact that they would be living under the same roof as him and the possibility of sharing his bed than the actual job. Alijah had been different.

He knew from her shocked expression that she hadn't known the job would require her to live with him, which meant that she hadn't read the entire ad. That should have annoyed him, yet it didn't. It only showed that she was there for the job and not for him. The fact that she was the only one with more than a few months of secretarial experience helped as well.

Kieran didn't have any more meetings for the day, which was a testament to how lax his last assistant had been. He was accustomed to having them scheduled three weeks to a month ahead of time. Not last minute as she seemed to like to do. This was something he would stress to Ms. Douglas.

Going over the numbers for the last quarter, he was more than pleased. Profit had gone up three percent and, by his calculations, was still rising steadily. He knew that if his current deals were to go through, he would gain a profit of over thirty-three percent this year.

It was well after eight o'clock when Kieran noticed the time. It wasn't unusual for him to stay at the office late. However, he'd meant to leave before the sun went down. He wanted to speak with Ms. Douglas about some things. Timothy had called him a little after three to inform him that he was driving her to his condo.

Sighing, Kieran picked up his phone calling the older man and informing him that he was ready. After putting on his suit jacket, he gathered the documents he'd been looking over and placed them in his briefcase before putting his cell phone into his breast pocket. Once he'd turned the lights out, he headed for the elevator.

Timothy was already standing by the car when Kieran walked out of the building. He nodded, acknowledging the older man as he opened the door for him. When he'd slid in, Timothy closed the door.

The ride from the office building took about thirty minutes. Once they arrived, Kieran stepped from the car and headed into the building. Going over to his private elevator, he stepped inside, inserted the access key, and rode it up to the fifteenth floor. Stepping off, he unlocked his door before going inside.

His living room was dark as usual, but a light came from down the hall.

Making his way to the light source, he stood at the open bedroom door. He watched her silently as she sat in the middle of the floor, her back to him; she folded the clothes she continued to remove from one of the few boxes littered around the room.

Kieran didn't feel inclined to alert her of his presence; instead, he stood and watched her for a few more minutes before he realized if she turned around and caught him, she would surely think he was some sort of creep.

Lifting his hand, he knocked lightly on the open door. He expected her to jump, startled by the noise. Instead, she turned slowly, placing the garment she had in her hands to the side.

"Mr. Cayman," she greeted, standing to her feet.

"Ms. Douglas. Settling in?"

"Yes, I'm almost done unpacking."

"Good. I'll return within the hour, and we can go over your duties."

Without waiting for a response, he turned and left, making his way to his home office.

Alijah exhaled as she turned away from the door. She could already tell that working for Mr. Cayman was going to be a chore. However, she was willing to put up with him and his standoffish demeanor. She didn't have much of a choice, and on top of that, the pay was too good to let slip away.

Closing the door, she finished putting away the rest of her clothes. She'd already put her underwear in the top drawers and hung up her work attire and jeans. All that was left was to place her sleepwear and casual wear into the drawers.

After all of her clothes were put away, she went to the box with her personal and feminine items. She carried it into the en suite and set about putting the contents away.

Alijah was finishing placing all of the boxes in the corner of the walk-in closet when the door to the bedroom opened.

"Come. We have work to discuss."

With her back to him, Alijah rolled her eyes to the ceiling and made a mental note to lock the door when she was getting dressed and sleeping — seeing as he didn't know how to knock. Deciding that cursing him out for it wouldn't get them off to a good start, she merely turned to find his steely hazel eyes penetrating her. She had to admit that it was honestly the first time she had seen such a soft color look so cold.

When she took a step toward him, he turned on his heels and headed down the hall. It took everything in her not to roll her eyes again. Instead, she followed after him into a home office. He gestured for her to take one of the seats across from him as he sat behind his desk. She watched as he opened one of the desk drawers and reached inside, pulling out a tablet and a phone.

"Keep these with you at all times. They're essential for your job. This phone," he started holding it up. "Should never go unanswered. No matter what is going on around you."

He placed the phone on top of the tablet and sat both items down in front of her. She then watched as he picked up a stack of papers.

"This is your employment paperwork," he stated, holding up a small stack of clipped papers. "This is a list of duties required of you," he then told her, holding up what appeared to be a few sheets of stapled papers. "This," he began, holding up the largest stack. "Is a list of my business associates and competitors. Familiarize yourself with this." He handed her all the papers. "Your employment paperwork is to be returned to me first thing in the morning." With that, he turned his attention to his computer screen.

Alijah mentally rolled her eyes at the dismissal before taking everything he had given her and exiting the office. Once back in her bedroom, she closed the door, remembering to lock it. She decided to go through the employment packet since he insisted on having it in the morning.

Most of it was standard, and she filled it out quickly. She then came to a Non-disclosure Agreement. She wondered for a moment what he would need this for but realized how stupid of a question that was. Of course, you needed one when you owned a multi-billion-dollar company.

When she was finished with those papers, she decided to look at the list of required job duties. Most of it was standard for a secretary as well. However, there were some things that she hadn't done at her other job. The list included accompanying him to events, running errands, and cooking. That one explained why he said her minoring in Culinary Arts would come in handy.

She noted from the list that he was an early riser and liked to be at the office by seven each morning. Alijah didn't have a problem with this. She had always been an early riser, preferring to start painting early before the sun arose. Five o'clock had always been when she rose.

Looking at the clock, she found it was a little after eleven, and she knew she would have a big day tomorrow. She rose from the bed and headed into the bathroom. There were a few towels on one of the racks.

Turning on the shower, she stripped from her clothes before grabbing her body wash and a face towel.

After her shower, Alijah dressed in a tank top and shorts before turning her light out and getting into bed. She double-checked her alarm before getting comfortable on the plush queen size mattress. She had to admit, if nothing else, the man had sweet tastes in furniture, at least what was in her room. She hadn't seen much outside of it aside from his office. She thought it would be best not to snoop around when she arrived without him being present.

It wasn't long before her eyes closed and sleep drug her under.

2

Alijah awoke to the chiming of her alarm clock. She quickly turned it off before turning on the lamp next to the bed. Getting up, she stretched and padded across the soft carpet to her walk-in closet. Turning the light on, she looked through her work attire before settling on a black pencil skirt, peach blouse, and peach pumps. She lay the outfit on the bed before going into the bathroom to wash her face and brush her teeth.

After taking care of her hygiene routine, she headed out of the bathroom and the bedroom into the hall. Making her way towards the living room, she continued until she came upon the kitchen. It took her a moment, but she finally found the light and turned it on.

Going through the refrigerator, she discovered there wasn't much in it. She did, however, find some eggs and cheese, along with a green pepper and tomato. There was no meat to go into it, but she figured a veggie omelet would be just as good. She went about making breakfast while making a mental note to tell Mr. Cayman that they needed, or rather she needed, to go grocery shopping, especially if he expected her to cook.

Alijah plated the omelets and placed them in the microwave to keep warm while she started on coffee. He looked like the coffee type, which was verified in her list of job duties, while she preferred tea. However, after searching the luxurious kitchen, she didn't find any. The coffee had just finished when she heard footsteps.

Turning towards the entryway, she saw him standing, watching her.

"Good morning," she stated, sitting the coffee on the bar before retrieving the omelets.

She placed one by the cup of coffee and gestured for him to have a seat while she put the other in the spot two down from it. She poured herself a cup of milk and got two forks before taking a seat. Closing her eyes briefly, she blessed her food before digging in.

They ate in silence, but Alijah hadn't expected him to make small talk. She preferred it that way. The less she had to talk to him, the less she dealt with his coldness. It sounded like a good plan to her.

Once she finished her food, she stood and took her plate over to the sink and rinsed it off along with her cup before putting it in the dishwasher. She then exited the kitchen and made her way into her new bedroom. She picked up her phone and glanced at the clock seeing that it was almost six o'clock.

Alijah made her way into the bathroom, brushing her teeth again before going back into the bedroom and getting dressed. Once done, she decided to leave her hair in its mass of curls. She put a bit of mousse in it before spraying it with a bit of water. It didn't take long for her curls to set back. She finger-combed them before doing her makeup, which only consisted of eyeliner, mascara, and light lipstick.

After slipping on her shoes, Alijah checked herself in the full-length mirror inside the closet door. She nodded in approval before grabbing the tablet and phone she had been given along with her personal phone. Placing them into her black Coach purse, which she'd gotten from Lawrence for graduation, she turned off her bedroom light before heading into the living room.

She saw Mr. Cayman sitting on one of the black couches, talking on his phone. She looked up at the clock on the mantel above the marble fireplace. Who could he possibly be talking to at six-thirty in the morning? When he saw her, he told whoever was on the phone that he would call them back and stood to his feet.

Bypassing her, he headed out of the door, and she followed. The entire elevator and car ride were silent, and again Alijah couldn't say that she minded. She would hold off speaking to him as long as possible. It was just something about the man that irked her so. She was sure it was his cold demeanor, and she almost wanted to assure him that it was alright not to be an asshole some time in his life.

They pulled up to the office five minutes before seven. Mr. Cayman led the way into the building and past security while Alijah followed him to the elevator. They stepped on, and the ride to the top floor of the building was one filled with silence, making the journey seem longer than it was.

When they made it to the top floor, Alijah allowed him to lead the way. He stopped at a glass top desk that housed a flat-screen monitor, wireless keyboard, wireless mouse on a sky-blue mouse pad, a lamp with a white shade, and a circular silver base. A comfortable-looking white chair accompanied the desk.

Alijah thought that the area was beautiful. The desk was pretty dull, but that was just fine with her. She would have plenty of time to fix it up with a few small paintings and drawings.

"This is your desk. Everything on your tablet is on your computer as well. I trust you read over your work duties and the schedule I provided you last night," he stated, his hazel eyes piercing her.

"I did," Alijah responded.

Mr. Cayman nodded curtly before walking off towards his office. Taking a deep breath, Alijah pulled her tablet out of her purse along with the phone he'd given her. She sat both items on the desk before placing her bag in one of the two drawers housed by the desk.

Once that was finished, she set about finding the break room. She'd read over her duties the night before and knew that as soon as the workday started, he liked a cup of coffee, black — no sugar or cream.

She found the breakroom and wasn't surprised when she saw how big it was. She hadn't expected anything different. The countertops were dark marble, and the stainless-steel refrigerator in the corner was spotless. There were two tables with marble that each housed four chairs. She was, however, shocked that there was a stove housed in the room.

After looking around for a few minutes, she found the individual cups for the coffee maker and put in a dark roast. She waited for it to fill the cup before grabbing it and returning to her desk. She picked up her tablet and phone before making her way to his office door. She knocked and waited for him to call her in before entering, closing the door behind her.

She knew as soon as she had given him his coffee, he would want to go over his schedule. The man had been meticulous in outlining her duties and when she was to do them. Alijah also knew this because of her experience as a secretary.

On the ride to the office in the silence, she'd decided to go through all of the things on the tablet and rearrange the applications to her liking; that way, she would know exactly where everything was.

She took a seat in one of the chairs across from his desk and sat his coffee down on the coaster to the side of him. She then pulled up the schedule for the day and began to run through it with him. He was quiet until she finished.

Once she did, he immediately began giving her meetings to reschedule for later in the day and appointments to schedule for the future, as well as calling a meeting for the department heads for the afternoon. He then told her she needed to set up the meeting room.

Alijah remained completely quiet as he spoke. She'd brought up the dragonfly app on her tablet and allowed it to pick up everything he was saying. She'd used the same thing on her other job and loved it. When he was finished, he turned his attention to his computer, and she took that as her dismissal.

Standing to her feet, she turned and exited the office, heading back to her new desk. It was a quarter past seven. Looking around at the other offices, she noticed they were empty. When she'd come for her interview, a couple had been occupied. She figured the other people who worked on the floor wouldn't be in until about eight, or they only worked on the floor on occasion. So, Alijah decided she would find the meeting room before emailing him the changes to the schedule.

Kieran sat at his desk, replying to emails, and wondering how competent his new assistant was. She hadn't taken a single note when he told her of his changes and what he needed her to do that day. It was going on eight, and she had yet to email him the changes to his schedule. Granted, his first appointment wasn't until nine; she had time, but that wasn't the point.

He was tempted to buzz her and see what was taking so long. That and he wanted to know if she'd found the headset he'd left in the top drawer of her desk. He was sure he should have told her it was there, but he wanted to know how observant she was.

Kieran returned to the emails that needed his response and continued to reply to them. He'd just finished the last one when he got another email. Checking the time, he saw that it was almost eight-forty. He opened the email to see that it was his schedule for the day with all of the changes he'd asked to be made. He continued to scroll and noticed that she'd also made most of the appointments he'd asked her to take care of. Kieran was a bit stunned until his phone buzzed.

"Mr. Cayman." Her silky voice came over the intercom on his phone. "I've spoken to both Mr. Richards and Mr. Waggoner about a meeting. Mr. Richards would like to know if you can conference call for the initial meeting since he's in Rome for the next two weeks but wants to meet as soon as possible about a merger. Mr. Waggoner wants to meet on Friday this week instead of next Monday since he's leaving the country Sunday."

Kieran was quiet for a moment. He had to admit that he was impressed, even if only to himself. He had asked her to contact the two men because while he did need to meet with them, he also knew that they would give her a challenge. Another way he was judging her competence as his assistant.

"That will be fine, Ms. Douglas," he stated after a moment.

"Alright, Sir." With that, she clicked off the line.

Shaking his head, Kieran began to go over the information he needed for his first meeting of the day once again. He knew the information inside and out, but you could never be too prepared. His computer chimed five minutes before nine, alerting him to another email. He opened it, noticing it was from Ms. Douglas. It consisted of times for the meetings she had mentioned before.

Moments later, she buzzed him again.

"Mr. Cayman, Mr. Russo is here for your nine o'clock."

"Escort him in."

Kieran's door was opened to reveal his assistant and Maxwell Russo a moment later. Ms. Douglas stood, holding the door open with her body, her tablet pressed to her chest, allowing Maxwell to walk in. Kieran stood as the older man came to a stop in front of him and extended his hand.

"Maxwell."

"Kieran." They both greeted simply.

He heard the door close and listened to the light tap of heels as they crossed the floor. He glanced over and saw his little assistant sitting on the couch on the other side of his office. Kieran said nothing, and he and Maxwell got down to business.

He noticed she sat on the couch, not saying a word the entire time. His meeting ended a quarter before ten. He watched as his assistant led Maxwell out of the office before coming back a few minutes later and taking a seat in front of him. He'd been interested in Maxwell's proposal and decided that going and touring the man's agricultural plant would be best before committing to doing business with him.

"I'd like to set up an appointment to tour his plant," Kieran told her.

"I suggest going on a Thursday. That's the only day that all parts of the plant are operating. Monday thru Wednesday, it's only two different departments each day, and they're closed Friday thru Sunday," she informed him. Kieran eyed her for a moment.

"How do you know this?"

"I did some research while the two of you were talking."

Kieran nodded his head, impressed. "How soon can we go tour?"

He watched as she pulled up his schedule on her tablet, her green eyes looking over the screen. He found himself shifting from her eyes to her thick pouty lips. His eyes rested there for a moment before trailing down the delicate curve of her neck.

"Well, I can move your afternoon meetings this Thursday to the morning, as long as you don't mind them starting at eight and having meetings back-to-back. Including a lunch meeting, and we can go this Thursday," she informed him, pulling his attention back to her gorgeous eyes.

"That's fine."

She nodded before rising to her feet. "I'll make the calls and necessary changes and get with you on lunch suggestions. Don't forget you have a meeting at ten-fifteen and then a meeting with the department heads at eleven. I set up the boardroom as well as hooked up the projector. I ran off presentations that I found on the tablet scheduled for today. I went through the contacts on my email and figured out the number of department heads. I'll email the list I came up with to you. If I missed anyone, please let me know."

With that, Kieran watched her walk out of the door. Again, impressed.

3

Kieran sat next to his assistant in the car as they headed back to the condo. They had gone and toured Maxwell's plant, and he had to admit he was impressed and sold on investing in the man's company. He knew that it would yield a significant profit for himself and Cayman Industries in the long run.

He'd been impressed with Ms. Douglas as well. She seemed to have done her research on Russo Agriculture and the man himself. She was efficient, that was for sure, and damn competent. Contrary to what he had believed at first.

They pulled up to his building, and he got out, led the way inside, and over to his private elevator. He had given Timothy an access card to it and a key to his condo when Ms. Douglas moved in. He was sure to get both of them back from him and gave them to his assistant.

When they walked into the condo, Kieran went straight to his office. He had spent the last half of the day touring the plant and knew he had several emails to respond to. He assumed that Ms. Douglas would do like she did every other evening. Change clothes and then prepare them something to eat.

He hadn't been in his office ten minutes when there was a knock on the doorframe. He looked up to find Ms. Douglas standing in the doorway, her head a mass of brown curls. It had been that way earlier, but now there was something else about them. They almost looked as if she'd just been thoroughly satisfied. His thoughts immediately went to her writhing beneath him, and he began to harden.

Bringing himself back to the present, he signaled to one of the chairs across from his desk. He tried not to watch the natural sway of her hips as she came in, but it was a bit of a challenge. Something had to be wrong with him. He figured it was just because he hadn't been with a woman in a few months, and his body was telling him it was time.

"What is it, Ms. Douglas?"

"We need groceries," she informed him.

"Why haven't you gone and gotten any?" Was his bright response, and from the look on her face, he could tell that it wasn't the right thing to say.

"Maybe because I've been working just like you have." She shot back, rolling her eyes.

Kieran felt his lips twitch slightly, and he cleared his throat to stop himself from smiling. He'd only been working with her for the last three days, and already he knew she was a bit of a spitfire. He had to admit that he liked her more than his past assistants. Unlike them, she wasn't one for holding her tongue when she felt it should be said, and she hadn't taken any of his crap.

"Well, why don't you go and take care of that now."

"I would, except I don't know what you like. You gave me a list of things you're allergic to. There was nothing on what you liked or disliked," she responded, folding her arms under her chest, causing the action to push her breast up and his eyes to roam there immediately.

"Just choose some things."

"Or you could come with me."

Kieran looked at her with a raised eyebrow. She couldn't possibly be serious and wanted him to go, but as he looked at her face, he knew she was indeed serious. He had never been grocery shopping before in his life. That's what his assistants were for, and his housekeepers and nannies when he was younger as his parents worked hard to give him a good life.

For some reason unknown to him, he found himself rising from his desk chair and heading around his desk. Ms. Douglas didn't seem to need words as she led the way to the door and down the hall. They left the condo and got into the elevator.

Instead of pushing the button for the first floor, Kieran pressed the button for the parking garage. He didn't bother with calling Timothy and just decided to drive himself. He unlocked the doors to his black Porsche and got in.

When they pulled to the parking garage opening, he paused for a moment, looking both ways, his face a mask of concentration, before turning his attention to Ms. Douglas.

"Which way?" He questioned.

She turned her attention to him, and the look on her face was pure shock and disbelief. Despite her seatbelt, she turned in her seat so she was looking straight at him.

"You've never been to the grocery store? Please tell me you're joking." When he didn't say anything, her eyes grew double in size.

He sighed, not sure if he liked her questioning him. "No, Ms. Douglas. I haven't. So, are we going or not?' He gritted out, hands gripping the steering wheel tightly.

Rolling her eyes, she corrected herself in her seat. "Don't get your panties in a wad. I was just curious. Go left."

Over the next twenty minutes or so, Kieran followed her directions until they were pulling up in front of the market. He found a park a reasonable distance away from the other cars, and they proceeded into the store.

He watched as she got a shopping cart and proceeded down the first aisle. She picked up a few standard things before turning to him and asking if there was anything on that aisle that he liked. He looked around for a few moments before shaking his head, and they continued. The rest of the shopping trip went this way. They went down every single aisle, and each time she would ask him if there was something he liked on that aisle. If there were, he would get the items and place them in the cart; if there weren't, he would say no, and they would move on.

When they'd come to the coffee aisle, he wasn't surprised to see her place a few different types of tea into the cart. Over the past couple of days, he noticed that she didn't like coffee and preferred tea.

By the time they had finished shopping, the cart was overflowing. They waited their turn to check out, and when they made it to the register, Kieran couldn't help but notice how the cashier looked at him. He had to admit she was mildly cute, but she wasn't his type. He would do nothing more than fuck her and be done were he to engage in anything with her.

Kieran pulled out his credit card when the total was given and swiped it. He signed the electronic pad and followed Ms. Douglas out of the store as she pushed the cart. When they made it back to the car, they placed the groceries into the trunk.

They were headed back to the condo when he felt her eyes on him. They made it to a stoplight, and he looked over to find that she *was* indeed staring at him.

"So, how did you like it?" She questioned.

At first, he thought she was trying to be funny, and his temper began to spike, but as he looked at her, he saw that she was genuinely curious. He reigned his anger back in before turning his attention to the stoplight that had now turned green.

"It was fine. I don't think I would want to do that by myself, but it was okay." He glanced over to see her nodding at his answer.

"Could we get takeout?" She then questioned. "It's already after eight, and I don't feel like cooking this late."

His first thought was to tell her no, that it wasn't part of their arrangement, but he made the mistake of looking over at her. She was biting her lip, and her brilliant green eyes were staring at him intently.

"What would you like?"

"Whatever is fine."

Kieran took out his phone and called for Chinese takeout. They had just pulled up to the front of his building when he ended the call. He watched as she got out of the car and headed into the building. Again, he couldn't help but watch the hypnotizing sway of her hips and her perfect, round ass.

He groaned out loud in the empty car. He needed to get a grip because she wasn't his type. The sooner he found some woman to fuck, the better. He would finally stop getting aroused by his assistant.

She returned with a trolley, much like the ones used at hotels. Kieran got out and helped her load all of the sacks onto it.

He then got back into his car and drove it back down into the parking garage as she wheeled the cart back into the building. He got on the elevator and hit the first floor. The doors opened, and she wheeled the cart in.

When they got back inside the condo, Kieran again retreated to his office. He still had more emails he needed to reply to, and he was more than sure that Ms. Douglas would be able to handle putting the food away.

Twenty minutes later, he heard the intercom beeping in the living room. Making his way there, he pressed the bottom and lifted the covering to see that it was the takeout he'd ordered. After having a brief conversation with the delivery boy, he allowed him access to the elevator but watched him the entire ride up.

Once the food was brought up, he handed it over to his assistant while watching the young man journey back down to the first floor and off the elevator. Once the empty elevator doors closed, he covered the screen and headed into the kitchen.

There he found Ms. Douglas fixing plates. He took a seat at the bar and waited patiently for her to finish. When she was, she handed him a plate and a water bottle. She grabbed her plate and water and took a seat at the bar, leaving a space between them.

They ate as they did most times, in silence. Neither of them felt inclined to speak. Him more so because he had never been one for idle chit-chat; her, he believed because more often than not in the last three days, he'd learned that she was usually irritated with him. However, that didn't bother him.

Once he was finished eating, he rose from his chair and headed into his office again. There were a few more emails he needed to read and respond to. Just because he wasn't at the office didn't mean work ceased. No, there was always more to be had, more to be made; therefore, there was still work for him to do.

When he finally headed to his bedroom, it was after midnight. Stripping out of his clothes, he stepped into the shower as the hot water tumbled from the showerhead. Over the past few days, his thoughts drifted to Ms. Douglas as he showered, and tonight was no different.

He could imagine her there in the shower with him. Her deep caramel skin glistening as the water ran down her frame. Her naked body there for his taking, to do with as he pleased. He could see her perky breast, beautiful nipples hardening under his gaze. His mouth watered at the thought of feasting on those nubs. His hand sliding down her body, resting between her legs as his finger massaged her clit.

Kieran was hard just thinking about all the dirty things he could do to his little assistant as he slid his hand across his dick. Only when he imagined her crying out her pleasurable release did he spill into his hand.

Taking deep breaths, he tried to calm himself. If he didn't do something about his sexual frustration quickly, he knew that he'd go insane. Between showers and the dreams, he was a ticking time bomb, and he didn't know when he was going to explode.

4

Alijah woke with a start. Sitting straight up in bed, she was sweating bullets, and her breathing was erratic. That, however, was not what had her main focus. No, her attention was on the wetness between her thighs and the person who had caused it; the sexy man who was probably lying sound asleep in his bed just down the hall.

She picked up her phone and checked the time, noting that it was just after midnight. After loading the dishwasher, she'd retreated to her room, showered, and settled into bed for the night. That had barely been over two hours ago. Alijah flung the covers from her body and got out of bed, taking a deep breath.

Going into the bathroom, she started the shower and turned the temperature to cold. Her body was hot, and she needed to cool off if she had any intentions of being able to go back to bed. She needed to get at least a few more hours of sleep. It was Friday, and she'd learned from some of the other people who worked on her floor occasionally for projects that Friday was just as busy as Monday.

Stripping out of her nightclothes, she stepped into the shower. The cold water instantly began helping lower the temperature of her flaming skin. She knew she needed to get a hold of herself. She had only been working for the man for three days, and already she was having wet dreams about him.

She had to get herself under control. She was meant to be Mr. Cayman's assistant, not another woman who got all hot and bothered over him. In her defense, however, he was wet dream-worthy. The man had a body and face that could make any woman catch a heat stroke.

Alijah shook her head as she began to wash her body. She needed to stop thinking about such things. Her focus was work. She would work and save as much as possible and then pursue her dreams. Though that required allowing more people to see her work. She would be getting paid tomorrow, and she planned on buying some canvases and paints. Her room was large enough to section off a small spot for an easel and her supplies. She'd also left a few selves in her closet empty to store her pieces.

After her cold shower, she wrapped a towel around herself. She dried off and slid on a pair of blue cotton panties and a tank top. Climbing back into bed, she turned off her bedside lamp and stared blankly into the dark. It was a while before sleep finally overtook her, but when it did, she was grateful.

Alijah's alarm woke her at five, as it had every other morning. After making her bed, she pulled her yoga mat from underneath it and engaged in her thirty-minute routine. She did yoga three times a week and cardio twice a week. She hadn't been able to do her cardio recently, however. She needed to find a gym nearby.

After her brief yoga session, she rolled her mat back up and put it away before slipping on some shorts, making her way into the kitchen. She washed her hands before deciding on French toast for breakfast. Taking the eggs from the refrigerator and the bread from the counter, she prepared the toast. As she put the last piece on, she started Mr. Cayman's cup of coffee.

Alijah had just finished plating the food and had started making her tea when he came and sat at the bar. He was fully dressed, as always. Taking her usual seat two down from him, they ate in silence. They'd finished eating a little after six, and she'd loaded the dishes into the dishwasher.

Going into her bedroom, she decided to put on a lavender pencil skirt with matching shoes and earrings and a black shirt with loose sleeves at the wrists. She added a necklace and grabbed her tablet and both phones placing them in her black purse. She had allowed her natural curls to draw up the night before in the shower, so she merely finger combed them.

When she made it back to the living room, Mr. Cayman stood by the door. She glanced at the clock on the fireplace and saw that it was just a few minutes after six-thirty. She followed him out of the condo and to the elevator.

Timothy was waiting for them outside. Like every other morning, Alijah greeted him and slid in. A few seconds later, they were on their way. Traffic was light, and they pulled up to Cayman Industries a few minutes before seven.

Once they reached their floor, Alijah went about her morning routine. She first placed her belongings at her desk before going into the kitchen to fix her boss a cup of coffee. Once it was complete, she took the cup and her tablet into his office.

After they had gone over his schedule for the day and she'd made notes for changes, she headed back to her desk to make said changes and email them to him. Once she'd sent the email, she made her way back into the kitchen to make herself a cup of tea.

For the next hour, she called to schedule or reschedule meetings. She also confirmed that he would be at the Furthered Education Gala tomorrow night. It was last minute, but he'd been intent on not going and working tomorrow night. He'd stated that he would send a check; however, after telling him how tacky it would be for him not to show up; and how bad it would look on his company, Alijah was able to get him to agree.

She ended up having a working lunch like always. She was sure that she would never get an actual lunch break. Her boss was a workaholic, and her employment information had explicitly said she worked when he worked. Unfortunately, he always worked.

When five o'clock rolled around, Alijah packed up her things and headed to Mr. Cayman's office. She knocked on the door and waited for him to grant her access. She heard him call her in and opened the door. He was sitting at his desk typing away on his computer, most likely replying to emails.

"Are you ready to go?" She questioned, taking a seat in one of the chairs on the other side of the desk. She had finished everything that she needed to for the day and had done a bit of Mondays as well.

"No." He simply replied.

Sighing, Alijah placed her purse in the chair next to her. She still needed to go and find a dress for the Gala tomorrow, and she didn't want to spend the rest of the day and all day tomorrow trying to do it. She would give him another thirty minutes, and if he wasn't ready, she was making him leave.

After thirty minutes, Alijah stood to her feet and grabbed her purse. She walked around to his desk, taking his wireless mouse from his hand and placing it to the side.

"Let's go. I still have to find a dress for tomorrow night," she informed him, pulling on his arm. She had dresses, but none she thought would be suitable for tomorrow's event, and since he insisted that she was to accompany him to every event, on the off chance that there would be business prospects, she needed to be prepared.

"I still have work to do," he informed her.

She rolled her eyes. "No, you don't. You're just trying to do all of next week's work in a day. I need to find a dress."

"I don't see what that has to do with me leaving work early."

"You're not leaving early. You're leaving at a decent time. Now get your ass up, and let's go," she stated, becoming a bit irritated.

She could tell by the look on his face that he wasn't used to people talking to him that way. She was sure none of his assistants had for fear of being fired. However, she was in a class all of her own. Alijah had always been one to speak her mind and tell you precisely what she was feeling, no bars held. She gave it to you straight with no chasers. You could either choke or swallow. So, he could fire her or leave with her.

When he seemed as if he was going to protest more, she turned off his computer screen and hit him with a look her mother always had to make her mind as a child. It took a moment, but it worked wonders. She watched him rise from his seat before turning towards the door and heading out. She wasn't concerned with whether or not he'd follow her. If he were smart, he would.

Kieran slid into the car after Ms. Douglas. He was coming to see that she was more than a bit feisty. In working for him the past four days, she had been able to do what many of his previous assistants had not, get him to leave the office at a decent hour. He knew she was more than competent and often started on the next day's work before the current day was over.

He stayed quiet while she instructed Timothy to drive her to the nearest dress shop. He was aware that she needed to find something to wear to the Furthered Education Gala she was forcing him to go to instead of allowing him to stay home and work.

Fifteen minutes later, they pulled up to a little boutique. Timothy opened the door, and they got out. She bypassed him and led the way into the small shop. Not feeling inclined to look around, he decided to sit in one of the chairs close to the two dressing rooms.

Pulling out his phone, he decided to continue replying to the emails he was working on in his office before his little minx of an assistant interrupted him. He was so engrossed in what he was doing that he hadn't realized someone was calling his name.

"Kieran!"

His head snapped up at the use of his first name, and his body began to harden as his eyes locked with green ones. It was the first time she had ever called him by his first name.

"What do you think?" She questioned, motioning to the dress she wore.

His eyes traveled down her body. She was wearing a pink dress that stopped a bit before her knees. It was a simple dress with gold at the waist. It hugged her curves in all the right places. He continued to allow his eyes to travel down to her shapely, caramel legs. It took him a moment to remember that he was eyeing her openly and that she had asked him a question.

"It's a nice dress," he stated after he cleared his throat.

"Is it appropriate?"

"Yes, it's perfect." He found himself saying before he could stop himself.

Kieran saw the look in her eyes when he said that, and even though he had said it, he was hoping she hadn't noticed. She didn't say anything as she walked back into the dressing room. Putting his phone back into his pocket, he waited for her to exit again.

When she did, he stood and followed her to the register. The sales lady rang up the dress, and before she could reach into her purse, Kieran pulled his wallet out, handing the lady his credit card. She swiped it, Kieran signed the pad, and she gave his credit card back before placing the dress in a plastic garment bag with the receipt.

He led the way to the car and allowed her to slide in before him. When he was in, and they had pulled into traffic, he felt her shift and turn to him.

"I could have bought the dress myself."

"I'm sure you could have, but it was for an event you're attending with me. You'll never have to pay for anything that has to do with me or my company," he informed her.

"Mr. Cayman, while I appreciate…."

"Kieran," he stated, cutting her off.

"I'm sorry?"

"Call me, Kieran."

"I think that would be unprofessional."

"And it would be, were we in the office at the moment, but we aren't."

He watched her think about it for a moment before coming to some conclusion in her head. When she did, she nodded at him before turning back around in her seat — the conversation they were initially having forgotten.

Kieran led the way inside and onto the private elevator when they pulled up in front of the building. Once on their floor, he opened the door and allowed her to walk in before going in after her. He couldn't help watching the sway of her hips and her plump ass as she walked away.

Shaking his head, he made his way down the hall behind her until she walked into her room, and he continued to his. Undressing, he decided to put on a pair of basketball shorts. He would be lying if he said he still wasn't slightly feeling the effects of her calling him by his first name. His mind instantly went to her, moaning his name in pleasure.

Deciding he needed to blow off some steam before dinner, he headed out of the front door and onto the elevator. He placed his keycard into the slot and pressed the button for the roof.

Getting off the elevator, he headed over to the door that led to the room housing his gym. Putting the code in, the door unlocked, and he walked inside.

An hour later, Kieran was dripping sweat. He placed the weight back on the bar and rose from the bench press. Making his way out of the room, he closed the door, ensuring the automatic lock clicked. Getting back on the elevator, he rode back to his floor before stepping off and going into his condo.

The smell of spices hit him immediately, and his stomach began to voice its hunger. He made his way towards the kitchen, wanting to glimpse what she was cooking.

"There you are." His little assistant stated as he came into view. He watched as she went to say something else, but whatever it was became stuck in her throat as she eyed him.

Kieran knew she was checking him out, and he damn well welcomed it. He'd been trying to convince himself that his attraction to her was only because he hadn't slept with anyone in a while. However, over the past few days of being in her presence, he realized it was because she was beautiful in her own right. The woman had sex appeal, and it was as if she didn't even notice it. It was nice to know that he affected her as she did him.

"Um…" She began clearing her throat. "Dinner will be ready in about twenty minutes."

"I'm going to shower, and I'll be right out," he responded before turning and heading down the hall to his bedroom.

He took a hot shower and decided to dress in another pair of basketball shorts and a t-shirt. He slid on a pair of socks and headed back into the kitchen. His plate was already in his usual spot, and he sat down, watching as she sat two places down from him. Kieran was sure she suspected that they would eat like every other time in silence, but he was going to change that tonight.

"So, Alijah, how did you like your first week?"

Kieran knew that he had caught her off guard. Not only with the small talk but with the question itself and calling her by her first name.

"It was pretty good. The more I get used to the things that go on, the better I'll be at my job."

He looked at her as if she had lost her mind. She was already outstanding at her job, better than any of the other assistants he'd had.

"You do an excellent job as it is," he informed her.

"Thank you."

They lapsed into silence again, and Kieran searched for another topic that wouldn't seem forced. Most people that knew him merely thought he was an asshole, and while that was true, he was capable of other things when he felt it was warranted, and at that moment, it was.

After racking his brain for the next five minutes over something to say, he finally decided to go with something safe that wouldn't be forced at all.

"So, tell me. What made you minor in Culinary Arts?"

He saw her face light up at the question and knew that he'd asked the right one. This, no doubt, would get her talking. He honestly didn't care what they talked about as long as he could hear that voice like honey.

For the rest of dinner, he listened to her tell him how her grandmother got her cooking when she was younger and fell in love with it—trying different recipes and learning tricks in the kitchen. She told him she loved taking Food and Nutrition in high school and knew she wanted it to be a part of her college curriculum.

When they finished eating, Kieran stayed at the bar and continued to ask more questions as she loaded the dishwasher and put away the leftover food.

"So, where were you earlier?" She questioned as she wiped off the countertops.

"I went to the gym," he responded, watching her intently. He saw the moment she stilled.

"Is it close by? I've meant to find one to keep up with my cardio regiments."

"How often do you exercise?" He questioned instead of answering hers.

"Yoga three times a week, cardio twice."

"It's on the roof. It's private so that no one will bother you. I'll give you the code, and you can use it whenever you like."

She smiled at him, and Kieran thought he'd been kicked in the gut. She had a beautiful smile, and it was simply arousing.

"Thank you," she responded as she turned the lights out in the kitchen and made her way around the bar. She told him goodnight and then excused herself to her room.

Kieran didn't linger in the living room and made his way to his office. It was a little before nine. He decided to check his emails and go over some papers he needed to sign. Tomorrow, he would ask Alijah to work out with him.

No matter how unprofessional it was, he wanted her, and he would have her: one way or another.

5

Kieran woke the following day at six o'clock. After having a shower, he dressed in a pair of basketball shorts. He made his way down the hall to Alijah's room and knocked on the door. He figured she would already be awake. She had been an early riser throughout the week, and he was hoping that rang true for the weekend as well.

He waited a few minutes before the door opened. There she stood, in a pair of black yoga capris and a black form-fitting tank top. White and black Puma's adorned her feet. Her hair was in its usual natural curls, haloing her head.

"Good morning, Alijah. I was coming to see if you wanted to go to the gym today."

He watched her eyes roam over the contours of his chest and abdomen before coming back to settle on his. He smiled at her, letting her know that he was well aware that she had been checking him out.

"Um…yes. Thank you."

Kieran stepped to the side and allowed her to exit her room. He then followed her to the door. His gaze locked onto the swaying of her hips. Once out of the condo, he followed her to the private elevator and allowed her on before getting on himself. Reaching into his pocket, he retrieved his keycard, placing it into the slot and hitting the button for the roof.

Once on the roof, he led the way to the gym and put in the code, allowing them access. He held the door open and stepped aside, letting her walk in before him. When he entered, he closed the door, hearing the automatic lock.

"This is your gym?" She questioned, looking around the room.

"Yes. You don't like it?" He inquired as he watched her curiously.

Alijah shook her head. "No, I like it. It's perfect. When you said you had a private gym, I thought you meant a small room with a few machines. This is an actual gym."

Kieran smiled, amused by her amazement. She should have known he would have nothing short of the best in every aspect of his life. Money was no object to him.

"Well, I'm glad it surpassed your expectations."

He headed over to the bench press and took a seat. He watched as Alijah made her way over to the treadmill. Kieran was aware of her muscle definition, but he also knew that it didn't come from free weights. She'd told him the night before that she was one for cardio, so it didn't surprise him.

He lay back on the bench as she began pressing in the settings she wanted on the treadmill. He figured it would be creepy to sit on the bench and watch her. In the middle of his first rep, he heard her feet begin to make steady contact with the treadmill.

Kieran finished his reps and decided to move over to the squats. They had been there for about thirty minutes, and she was still steadily jogging on the treadmill.

Making his way over to do his squats, he ensured he was at the best angle to watch her. Her hair moved up and down with each step that she took. Her ample breast bounced ever so slightly as well as her perfect, round ass.

Shaking himself from those thoughts, he put all his energy and focus on his workout for the next hour.

He glanced over at Alijah and saw that she was getting off the elliptical. Making his way to her, he admired the way her body glistened with perspiration.

"Are you ready to head inside?" He questioned. She merely nodded, and he led the way out of the gym.

Once inside the condo, he made his way to the kitchen and removed two bottles of water. He handed her one before opening his own and taking a generous drink.

"I'm going to shower, and then I'll start on breakfast," Alijah informed him before turning and heading down the hall.

Kieran turned to look at the clock on the mantle. It was a little after eight. He headed down the hall to his bedroom to have a shower.

After his shower, he felt refreshed. He dressed in a pair of dark jeans and a Versace t-shirt. He slipped on some socks before making his way down the hall to the kitchen. There he found Alijah preparing a cup of coffee for him.

Sitting at the bar, Kieran decided to watch her as she cooked. She handed him his cup of coffee and went about her task. Once she'd gotten all the ingredients out, he watched as she went about making omelets.

When she finished, she handed him a plate before taking a seat with her cup of hot tea. They ate in silence, and when finished, he offered to help her clean the kitchen. He knew that he had caught her by surprise with his offer. However, she declined, telling him that it wasn't much and she would be done in a matter of minutes.

Kieran contemplated staying and making small talk with her but decided to retreat to his office. He had a bit of work he wanted to get done before the gala that night.

He'd been in his office for a couple of hours working when his phone rang. He glanced down at it to see that his close friend Nik was calling.

"Hello." He answered after another ring.

"Hey, man. What's been going on with you? You haven't been to our weekly games." Nik stated, getting straight to the point.

Kieran had known Nik since the summer after his first year in college, being introduced to him by Paetyn, another one of their friends. He was used to his friend's always direct approach. He had never been one to beat around the bush.

"I've been working. I'm looking to expand before the year is out." Kieran informed him.

"You work too much. I bet you're working now."

"When you have a company to run, your life consists of it, but I wouldn't expect you to know about that since you play more than you work."

Nik snorted on his end of the phone. "I work just as hard as you. I know how to balance work and play."

"Yes, and you play more than you work."

Kieran spoke to Nik for a bit longer before getting back to work. It wasn't long before delicious smells were wafting into his office. He glanced at the time on his computer and saw that it was twelve-thirty. He knew his little assistant was in the kitchen cooking something delicious. Deciding that she would come to get him when it was ready, he went back to work.

Just as he suspected, there was a knock on his door about fifteen minutes later. He called for her to come in, and she opened the door.

"I made lunch if you can drag yourself away from your computer screen long enough to eat it," she informed him.

Kieran cocked his head to the side. He was well aware that she was teasing him. The smile on her face gave her away, but it also made him want to tease her in other ways.

"I'm sure I can spare a few minutes for your mediocre cooking." He then threw back. Alijah simply rolled her eyes and left down the hall. Kieran smirked to himself before following behind her.

Kieran sat on the couch in his living room while waiting for Alijah. It was six o'clock, and the gala was due to start at seven. He was dressed in a black Armani suit with a black shirt. His shoes were black and of the same designer as well. His wrist housed his black and gold Hugo Boss watch.

It was another ten minutes before he heard steps coming down the hallway. He turned his attention in that direction, and his breath caught in his throat. Yes, he had seen Alijah in the dress when she tried it on at the store; however, now she looked stunning.

She had paired the dress with a gold doubled chained necklace and gold dangling earrings. She had on a pair of white and pink shimmering heels and a matching purse. Her hair was in its usual curls, but she'd pulled them up on the side and pinned them out of her face for tonight. Kieran was speechless.

"I'm ready," she informed him as she smoothed her dress down with one hand while holding her clutch in the other.

He couldn't speak. Kieran was too entranced by the deep caramel-skinned goddess before him. To keep from making a fool of himself, he took the safe approach and just nodded at her words instead of attempting to speak. Opening the front door, he gestured for her to lead the way out. As always, Kieran found himself focusing on her perfect ass.

They took the short ride to the lobby in silence. Once outside, Timothy opened the door, and they slid into the back of the luxury vehicle. The car slowly pulled into traffic, making its way to the event.

"Did you bring your tablet?" Kieran asked after a few moments of silence. When he didn't get a response, he turned his attention to Alijah, only to find her looking at him as if he was stupid.

"And where exactly would I have put it?" She questioned, looking over her person dramatically.

Kieran could feel his lips twitching but stopped himself from smiling. "How do you expect to do your job effectively if you aren't bringing the tools you need?" He questioned. His tone was a bit clipped, but he was a little annoyed with his assistant for the first time. She was showing her first signs of incompetency.

"I guess I didn't plan on doing it." Came the smart response that greeted him.

Kieran turned in his seat to glare straight ahead. It wasn't lost on him that his mood had gone from hot to cold, which was usually the case. His closest friends often stated that they thought he was bipolar. While Kieran always adamantly denied it, it might have been mildly accurate.

The rest of the ride was silent. The only sounds were that of the wheels on the road and the surrounding traffic. It was half an hour or so before the car came to a stop. Instead of waiting for Timothy to come around and open the door, Kieran opened it himself and stepped out. He headed directly for the entrance leaving Alijah behind.

He was mad. Alijah could tell from the tensing of his body. She would have said to him that she was only messing with him if it weren't for the fact that he seemed to be giving her the silent treatment like a child. So, instead, she allowed him to think that she had no intentions of doing the job she'd been hired for.

When they reached the building, the gala was held in; instead of waiting for Timothy like he usually did, Alijah watched Kieran open the door and storm out of the car. At that moment, she decided that she would put him out of his misery, but not before giving him a piece of her mind and telling him where he could put his little attitude.

Getting out of the car, she smiled at Timothy as she bypassed him, walking hastily to catch Kieran. When she made it to him, he was about to open the door. She placed her hand over his, and he immediately snatched his away before glowering down at her.

Alijah, never one to be intimidated, leveled him with a glare of her own. Her clutch tucked securely under her left arm; she placed both hands on her hips.

"I understand that you may be menstruating, but you need to come off it. You hired me because I'm good at what I do. Just because I didn't bring that stupid tablet doesn't mean I don't plan on doing my job. It means that I have another means of doing it. You also need to learn how to take a joke." She gritted out before batting his hand, which he'd placed back on the handle, away and making her entrance.

A few photographers were inside taking candid pictures when she walked in, but Alijah paid them no mind as she followed the elegant signs leading to her destination.

When she arrived, she found that the large room was decorated beautifully. She stood in the entrance for a moment just admiring the décor. There were people all over, dressed in various colors.

Alijah felt a presence behind her, and she knew it was Kieran. The man just gave off an aura of power, and when he was pissed, you could feel it tenfold. At that very moment, she felt like it was suffocating her.

Instead of acknowledging him, she made her way into the room and began to walk around. It only took her a moment to spot one of the three people she'd hope to encounter at tonight's event. Nathaniel Golding.

Nathaniel was in his mid-fifties, had no kids, never married, and had a thing for the younger woman. He was also the Chief Founding Operator of Golding Technologies. His company was the number one leader in overseas technological advances. However, what made his company special was that production took place in the United States and was merely sold and marketed there and overseas.

Alijah knew that Kieran wanted to become an investor in the company that had, in fifteen years, become known around the world. She knew he wanted to sit on the board as well, but tonight, she would be taking baby steps.

Making her way over to the bar, she ordered a Scotch and coke and a glass of champagne. With her clutch still tucked neatly under her arm, she grabbed both drinks and made her way over to Nathaniel. She stopped a few feet from him, and when he turned to look at her, mid-sentence with whoever he was talking to, she smiled at him and raised the glass of Scotch slightly.

She could only assume that he'd excused himself from the young man he was talking to as Alijah watched him pat the man on the back before closing the short space between them. She extended his drink and watched him take a sip as he eyed her.

"Scotch and coke," he stated after taking his sip. "How did you know?"

Alijah shrugged indifferently. "It's a real man's drink," she replied before taking a sip of her champagne.

Truth be told, Alijah had done a bit of research when the invitation to the gala had first been presented to her boss. She felt that it was her job to know about the possible business opportunities beforehand. It's what made her good at what she did. She researched each person. Got to know them a little intimately without their knowledge, but when presenting it to said person, it was almost as if it were coincidental—second nature.

"Well, Miss..." Nathaniel started, trailing off.

"Douglas." Alijah supplied.

"Ms. Douglas. To what do I owe the pleasure of such alluring company."

"I wanted to congratulate you on opening your new technical research center, Mr. Golding," she replied casually, taking another sip of the cold liquid.

"Thank you, and please, call me Nathaniel."

Alijah smiled at him. "I would love to, Mr. Golding; however, I'm here on business," she responded, gazing up at him.

"I see, and what is it that you're going to offer me?" He inquired.

Alijah took another drink of her champagne, slowly swallowing to build the anticipation. Her eyes locked on his when she brought the glass down from her lips. "A big fish."

Alijah had spent the past hour and a half talking business. The first thirty minutes of it had been to Nathaniel Golding. She'd spoken to him about what an asset Kieran would be as an investor while also pointing out to the man what he could gain from such a business relationship. She had made it sound like he was the one gaining everything, and Kieran would merely get a small piece. When in all actuality, it was a win for both of them.

She did not doubt that all Kieran would need was an initial business meeting with the older man to get his foot in the door as far as being on the board went. Being ever effective at her job, she was able to get a meeting scheduled. It wasn't as soon as she wanted and was actually over four weeks away, but she knew that Mr. Golding was a busy man and, therefore, she would take what she could get. After all, it was better than anything Kieran had accomplished on his own or with his other assistants.

However, there was a catch. Alijah had to agree to be present when the meeting took place. That wasn't a big deal to her. She was always present at her boss' meetings, taking notes and doing fly by her seat research. The difference this time was that he wanted to have a meeting at the country club, and she knew that meant golfing.

The next forty-five minutes had been spent talking to Wayne Farley. Wayne was a man around Kieran's age who'd just taken over his family's solar energy company. They were currently looking for ways to maximize the solar industries and lower the costs of everyday products while going green.

Alijah knew that Kieran was looking to get into the organic fruits and vegetable business. It was one of the reasons he'd made the trip to the agricultural plant earlier in the week. He wanted his entire building to run on solar panel lighting. Farley Solar Enterprises was leading the way with their revolutionary products, and she knew these were the people Kieran would want to enlist to get the job done.

Her approach with him had been different than it was with Mr. Golding. Wayne was far more interested in looking at her breast than hearing what she had to say. She grabbed his chin at one point, forcing him to look at her. She told him if he wasn't going to take her seriously, she could take her chance of a lifetime business somewhere else and give it to someone more deserving.

He had sobered up and given her his undivided attention at those words. Just like with Mr. Golding, she knew that getting the initial appointment was the thing standing in the way. There was little time to take on new projects with control switching hands recently without Wayne getting overwhelmed.

However, she persuaded him to sit down, even if it was only for half an hour, and listen to the idea Kieran had. She hadn't gone too much into detail, feeling that wasn't her place.

After a while of thought, he agreed and set their meeting for two months. Alijah wanted to push for something earlier but knew that Kieran was just in the beginning phases of finding the contractors for his latest business endeavor.

Unfortunately, she hadn't seen Corey Wexler. Then again, she knew she shouldn't have expected to. She had heard the man was hard to get in touch with, and the rumors were proving to be true.

Making her way to one of the tables, she grabbed a glass of champagne off of the tray of a passing waiter before having a seat. She had already put the meetings in her calendar and saved their contact information. Each had given her their direct office line, claiming to have liked her drive. She was sure Mr. Golding probably had. Wayne, however, she figured liked her breast more than anything.

Alijah sat sipping her champagne and listening as they called out the names of the businesses in attendance and the hefty amounts they gave in the pursuit of higher education. She was impressed by the amount they had raised in that single night.

She had just finished her glass when she felt that presence again. Kieran's aura was unmistakable, and he was just as mad, if not more so than he had been in the car.

"We're leaving." Was the only thing he said before she felt that dominating aura retreating.

Sighing, Alijah rose from her seat and followed him leisurely. She'd had about enough of his attitude. When she made it outside, he was already seated in the car, on the far side by the door.

She smiled at Timothy as she got in, and he closed the door behind her.

The silence was thick in the air, but she wasn't going to be the one to break it. She didn't feel inclined to apologize to him for her earlier words, and she wouldn't. It wasn't her fault that the man couldn't take a joke and seemed to have rattlesnakes up his ass.

When they arrived back at the condo, the ride on the elevator was pure agony. Alijah could feel him staring a hole into the side of her head, but she refused to acknowledge him, and it took everything she had not to snap at him. As they walked into his condo and the door closed, the silence was broken.

"Do you want to lose your job?"

Turning on him, Alijah had fire in her eyes from his audacity to ask her that question. "Are you serious right now?" She fired off.

"I told you that your purpose in accompanying me was for business prospects. I didn't even want to go to that damn thing in the first place." Kieran grounded out through clenched teeth.

Alijah looked at him as if he were crazy because she just knew he had to be. Bringing up the calendar on her phone, she pulled up both of the meetings she'd set up for him before slamming the phone into his chest. She then brushed past him, heading to her room.

"What the hell is this?" Kieran snapped.

Alijah stopped walking and took a deep, calming breath. "Meetings I set up for your ungrateful ass with Nathaniel Golding and Wayne Farley. You're welcome." She threw over her shoulder, adding the ever-present sarcasm to her last two words.

Once in her room, Alijah began to undress and headed into the bathroom. She felt that she deserved a much-needed shower and the privilege of sleeping in tomorrow. He could find himself something to eat for breakfast, and if not, she was happy to watch him starve.

● ● ●

6

Four weeks. It had been four weeks since the Furthered Education Gala. Meaning it had been four weeks since his little assistant had said anything to him if it wasn't work-related. She went out of her way to avoid him. When he woke in the morning, she would have breakfast already done and set aside for him, but she would be nowhere in sight.

That is...after she started back cooking breakfast. For a week, she hadn't even bothered. Kieran was undoubtedly mad the first couple of days, but he figured he deserved it for the way he acted. He wouldn't, however, admit to this aloud.

He noticed reasonably soon that it didn't matter what he said to her; if it wasn't regarding work, she wasn't answering him. It was frustrating, and if she were anyone else, he would have fired her. However, she'd proven to be his best assistant yet and had succeeded in doing something his others hadn't been able to do, get him meetings with two of the hardest to reach men in the business world.

While he put up with her behavior, it didn't mean he liked it. Kieran often wanted to bend her over his desk and spank her caramel ass cheeks until they were warm and red. Each time he thought this way, he had to deal with his hardening dick.

Sighing, he stood and walked over to the floor-to-ceiling windows. He looked out over the city. As always, he enjoyed the view. It was well after seven o'clock, and the sun was beginning to set. There was still work that he wanted to do, but that wasn't to say that it needed to be done right at that moment. He was ahead by a few days, but it wasn't his nature not to be busy.

Kieran had started his company from the ground up right out of college, and it wasn't from him slacking. Now, fourteen years later, he could honestly say he was a self-made man. His company was booming, and he intended to keep it that way.

He heard the door to his office open, and he knew that it was Alijah. She decided she wouldn't knock on his door since she was pissed at him, and Kieran didn't care. He knew that he should apologize. He knew that he probably should have that night, but he was stubborn, and unfortunately, it was standing in his way.

"We have the meeting with Mr. Golding tomorrow morning at nine. It's at the country club." He heard her smooth velvet voice, but he didn't turn to acknowledge her when he spoke.

"I hate golf," he stated simply. If he were honest, he would admit to trying to rile her up. She was feisty. The more he riled her up, the more he imagined what he could do to punish her and put her in her place.

"Well, suck it up for a few hours or blow a potential deal. Your choice."

He could tell by the tone of her voice she was annoyed with him, but that was the norm as of late. It was silent for a few moments, but he knew she hadn't left. He hadn't heard the sound of her heels or the door closing. His theory was proven correct when she spoke.

"I'm leaving." That was all she said, and then he heard her retreating.

Kieran continued to look out of the windows for a few more minutes before going back to his computer to get a few more hours of work done.

The ride was silent the next afternoon, but Kieran had become used to it by this time. They were heading to the office after they met with Nathaniel Golding. He'd stayed out with the older man for a few hours. His little assistant was ever-present, sitting in the golf cart. While the activity hadn't been too strenuous, Kieran needed to change and decided to have a shower as well when he got to the office.

Once inside his office, Kieran went straight to the bathroom after closing his office door behind him. He started the shower, looked through the closet, and chose one of the suits he kept there. It wasn't unusual for him to work through the night and need a change of clothes and a shower the following morning or go out of town at the last minute and not have time to go to the condo and pack.

Kieran stripped out of his clothes, stepped into the shower, and began to wash his body. He grabbed a towel and wrapped it around his waist when he finished. He stilled when he heard what he thought was his little assistant calling his name over the phone intercom. He opened the door to ask her to repeat herself. He was halfway to his desk when his office door opened.

He turned, finding his assistant standing there with her eyes on him. He watched her as her eyes roamed over his chest since he stood in nothing but a towel.

"Was there something I could help you with, Ms. Douglas?" He inquired, bringing her eyes' exploration of his chest and abdomen to a halt and snap back up to his own.

"Yes, you have a call on line two."

Kieran watched as her eyes flickered back down to his abdomen before coming back up and landing on his. She then turned to leave the office.

Making his way over to his desk, he picked up the receiver, bringing it to his ear. "This is Kieran."

"Yes, Mr. Cayman. My name is Alex Connolly. I'm Victor Finch's assistant. I was calling on behalf of Mr. Finch to try and set up a meeting with you. He has a proposal that he is sure you would be interested in."

Kieran gritted his teeth as his grip on the receiver tightened. He was witnessing his assistant's first act of incompetence. He knew that she was upset with him, but to pass along a call that was her job to handle was not excusable, no matter how mad she was. Kieran had tolerated everything else she had done or had not in defiance of her job description. However, it had never been with something that related to his company.

Taking a deep breath, Kieran agreed to meet with the man and set the meeting for three months. For the past four years, Victor Finch had been trying to get in bed with Kieran on some business deal or another. However, Kieran wasn't a big fan of the man. His business sense was mediocre, and he was sure that had the man not inherited the company, he would have never been able to start it independently. Kieran figured it would be best and that it was just time to let the man know in person that he was not interested.

Making his way back to the bathroom, he proceeded to get dressed, all the while miffed with his assistant. When he was fully clothed, he walked over to his desk and pressed the intercom button, asking her to come into his office.

It only took a short moment before there was a knock at his door, and he found himself slightly amused. Alijah hadn't knocked to gain entrance since he'd ticked her off; now, she wanted to be the picture of manners. He called her in, and when she sat down in front of him, he leveled her with his cold gaze.

Kieran could detect the exact moment she read his mood through his eyes because he watched her green irises spark slightly and prepare for war.

"Is it not your job to handle all appointment setups and deal with other people's assistants?" Kieran questioned flatly.

"Yes, it is, and I pride myself on doing my job thoroughly," she responded.

"Well, your incompetence is showing. Why would you pass a call on to me from someone's assistant?"

He watched as she opened her mouth to protest but closed it a mere second later when realization dawned on her.

"I'm...sorry," she stated. "They told me they were a friend of yours. Otherwise, I wouldn't have passed the call on."

Kieran saw the honesty in her words. He nodded his head slightly before leaning back in the seat.

"Any friend of mine has my direct office number and cell phone number," he informed her. She merely nodded before shifting in her seat.

"Simon needs you to approve the expense reports he sent up on Monday. You've been putting it off, and it needs to get done. We also need to get the presentation together for the next department heads' meeting concerning your new business venture," she stated.

"That's fine." Kieran agreed. "Order lunch in for the both of us," he informed her. He was more than sure she was tired of working through her lunch, but it came along with the job more often than not.

Alijah sighed, rising from her chair. "I already did. It should be here any minute. I'll bring it along with the expense reports," she stated, turning her back to him and heading out of the door.

"Thank you, beautiful," Kieran responded before he had time to stop himself. He watched as her steps faltered, but she didn't turn around to look at him. Continuing out, she closed the door behind her.

Alijah was in a haze. Her mind was in a fog as her body went about the task at hand. She went over the expense reports with Kieran, but she wasn't hearing him or seeing what she was doing, for that matter. No, the movements were familiar, and she went through them with little effort on her part. It had become second nature to her over the last few weeks.

Boredom, however, was not what was causing her mind to be in an entirely different place. No, what had Alijah preoccupied was the man sitting across from her, or better yet, the words he spoke a mere hour ago. A single word if she wanted to get technical.

He had called her beautiful, and Alijah had been stuck on that fact ever since. She didn't know if he meant to say it or not, but he had, and now she wondered why.

It wasn't as if she hadn't heard it before. Throughout high school and especially in college, she had heard it slip from the mouths of multiple boys. Granted, she had never been interested in most of them. She knew their types. Telling a girl what they thought she wanted to hear to get into her pants. Alijah had never been that girl. Never one to fall for simple words.

To her credit, she knew she was pretty, but she didn't go around trying to flaunt it and throw it into people's faces. She simply had self-confidence. That was enough to keep her from falling for any juvenile compliment thrown her way — that and self-respect.

So, the fact that her boss had called her beautiful was something she didn't quite know how she should handle because they worked together; it was unprofessional. She was going to stop dwelling on it and pretend to the best of her abilities that it hadn't happened. That is, whenever she could force her uncooperative brain to shake the thought.

Alijah had been so deep in her thoughts that she didn't notice at first that Kieran had spoken. It took her a minute to process what she thought she heard.

"Will that work?" Those were the words that caught her attention.

Alijah thought hard about what he could have been talking about and came up empty. She was so far spaced that she hadn't even been able to store his words in the hollow of her mind while her brain was otherwise occupied.

She contemplated asking him what he was referring to for a minute, but after the blunder she'd made earlier, patching someone's assistant through, she didn't want to seem incompetent. She thought about briefly telling him no. Then, if fire sparked behind those hazel eyes, she would know that it was something he needed her help with. She decided to stick closer to the safe side and gave him the answer she knew he expected. Even if she didn't know what he was talking about.

"Yes, that should be fine."

"Good, because Francis Deveaux will be in town for a few hours tonight, and he is willing to meet."

At that, Alijah was happy she hadn't deliberately told him no. She knew that Kieran wanted Mr. Deveaux as the architect for his new project. She couldn't blame him. The man's work spoke volumes in itself.

She had done in-depth research on him when Kieran first stated he wanted him as his architect. Alijah had found over the last few years in her time as a personal assistant that when you connected with someone on one or more of their interests, it was often easier to get them to open up and speak with you. You seemed genuine and not as if you were trying to poach their time.

So, as always, she'd looked into the man, spent several hours going over the personal information offered by the internet and looking at his works. While his new projects were exquisite, Alijah found herself more partial to his earlier works.

As an artist, she could tell that it was before he had entirely found himself, fully discovered the type of architect he wanted to be. Therefore, when she'd contacted him inquiring about a moment of his time, she told him as much. He hadn't been offended that she wasn't as big a fan of his modern structures, to her surprise. He'd laughed and told her he liked a person that spoke their mind.

However, while their conversation had been good, he hadn't promised her a meeting. More so to say, he hadn't been able to nail down a date. He merely told her that he was a busy man and would drop in when he had the time. That had been three weeks ago, and she had to say she was happy he had the time so soon.

"So, what I'm going to need from you is working late into the night. Order something for dinner and have it delivered.

I've got one night to make my initial pitch, and he's on a red-eye out of here."

Alijah was quiet for a moment. While she knew this was last minute notice for both of them, she felt there was something they should be able to do to make this meeting magical. To make sure that he remembered his time at Cayman Industries and wanted to jump on board.

"Did you offer him the use of the company jet? That way, it gives you more time to talk to him?" Alijah finally asked.

"Yes, but the man is eccentric and dead set on keeping his schedule the way it is."

Alijah nodded before speaking again. "Alright, well, let me cook something for the meeting. It'll show him that we went out of our way to make something for him. I can even find out what his favorite dish is."

"I'm not going to allow you the rest of the day off to go shopping and then to the condo to cook."

"No one said I needed the rest of the day. I can give a list to Timothy and have him run to the market for me if he doesn't mind, and I can cook it here. Did you forget that there was a full kitchen in the break room?"

She watched him as he thought for a moment. Those hazel eyes were unblinking at her. It felt like an eternity before he answered her.

"Alright, as long as it doesn't interfere with your work."

"It won't. I'll start cooking at about seven or so. That should give me plenty of time to have it done before he gets here."

Kieran nodded his agreement. With that, Alijah gathered the completed expense reports and rose from her seat to take them to Simon before researching precisely what types of foods Francis Deveaux indulged in.

It was going on seven o'clock as Alijah sat in Kieran's office researching on her tablet. She had given him a few companies to look over that could supply materials for the greenhouse he was going to build, and she was waiting on him to provide her with a decision so she could contact them. While she waited, she looked at the different land areas for sale. Alijah didn't know how big Kieran was planning to build his greenhouse. She hadn't seen the blueprints yet.

"I want this company," Kieran stated, pulling her from her research. She looked at the file he set across the table in front of her.

Alijah frowned slightly. She hadn't expected him to choose that company. She had presented him with several large companies that could, without a doubt, supply all of the materials he needed. However, he had chosen the smallest of the companies. She had included them because they had terrific reviews, but all of their projects had been small. She wasn't sure they could handle his demand.

"Why this one?" She knew it was probably none of her business, but she had to ask.

"They're small, family-owned, and would appreciate the business more than a bigger company which is probably corporately owned. Which means they would do a better job and supply the best materials," he told her without looking up from the business plan she was sure he knew by heart.

Alijah nodded, though she knew he wasn't paying her any attention, and returned to her research.

When she looked at the clock again, it was going on seven-thirty. She placed her tablet on the table and stood to her feet, informing Kieran that she was about to start dinner. Francis was due between nine-thirty and ten, which gave her about two hours to get everything ready.

Her research revealed that he was a big fan of Greek food. One of his particular favorites was Lemon Chicken and Potato Bake. It was a simple recipe. She'd only made it once while in school but was more than sure it would be delicious.

The dish would be served with potatoes as was suggested and green beans. Alijah had also deiced to make a green salad and whip up a simple salad dressing. She would serve their meal with a glass of red wine she had chilling in the refrigerator.

Timothy had been kind enough to take the list she'd made and retrieve everything she needed from the store.

Washing her hands, Alijah went about the task of preparing the chicken. It would take about an hour and a half to cook, so she wanted to get it on first. After turning on the oven, she went about washing the chicken before laying it out and seasoning it.

Once that was done, Alijah placed the chicken breast on a pan and waited for a few more minutes for the oven to heat up. She rewashed her hands, removing the seasoning before grabbing a knife and the potatoes. She'd asked Timothy to buy small potatoes, and he had, but she needed to cut them in half. She placed the cutting board, knife, and potatoes on the countertop before putting the chicken in the oven.

She cut potatoes for about ten minutes before she thought she had enough. She then placed them in a bowl and washed them off, letting them sit in the sink. Kieran walked in at that moment, spreading the blueprints over the table and looking over them again.

Alijah shook her head slightly. She knew for a fact the man could draw those with his eyes closed and, if he so wanted, build the structure in his sleep as many times as he had looked over them.

The food was nearly ready. All Alijah had to do was finish making the salad dressing. She'd decided to make her signature dressing from scratch. She had finished mixing it and was in the midst of tasting it when Kieran returned from retrieving her tablet, which he planned to use in his pitch. He caught her as the tip of her tongue traced up her finger.

Alijah turned to find him looking at her. She watched as he placed her tablet down and slowly walked to her. When he stopped in front of her, Alijah was forced to look up at him. He was crowding her space.

Suddenly, he brought up his thumb and wiped it over the corner of her mouth before bringing it to his lips. It was then that Alijah realized that she must have had a bit of dressing there. She watched as he licked it off slowly.

"Delicious," he stated in a husky voice.

Time seemed to have stopped, and Alijah was frozen in place as she watched him lean forward. Her breath hitched as she waited for his lips to meet hers, but they didn't. He stopped a hair away from her lips. His hazel eyes were staring into her green ones.

It was as if he was waiting, and she realized that he was. He was waiting on her to make that move and close the tiny gap that separated their lips.

Alijah knew she shouldn't, but she wanted to. Damn, did she want to. Even though he was her boss, she couldn't deny his sex appeal. Just as she had talked herself into moving that minuscule distance, his phone rang, causing her to jump back, startled.

Heart rapidly beating and a little embarrassed by what she had almost done, Alijah turned her back to him—going back to stir her salad dressing aimlessly. She heard his side of the conversation and figured that Timothy was about to arrive with Mr. Deveaux.

"They should be here shortly," Kieran stated.

Alijah was unable to find her voice, so all she could manage was a nod. She heard him walk out of the kitchen and exhaled silently. She couldn't wait for the night to be over.

Kieran was packing up his blueprints while Alijah went about cleaning the kitchen. His meeting with Francis had been very productive. The man had not only been interested in his designs but also impressed by the knowledge his little assistant held regarding his work. It shouldn't have amazed him how much she knew about Francis' work, but it did.

He had informed Kieran that he was about to start working on a project and anticipated that it would take several months. Kieran was alright with that. He was in no hurry at the moment to begin construction. He needed to get the rest of his ducks in a row. He was just glad to know that he had that part out of the way.

Once his blueprints were packed up, he turned to see Alijah rinsing the dishes. He didn't know what had come over him earlier. He'd seen her licking her finger and wanted to know precisely what her tongue tasted like. He didn't know what was coming over him at that moment either as he made his way to her.

He placed both hands on her waist, feeling her jump at the contact. Her body stiffened, and he knew he should have let her go, but something had taken over him. That was his only excuse. Removing his left hand from her waist, he reached over and moved her hair, exposing her right shoulder.

Kieran leaned in and placed his lips on the heated skin of her neck. He allowed them to linger there for a moment as he wrapped his right arm around her waist. He pulled her back against him. Hearing her gasp at the action, Kieran released her, taking a step back.

"I'll gather our things, and we can leave," he informed her before walking out of the kitchen.

Kieran did as he said and waited for her at her desk. He'd only been waiting a few minutes when she walked out. He watched as she grabbed her tablet and phone from the desk where he'd laid it and slid them into her purse.

When they stepped onto the elevator, it was like stepping into a sauna. The difference was it wasn't thick with steam; it was packed with tension. Sexual on Kieran's end, he was more than sure it was the same on hers.

Once in the car, Kieran watched as Alijah rolled the window down. He was sure she was attempting to alleviate some of the tension between them, a feat he knew wasn't possible that way. He was sure she knew that as well but had tried it, nonetheless.

When they walked in the front door, all he saw was a mass of brown curls blurring by him before he heard her bedroom door slam.

He made his way into his bedroom and headed straight into the bathroom. It looked as if he would continue his pre-slumber ritual of a cold shower. The one he started the day she stepped into his office.

7

He was testing her. Of that, Alijah was positive. She didn't know what she was supposed to do. What she wanted to do, yes, she knew that. However, she wasn't sure how he expected her to respond. So, she had decided to steer clear of him. As much as she tried, the man made it next to impossible. She should have known better, considering he was her boss and she lived with him.

Kieran was always flirting with her. Alijah knew she wasn't the most experienced when it came to men. She had pretty much ignored most of them while she attended college, but she knew when a man was flirting with her, and her boss was doing just that.

At first, Alijah wanted to believe his actions were innocent, but she knew better. After he'd done what he had in the kitchen the night of their meeting, she knew there was nothing innocent about it.

The man would make some comment, openly flirting with her, but say it just as casual as if he was telling her the weather. He would touch her some simple way.

What pissed Alijah off was that her traitorous body would respond to his comments, compliments, and touches. She wished nothing more than to be a robot of some sort so she could turn her emotions off.

The worst of it was the fact that she knew he was testing her. While Kieran would flirt with her or compliment her, there was never the playful glint in his eyes that most got when flirting. No, he remained just as withdrawn as she had ever seen him.

Unfortunately, she was at her wit's end. This had been going on for the past two weeks, and she was close to strangling Kieran. Her mind had resorted to violence and convinced her that it was the only way to handle the situation at hand.

Alijah looked at her watch. It was fifteen minutes to seven, and Kieran was in his office working. He'd been in there, to her knowledge, since she woke up. He even passed on breakfast.

She didn't want to, she knew that he would probably say something to get her blushing and her body responding, but she knocked on his office door before opening it. If she didn't get him now, they would be late, and she didn't need him saying it was her fault.

"We need to go," she stated when he didn't look up and acknowledge that she had walked in.

"Give me a minute," he responded.

Alijah sighed. The man was impossible. She didn't know how she put up with him because all he wanted to do was work, and his mood while working, most of the time, was insufferable. So, Alijah did the only thing she knew would get his attention. She walked over to him and turned off his monitor, swatting his hand away when he went to turn it back on.

"We have to leave now. If I let you keep working, we'll be late, you'll blame me, and I'm not about to allow you to do that."

Kieran sighed, standing to his feet. "I wouldn't blame you."

Placing one hand on her hip, Alijah cocked it to the side while simultaneously rolling her eyes.

"Yes, you would."

"No, I wouldn't, gorgeous." With that stated, Kieran passed her and headed out of his office.

Alijah stood there a moment in stunned silence though she didn't know why. He had been doing things like that consistently. She was brought out of her temporary daze when she heard Kieran's voice.

"Come on, Alijah, before you make us late."

She rolled her eyes and huffed before heading out of the door and down the hall. He dared to be standing there with a slightly irritated look on his face. She took a deep breath, and it took all she had to keep her hands at her sides and not reach up and smack him in the back of the head.

Alijah sat taking notes while Kieran and his department heads discussed the upcoming quarter and projects. Whatever was said went into her ears and came out on her tablet, but she didn't hear it. Admittedly, her body was merely on autopilot. It was more a learned behavior. Having done it over time, her body was equipped to go about the task.

She had been sitting in the meeting for almost an hour; her focus hadn't been on it once. She was more focused on listening to the deep baritone that sounded from Kieran whenever he spoke. Alijah knew she shouldn't have been, but she couldn't help herself. All of his testing had caused her to act in such a way.

The man's voice was deep and commanding but smooth like silk all at the same time. If she had to give a flavor to his voice, it was milk chocolate—smooth, creamy, yet always in control.

His voice seemed to make most of his employees shiver with fear. It made Alijah shiver, but it wasn't out of fear.

She was more than happy when the meeting was over. Gathering her things, she stood and made her way out of the conference room. She wasn't watching where she was going. Instead, she was looking down at her tablet, preparing to send her notes to her boss, when she bumped into a hard chest.

Alijah took a step back, and she probably would have fallen had it not been for two hands grasping her forearms, reaching out to steady her. Looking up, she was met with deep brown eyes.

"Are you okay?"

"Yes, it was my fault. I should have been paying attention." Alijah stated as she took in the man's facial features.

He was handsome. His deep brown eyes set against his mocha skin nicely, a slightly darker contrast than hers. He stood at least five-ten with short curls on top of his head.

"No, I shouldn't have been standing in the doorway," he responded with a small smile. "I'm Trevor, by the way. I work in marketing."

"Alijah, I'm Mr. Cayman's assistant." Trevor nodded slowly, and Alijah shifted her weight. "Well, I better get going. I have a few calls to make."

Trevor moved aside and allowed her to pass. "It was nice meeting you, Alijah."

"You as well," she stated as she headed back towards her desk.

Once at her desk, Alijah sent her notes to Kieran after making sure they were organized. She then went about replying to some emails. She was happy that it was Friday and she would have the next two days off. Her boss may have been an extreme workaholic, but he didn't make her work on the weekends when he did unless there was an event, and she was happy about that.

This weekend she had plans. She hadn't hung out with Lawrence since moving out of his apartment. They talked several times a week, but it was almost impossible to get together with both of their schedules. However, he was off for the first weekend in a long time, and Alijah thought it was best to catch up with her friend.

She was in desperate need of someone to talk to about what was going on with her boss. She needed an opinion on how to handle it. If anyone gave it to her straight, it would be Lawrence. He'd always been blunt about everything, and if you associated with him, you merely had to take it — no chasers as was the case with their small group. She could use his honesty for the current issue she was having.

Kieran sat at his desk, going over the reports from the different departments. He was pleased so far with everything he saw, except for the marketing department's concept for a product he'd purchased the rights to six months ago.

It was a unique product. It was a self-aware carpet and floor tool. Not only did it vacuum up messes on the carpet, wood, and tile flooring. It also mopped the hard floors as well as shampooed the carpet. It then went behind itself and dried the floor afterward to reduce the chance of slipping.

He'd purchased it from the creator, who had some troubles with the power core. He made the man more than a fair offer and gave him ten percent of revenue garnered, paid quarterly for the rest of his life. He was well set.

Kieran had gotten his team on the power core issue and they had it figured out within three months. Over the next three months, they tested the prototype. Putting it to whatever test they could think of. Now he was ready to start marketing it so they could get it in stores and on the shelves.

His finance department had come up with a reasonable budget that would give the product the push it needed without spending more than it may garner in the first six months of selling it. He had figured the product would be relatively easy to market. However, he'd left the strategical matters and the overall concept to his marketing department. They had fallen short.

The concept, in his opinion, was not enough to catch the attention of anyone — not even a child. He was going to make them do it again, and they would be on a strict deadline. The product was going out on the first of September and needed advertising to take place at least a month prior. With it being almost the end of June, that gave them a month to get their shit together, or heads were going to roll. He would clean out the whole department if he had to and hire an entirely new team if he had to push the shelving day back.

Speaking of the marketing team, Kieran's thoughts went back to right after the meeting when he'd seen Trevor talking to Alijah. For lack of a better word, the young man was promiscuous. Kieran had seen him flirt with several female employees and did not doubt that he'd slept with several of them.

He didn't have a massive "no fraternization" policy. He more so didn't want it to interfere with anyone's work or cause any tension. If it affected someone's job performance, then it cost him money. Therefore, both parties would have to go.

In this aspect, when it came to Alijah, it would be best for Trevor to keep his distance. Kieran was still determined to have her. He was easing her into it. It was much like a business acquisition, and he didn't get where he was without knowing how to go about things.

At thirty-five, Kieran had been running his company successfully with no profit losses for the past eleven years. He started it right out of college with the life insurance money he'd gotten from his parent's death. It was a struggle, and every day had been hard, but Kieran had three great friends that helped him get off the ground. In return, when they had decided to go into business for themselves, he was more than happy to help them.

His three friends were his family after his parent's passed away. He had no one. They had both been only children. His father had grown up in the foster system, never knowing his parents. His mother's father had disowned her for marrying his father. The old man was still alive, to Kieran's knowledge. He was probably too damn stubborn to die, but he had nothing to do with him. Not from the way he treated his mother.

Sighing, Kieran shook the memories away and rose from his seat. Making his way to the window, he looked out over downtown Denver. He loved his city. It always seemed so peaceful and serene. He had never been one for the hustle and bustle of huge cities. This one fit his needs just right.

While Denver was large, it was private. Therefore, there weren't many people trying to take his pictures at every turn like there were in other cities. He enjoyed that fact, and though he liked to travel for work and pleasure, he didn't like being hounded if he allowed himself that luxury. He would have to get over the discomfort considering he had many out-of-town business meetings scheduled over the next few months.

Making his way back to his desk, he began to mark up the marketing campaign sent over. He was sure that there would be more red than anything else on the screen by the time he finished.

Kieran didn't need to glance at his clock when his door opened, and Alijah walked in to know that it was after five o'clock and she was informing him that she was leaving. He also knew she would try to get him to leave work early as well. Sometimes, he gave in to her. This would not be one of those times.

"Quitting time," she announced as she stopped in front of his desk.

"I still have work to do," he stated simply, typing away on his keyboard.

He listened to her sigh, and he didn't need to look at her to know that she was rolling her eyes. The corners of his mouth twitched as he fought a grin. Kieran all but expected her to give him lip like she usually did. However, he was surprised when she conceded with no fight at all.

"Fine, you stay and work. I'm leaving."

"Timothy is waiting for you downstairs," Kieran informed her. He paused in his actions long enough to look up into her green eyes. "I'll see you later tonight, baby."

With that, he turned his attention back to his previous task, but he didn't miss the hitch in her chest as she seemed to stop breathing for a moment.

Alijah didn't mumble a reply to him. She merely turned and walked out of the door. With her back to him, Kieran looked up and admired the sway of her ass as she left. He smirked to himself, enjoying the effect he seemed to be having on her.

He had been teasing her for over two weeks, and he had thought she would have broken by now. Come begging for him to pleasure her body in numerous ways. However, that hadn't happened. He had to give it to her. She had willpower—much more than he possessed.

Kieran was growing closer to simply bending her over his desk and taking her from behind. The thought had crossed his mind several times, but when he gave it to her, it would be more than an office quickie. He was going to fuck her to the extent she forgot her own name.

He worked a bit longer before finally deciding that it was time for him to leave the office. The sun had set, and the city's lights twinkled below — another reason he loved the view. He could see out, but no one could see inside due to the outside tint on the window.

Making his way out of the office, he closed the door behind him on his way to the elevator. He'd called for Timothy twenty minutes before and knew he was waiting on him.

Sliding into the car, Kieran sat back in the seat as he loosened his tie. He had plans to go to, what was supposed to be a weekly basketball game with his three closest friends. Admittedly, he hadn't been going lately, and they were all giving him hell.

So, instead of working all day tomorrow, he planned to play a few games and maybe get a few drinks. Then, he would go back to the condo and work.

He pulled up a short while later and headed to the top floor. It was close to nine, and the lights were out in the living room. The light over the bar was on, and he walked over, finding dinner left out for him. His little assistant had thought enough to make him a plate. He decided to eat it before heading to his room.

* * *

As he passed by Alijah's door, he noticed the light coming from underneath. He hadn't suspected she was sleeping, but she had been locking herself in her room for the past few nights. Kieran hadn't felt inclined to ask what she was doing. What she did with her free time was her business. Though, he planned to be the only thing she did starting very soon.

Going into his room, he began to strip. He would take a shower and then start researching other potential business endeavors. Money could be made, and he had every intention of making it.

8

Kieran stepped out of the shower and wrapped a towel around his waist. He'd slept in until about nine-thirty and then made his way onto the roof for his workout. Time had slipped away from him, and it was nearly lunchtime when his stomach demanded that he stop and get some food. Considering he'd skipped breakfast.

Deciding that there was no need to get dressed up since he was going to play ball later, Kieran put on a pair of gray Nike shorts with a matching top, socks, and shoes.

Once he was dressed, he made his way to the kitchen, where he could smell the scent of seafood. He took a seat at the bar and watched as Alijah moved around the kitchen. He couldn't see what she was making, but it smelled like shrimp.

She hadn't noticed that he sat behind her at the bar, so he was amused to see her jump when she finally turned to see him. Her hand went to her chest as it rose and fell. Instinctively, his eyes went there.

"Are you trying to give me a heart attack?" She questioned him. Her eyes were tiny slits as she glared at him.

"Not at all, baby," he responded, waiting to see that catch in her chest, which was almost instant.

She didn't say anything. Instead, she turned back to the task at hand. Kieran didn't mind. He was a great fan of her ass and found he enjoyed watching it more than any show he'd ever seen. It was hypnotizing, and he loved being under her spell.

He knew she could feel him watching her by her stiff movements, but it wasn't enough to stop him. His view at that moment was spectacular, and he planned on taking it in as much as possible.

When she was finished cooking, he watched her place the shrimp pasta she'd made onto plates before sitting one in front of him with a fork and hers two seats down from him. When Alijah turned her back to retrieve bottled water for both of them, he moved her plate down to the place right next to him.

He knew she noticed just as soon as she turned around, but she didn't say anything. Instead, she placed the water on the bar before walking around and sitting beside him stiffly. Kieran knew that wasn't because she was uncomfortable; it was because of the sexual attraction and tension between them that she was trying to deny.

Silence lingered between them. Typically, he didn't mind silence. It was a delightful welcome. At the moment, however, he wanted to hear her voice. It seemed to do something to him. The sound was as sweet as honey.

"Tell me about yourself, Alijah," Kieran stated when he couldn't bear the silence any longer.

As he made his statement, he realized that he was curious to know more about his assistant. He didn't know much more than what her resume and a background check had informed. He hadn't felt the need to know anything else beyond that. However, if he was going to bed with her, he needed to know at least the basics and perhaps about a few of her past relationships.

He could tell that he had shocked her with his question when his eyes met hers. He could see the wheels turning in her head, probably wondering why he wanted to know. He thought she wouldn't answer him for a moment, but she finally responded.

"What do you want to know?"

Kieran thought for a moment. "Do you have any siblings?"

"No, not by blood. I have a cousin, Chayse. We were born two weeks apart, and we're close. My best friend Erin and I are close as well. Even though we don't get to see each other often, we still speak frequently, and my friend Lawrence."

"What about your parents? What do they do?"

Kieran heard her scoff and watched as she pushed her pasta around on her plate. He opened his mouth to retract his question and ask another one, sensing that it was a sour topic, but she spoke before him.

"Cornelius, my sperm donor, is a chronological cheater. Has been for as long as I can remember. Anya, my egg donor, is a manipulative, pathological liar."

It was silent once again when she finished speaking, and this time the air was filled with awkward tension. Kieran had asked the wrong question, and he didn't want to worsen the situation by asking another wrong one or saying the wrong thing. He did, on occasion, have some sense of decency.

"What about you?" She finally asked, still pushing her food around. It was clear that she had lost her appetite. "Do you have any siblings? What do your parents do?"

"I don't have any siblings either. I have three friends that are like brothers." He answered slowly, debating whether or not he wanted to tell her about his parents but deemed it was only fair. "My parents both died in a car crash right before my junior year of college."

Her response to his admission wasn't what he had expected. He'd expected her to tell him she was sorry for his loss like everyone else did when they found out, but she hadn't. Instead, she placed her hand on his arm and squeezed it gently.

"I'm sure they're proud of everything you've accomplished." With that said, she took small bites of her food as Kieran finished his. He sipped his water slowly, trying to linger in her presence without seeming as if it was his goal.

When Alijah had decided she'd had enough of the pasta, she rose, collecting her plate and his. He watched as she went about loading the few dishes in the dishwasher. Once she finished that, she began to wipe off the counters and the stove.

Making his way behind her, Kieran wrapped his arms around her waist. She halted in her movements, and he pulled her back against him before leaning down and nuzzling her neck.

"I'm going to head out to meet the boys for a few games of basketball. Save me a plate of whatever you cook tonight. It may be late when I get back." He then kissed her neck lightly.

"I'm going out later today myself. So, I won't be cooking anything since I'll probably return late," she informed him, maneuvering out of his arms.

Kieran stared at her for a moment before opening his mouth. He had every intention of asking her where she was going, but she told him she would see him later as she threw the towel in the sink and exited the kitchen. He stood there and wondered for a moment where she was going and if she was going alone before he headed towards the door and grabbed his keys.

It didn't take him long to pull up to the gym they like to play at. He saw Cruz and Paetyn's car, but Nik was nowhere in sight. He wasn't surprised, though. Nik was seldom on time for anything.

Kieran found them shooting the ball leisurely as they waited, making his way inside. He walked over and joined them, preparing to wait at least another half hour for Nik.

Alijah sat across from Lawrence as their waitress took their menus. She didn't miss the look the young woman threw her friend's way before she went to put their order in.

They were seated outside of a small café downtown. The weather was beautiful, and instead of being inside where every Nosey Jack and Jane could hear what she needed to speak with Lawrence about, she opted for them to sit outside. The tables were spaced a reasonable distance apart. There were only two other tables occupied — neither in hearing distance of the conversation about to be had unless she decided to start yelling.

"So, how's everything been since we last spoke?" Lawrence questioned before taking a sip of his tea.

"Honestly? Stressful and confusing."

"The job's stressing you out?"

"I wish. Then it would be a matter of having a spa day. No, it isn't the job. It's the employer himself."

Lawrence sighed. "I told you before you even applied for the job that the man was an asshole."

"No…I mean, yes. He is, but that's not why I'm stressed and confused. He's been testing me."

"Testing you how?" Lawrence inquired cocking his head to the side.

Alijah proceeded to tell Lawrence everything that had happened over the past week. She told him about Kieran's flirty, suggestive words. The touches that she knew were more than innocent. The way he would walk up behind her, wrap his arms around her, or the way he would ghost his lips over her shoulder or neck. She told him about the night in the break room when they almost kissed.

She expected Lawrence to have something to say right away when she finished. He often did. Instead, he picked up his tea and took a few drinks before sitting it back down and looking at her. He let out a deep breath before speaking.

"I don't think he's testing you, Lioness," Lawrence stated as Alijah leveled him with a glare. He knew she hated when he called her that. He continued before she had time to address it. "I think the man is genuinely flirting with you. It sounds to me like he wants you as more than his assistant. Before you try to deny it or poke holes in it, listen." When he was sure she wouldn't say anything, he continued. "Another friend of mine used to work for him, and she never complained about him flirting with her. She often stated how big of an asshole he was, and he worked her way too hard, and it was unfair, but he never tried to get with her, and she was attractive too."

"I don't know, Lawrence."

"Tell you what. Stay with me tonight."

"What? Why?"

"Because I'm sure when I drop you off tomorrow in the same clothes you left in, he will be fuming. Then that will show you that he's interested in more than your efficiency and clerical skills, and if he isn't fuming, I was wrong. However, I doubt I'm wrong."

Alijah thought about it for a moment. She did want to know if Kieran wanted her the way she wanted him, but Lawrence's plans had a way of backfiring. Whether that be on the person, he thought he was helping or himself. However, her curiosity and need to know won over her common sense, and she agreed. She just hoped that this was one time where curiosity didn't kill the cat.

Alijah was seated on Lawrence's couch, and she wanted nothing more than to kill him. She knew that agreeing with him was a bad idea, but she'd done it anyway. It was a little after ten o'clock, and he'd just taken both of her cellphones and turned them off. They'd wrestled over the phones for a few minutes, and even as she tried, she knew her efforts were futile. Lawrence had kept them from her and had even gone as far as to lock them in a small safe he had in his bedroom.

She wanted nothing more than to take something sharp and impale him with it. However, she realized she would miss him too much once she had killed him, so she settled on being pissed to the extreme. He had claimed it would make the message he was trying to help her get across more convincing if she didn't answer her phone if he happened to call. Then Lawrence thought it would be even better if it went straight to voicemail. In the pit of her stomach, she knew that things would go very wrong if Kieran tried to call her. She could only hope that he wouldn't.

Alijah decided to put the thought out of her head, but it wasn't an easy feat. She admittedly wasn't seeing whatever she and Lawrence had been watching and opted on going to bed at around eleven-thirty.

She took a shower and changed into a pair of panties and a t-shirt — some of the few items she left behind when she'd started working for Kieran. She threw her dirty clothes in the washer and started it before bidding Lawrence a clipped goodnight and retreating to the room she once occupied.

Laying down, her mind wandered to Kieran and what he was doing at that moment. She sighed before turning onto her side. The man had a way of invading her thoughts no matter what she was doing. As her eyes fluttered closed, a small part of her hoped that he was at least a little ticked off tomorrow when she returned to the condo.

It was a little after midnight, and Kieran's friends had just left. It was only then that he'd noticed his little assistant had not yet returned. After playing a few games on the court, the four had come back to his place. They had a few drinks and watched the game before ordering pizza and starting, what turned into, an intense dominos tournament.

Grabbing his cell phone, he went to her name in his contacts and called her. The phone went directly to voicemail. Ending that call, he then called her work cellphone. Again, the phone went straight to voicemail.

Frustrated, Kieran tossed his cellphone on the couch. He sat down and rubbed his temples. One of his requirements was that she always kept her work phone on her…charged. He knew he shouldn't have been too pissed off about it. This was the first weekend, other than the first one she'd been employed with him, that he had called her, but it was no excuse.

Taking a deep breath, he tried to calm down. He stood to his feet and headed into his office, deciding to do some work since he hadn't gotten to earlier. Sitting down in his chair, Kieran got to work. She would be back any minute. He was sure of it.

The next time Kieran looked at the clock, it read four-thirty. He'd lost himself so much in his work that he hadn't realized how much time had gone by, and still, Alijah was not back.

Making his way into the living room, he grabbed his phone from the couch and proceeded to call both numbers. Again, he was met with the same results. His anger flared as he turned and headed into his bedroom.

Tossing his phone on the bed, Kieran made his way into the bathroom. He needed a hot shower. Maybe that would calm him down. For her sake, he hoped it would because when she made it back, he was letting her have it.

His shower had done little to calm his nerves, and as he heard the chime in the condo signifying that someone had accessed the elevator, his anger decided to make itself known again. It was now almost ten, and while the sun was shining, birds were singing, and the promise of a beautiful day was all outside of the condo; a war was about to wage inside it.

Kieran stood in front of the panel and watched as Alijah rode the elevator with some man close to her side. The sight alone had a slow burn of anger building within him. It seemed as if he had watched them for hours. When in all actuality, it had only been about a minute.

When the elevator stopped on his floor, he watched as the man leaned in and kissed Alijah. With that, his anger was no longer slowly burning. He was seething.

He stepped away from the panel once she stepped off, and it had begun to descend again with the man in it. Kieran listened to her put her key in the door, and when it opened, he was there glaring daggers at her. His eyes were filled with rage, which stopped her in her track.

"Where have you been?" He questioned through clenched teeth. He watched as she swallowed a lump in her throat and knew she was frightened. She should be.

"I told you I was going out," she finally answered.

"You told me you were going out yesterday. Yesterday has come and gone."

"I told you I would be back late, Kieran."

"Late. Not a whole fucking day later." Kieran saw those green eyes spark and knew she was about to fire back at him, but he didn't give her a chance. "I called trying to see if you were alright, and both of your phones went to voicemail every time. It's your responsibility to make sure your work line is always charged, and you couldn't do that. Something could have happened to you. You could have been lying in a ditch somewhere. Was it too much for you to let me know you weren't coming back? Clearly, it was." With that, Kieran turned and headed down the hall. He stopped again briefly to throw over his shoulder, "Thanks for being so damn inconsiderate."

Making his way into his room, he closed the door and laid down on his bed. He was tired. He'd been up all night wondering where Alijah was, and now that she was back and he had gotten most of his anger out, he was tired.

Placing his hands behind his head, he cursed at himself. He should have known that she was involved with someone. While she hadn't always been receptive to his advances, she hadn't told him to leave her alone either or that she was dating someone.

As bad as he wanted her, he wasn't about to step foot knowingly into another man's territory. He was a lot of things, but that wasn't his style. He didn't share either, whether he was sleeping with a woman or having a casual dating relationship with her. He had always left that to Cruz and Paetyn.

Sighing, Kieran closed his eyes. He needed a nap — an extremely long one.

9

The roles had significantly been reversed. Two weeks ago, it was Alijah ignoring Kieran, and now he was ignoring her. She didn't like it. After he'd all but chastised her like a child four days ago, he hadn't said much to her unless it was regarding work. It was the same way she had done him previously.

So many times, she found herself wanting to explain what happened. Tell him about how she thought he had been testing her and coming on to her and how Lawrence had come up with that stupid plan. She wanted to, but every time she would open her mouth to say something, he would level her with those hazel eyes. They were just as hard and cold as they had been when she'd first started working for him.

While it hadn't affected her when she first started working, it now sent chills down her spine. She had forgotten how cold Kieran could indeed be. It terrified her to know that she was the cause of that stare. Her actions, or better yet, what she let someone talk her into doing, were the cause of such chill.

Alijah sighed, trying to focus her attention back on her work. She was supposed to be rescheduling a few meetings and then making travel arrangements. Kieran was going to Paris on business in three weeks and then Rome two weeks later. She had been tasked with letting the company pilot know so he could file the flight plan ahead of time since they were traveling international so there would be no hiccups. She also had to book a hotel for them to stay at.

Usually, Alijah would have been excited about the prospect of visiting Paris and Rome. Even though she would have been working, it would have been an excellent opportunity to view some of the world's most remarkable buildings and art pieces.

However, with him being in the mood he was towards her, she didn't even think she wanted to go. It would merely be unpleasant, but as his assistant, she knew she didn't have a choice in the matter.

Alijah glanced at the clock and saw that her lunch break was rapidly approaching. She shook herself mentally. Focusing back on rescheduling meetings, she finished it in twenty minutes and then began looking for hotels for them to stay in. Granted, Kieran had told her which ones he wanted. She felt it would be better to switch it up.

She knew he stayed in those whenever he visited the city, and the paparazzi were bound to know that. Alijah had learned that her boss was not one for considerable amounts of attention. Therefore, she reasoned as she booked two completely different hotels, he would see the logic in what she had done. If not, he was already pissed with her, so it wouldn't make much difference.

It was a few minutes after twelve when she got it all done. Rising from her seat, she headed to Kieran's office and knocked on the door. She heard his voice granting her access and slowly pushed the door open. He glanced up when she entered but turned his attention back to his computer screen.

"I'm going to head to lunch unless you need me to order in and work through-"

"No," Kieran stated, cutting her off.

Alijah took a deep breath. "Okay, would you like me to order you-"

"No." He cut her off again.

It took everything Alijah had not to snap back at him. For some reason, she knew that if she had, a war would have broken out at Cayman Industries, and she wasn't sure she would have won. She was smart enough to know to never go into battle if you didn't think you could win.

Instead, she turned and headed out of the door, closing it behind her. Going over to her desk, she grabbed her purse from the bottom drawer, dropped her work phone in it before taking out her phone, and headed to lunch.

As soon as she was off the elevator in the lobby, she placed her cellphone to her ear. She listened to it ring before it was picked up after the fourth one.

"Hello."

"Chayse," Alijah stated with a relieved sigh as her cousin answered the phone. "Are you busy?"

"No, what's wrong?" Her cousin questioned from the other end of the line. Alijah could tell that she was shifting the phone.

"I did something stupid," she responded as she made her way down the sidewalk to a little bistro a few blocks from the office. "I listened to Lawrence and-"

"Yeah, you did something stupid." Chayse agreed. "Anytime anyone does anything, Lawrence says they're doing something stupid."

"Chayse, I'm serious."

"Sorry. Tell me what happened."

By the time Alijah finished telling Chayse everything, from when Kieran had come on to her in the company break room to when he had started ignoring her, she was seated at a table in the bistro eating her lunch.

"Well, as much as it pains me to say this, and it does to my core. I think Lawrence was right. I don't think the man is testing you, Ali. I think he likes you, or he at least wants to fuck you. No, no. I'm pretty sure that he likes you. He was all worked up when he thought something happened to you."

"Even if that had been the case, he hates me now." Alijah countered with a sigh.

"He doesn't hate you. If that elevator has a camera in it, as you've said, then I do not doubt that he saw Lawrence kiss you, and he's jealous."

"I don't know, Chayse."

"Trust me. I know men. Just talk to him. Tell him what he saw with Lawrence was a misunderstanding and apologize for worrying him."

"I've tried. Kieran won't let me get a word out."

"Try again, and don't back down. Now, I have to go. I lied when I told you I wasn't busy. I have a shoot in twenty minutes, and I need to finish setting up."

"Okay, thanks for listening. I'll talk to you later." With that, they said their goodbyes and hung up.

Alijah sat, finishing the rest of her lunch and thinking about what her cousin said. Chayse was right. She just needed to explain the situation to him. Let him know that she wasn't with Lawrence and sincerely apologize for worrying him. Though she knew that was easier said than done.

Kieran ended his conference call with a sigh. Leaning back in his seat, he began to rub his temples. He'd been excellent at the beginning of the call, but he was suffering from a headache at the moment. This venture was becoming one of his most stressful.

For the past four months, his Vice-President of Operations, Remy Price, had been in Altay, China trying to broker a deal with one of the factories. It was the leading producer of Bluetooth headsets. When he heard they were looking to expand, Kieran did his research and knew that it would be one of the best investments he had ever made. The company's profit to cost margin was impeccable.

He sat down with his Vice-President and his finance team, and they came up with a sound business pitch.

Kieran knew that the deal's closure would take at least a few weeks, and he didn't have time to be gone that long so instead, he sent Remy. The man was more than competent, and he didn't think it would take this long for the deal to close.

However, unfortunately, it was taking more time than Kieran was beginning to think it was worth. He was ready to pull out of the process. The owner of the company was hell-bent on keeping all manufacturing within Altay.

Kieran didn't want to do that. The point of expanding, in his opinion, was to put another facility in a place you previously didn't have one. The United States would be just that place. It would also bring in hundreds of jobs.

There was no way he would go into business with the man only to open another factory in China. It just wasn't happening. He would wait a few more days to see if things would change. If not, he would call Remy and tell him to pull out.

Rising from his chair, Kieran made his way over to the wall of windows. He looked out over the city. He was stressed and needed to relieve it.

His first thought went to Alijah, but he immediately shook it from his head. He was still pissed with her for worrying him. If he were honest with himself, he would admit that he was pissed with her for being involved with someone and not telling him.

However, that didn't stop him from wanting to have her mount him and ride him into tomorrow. No matter how much he would have liked that, he knew that it wasn't something that could happen. He wouldn't cross into another man's territory. No matter how much he wanted to.

If this were a business conquest, he wouldn't care. He would have infiltrated and taken over by now. However, regardless of whether he wanted it to be or not, it wasn't, and he would respect that.

Looking at the clock, he saw that it was almost six o'clock. He knew Alijah had left an hour previous. She hadn't come to tell him she was leaving, but he'd heard her. Kieran knew he was probably too hard on her, but he couldn't bring himself to let it go just yet.

Sighing, he made his way back over to his desk and called Timothy. While he was waiting, he packed up what he'd been working on and headed towards the elevator after turning out his light. He made it down just as Timothy pulled up. Not feeling the need for the older man to get out of the car, Kieran opened the door and slid in. He'd decided to head up to the gym when he made it to the condo.

By the time Kieran finished his workout, he was dripping in sweat. He knew he had pushed himself a little too far, and he would be sore tomorrow, but he needed the release. Kieran made his way back into the condo and headed to his room to shower.

When he finished his shower, he dressed in a pair of sweatpants and socks before making his way into the kitchen. He'd thought mildly for a moment about doing some work, but he was honestly too exhausted. Instead, he grabbed a beer from the fridge and headed to the living room.

Sitting on the couch, he turned on ESPN and decided to watch the game highlights. He sat drinking his beer for the next twenty minutes. He decided he needed another one when it was empty and rose from his seat. Kieran didn't care to see that the Cubs had beaten the Dodgers.

He had just turned around from retrieving his second beer to find Alijah standing behind him. She stood there in cotton Capri pants and a black tank top. Her feet were bare, and Kieran couldn't help the fact that he wanted her even in something so simple.

"Can we talk?" She questioned.

"There's nothing to-"

"I'm sorry, Kieran," she started, cutting him off. "I should have been more responsible and made sure both of my phones were charged. I should have been more considerate and called you to tell you that I wasn't coming back that night," she said, walking towards him. She placed her hand on his chest and looked up at him from under her lashes. "I apologize."

At the sight, Kieran could feel himself hardening. He wanted nothing more than to lean down and mold his lips with hers. For a moment, his wants got the better of his judgment as he began to lean down. Then Kieran remembered the man that had kissed her in the elevator and took a step back — her hand falling quickly from his chest as if it had burned him.

He had every intention of walking away from her, but she got up on her tiptoes, placing her arms around his neck. Her green eyes bore into his, and Kieran had to take a breath to keep his willpower and control himself. He removed her arms from around his neck with one hand, placed the beer in the other on the bar, and walked past her towards the hall.

"Your boyfriend wouldn't appreciate what you're trying to do, Alijah," he told her through gritted teeth, back still turned.

"I don't have a boyfriend."

Those words stopped him in his tracks and his shoulders tensed. She was lying to him. He knew what he'd seen. Yet, she had the audacity to sit there and try to tell him something different.

"I saw you with him," he bit out. "I saw the two of you kiss."

"Lawrence isn't my boyfriend. He's a friend of mine from college. We aren't dating." There was silence before she added, "I'm not his type."

Kieran turned around, scoffing. "I doubt that."

"It's true. We're nothing more than friends. I promise."

He studied her for a moment. In his line of work, it was best always to be able to tell when someone was lying. As he stood and looked into Alijah's eyes, he knew she was telling him the truth. His eyes narrowed as he took predatory steps towards hers, circling out, causing her to mimic his motions before advancing on her.

"What are you doing?" Alijah questioned him as she backed into the door.

"What I've wanted to do since the first time you walked into my office," Kieran replied with a husky tone.

He closed the distance between them, trapping her luscious body against his and the door. He left nowhere for her to go, and that was his intent. He'd been fighting his desire for this woman long enough, and he wasn't going to do it anymore. He was going to fulfill his every need and hers. Her body was calling to him, begging him to touch her, and he was going to do just that.

Picking her up, her legs instinctively wrapped around his waist. He pressed his hardened dick between the apex of her thighs and allowed her to feel his need for her, his desire.

Without a word, he captured her lips with his and dominated the kiss. He was hungry for her and was damn sure going to get his fill of her even if it took all night.

With her still in his arms, lips again moving together, Kieran turned and began to head down the hallway. When he came to her bedroom, he walked inside before they stumbled onto the bed. He laid her down, and his body followed hers only a second later.

Her legs disengaged from around his waist, but Kieran barely noticed as his lips moved with hers. They were so soft. His fantasies and imagination did not do them justice, had not prepared him for the actual thing. They were addicting, and all he wanted to do was drink from them, but he knew he needed to let her breathe.

Reluctantly removing his lips from hers, he began to trail them along her jawline to her neck, giving her time to take in much-needed air. Kieran nibbled on Alijah's neck, drawing small moans from her as he snaked his hand down over her side to her hip. He moved it to her lower abdomen and had every intention of continuing his explorations when he heard the small chime reverberate through the condo — the sound that someone had accessed the elevator for his floor.

Stopping his movements, he rose from the bed, reaching out and pulling Alijah up. With one of her hands in his, he led the way down the hall into his office. He sat her in his chair.

"What's going on?" Alijah questioned. He could see she was confused by his sudden change in mood.

"Someone is on their way up to the condo," he stated, keying in the code to the small safe underneath his desk.

"Okay..." Alijah trailed off as he opened the safe and pulled a .9mm from it. "Kieran," she stated, puzzled. Her green eyes were big as she stared at the gun in his hand.

"Someone is on their way to the condo, but the only two people with an access card for the elevator are you and I." Kieran further elaborated. He realized it was taking her longer to come out of her sexual haze. She stood from the chair as he watched realization dawn on her. "Where are you going?" He then questioned.

"I'm coming with you."

"No, baby. Stay here. Lock the door behind me. If I'm not back in five minutes, call the police," he stated before placing a soft kiss on her lips and heading out the door. He waited to hear the lock click into place before making his way down the hall.

He hated now that he hadn't gotten cameras placed outside of his front door or that there wasn't a peephole in the door. However, he never thought he'd need either of those when he controlled who could and couldn't have access to his floor. He was wrong.

He took a deep breath and took the safety off the gun but kept his finger away from the trigger. Aligning it instead to the side of the weapon. He pulled the door open and frowned.

"Really, Kieran? You're going to shoot me?" Cruz questioned on the other side of the door.

Kieran quickly lowered his gun and put the safety back on. "What are you doing here? And how did you access my floor?"

"Seriously? It isn't that hard when you create the security software." Cruz informed him. "Besides, my assistant was supposed to call you and tell you I was coming over to inspect it and make sure it was in perfect working order," he finished pushing past Kieran into the condo.

Kieran placed the gun on the table as he closed the door. Turning to see Cruz sitting on his couch. "No one called me."

Cruz scoffed. "Figures. I'm firing her ass tomorrow."

"Is that all you wanted, Cruz?"

"No, I also wanted to remind you of Nik's opening tomorrow. I know how you are, and I figured a face-to-face reminder was best."

Kieran nodded. In all honesty, he had forgotten about Nik opening his new lounge, but regardless of what he had scheduled for tomorrow, if anything, he would make time to support his friend.

While he had Cruz there, Kieran decided to talk to him about getting cameras placed outside the door. This incident had opened his eyes to the possibility that someone could hack his elevator, though Cruz swore it to be impossible. Claiming he was the best at what he did and could not be hacked.

"Seriously, Kieran?"

Alijah's voice made Kieran halt his conversation and turn to look at her. Those green eyes held that spark, and he knew she was about to go to war with him. So, he beat her to it.

"Why did you come out?"

"I was coming to make sure you were alright, and I heard you talking to him," she stated, gesturing to Cruz.

"I could have been out here, tied to a chair, preparing to be tortured. What would you have done then?" He questioned. She glared at him, and Kieran had to admit she was damn sexy when she was mad.

"Screw you, Kieran." With that, he watched as she turned and headed back down the hall. None too pleased with him.

He turned his attention back to his friend to see him giving him a questioning look. Kieran raised his own eyebrow in question. Cruz simply shook his head, telling Kieran he would see him tomorrow night before heading out of the door.

Kieran locked the door behind him and grabbed the gun off the side table. He made his way into his office and placed it back into the safe, closing it. He then backtracked to Alijah's room. He tried the door handle and found it locked but wasn't surprised. He was, however, irritated.

Sighing, he made his way down the hall. Resigning himself to the fact that it would be another cold shower for him tonight.

10

Alijah sat at her desk, going through emails. She had to admit to herself honestly; it was one of the least favorite tasks of her job. She was responsible for going through all the emails that came in as business propositions. She then had to determine which were legitimate and which were merely a waste of time before forwarding the actual proposals to Kieran.

Every day, it seemed as if more and more of them came in. She was starting to think there was a damn Submit Your Business Proposal section on the website. Had she not known for herself that there wasn't, she wouldn't have ruled it out.

She'd just finished reading one proposal about genetically engineering honeybees to gather the world's fecal matter and reproduce it into honey. She was getting frustrated with all the stupidity that was apparently in the world. It took all she had not to email the man back and ask him how many sandwiches short of a picnic he was. Instead, she promptly sent that email to her trash folder.

Alijah had known before that people would do anything to make a quick buck, but she hadn't known they would go to the extent of losing all common sense and spewing the first ridiculous thing that came to their mind. Placing her head down on her desk, she groaned.

"Ms. Douglas, can you step into my office, please?" Kieran's voice questioned over her phone's speaker.

Standing to her feet, Alijah smoothed out her knee-length skirt before proceeding into her boss' office. She didn't bother to knock since he had requested she come and just opened the door, allowing it to close gently behind her.

He was standing looking out the bank of windows, his back to her as she made her way across the office in his direction. She was halfway there when he turned, and those hazel eyes locked her into place.

It was as if the distance between them had never existed as he closed it quickly. Placing his hands on her waist, her body was pulled flush against his. Alijah gasped at the sudden action, but his lips promptly swallowed it.

The kiss was vigorous, and it seemed to help Alijah relieve some of the stress and frustration she was holding on to as she battled with him for dominance. She was sure he expected her to let him have it, but she wasn't about to do that.

His right hand began to travel up the inside of her right thigh. She felt her skirt rising, starting to bunch up with the action. As his hand came into contact with the fabric of her panties, Alijah grabbed his wrist and removed his hand from under her skirt.

He groaned against her lips, and Alijah did everything in her power not to laugh. He had been calling her into his office all day. Each time ravishing her lips, but she wouldn't let him get much farther than that. Determined that the first time anything happened between them, it wouldn't be some office quickie.

Kieran's hand began to snake down her back until he was cupping her ass as he punished her lips with his. He brought his right hand down on her left cheek, and Alijah moaned into the kiss. He then proceeded to do the same with the opposite side before slapping both of her ass cheeks — the final action causing her to latch on to his lower lip with her teeth.

She released his lip and took a step back, breathing deeply. She looked up into those hazel eyes and saw they were dark with desire.

Kieran leaned back down and whispered against her lips, "You better stop teasing me," he then smacked her ass again before releasing her and making his way back to his desk. "We're going to *Mirage* tonight," he informed her.

"The new club that's opening up? I never pegged you as a club-goer."

"I'm not normally, and it's more of a lounge than a club," Kieran replied.

Alijah nodded her head. She had read an article about the new place in a magazine and thought it had been called a club, but perhaps she was wrong.

"What time are we going?"

"Ten. Traffic will be hell since its opening night. Not to mention it's Fourth of July weekend, so be ready by nine."

Again, Alijah nodded before heading out of his office and back to her desk. She was in no mood to finish going through the email proposals, but she knew it had to be done.

Alijah had finished going through all of the proposals and had attended two afternoon meetings by the time four-thirty rolled around. Pulling up Wayne Farley's contact information, she dialed his number, waiting on him to pick up. She was just about to hang up when she heard his voice on the other end.

"This is Wayne."

"Hello, Mr. Farley. This is Alijah Douglas, Kieran Cayman's assistant."

"Yes, Ms. Douglas. How are you?"

"I'm well, thank you. How are you?" Alijah questioned politely.

"Can't complain. To what do I owe this pleasure?"

"I was calling to ensure that your meeting with Mr. Cayman was still on for next week?"

"It sure is. I'll see you both at ten sharp."

"Thank you, Mr. Farley. You enjoy your weekend."

"You do the same, Ms. Douglas." With that, the two of them ended the call.

For the next twenty minutes, Alijah made a list of things to do Monday and placed appointments, conference calls, and meetings into her calendar with reminders. At five, she shut everything down and locked up anything that contained pertinent information before gathering her things and heading toward Kieran's office. He was opening his office door and coming out, briefcase in hand, to her surprise.

"Well, this is new," she stated. "I didn't think you were capable of leaving at a decent time without being dragged away." She then teased as they stepped onto the elevator.

He leveled her with those hazel eyes, and the look he gave her was one more deadly than if he'd been glaring at her. It was filled with pure unadulterated lust.

"Keep teasing me. I dare you," he responded as the elevator opened on the first floor.

Alijah stared at his back for a moment before following him off the elevator and out of the building. Timothy was waiting for them and opened the door immediately when he saw them.

Kieran stepped aside, allowing her to get into the car first, and Alijah knew it was because he wanted to stare at her ass. Once he had climbed in and was settled, Timothy closed the door making his way to the driver's side. No sooner than he had pulled into traffic, Kieran raised the partition between them.

Alijah was pulled into his lap when it was up, straddling him, which caused her skirt to bunch at her thighs. His hand went to the back of her neck and pulled her forward, causing their lips to touch barely.

"Tease me now," he stated, his lips brushing over hers before capturing them in a solid kiss.

Their lips moved in synchronicity, fluid against one another. Kieran pulled away long enough to bite her bottom lip. Eliciting a gasp from her before he claimed her mouth again, snaking his tongue inside.

Alijah groaned as their tongues battled for dominance. They both wanted control. She could tell it was going to be an everyday thing for them. Neither one wanted to relinquish their control, which made it even more exciting and immensely turned her on.

When Kieran removed his lips from hers again, she wanted to groan out her protest but stopped short when she felt his lips leaving kisses up and down the side of her neck. She felt his fingers in her wild curls and gasped as he gripped them, pulling her head back. He moved his lips to trail up the column of her neck before nipping it lightly.

"Tease me now, Alijah."

She couldn't even respond. Alijah knew he was getting her back for teasing him throughout the day, as he had put it, but she didn't care. With his hands gripping her hair and his lips on her body, she could care less that he was essentially teasing her. She just didn't want him to stop.

Unfortunately, she would not be getting what she wanted. Placing one final kiss on her lips, Kieran lifted her from his lap and straightened his shirt. Alijah hadn't been aware she had been gripping it.

While he did that, she went about straightening her skirt. She glanced outside the window and noticed that they were only moments from the condo.

Once they arrived, Kieran informed her of a video call he had, stating he didn't know when it would be done and reminding her to be ready by nine.

Making her way into her room, she decided to find what she would wear later that night. She didn't know if they were going for business but figured they most likely were. She knew she needed to look professional, but she also wanted to look sexy. He claimed she had been teasing him all day; she wanted to *really* tease him tonight.

Going through her closet, she finally decided on a blue dress. It would come down to her knees while clinging to her body. The straps were about two inches wide, and while the dress would push her breast up and wasn't overly revealing — sensual ... that's what she planned on being for the night. The dress would also cover her tattoos, and she wanted him to be surprised to see them when he peeled her out of it. Alijah decided that she would pair the dress with silver shoes and accessories.

Once she had everything laid out, she decided to sit in her window seat and paint a little before she began getting ready. She made a mental note to put her painting away just in case they ended up in her room tonight. She couldn't be sure how tamed they would be.

Kieran was very close to saying to hell with the opening. At that moment, he would have much rather bent Alijah over the back of the couch and fucked her until she couldn't walk. The dress she wore hugged her body in all the right places, and her heels gave the illusion that her legs were two miles long. Her hair was in its naturally curly state, and she wore little makeup.

He was in front of her in three long strides, pulling her body against his. He had every intention of devouring her lips, but her hand on his chest stopped him as she pushed him back.

"You're going to mess up my lipstick," she informed him.

Kieran raised an eyebrow at her, wondering if she thought he cared. If she did, she was sorely mistaken. He placed his hand on the back of her neck and brought his lips down to hers. Ignoring the fact that she pushed against him for him to stop. After a few seconds, she stopped fighting him and began to kiss him back with just as much vigor as he was kissing her.

When he pulled back, he slowly watched as her green eyes opened. They then narrowed at him. He knew it was because he hadn't listened to her, but he didn't care. He enjoyed her attitude at times.

Kieran watched as she reached up and began to run her thumb across his lips, he assumed, to remove the lipstick from them. She did his top lip first and then his bottom. Before she could pull her thumb away, he caught it between his teeth and began to suck on it lightly.

"We're going to be late," she informed him after a second. Releasing her thumb from his lips, Kieran stepped aside and allowed her to lead the way. As she did so, she fixed her lipstick.

Once on the elevator, Kieran pressed the button for the parking garage instead of the first floor. He had decided to drive tonight. Not knowing what time they would return. He didn't want to keep Timothy up at all hours of the night.

They made their way over to his Porsche, and Kieran opened the door for her before going around and getting in on the driver's side. He started the car and headed towards *Mirage*.

The ride was quiet except for the soft murmur of music on the radio and the sound of the tires on the road. What usually would have been a thirty-minute drive took them almost an hour by the time they got to the front of the club where the valet was for the opening.

• • •

Kieran got out and handed the young man the keys before he walked around and opened Alijah's door. He helped her out, placing his hand on the small of her back and leading her toward the front of the line.

There were photographers everywhere taking pictures. A few of them shouted his name and asked him questions, but he ignored them and continued to the door. The bouncer nodded at him before stepping aside and allowing them in.

As they stepped inside, Kieran looked around. It never ceased to amaze him how Nik could give a place a club and lounge effect, but his friend did it effortlessly. The music was loud, but not overly so. There were two bars — one on each side of the building. The right side was definitely for all the people that came merely to dance and drink, while the left was for those who wanted to drink and lounge around.

Looking up, Kieran saw what he knew was Nik's office. The wall facing the club was mirrored glass. He also noticed that Cruz had provided the security equipment, but he wasn't surprised. Cruz's security company was one of the best in the world, in his opinion, and they each utilized it.

There was one thing about Nik's clubs that were forever consistent, and that was where he placed his VIP section.

With his hand still on the small of Alijah's back, he guided her through the crowd of bodies and the many tables occupied by people to the back. When he got closer, he noticed Cruz and Paetyn were already there, sitting in one of the sections. A few other people were seated in different sections. He recognized a few, but he didn't feel inclined to speak to them.

As they stopped in front of the couches, the two men rose to their feet. Their eyes were on Kieran before shifting to Alijah.

"Paetyn, Cruz...this is Alijah Douglas. Alijah, these are friends of mine, Paetyn, and Cruz," he introduced over the music. The music wasn't as loud in the back where they were, so he didn't have to battle with it to be heard.

"You mean you have friends?" Alijah questioned him with a raised eyebrow, those green eyes shining with mischief.

Paetyn began to laugh at her statement while Cruz wore a look of amusement but didn't say anything. Shifting his eyes down to look at her, he gave an irritated look, though he didn't feel that way. Only to have her wave him off. She then stuck her hand out for each man to shake.

"It's nice to meet you both," she stated politely.

Kieran gestured for her to sit, and when she did, the three men followed suit. Kieran stopped a passing waitress and asked that she bring them a bottle of *Chateau Palmer* and a bottle of *Inverleven Duncan Taylor*, and glasses. He knew Nik would have a supply of both since they were his favorites.

Kieran began to look around *Mirage* some more. He had always been one to check out his surroundings. If something was going to happen, he liked to be the first one to know. He didn't know how long he had been looking around, but Paetyn's voice pulled his attention back.

"So, Alijah…how do you know Kieran?" His friend questioned.

"Well, I have the grave misfortune of working for him. I'm his assistant."

Kieran turned his attention to her and saw she had a smirk on her face.

"That must be terrible. He's a hard-ass." Paetyn told her.

"It isn't too bad. I'm not easily intimidated, so we bump heads…a lot. I win most of the time. I let him rest the time, so he doesn't feel bad."

Kieran's mouth twitched as his friends both laughed. Paetyn stating through his laughter that he liked her. Leaning in, he brought his lips to her ear.

"Are you teasing me, Alijah? Because if you are, I will be forced to reciprocate," he pulled back and found her looking at him with desire-laced eyes.

"You promise?" She questioned.

Kieran's first instinct was to attack her lips with his. However, the arrival of his ordered drinks stopped him, and he watched as the waitress sat down the wine he'd ordered in a bucket of ice. She then sat down the bottle of scotch and then another bucket of ice: four wine glasses and four scotch glasses. She fluttered her eyelashes, asking Kieran if that would be all.

● ● ●

He merely nodded and turned his attention to the wine, preparing to uncork it.

After he poured them a glass, he passed them out before taking his own. He watched as Alijah swirled hers in her glass before smelling it lightly. He then watched as she brought it to her lips and sipped it.

Kieran took a sip of his own wine before turning his attention back over the crowd, but not before Cruz caught his eye and gave him a knowing look. He ignored his friend and swept the room again.

They'd been sitting for about thirty minutes. Kieran had been otherwise silent, but he'd been listening to Paetyn and Alijah's conversation. Cruz would comment now and then, but he wasn't one for many words often, especially first meeting a person.

He had just finished his second glass of wine when he saw Nik approaching through the crowd. He stopped at the section before theirs, checking on his customers before making his way over. Kieran stood and greeted his friend, congratulating him with a man hug. He then held his hand out to Alijah, which she took and stood.

"Alijah this is my friend Nik. He owns *Mirage*. Nik, this is Alijah."

Alijah held out her hand. "It's nice to meet you."

Nik took her hand in his before bringing it to his lips and brushing a soft kiss against it. "Trust me. The pleasure is all mine."

Kieran watched as Alijah slowly removed her hand from Nik's before reclaiming her seat. Everyone else followed suit, and Nik took up residence on the last couch by himself.

"Alijah," Nik started gaining her attention after he'd been looking at her for a few moments. "How do you know Kieran?"

Kieran watched as Alijah took a small sip of her second glass of wine before setting it on the table and giving him her attention.

"I work for him," she stated simply,

"I figured as much." Was Nik's response.

"Oh?" Alijah questioned and uncrossed her legs to lean forwards and stare straight at him. "And why is that?"

Nik was about to answer, but Kieran leveled him with a gaze that would stop a bullet cold in its tracks. He knew that whatever Nik was about to say would piss him off. He knew his friend well enough to know that, even when he was playing, as Kieran suspected he was doing now, Nik didn't know when he'd gone too far.

"I just did," he stated with a shrug.

Kieran watched as Alijah went to say something. No doubt it was something smart and would put Nik in his place, but at that moment, some song came on with an upbeat tempo, and he saw her whole-body language change. She sat back and turned her attention to him.

"Will you dance with me?" She questioned hopefully.

"I don't dance." Was his simple reply. She pouted at him, and as cute as it was, Kieran was not giving in. "The answer is still no."

She glared at him. "Fine." It was her only response before she rose from her seat and headed out of the section and towards the dance floor.

Kieran watched her as Paetyn began filling the scotch glasses with ice from the second bucket brought and pouring scotch into all four of the glasses. Nik cocked his head to the side as each man grabbed one, looking at Kieran.

"Are you fucking her?" Kieran ignored Nik's question, opting to sip the scotch instead. It was smooth and went down easy. "Do you plan on fucking her?" Nik then questioned. Not at all phased by the fact his first question wasn't answered. "If you plan on it, I don't blame you. She's sexy as hell. Not your usual type, is all. So, if you're not going to sleep with her, I'd like to. You know I love all women in general, but chocolate is my favorite candy."

Kieran gritted his teeth. While he knew Alijah wasn't the type of woman he usually would pursue, she was the only woman he could see himself pursuing at that moment. Regardless of Nik's "love of chocolate," as he essentially said, he wasn't about to let the other man think he had a chance. So, without words, Kieran gave Nik an even more fierce glare than he had previously given him. It said everything it needed to, and his friend put up his hands in surrender.

He took another sip of scotch before turning his attention to the dance floor. When he did, his eyes narrowed. She was dancing, but she wasn't alone. Some guy had walked up and started dancing with her. When he stepped closer, Kieran almost rose from his seat but stayed put as he watched Alijah place her hand on his chest and step back.

He couldn't tell what was being said, but from the looks of it, the man had started an argument with her, and Kieran almost felt sorry for him. He knew Alijah would not take whatever he said lightly.

When he saw her place on hand on her hip and point her finger at him, he knew the other man was about to receive a lashing. She finished what she had to say, then turned her back on him and headed back towards the VIP section.

Alijah had just made it back to them when the man that had tried dancing with her grabbed her arm and spun her around.

Kieran didn't think; he just rose to his feet and grabbed the man's hand, placing more force on it than he needed to before removing it from her arm. He then realized the young man had been seated at another section when they entered.

"Are you okay, Alijah?" He questioned. Instead of answering him, Kieran listened to her fire off at the man in front of them.

"Don't you ever put your fucking hands on me again. I will break every single one of your fingers," she snapped out.

The young man sat there looking at her as if she was crazy, and for a moment, Kieran thought she was, but he knew that women tended to get violent when you pissed them off or invaded their space unwantedly.

"Why are you still standing here?" She bit out again when he didn't immediately turn and leave.

Kieran wrapped his arm around her waist, his fingers splaying against her stomach, and pulled her back into his body. It seemed that he didn't need to worry about her. She was perfectly capable of fighting her own battles. Though had the situation elevated, he wouldn't have hesitated to place the young man on his ass.

As he began to walk away, Kieran retook his seat, pulling Alijah down into his lap. If Nik had any more doubt about his intentions with Alijah, they were shattered upon that action. His friends knew him well. Knew that he was never publicly affectionate with anyone he wasn't pursuing, and even when he did, it was minimal.

He picked his glass back up and brought it to his lips, taking another sip while he reached up with his other hand and pulled one of her natural curls, watching as it sprung back into place. He loved her hair, liked the way it always looked as if she'd been thoroughly satisfied yet kempt all at the same time.

"What are you drinking?" She questioned as he grabbed another curl.

"Scotch. Do you want some?"

"No, I don't like the way it feels going down my throat."

"This is smooth. I promise you'll like it," he stated, placing his cup to her lips.

Kieran tipped the cup, and Alijah tilted her head back slightly, and he watched as she allowed the liquid to slide down her throat. He was so caught up in watching that he tipped the cup too much and caused a bit to slip down her chin.

He placed his cup back on the table and kissed her chin before trailing his lips up. Removing the liquid as he went. He then placed a soft kiss on her lips, fully aware that his closest friends watched him the entire time. When he pulled back, her bright eyes had darkened.

"Can we leave?" She whispered, and Kieran knew precisely why she wanted to. It was the same reason he'd almost not made it when he saw her in her dress, but he didn't want to dip out too early on his friend.

"Give me another hour, baby, okay?"

Alijah nodded her head in agreement and turned on his lap to face his friends, sparking up a conversation with Paetyn.

"So, Paetyn, tell me what you do for a living."

"I'm a Restaurateur."

"Really? Do you own any restaurants in the city?" Alijah then inquired.

"I do. You'll have to have Kieran bring you some time." Was his friend's response. Kieran watched as Alijah nodded before turning her attention to Cruz.

"What do you do, Cruz?"

"Security."

Kieran drank the rest of his scotch before leaning forward to place the glass on the table. This caused Alijah to lean forward as well, making her slide backward in his lap over his groin. When he leaned back, she slid forward a bit to regain her previous position, and he placed his hands firmly on her waist to stop her.

At that moment, the waitress walked by, and Alijah flagged her down. The woman stopped and looked at Alijah before her eyes fell on the four men. Kieran was sure she was about to flirt with one of them, despite Alijah being in his lap, when she realized her boss was one of the men sitting among them.

"What can I get for you?" She questioned Alijah.

"Can I get a White Russian? Made with milk instead of cream."

"Yes, ma'am. Anything for the rest of you?" The waitress then questioned. The men shook their heads, and she headed away to place the order.

"So, Alijah," Nik started. "You're rather comfy there...sitting on your boss' lap." Kieran shot Nik a look, but his friend ignored him. "I mean, it isn't all that professional, is it?"

Kieran watched as Alijah turned her head to Nik slowly, and he almost felt sorry for his friend. He couldn't see her face, but he knew those green emeralds were smoldering with fire.

"I could say the same of you and the number of female employees you've slept with. We could play a guessing game to see just how many there were. However, I don't think I could guess a number high enough." Alijah bit out.

Kieran saw the shocked look on Nik's face as his other friends began laughing uncontrollably. Nik wasn't used to women not falling all over him. Regardless of what he said to them. So, Kieran knew that the fact that Alijah snapped at him caught him off guard.

"What makes you think I sleep with my employees?" Nik asked, trying to recover.

The waitress came back and handed Alijah her White Russian at that moment. Alijah thanked her and took a sip as the waitress walked off before turning her attention back to Nik.

"Because you're that type," she told him simply.

Kieran found himself laughing as he slid Alijah off his lap before leaning forward and placing more ice into his cup. He then refilled it with scotch. Alijah's eyes watched him as he drank half of it before sitting back.

"You do realize you drove tonight, right? Timothy didn't bring us."

"I'm perfectly fine to drive, and even if I wasn't, you could. We're fine," he responded.

She didn't respond to him as she slowly sipped on her drink and once again began talking to Paetyn.

11

Kieran slid behind the wheel of his car after tipping the young valet. They stayed a little longer than he intended, but they were now headed back to the condo.

Slowly, he maneuvered into traffic. The street was less busy than it had been when they arrived. Many of the patrons still having a good time inside. He, however, was trying to have an even better time away from public eyes.

At the thought, Kieran glanced over and caught Alijah shifting in her seat. The action was making her dress rise the tiniest fraction. His attention went back to the road until they came to a stoplight. He then allowed it to venture back over to the alluring woman in the passenger seat of his car. Her legs were exposed.

Reaching over, he placed his hand on her left thigh. The action caught her off guard, and Kieran watched her jump slightly before turning to look at him. He held her gaze for a moment before turning back to the traffic light and proceeding through it when it changed.

As he drove, Kieran began to massage her thigh lightly. He wanted to feel her skin under his hand. So, in one swift motion, he removed his hand from her thigh and replaced it under her dress in the same place. Her skin was silky smooth, just as he imagined it would be.

Again, he began to massage her thigh, causing her breath to hitch lightly. It took everything in him not to allow his hand to trail upwards, but he would have plenty of time to play with her in just a few minutes. So, instead, Kieran focused on the road and getting them back in one piece.

When he pulled into the parking garage, he was reluctant to remove his hand but reasoned that the faster he did so, the quicker he could get her upstairs and naked.

He got out of the car before making his way around to help Alijah out. With his hand on the small of her back, he led her into the elevator before placing his access card in the slot for his floor. As soon as the door closed, Kieran yanked her body to his, causing a gasp to leave her lips before he smothered it with his own.

The kiss was slow, methodical. Kieran wasn't in any hurry. He had all night to sample her, and he planned on taking advantage of every second. So, instead of kissing her with a torrid frenzy, he kissed her with slow, heated lust. His aim: to take her breath away.

Kieran's fingers laced in her hair, pulling slightly to angle her head more. He felt her moan against his lips at the action and gripped it marginally tighter, testing her response. Again, he was greeted with a sensual moan against his lips.

As the elevator rose higher, taking them to their destination, so did the temperature inside it. Their kiss was full of passion, and he was more than sure that if it were made entirely of glass, it would have been fogged up by the sheer heat radiating off their bodies.

When the elevator stopped, Kieran backed her out of it and directly into the condo door. He finally removed his lips from hers to unlock the door. They were both breathing heavily, chests rising and falling.

Once the door was opened, he gazed down into her eyes before recommencing his onslaught of her lips. He then picked her up. His right arm under her ass, left hand tangled once again in her hair while her legs hung down the length of his body. He pushed the door closed with his foot and preceded down the hall.

Kieran made his way into her bedroom, stopping at the foot of the bed. He slid her down his body, allowing her to feel his need for her. Once she was on her feet, he removed his lips from hers, admiring how they were swollen from his kisses.

For a long moment, he just took her in, drank in the sight of her in that tight blue dress. She was breathtaking in it, but he knew she would be sinful out of it.

He reached up and removed the straps of her dress slowly from her shoulders. His eyes locked on hers; he watched in fascination as they darkened with desire. She hadn't said anything, and Kieran was perfectly fine with that. He would have her making plenty of noise in the hours to come.

Once she'd pulled her arms free of the straps, Kieran placed his hands inside the dress and pushed it down until it fell, pooling at her feet. He took a step back, removed his eyes from hers to roam over her body, and when he did, his breath caught in his throat.

"Fuck me," he groaned out as he looked at the intricate tattoos that adorned her waist, sides, hips, and upper thighs.

If he thought she was sexy before, she was even more so at that moment, ink brandishing her body and standing in only her black boy shorts, a strapless bra, and silver heels. He just needed to take her in for a moment.

His plan was cut short when she stepped over the dress at her feet and placed her hands on his chest. Kieran watched her with darkened eyes as she pushed the jacket he'd been wearing from his shoulders, and he allowed it to hit the floor. She then went about unbuttoning his shirt. Her hands moved slowly, but they weren't unsure of their actions as the buttons came undone one by one.

Alijah pulled the shirt from his pants and finished with the buttons before pushing it off his shoulders. Kieran allowed it to hit the floor, watching her as she stood there admiring him. Then she leaned in, and her soft lips made contact with his chest.

Slowly, she skimmed them across his chest as she ran her nails tauntingly down his stomach. Kieran let out a slow breath before looking down and finding her green eyes staring up at him as she darted her tongue out and trailed it up, rising on her tiptoes, causing his head to fall back as she licked the hollow of his neck.

Kieran growled within his throat before he hoisted her up by the waist, causing her to gasp and wrap her legs around him. They were doing this his way, and he would not allow her to tease him tonight.

He unclasped her bra with one hand before descending her back to the bed. He removed the material that hid her chest and gazed down at her beautiful breast.

Wasting no more time, he leaned down and flicked his tongue across her left nipple before latching onto it and sucking as he rolled her right nipple between her fingers. He bit down on her nipple, and her fingers came up to weave into his hair. He was sure she would push him away, but she pulled him closer. His little assistant liked a bit of rough play.

Testing his theory, Kieran pinched her right nipple, drawing a sharp gasp from her as she arched off the bed, placing more of her breast into his face. She liked it, and he planned on utilizing that fact.

Releasing her left nipple from between his teeth, he laved the sensitive bud with his tongue. After a few moments, he turned to give her right nipple the same attention. He snaked his hand down her stomach and into her panties as he did so. He wasted no time dipping his finger into her center and was greeted with a pleasurable moan.

She was soaking wet for him, and Kieran was surprised that it hadn't been dripping down her leg, and she was so tight. He wondered if he'd fit. Trailing his finger up, he began to circle it over her clit. Her soft moans music to his ears.

Pausing only shortly in his ministrations, Kieran took a second to remove her panties before throwing them on the floor with the rest of the discarded clothing. He then set back to work. Again, worshiping her breast and nipples with his tongue and fingers while his other hand played with her clit. Pinching it before dipping his fingers into her depths and coming out, using her juices to assist in pleasuring her.

The next time Kieran dipped his finger into her, she began to thrust against it, and he knew exactly what she wanted. He slowly added a second finger and started to finger her at a steady rhythm. She reached down and grabbed his wrist as she began to move against his fingers faster. He matched her speed as he felt her tighten around his fingers. She was on the brink, and as he bit down on her nipple, he sent her toppling over the edge.

"Kieran!"

His name on her lips was like music as he slowed his fingers, extending her orgasm. Pulling back, he looked into her face and saw pure bliss. He waited until she opened her eyes to remove his fingers from her. Kieran slowly placed them to his lips when she was looking at him and licked them clean.

Getting off of the bed, he grabbed Alijah's ankles, quickly pulling her to the end of the bed. A small gasp passed through her lips, and he sank to his knees. He looked up at her momentarily to find her watching him. Kieran gripped both of her thighs in his hands and parted her legs, diving in tongue first.

He flicked his tongue over her clit slowly. Eliciting long, drawn-out moans from her. He loved her moans, liked that she didn't try to hold them back. They were enticing and urged him to pull more from her.

When her hands came down to grip his hair, the flicking of his tongue turned to circular motions on her clit, and she moved against it. Gradually, he began to speed up his actions. Her breathing had changed, and her breaths were coming out hitched. As she arched off the bed, thrusting her core into his face more, Kieran pulled her clit between his lips and sucked on it, bringing her to another orgasm.

"Fuck!" Alijah screamed. Her word choice was making his hardened dick twitch.

Kieran released her clit, blowing on it before giving it a slow lick. He knew she was sensitive as she tried to run away from him, but he wasn't having it. Placing his arms around her thighs, he pulled her back down. Licking her clit before looking up at her.

"Don't run from me." With that said, he lowered his head to her pussy again.

"Kieran, please! I can't take anymore! No more, please!"

Alijah's voice rang through his ears as he drank from her center. He'd licked and sucked her to four orgasms, and he knew she was oversensitive, but she tasted divine, and he didn't want to stop just yet.

"One more baby. Just give me one more," he mumbled against her sex before latching onto her clit.

She began to run again, and Kieran pulled her back. Releasing her clit and dipping his tongue inside her pussy. He stroked his tongue inside her as he breathed slowly through his nose onto her clit.

Kieran felt the moment her legs began to shake, and he could feel her tightening around his tongue. Releasing one of her legs, he began to rub her clit frantically. He felt her tense up and leaned back to watch as her orgasm overtook her, but he wasn't prepared for the gush of liquid that hit his lips and chin sporadically before ceasing as Alijah's chest rose and fell.

"Damn, baby. You didn't tell me you could squirt," he stated, licking his lips and wiping his chin as he rose to his feet.

Kieran took in her beautiful body and the ink that adorned her skin as he removed the belt from his slacks. He dropped it to the floor, reaching into his back pocket to pull out his wallet, where he then removed three condoms. He threw two on the bed before taking the corner of another wrapper between his teeth.

He stepped out of his shoes, never taking his eyes off her, watching as she watched him. He unlatched the button on his pants before unzipping them and pushing them to the floor along with his boxers, his dick standing up at attention as he stepped out of them.

He watched as Alijah's eyes traveled to his exposed member. Her breath hitched as she caught sight of it before biting her lower lips.

Kieran had never been one to brag about his size, but he wasn't by any aspect a small man. He was bigger than average, at ten inches. She would fit him like a glove, but they would enjoy it. Opening the Magnum XL wrapper, Kieran removed the condom and slowly rolled it on as she watched.

Once he had it on, he pulled her up by her arm before leaning down to taste her lips. He laced his fingers in her hair and moved forward as they kissed, backing Alijah up. He broke the kiss to settle between her legs when she was at the top of the bed.

He took his dick in his hand and rubbed it up and down her dripping slit before slapping her clit with it. This caused Alijah's lower body to jerk up as she moaned in pleasure. Still very sensitive from his oral assault.

Again, he ran his dick up and down her slit. Then, he pressed the tip to her opening. He slowly worked it in, looking down at her before pulling it out. He continued this action — each time adding just a bit more than before until he was a third of the way in. Then he pulled back, laying his body over hers.

Kieran stared down into those green jewels before kissing her softly. He then moved to kiss her jawline before kissing down to her neck and, finally, up to her ear.

"I'm going to fuck you until your legs shake, until you're worn out, completely drained of energy, sore and begging me for no more," he stated as his lips brushed her ear. He then licked her earlobe before biting it gently. "Then… I'm going to fuck you again."

Kieran snapped his hips with his last statement and seated himself entirely in her depths. A loud moan fell from Alijah's lips as her chest arched upwards, and her nails instantly went to his shoulders, digging in.

Burying his face in her neck, he closed his eyes. He'd known she would be tight, but he hadn't known she would immediately begin sucking the life from him.

"You're so fucking tight," he stated through clenched teeth into her neck.

Pulling out after a moment, he stopped when only the tip remained before snapping his hips and driving deep within her. He swiveled his hips, which caused her to bite her bottom lip before repeating the act. He was giving her long, slow strokes.

After a few minutes, he removed his face from her neck and looked down at her. Her eyes were closed, but he wouldn't have any of that. He wanted to see those green eyes drowned in pleasure.

"Open your eyes," he demanded. Alijah opened them momentarily, but they fluttered closed as he thrust into her again. Getting up on his hands, Kieran retreated before driving into her hard.

"Kieran!" She screamed, her hands going to his chest, pushing him slightly.

Kieran removed her hands from his chest and put them above her head. He aligned his body with hers again and began to pound into her.

"Open your fucking eyes, Alijah."

Her eyes snapped open to meet his, but Kieran wouldn't stop his assault. He was relentless, and he wanted to see her cum, wanted her pussy to tighten and squeeze him as she submitted to bliss.

"Please, please, Kieran, please." Alijah panted as he slammed into her.

"Please what, baby?" He whispered against her lips. "Tell me what you want."

"Don't stop. Please don't stop."

Kieran swirled his hips as he slammed back into her, and he watched as she found release. Her legs locked around his back as her eyes darkened, and she screamed her release.

"Yes!"

Kieran didn't stop; he merely slowed his strokes, forcing her to ride out her orgasm, lengthening it when he'd brush her g-spot.

When it finally subsided, Kieran moved them around, still embedded deep within her, and sat on the side of the bed with her straddling him. He smacked her ass before leaning back on his elbows.

"Ride this dick," he commanded — his voice filled with pure lust.

He watched as Alijah placed her hands on his chest and began bouncing up and down. Kieran groaned, throwing his head back. It didn't take her long to get into a rhythm, and Kieran enjoyed every minute of it. Her walls began to contract around him, and he knew that her next orgasm was approaching.

Placing his hands on her hips, he began to bounce her harshly. Thrusting up to meet her every time he pulled her down. He sat entirely up, and Alijah wrapped her arms around his neck as he continued to bounce her faster.

"Yes, yes. Right there, baby. Don't stop, please don't stop!" She pleaded as she tightened around him.

"Cum for me," Kieran demanded, slamming her down onto his dick. "Come on, baby. Cum for me."

Alijah's body began to shake at those words, and she tightened her hold on him. He could feel her juices leaking down onto his thighs and knew that she would have squirted all over him if he hadn't been planted deep within her. He stopped bouncing her and began to rock her back and forth, grinding her onto his dick.

She was breathing heavily, and Kieran reached up and pulled her face out of his shoulder. Lacing both hands in her hair, he held her hostage, and he began to kiss her. It was frenzied, hurried, and he was in complete control. He was overwhelming her, and that was just how he wanted it.

Standing up, their lips still connected, Kieran walked to the wall, placing her back against it. He removed his hands from her hair. Taking her arms from around his neck, he put them above her head, pinning them to the wall. He knew the look in his eyes told Alijah precisely what he had planned.

He snapped his hips, pushing into her, causing her to rise slightly off his dick before sliding back down it. Again, he repeated the action, groaning against her lips as she moaned. He tried to keep a slow pace, but he found himself gradually speeding up after a few minutes.

"Kieran! I'm cumming. I'm cumming. Yes!"

At this point, Alijah was bouncing up and down on his dick, using the wall to support her back while Kieran stood still. She was chasing her release, and he wouldn't deny her. When she came, her body slumped, and Kieran released her hands, wrapping his right arm around her waist and using his left hand to hold the condom in place as he slid her off his dick.

Placing her on her feet by the bed, he turned her around and pushed on her back, bending her over. He then slid back home. With both hands on her hips, he wasted no time. His thrust started fast and powerful. He'd given her damn near ten orgasms, and it was his turn. At this moment, he was thinking of only his pleasure.

As he thrust into her, he pulled her back against him. Her moans were loud, filling the room, and Kieran did not doubt that if he had neighbors sleeping in close vicinity, Alijah would have woken them up. He hit the spot deep within her, and she screamed his name, scrambling off his dick onto the bed. He followed, grabbing her waist again.

"Don't run from me," he bit out. Lifting her to her hands and knees and sliding back into her. "Take this fucking dick."

He began to thrust again, placing his hand in the middle of her back, pushing Alijah's upper half down. She complied, and Kieran almost lost his damn mind. With her hands stretched out in front of her, she was almost at a ninety-degree angle. Her arch was practically unbelievable. Kieran admired it while he drilled into her.

Slapping her ass, he reached down and grabbed her hair, pulling her body up against his. Never stopping or slowing his thrust.

"Whose pussy is this?" He whispered in her ear, punctuating his question with a hard thrust. Alijah's only response to him was a whimper. "I can't hear you, Alijah. Tell me who owns this pussy." He snaked one hand up her chest to lightly grasp her neck.

"Shit! You do. It's yours!"

"What is?" He questioned, slamming into her. "What's mine? Say it," he demanded.

"It's your pussy! Oh, fuck! It's your pussy!"

Kieran reached down with the hand that wasn't around her neck and began to slap her clit, causing her to moan uncontrollably.

"What's my name, baby?" He questioned as his clit slapping began to match his thrusting. "Say my fucking name."

"Kieran, Kieran, Kieran." She chanted breathlessly as he pounded into her. Kieran felt his balls tightening at the same time he felt her tighten around his dick. "Oh, Daddy!" Alijah then screamed as cum gushed from her pussy.

At that same time, Kieran grunted his release. "Fuck, Alijah."

He released her, and she fell flat on the bed as he slipped from her warmth. Kieran stood from the bed and removed the used condom before throwing it into the trash. His dick, still hard, bobbed against his stomach. He reached onto the bed and grabbed the other two condom wrappers.

Throwing one on the bedside table, he opened the other and rolled it on — the sound of the foil drawing Alijah's attention. She rolled onto her back and began to back away as she looked at him.

"Kieran, no, wait, stop."

Kieran smiled. His eyes darkened as he reached out and grabbed her ankle, pulling her to him. He positioned himself between her legs and sank home.

"I can't…I can't take anymore tonight." She pleaded as she moaned.

He looked into her eyes, pulling out. "You can," he began before snapping his hips forward, causing her to groan loudly in pleasure. "And you will," he whispered against her lips as he hooked her legs in his arms.

12

Alijah sat at her desk and crossed her legs. Finally, able to do so without the action causing her once sore pussy to protest. Kieran hadn't been playing with her. He had ravished her body the entire weekend. Simply giving her more when she stated she couldn't handle anymore.

It had been well over a year since her last sexual encounter, and she hadn't known if her body could take what he was dishing out, but Kieran had known—giving her just enough to stretch her limit, stopping right before stretching it too far.

She hadn't been prepared for what he was going to give her, which was why he'd completely dominated her body over the weekend and had utterly controlled her. She wasn't going to let it happen again. She knew his game now. Well, at least some of it. She would be prepared next time.

Alijah had to admit she was a little upset, however. He hadn't touched her since the weekend. He had kissed her but hadn't taken it any farther than that. Even though she was sore, she loved the feel of his body on hers. She'd become addicted over the forty-eight hours he'd practically kept her in bed.

She knew he was giving her time to get over her soreness and adjust to his sex, but it was already the middle of the week. She felt as if she'd had more than enough time.

Sighing, Alijah focused her thoughts back on her computer screen. It was almost eleven, and Wayne Farley was due to arrive at any moment to hear Kieran's proposal. So, she needed to finish going over the presentation Kieran would be giving at a meeting he was holding with the department heads that afternoon at two-thirty. Not knowing how long his meeting with Wayne would be, she wanted to be finished beforehand.

Fifteen minutes later, she had just finished syncing the presentation to her tablet when she heard the elevator ding. Looking over, she saw Wayne get off the elevator and head her way.

"Mr. Farley," Alijah stated. "Good morning. It's nice to see you again."

"Please, call me Wayne. It's a pleasure to see you this morning, Alijah," he responded, taking her outstretched hand and shaking it lightly.

"I'm sure Mr. Cayman is ready for you. I'll buzz him and let him know you've arrived. Can I get you anything? Coffee, tea, water?"

"No, thank you. I'm fine."

Alijah nodded before picking up her phone and buzzing Kieran. "Mr. Cayman. Mr. Farley is here to see you."

"Bring him in, Alijah." Came the response on the other end.

"Right this way, please," Alijah stated while picking up her tablet and leading the way into Kieran's office.

Once inside, she sat on the couch like she usually did when Kieran conducted a meeting. She listened to him, and Wayne talk, allowing her Dragonfly program to note what was being said while voice recording it and making notes of critical points she wanted to research more or ask Kieran about later.

They had been discussing business for almost an hour when it finally began to draw to a close. When Alijah was sure nothing else of importance would be said, she turned off her recorder and Dragonfly.

"I'll get with my teams about your time frames and get back to you as soon as possible. I'm sure it shouldn't be a problem, but I don't want to tell you one thing and then not be able to deliver." Wayne stated to Kieran as he glanced over at Alijah.

"That's understandable. Just get with Alijah when you want to meet again and talk more about the figures." Kieran informed him.

Wayne nodded, and Alijah noticed him glance in her direction again. She didn't think much of it, chalking it up to the fact that he was sparing her a glance since Kieran had mentioned her. However, that theory went out of the window with his following words.

"Kieran, you wouldn't mind if I took Alijah out for lunch?"

Alijah's eyes widened before she looked over to Kieran. "Why are you asking me? She's the one you're trying to take. Ask her."

When Wayne turned his full attention to Alijah, she felt a lump in her throat. "How about it, Alijah?"

Alijah swallowed and put on a smile. "Thank you for the offer, but that isn't necessary."

"I insist. It would be my pleasure."

Alijah again glanced at Kieran, but his attention was on his computer, and it was apparent she wasn't getting any help from him. She contemplated for a moment. Wayne seemed kind enough, but so did most people to reel you in.

After a moment of thought, she didn't see the harm in it. They would be in a public place, and it was just lunch between two acquaintances. There was no harm in that.

"Sure. I'll grab my purse, and we can leave."

Standing from her seat, Alijah made her way out of the office. She put her tablet away and dropped her phones into her purse before closing it and waiting by the elevator. It was only a moment before Wayne emerged from the office and headed her way.

As they stepped into the elevator and the doors closed, Wayne turned to her.

"Do you have a preference on where you'd like to eat?"

"There's this little café about a block or so away. We could go there." Alijah stated, informing him of the café she liked to frequent on the days she could have lunch outside of the office.

"Perfect," Wayne stated as the elevator came to a stop.

Alijah stepped off the elevator before him as he motioned her to do so and led the way out of the building. The walk to the café was silent, but it wasn't uncomfortable as she listened to the other people walking around her and the hustle and bustle of cars as they drove by.

When they made it to the café, they both ordered, and though Alijah insisted on paying for her lunch, Wayne would not have it. So, while he paid the cashier, she found them a table by the window and took a seat, waiting for him to join her. Once he did, he looked at her for a moment before speaking.

"So, Alijah, are you from Denver?"

Alijah shook her head. "No, I'm originally from Gainesville, Florida."

"You're a long way from home. How did you end up here?"

"I went to the Art Institute in Utah and met my friend Lawrence. He's from here. I came home with him my Sophomore year for Spring Break and loved it. When I graduated in December, I moved here."

"Do you live with Lawrence?"

"I did for a few months while I looked for a job. When Kieran finally hired me, I moved out of Lawrence's apartment." Alijah answered, hoping he didn't try to pry further and ask her where she lived now.

"What was your major in college? Fashion?

Alijah smiled at him. "No. I paint."

"Really? Are you any good?"

"I would like to think so."

He was about to ask her something else when their order was called. Alijah watched as he got up to retrieve it before glancing out of the window. Wayne was back a moment later, setting the tray on the table.

They each took their food and ate with a bit of small talk. Wayne dumped the trash when they were finished as Alijah waited for him at the door.

Once outside, the sidewalk was even busier, with the one o'clock lunch hour approaching. She felt Wayne place his hand on the small of her back and gently guide her through the crowds of people.

"So, Alijah, you said you graduated in December. How old are you, if you don't mind me asking?"

"I don't mind. I'm twenty-four."

"Did your birthday just pass?"

"Coming up."

"When?" Wayne inquired.

"August," Alijah stated.

Wayne simply nodded, and they fell silent for the remainder of the journey back to the office. Once inside the building, he walked her to the elevator and even got on with her, though she told him it was unnecessary.

"Thank you for lunch," she told him as they ascended.

"You're more than welcome," Wayne responded before continuing. "I have to go out of town on business for a few days, but I'll get with you to set up a meeting about the numbers for Kieran's proposal once I'm back."

"Okay," Alijah responded just as the elevator doors opened.

"I'll talk to you soon then," Wayne stated as she stepped off.

Alijah nodded. "Bye, Wayne. Thanks again."

"It was definitely my pleasure."

With that, the elevator doors closed, and Alijah made her way to her desk. It was one on the dot, and since she had the time, she decided to print out the presentation for each department head and put it together. Sitting her purse in her desk drawer, she took her headset out and put it on, getting down to the task.

It was two o'clock, and Alijah was finished putting together the presentations and had started sorting through emails. She had only done a couple when Kieran buzzed her into his office, telling her he needed her to make copies of some financial reports for him.

Standing from her seat, Alijah made her way to his office and walked in. She hadn't been expecting him to be standing a few feet from the door, which startled her.

He stalked towards her and pushed the door closed, reaching around her to lock it. Alijah looked up into his eyes and swallowed. She knew that look and had gotten used to it over the weekend. She backed up, and it only took three steps before her back hit the closed door.

Alijah cursed herself in her head as he placed both hands on either side of her head, trapping her. Why was he trying to have sex with her now and in his office of all places, less than thirty minutes from his meeting?

"Kieran, we're at work."

"I don't care," he told her, leaning down and placing his lips on her neck.

Alijah held in a moan. "You have a meeting in thirty minutes." She tried again.

"I'll be done before then."

"Someone may come by and hear us."

"What are they going to do?" He questioned before he pulled her earlobe between his teeth. "Fire me?" He finished sarcastically.

Alijah's body was becoming hot as his lips returned to her neck. She wanted this, wanted him, had wanted him to touch her for the last few days, but she knew now was neither the time nor the place.

She didn't know how, but amazingly she mustered up the strength to duck under one of his arms and back away from him. He growled lowly as he turned to her, stalking her like prey. Just when Alijah decided to make a run for it and lock herself in his bathroom until the meeting, it was too late.

Kieran reached out, and she felt his hand wrap lightly around her neck before he pulled her to him. His lips instantly descended on hers. He kissed her fiercely, biting her lip now and then.

Alijah was so caught up in the kiss; she hadn't noticed when he removed himself from his pants. It was only when he used his free hand to guide one of hers around his dick did she realize. He was heavy in her hand, thick and warm like he had been over the weekend. She was still astonished by his size. She had never taken anything that big and was a bit worried when she had first seen it, just knowing it wouldn't fit, amazed when it had.

Slowly, as he continued to kiss her, Alijah began stroking him. He groaned into her lips, and she felt him raise her skirt. Removing his hand from her neck, he grabbed either side of her panties and quickly ripped them, drawing a gasp from her.

Kieran pulled away from her lips, and she watched as he stuck her panties in his back pocket before reaching in his front and pulling out a condom. She had no doubt he'd put it there before calling her into his office.

While he was distracted by those two things, Alijah could drift down a bit from her high, and again, she knew they didn't need to do this. She slowly began to take two steps back, thinking she would be able to get to the bathroom before he noticed. She was wrong.

"If you run into that bathroom, Alijah, I will break that door down and fuck you into the tile for running from me," he stated as he rolled the condom down his length, looking up at her.

Kieran's words had her frozen. She loved his crass language when he was turned on. Hearing it tumble from his lips in that deep baritone got her wetter than a tsunami. He closed the space between them, and Alijah didn't back away.

"Good," Kieran stated. "Now turn around and bend that ass over."

Doing as he asked, Alijah turned around and slowly bent over. She felt his hands on her as he pushed her skirt up to her waist.

"Damn, baby." She heard him mumble as he palmed her ass. "I love this view."

She felt him run a finger over her moist slit and moaned when he slid it between her folds and into her. He worked his finger in her for a moment before pulling out. She then felt his dick pressing at her opening. He pushed it in slowly until he was buried to the hilt as Alijah groaned out in pleasure.

Alijah felt his hands on her hips as he slowly withdrew himself until only the tip was left in.

"Hang on, baby."

Alijah felt his hips snap forward as he buried himself deep inside of her again. She moaned as he pounded into her. She hadn't expected him to be gentle, but she also hadn't expected him to drill her off the bat.

Alijah threw her hands over her mouth, trying to stifle her loud moans. Hardly anyone ever came to Kieran's office unless they had scheduled a meeting, but she didn't want today to be the day someone did, and they heard her moaning loudly. She had learned the offices occupied when she interviewed had only been temporary due to a product release that was taking place.

He had been pounding into her for the last ten minutes, never breaking his pace or aggressiveness. The man was blessed with stamina.

Alijah felt herself tighten around him as she felt her orgasm build. His hand in her hair pulled her head up as he slapped her ass.

"Whose pussy is this?" He questioned, leaning over to whisper in her ear.

Alijah removed her hands and softly gasped out, "Yours."

"Who does it belong to, Alijah? Tell me. What's my name?" Kieran questioned, a brutal thrust punctuating each sentence.

That was all it took to send Alijah over her edge. "Fuck! Kieran, it's yours!" She responded, feeling her juices leak out of her. Her muscles contracted and squeezed around him.

"Shit, baby." Kieran groaned, and Alijah knew he had released himself into the condom. "Mine," he leaned over, speaking into her ear.

Slowly, she felt him pulling out of her as he released her hair. He turned her around and kissed her softly on the lips before taking her hand and leading her into his bathroom.

"Let's get you cleaned up, gorgeous. We have a meeting in a few minutes."

Kieran was frustrated. He was ready to break something and take his frustrations out or fuck something. Unfortunately, Alijah wasn't at the condo. She'd left work at five, but he had stayed to finish a few things, not leaving until after seven. When he'd arrived at the condo, she was nowhere in sight, but a plate was left sitting on the bar for him. He had immediately sent her a text asking where she was. She had responded that she was shopping and would be back. That had been two hours ago.

During that time, he had eaten, worked out, and showered, yet he was still frustrated. Before leaving the office, Remy had called him, informing him that Mr. Lao had decided the only person he would speak further with about the business venture was Kieran himself and settle for nothing less than a face-to-face meeting.

For a moment, Kieran had been very close to saying fuck it and bringing Remy back to the states. However, after thinking about it for a while and speaking to Remy, he realized that he had already put an obscene amount of work and time into trying to get this deal to go through. Not only that, but it would result in a significant profit gain for him and his company. His finance experts and statistics team had also seen a twenty percent growth margin, and Kieran liked those numbers.

So, despite his irritation, Kieran had agreed to a meeting the coming Monday. That meant that he had to push some of his appointments for next week back to accommodate his trip. He was even less happy about this trip because it meant that he would be out of the office at the same time Remy was.

Kieran wasn't very fond of those times. It wasn't that he didn't trust the rest of his staff to perform their jobs accordingly in his absence. He just needed to be sure that things were being done correctly. He could leave Simon, the head of his accounting department, in charge, but the man was soft. Kieran wasn't sure that some wouldn't try to run over him in his absence.

Had he just been leaving for a day, he wouldn't have worried about it as much. However, that wasn't the case. He would be gone at least three days, and that was if negotiations went smoothly at Monday's meeting. If not, he would be there longer and have to push back all of his meetings.

Sighing, Kieran stood to his feet and headed to his bedroom. He grabbed his phone from the bedside table and looked at the time. It was almost ten. He found the contact he was looking for and waited as the phone rang.

"Yeah?" Came the answer on the other end.

"Paetyn, are you busy next week?"

"Not at the beginning of the week. I have a company renting out *Afenity* for a party they're throwing Friday, so I'll be running around then trying to make sure everything is past standards. What's up?"

"I'm going out of town for a few days. I have to head to China and close a deal. Remy is already there, and I need someone to check in and ensure everyone is still working diligently while I'm gone."

"Not a problem," Paetyn responded. "I can take care of it. You need me to check in tomorrow?"

"No, my meeting isn't until Monday, so from then until Wednesday. I should be back by Thursday morning." Kieran informed.

"Not a problem."

Kieran spoke to Paetyn for a few more moments before hanging up the phone. He sat it on the bedside table again before laying back in his bed.

He had fallen asleep he surmised after he had woken up. Kieran glanced over at the clock and saw that it was a little after one in the morning. He sat up, rising to his feet and stretching. He knew Alijah had to be back, and his libido demanded that he pay her a visit.

Reaching into his bedside table, he retrieved a condom before walking out of his bedroom and down the hall. He gently turned her doorknob, checking that it was unlocked. He pushed it open slowly before stepping inside when he found that it was.

He could see her in her bed, the soft light from the lamp in the hallway spilling into the room. She was lying on her side with her back facing him.

Kieran removed his clothes before slowly opening the condom and rolling it down his length. He wasn't sure what Alijah had done to him, but it was as if he could never get enough of her.

Sliding into bed behind her, Kieran wrapped an arm around her waist, pulling her to him before dipping his hands into her panties. She was only wearing them and a tank top, and for that, he was grateful. He didn't feel like wrestling with her clothes.

He began to stroke her slowly while placing kisses on her shoulder. It wasn't long before she started to stir and get wet — her body responding to his ministrations. She let out a sigh, and Kieran stopped his movements, placing his hand on her waist and turning her to face him.

"You were asleep when I got back."

"I'm up now, baby," he informed her, showing her his double meaning as he pulled her close, pressing his hardened dick into her thigh. "Panties off."

He began to stroke himself slowly, waiting as she removed her panties before facing him on her side again. Lifting her right leg, he brought it over his waist before positioning himself at her entrance. Kieran leaned in and kissed her as he slowly slid inside of her.

Alijah moaned against his lips, and he bit her bottom one once he was entirely embedded. He didn't move for a moment, just enjoyed the feeling of her gripping him. It amazed him every time she took all of him. He was sure he'd never get used to how tight she was.

Kieran pulled back from the kiss and slowly moved inside of her. Though he knew his slow pace wouldn't last. He seemed to always lose control with her. Giving in to his carnal desire and allowing his body to establish the rhythm, instead of his brain as he had with any other woman, Alijah wasn't any other woman.

As he expected, his slow pace only lasted minutes before it gradually picked up. Before long, he was slamming into her. Listening to her moans and screams fill the room. Alijah was always so expressive, and that fact was what usually led him to talk so salaciously to her during sex. He'd never been one to do much of it before, preferring to get his rocks off and get up to shower away whatever woman had assisted him before climbing into his bed and going to sleep or getting back to work. Alijah made him do things out of his character, and he couldn't say that he didn't like it.

Kieran reached up as he continued to pound into her and wove his fingers through her hair, bringing her face back to his. Their lips barely touched, but they weren't kissing.

"Tell me you like it," he demanded, lips ghosting over hers.

"I like it. You know I like it, Daddy."

"Tell me you want more," he then demanded, still pounding into her deeply.

"Yes, yes. I want more. Please give me more."

At that, Kieran began to jackhammer into her, his actions making her scream out. He could feel her tightening and knew she was close to release. Her walls were milking him, and Kieran could feel his own release on the horizon. His name tumbled from her lips, and Kieran kissed her. Claiming her mouth as he released into the condom.

When the last rope of cum had squirted from him, Kieran slowed the kiss down, gently removing himself from her. He released her, rolling out of bed to remove the condom and throw it away before joining her again. He pulled her to him and kissed her forehead.

"In the morning, I need you to call the pilot and have him file a flight plan for Altay, China. Something just came up that I need to handle. You also need to pack tomorrow after work. We're flying out Friday night," he informed her.

"Okay." That was all she said before snuggling closer to him.

Kieran had never been one to be affectionate. Even less so after sex, but he didn't mind with Alijah. He knew she wasn't after him for his money like most of his past sexual partners, which allowed him to be comfortable with her.

Closing his eyes, Kieran tried to get some sleep and not think about the half-naked beauty he held in his arms.

13

Alijah stepped off the plane in Altay, China. It seemed as if her body was giving out on her right away. She had known she would have a bit of jet lag but hadn't expected it to kick in right away. After calling the pilot Thursday morning as Kieran had asked her to, she did some research on Altay. She had learned that it was a twenty-three-hour flight. That at first had worried her, but Kieran told her it would be fine. In Moscow, they would stop halfway to refuel and do whatever else needed to be done.

Her subsequent discovery was that Altay was fifteen hours ahead of Denver. So, while they had left Friday night, they didn't arrive until Sunday afternoon. Alijah figured that was another reason her body was so out of sorts, and she hadn't even been off the place more than a few minutes. To her body, it was supposed to be nighttime.

Sighing, Alijah followed Kieran as he made his way to the car that was waiting for them. She slid in first, and once he was in and the driver was going around to get in as well, she leaned over and lay her head on his shoulder. She just wanted to sleep the rest of the day. As if reading her mind, Kieran's voice broke the car's silence.

"You can't go to sleep, Alijah."

Alijah contemplated rolling her eyes for a moment but then decided against it. He couldn't see her so the act would be done only for her benefit, and she honestly did not have the energy.

"Like hell, I can't. When we get to the hotel, I'm taking a hot shower and going straight to bed." Even though she'd showered on the plane, she felt she needed another one.

Kieran didn't reply to her surprise and relief. She didn't have the energy to try and argue with him. She just wanted to rest, even if it was only for the ride to their hotel.

He hadn't been specific about where he wanted to stay, so Alijah decided to book a two-bedroom suite at the Sheraton Urumqi Hotel. When she informed Kieran of as much, he hadn't seemed to mind either way.

Alijah hadn't remembered falling asleep, but she was awakened by Kieran shaking her. She slowly opened her eyes, and she would have sworn it was one of the most challenging acts she'd performed in all her life. She was beyond tired.

As Kieran helped her out of the car while the bellhop retrieved their bags, she wanted to smack him. Her body was going through war trying to deal with the drastic change, yet he seemed to be handling it without a hitch.

She wondered if he'd done anything special. She couldn't be sure but figured he was okay due to the fact that the man hardly ever slept anyway.

Alijah hadn't interacted with Kieran a lot on the plane. She spent most of her time in the small bedroom the plane housed, while he spent his in the front, going over work as usual. She saw him when he came to shower, and she contemplated joining him, but she'd already used the shower herself and knew there was no room for that. She had wanted to join the mile-high club, but his constant work stopped that.

Once they were checked in, Alijah found herself in their suite. She wasn't sure how she'd gotten there but chalked it up to her body being on autopilot. She was vaguely aware that Kieran was tipping the bellhop as she made her way to, what she assumed, to be one of the bedrooms.

She stumbled in and flopped down on the bed unceremoniously. Alijah let out a sigh of relief as she allowed her eyes to drift shut and her body to relax.

Alijah groaned in her sleep. She knew she hadn't been asleep very long, and here she was being awakened again. She wasn't going to give in. She planned to ignore him. She figured he would go away and leave her alone if she did. Unfortunately, that didn't happen.

She was lifted off the bed and placed on her feet. She didn't know where it came from, but she mustered up the energy to glare at Kieran. Of course, he didn't seem fazed. Alijah was so intent on glaring at him; however, she almost missed the fact that he had undone her jeans and was now attempting to pull them down. She placed her hands on top of his to stop him.

"I'm not in the mood for you to try to fuck me right now."

Lifting a brow as he gazed at her, Kieran used one of his hands to restrain both of her wrists and continue to remove her jeans.

"If I were trying to fuck you, you wouldn't protest. We both know that," he responded as he released her wrist, having gotten her pants down to her ankles. He pulled her shirt over her head so quickly that Alijah didn't know what hit her.

"Kieran, I'm serious." She gritted out, trying to take her shirt from him.

She watched as he threw it behind himself before picking her up.

"If you don't put me down, I promise I'm going to..."

Her words trailed off as they made it into the bathroom. There she found the large spa tub was filled. There were also a few candles lit, and she could smell the lavender in the air.

"You're going to what?" Kieran questioned, placing her slowly on her feet. When she didn't say anything, he reached out to unhook her bra. "Finish getting undressed and get in."

"So, you do have a soft spot somewhere in you." Alijah teased as she pulled her bra off.

"No," Kieran stated simply, and Alijah couldn't tell if he was joking but figured he was. "I'll be back to get you in a little while." With that, she watched him walk off.

Kieran left Alijah to her bath and headed back into the suite's living room. He knew she was tired and wanted to sleep, but he couldn't let her just yet. He wasn't trying to be an asshole...for once. He knew, however, that if she slept now, there was a possibility she would be up all night, and he didn't need her tired at their meeting tomorrow morning.

He took out his phone and decided to call Paetyn and let him know that they had made it safely.

"Hey," Paetyn answered on the third ring. Kieran could hear the noise in the background and knew that his friend was at one of his restaurants.

"Hey. Just letting you know we made it."

"Great." There was a pause. "Have you talked to Cruz?"

"No," Kieran responded. "Was I supposed to?"

"I was just wondering."

Kieran's suspicions were instantly kicked up, but he knew whatever it was, he wouldn't get it out of Paetyn. At least not until he was ready to tell him. So instead of asking his friend what it was, he spoke to him a few more minutes before ending the call.

He sat for a few moments, just enjoying the quiet. Not that the plane hadn't been relatively quiet. He didn't like the sound of the engines. Despite how soft they were, he could still hear them. After a few more minutes, he picked up the room service menu by the phone.

After perusing it, he decided to order their fruit medley. He knew that Alijah needed to eat something but knew that something substantial would not sit well with her in her body's current exhausted state.

Once his order was placed, he headed back into the bedroom she'd claimed and peaked into the bathroom at her. She was lying back with her head resting against the bath pillow. The bubbles were up to her chest, but he could see her chest rising and falling steadily, so he knew she was sleeping. He thought about waking her but figured a short nap wouldn't hurt.

Making his way back out of the room, he grabbed the suitcases he'd had the bellhop leave by the door and wheeled them into the room. He thought about going through her bag and finding her something to put on when she got out of the tub but figured she probably didn't want him in her things. So, instead, he looked through his suitcase and pulled out one of the two t-shirts he'd brought with him and laid it out for her. He also pulled out a pair of boxer briefs and shorts for himself.

As he placed their suitcases into the closet, his mind wandered back to her statement about him having a soft spot once pulling the items out. He had told her no, and he wasn't lying. He'd never run a bath for a woman before or chosen something for her to wear when she got out. To him, that hadn't been his job with the women he'd dated, but she did things to him. He was sure that most of his actions were because he knew what the end result would yield. Alijah under him. So, he was more than certain his dick was doing most of the thinking for him, and the actions were coming off as sweet and romantic.

Kieran was brought out of his musing by a knock on the door. He opened it after looking out of the peephole and seeing that it was room service. He allowed the young man to wheel the cart in and tipped him before he left.

Once the door was locked again, Kieran went into the bedroom and grabbed his clothes before making his way into the other bedroom to use the shower. When he was finished, he dried off and got dressed before going to get Alijah from the bathtub. She had been in there almost an hour.

Leaning over the tub, he pushed some of her wild curls from her face before grabbing one of the plush towels. He sat at the edge of the bathtub and ran his knuckles slowly down the column of her neck. He did this a few times before she stirred. When hazy green eyes stared at him, he held up the towel.

"Let's get you out."

He watched as she nodded slowly before standing to her feet. Kieran had to tell his body to simmer down upon seeing her dripping with water. He decided then that he would be taking her in the shower very soon.

Wrapping the towel around her, he easily lifted her from the bathtub, sitting her on her feet on the thick rug. He helped her dry off before leading her to the bedroom and pulling his shirt over her head the whole time, trying to keep his dick under control.

"Where are my panties?" Alijah asked as she tossed the towel onto a chair.

"I didn't think you'd want me going through your things. You don't need them anyway."

"Kieran, I wasn't playing. I'm too tired."

He merely stared at her and blinked before taking her hand and leading her to the living room. He had sincerely hoped she had realized by now that if he wanted her, he would have her, and she would love it. He almost wanted to prove that fact to her as she protested the whole way to the living room. As soon as he released her, she turned to go back into the bedroom.

"I'm going to bed."

He wrapped an arm around her waist and pulled her back to him. "You need to eat something first."

He released her and removed the lid from the tray only after she nodded. While she piled the different fruits onto her plate, Kieran pulled his laptop from its bag and decided to do some work. He had been working for about fifteen minutes when Alijah's voice cut through his focus.

"Aren't you going to eat?

"I had planned on it," he stated, still typing on his laptop. "But you keep telling me you're tired, so I guess I'm going to have to wait," he finished, looking up and locking his hazel eyes with hers. He watched her slowly chew the strawberry she had taken a bite of before going back to what he had been doing.

It was quiet for a while, but her voice rang out again, pulling him from his work.

"Kieran," she stated.

"Yes?" He questioned, looking over the modifications Mr. Lao had told Remy he wanted.

When she didn't say anything, he looked up. What he found was her, one leg draped over the side of the chair. The other spread open. Her slit was glistening at him as she picked up another strawberry.

"It wouldn't be right of me to let you starve."

Smirking, Kieran placed his laptop on the table, standing. He made his way over to her and dropped to his knees. "No, it wouldn't," he stated before diving in.

Alijah sat at the conference table beside Kieran. As she did, she took notes on the conversation being had. It was amazing to her that the entire ordeal hadn't turned into a screaming match by now. She was sure that had something to do with Remy. She'd met the man that morning and had quickly discovered that he was Kieran's opposite. Where Kieran was short-tempered and quick to react, Remy seemed to have the patience of Job.

Each time a storm began to brew within Kieran, Remy would step in and take control of the conversation for a few moments to let Kieran simmer down a bit.

In his defense, Alijah could understand why Kieran was often losing his already short patience. Mr. Lao was a ridiculously impossible man. She had discovered this at the beginning of the conversation. He stood about five-four and was averagely built. The Americans in the room towered over him— even Alijah in her heels. However, with the way the man carried himself and was being outright belligerent, you would think he was the most prominent man on the planet.

His accent was thick, which at times made his English hard to understand, but it wasn't something that was hindering the meeting. Remy had brought along the translator he'd employed as well, but the young lady was sitting in the corner. Her eyes stating she was as bored as Alijah was.

Slowly, Alijah shifted in her seat. She'd been shifting often, and every time she did so, Mr. Lao and his associates' eyes would snap to her as if her movements were somehow an offense to them. She was sure they were, in a way. Hell, she had discovered that her very presence was offensive to them. Well, him, at least.

He was the old-fashioned sort. A feat Alijah learned after introducing herself and holding her hand out to shake his. He'd completely ignored her as if she hadn't been there and began speaking to Kieran. She wanted to snap at the little dwarf of a man, but a light touch to the small of her back had her looking into Remy's dark eyes. He guided her to the conference table and pulled her chair out for her.

As she had expected, her shifting garnered Mr. Lao's attention, and he sent her an impatient look. Alijah gritted her teeth and gripped her pen tighter. Placing more force than necessary on the pad, she was writing on. This was one of those times she couldn't use her Dragonfly applications. With the thickness of Mr. Lao's accent, she knew everything he said would be registered wrong.

Alijah felt a warm hand on her bare knee, and she relaxed a little. The meeting had been going much that way since it started. The little man would do something, say something, ticking one of them off, and they would have to calm each other down. Well, as much as she could calm Kieran.

They had been in the meeting for three hours, and nothing was getting accomplished. At this point, she even thought that Kieran should give up on the whole deal. She understood he'd put a lot of his time into it, but she didn't think it was worth it, especially if he often had to deal with Little Satan.

"You know what, ladies and gentlemen. I propose we break for lunch." Remy stated, his accent just barely noticeable. If she had to guess, she would say he was Haitian.

Everyone seemed to agree with this due to the ever-rising tension in the room. Alijah wanted to be out of this man's presence for a while. Unfortunately for her, Mr. Lao informed them that he had lunch catered and sent his assistant out to retrieve the caterers.

As she watched the young man go, Alijah sat her pen down and turned to Remy, who was seated to her right.

"Could you point me in the direction of the restroom?"

"I'll show you. It's challenging finding your way around here."

Remy stood, excusing them both, and Alijah followed suit, following him out of the conference room. As they walked down the hall, she let out a sigh she didn't know she had been holding in. She heard Remy chuckle next to her, and she turned to look at him.

"I feel the same way after talking to him."

"He's just so disrespectful. It's the twenty-first century. Women have rights. I wanted to smack him. The little twerp of a man."

At that, Remy began to laugh again. "Believe me. You aren't alone."

The rest of the walk was silent as Remy led her to the bathroom. Alijah took care of business and washed her hands before leaving back out. She didn't want to go back into that room, but she knew it was part of her job. So, she sucked it up and walked back the way she had come with Remy.

"So, how do you like working for Kieran so far?" He questioned a moment after they were headed down the hall.

"It's...different. Challenging."

"Because he's an asshole?" He questioned with a smirk.

"That's one of the reasons and because he seems to work more than he sleeps." Alijah agreed with a chuckle.

"Well, I can say you'll probably last the longest. It's the middle of July, and you're still here. That's what? Two months? Most of his assistants are raged and ready to quit by this time."

"What can I say? I'm a tough cookie," she stated with a smile as they made it to the conference room door. She took a deep breath and walked through the door as Remy held it open for her.

When she entered, the first thing she saw was the food that was spread across the tables. There were sandwiches, salads, and what appeared to be soup.

Making her way back over, she reclaimed her seat beside Kieran, who was checking emails on his phone from the looks of it. The caterers came around and placed lunch in front of everyone. Alijah said a quick prayer over her meal before taking a bite of the soup. It took her only a moment to realize it was Bean Cured Soup. She reached over and took Kieran's from him just as he was about to lift his spoon.

"Alijah," he stated. His tone was more demanding than questioning.

"You can't eat this, Kieran. It's Bean Cured Soup."

Kieran let out a sigh like he was irritated with her like most of the other men in the room. "Is that supposed to mean something to me?" He questioned through gritted teeth.

Alijah thought about just giving it back to him and letting him eat it for a moment. It would be his fault if he had a reaction. She was trying to save him some trouble. However, she knew that his irritation wasn't targeted towards her per se. Therefore, she took a breath to calm herself down before replying to him.

"It has fennel seeds in it, Kieran."

She saw the look of realization on his face. Fennel seeds had been one of the items he'd listed in her hiring information that he was allergic to. Instead of saying anything, he merely nodded his head and turned back to the rest of his food.

"It's rude to call one's boss by the first name." Mr. Lao stated, and Alijah had to resist the urge to roll her eyes. "You lose respect from employees. Too intimate when should be all business," he then stated, looking at Kieran.

Buddy, you have no idea how intimate we are, Alijah thought as she took another bite of her soup. She had decided to ignore him for the rest of the meeting.

"Negotiations are not finished, Mr. Cayman."

"There will be no more negotiations." Kieran ground out. Mr. Lao had pushed him to the edge, and Alijah could see it. "That is my final offer. Those are my terms. You can take it or leave it." The smaller man opened his mouth to speak, but Kieran cut him off. "You have forty-eight hours to make your decision."

He stood, waiting for Alijah and Remy to follow suit, and the four of them, the translator included, exited the room. Alijah quietly followed him to the car he'd hired and slid in to wait while he spoke to Remy.

He slid into the car when he was done, and the driver pulled off. Kieran grabbed her chin lightly, and Alijah turned to look at him. He leaned in and kissed her forehead.

"Thank you," he stated. "If you hadn't been there today, who knows what could have happened."

Alijah had long ago stopped being shocked by his sweet actions when he was with her. She was coming to expect the contrast of public Kieran and...well, and *her* Kieran.

"I'm also sorry that Lao was such an ass."

She smiled at him. "I deal with a bigger one on a daily basis." She teased.

Kieran raised an eyebrow at her. "When we get back to the hotel, I'm going to show you my gratitude for the next forty-eight hours."

Alijah's breath hitched. She had no doubt he would make good on that promise, and she was looking forward to it.

14

"Come on, Kieran. Be a man." Alijah taunted. "Unless that's difficult for you." She then concluded, receiving a grunt as her reply.

Moments before, she and Kieran had been having a...friendly debate about him manhandling her in the bedroom. He'd stated it wasn't his fault she was tiny compared to him. While that was indeed true, Alijah wouldn't admit that she was small. She was over the average height of women, and she had a stable weight that consisted of less fat than muscle. In her attempt to defend herself, he merely told her she was cute before walking from the kitchen into the living room.

For some reason, after that, she'd thrown out this ridiculous challenge to him. She wanted to test their strength against each other. She knew she would probably lose, but if Alijah were honest, she would have to say she was bored and needed something to entertain her this Saturday afternoon. He had agreed. Only on the condition that he got to choose her challenge since she wanted to pick his. Which is how five minutes later, Alijah found herself lying across his back. Her head on his shoulder, her arms wrapped around his stomach as he did thirty push-ups.

To her dismay and delight, he finished them with ease. She removed herself from his back when he was done and sat down on the couch.

"Okay, macho man. What's my challenge?" She questioned.

She watched as Kieran looked down at his watch. "I'll think of something. I have to go. I'm meeting the guys to play ball," he informed her before walking over and kissing her gently on the lips. He then headed for the door but stopped and turned back around. "Are you going to be here when I get back?"

Alijah furrowed her brow. "I plan on it. Why would you ask me that?"

"Because last time I went to play ball with them, you didn't come back that night."

She sighed and rolled her eyes. "Whatever. I'll be here. If I'm not, know that I'm going back."

Kieran didn't respond, only turned and walked out of the door, and honestly, Alijah was glad he didn't. She didn't need him bringing up the things that happened about a month ago.

Getting up, Alijah decided to paint since she had time. She hadn't been up on the roof to paint yet and figured today was as good a day as any.

She contemplated how she would get everything to the roof in one trip and remembered that Lawrence had bought her one of those pop-out rolling carriers. She found it in her closet and loaded it with her paint supplies and stuffed her easel in once she'd folded it down. Alijah placed her phone in her pocket and put her earpiece in her ear. She then reached for a canvas and noticed it was her last one. Making a mental note to buy more when she got the chance, she opted on carrying it and headed to the roof.

Once she'd set up her materials, Alijah looked over the skyline. It was a beautiful day. The sky was clear and radiant, so she decided that's what she would paint.

Art had always been a solace for Alijah. She would find herself drowning out her parents' arguments as a child. They were usually centered around her mother and why she hadn't done one thing or another that her father deemed necessary before he got home. As well as being a chronological cheater, the man was mentally and verbally abusive.

He would often berate her mother for not doing something or not doing it the way he thought she should. Whenever her mother would try to defend herself against his onslaught of words, it would quickly turn into an argument that didn't end until well into the night.

During those times, Alijah would hold up in her room and draw. If it weren't for her parents, she never would have discovered her love of replicating beautiful things. So, she supposed she had at least that to thank them for, especially as she got older.

As a pre-teen, her father's abusive words began to target her. The argument would start between her parents, but she was quickly brought into it if she happened to be in the room. He would make cracks about the wildness of her hair and the fact that they needed to do something about it. Often, he would even question her mother, in front of Alijah no less, whether or not she was his daughter. Siting her green eyes as the reason he had his doubts, considering both of her parents had brown eyes.

Sometimes, she wondered if physical abuse would have been better. At least those bruises healed over time. The damage that her father inflicted did not grant her that luxury. So, Alijah learned to give as well as she got. She would do her damnedest to let her father's words roll off her back and shoot back something just as harsh at him once she was a teenager. For her actions, she always stayed grounded, but she didn't care. Her needle-sharp tongue was how she had come to protect herself from him. As she got older, the habit didn't fade.

She never honestly got over what her father would say to her, and she knew those scars would forever run deep, but she buried them down deeper. Alijah covered them with a band-aid that had been holding firm ever since.

Alijah was brought out of her thoughts by the feel of her phone vibrating in her pocket. Reaching up, she pushed the button on the blue tooth to answer it.

"Hello."

"Hey, And."

Alijah rolled her eyes but smiled nonetheless at the nickname her best friend had given her upon meeting and realizing it was what her initials spelled.

"Hey, Erin. How are you?"

"I'm pretty good. You know, just working. I've been so busy; I feel like we haven't spoken in quite some time."

"That makes two of us. So, how's work going?"

"It's going well. I'm bringing a lot of customers into the shop."

"That's great. Any word on whether or not they're going to make you a partner?"

At that question, Alijah heard her friend sigh and knew she had asked the wrong one. She scrambled to find another topic but heard Erin speak before she could.

"I don't know, And. I mean, they should. I work harder than anybody else in that place, and I'm pretty good at what I do." Erin responded.

Alijah snorted. On that, she had to disagree. Yes, her friend worked harder than anybody else in that shop, but she wasn't just pretty good. She was damn good. Hell, she was even beyond that. She was better than the two co-owners themselves. Erin had done all of Alijah's tattoos, and whenever someone saw them, they always complimented her on the cleanliness of the lines and the beautiful intricacy.

She had seen a lot of the other shop artists' work and having an eye for art; she knew that her friend was the best. Alijah honestly felt as if Erin was being held back.

"You should just open your own shop, Erin."

"Believe me, I've thought about it, but no bank is going to give me a loan with my credit, and we both know the cost of living in Florida is no joke. It will take me forever to save for a building and all the equipment I would need."

"Yeah, I don't miss the cost of living there. Have you tried finding a building to rent?" Alijah questioned as she paused in her painting to grab a smaller brush.

"I've looked at a few places, but I suppose space should be an afterthought until I get all the equipment I need." Erin sighed. "Enough with that; tell me how you've been."

"I've been good. I just got back from China."

"China?"

"Yeah, I had to go for work."

"How is work with your sinfully handsome boss?"

At that, Alijah laughed. "He's still a hard-ass most..."

"Even though you're letting him lay the pipe?" Erin cut her off.

"Wow," Alijah stated, rolling her eyes. "He's still a hard-ass most of the time. Especially at work. He's a bit better at the condo."

"I was about to say. If he's still that way all the time, you need to restrict his pussy playtime."

Alijah fell into a fit of laughter. Leave it to her direct friend to say something like that. They had practically grown up together, yet Erin was always finding new ways to shock her.

"Don't laugh, And. I'm serious." Erin paused for a moment. "Anyway, I'll be in town the week of your birthday. We have to celebrate big. Twenty-five is a big deal. We're going to party all weekend."

Alijah was a little horrified by that fact. Her birthday was a little over two weeks away and fell on a Sunday. She remembered when they'd celebrated last for Erin's twenty-fifth birthday. They'd all had a hangover for two days. She did not want to repeat that.

"I don't know, Erin. Let's just go out and have dinner and then go to a lounge or something."

"I'll think about it." Her friend responded, and Alijah rolled her eyes. Erin was going to think about it like it was her birthday. Typical.

Alijah spoke to her friend, catching up on what they'd missed out on over the two weeks they hadn't talked. When she hung up the phone, Alijah noticed she was finished with her painting and had just been staring at it. She began to pack up her materials before carefully taking the painting off the easel and folding it down.

She made her way back onto the elevator and back to the condo. Once inside, she put her items into her bedroom and checked the time. It was after five, and Alijah decided to start dinner. She was in the mood for salmon and decided to pair it with sautéed asparagus, butter squash, and rolls.

She set about preparing the food as she thought over Erin's dilemma. She wanted to help her friend because she believed in her talent and knew that all she needed was a start in the right direction.

Alijah was making more than enough money working for Kieran, and the fact that she didn't have anything to pay for other than her phone bill and whatever personal items she desired, she could help her friend in some capacity. She decided that she would look into how much tattoo equipment would cost once she was finished cooking and eating.

She was sure Erin wouldn't need more than three stations starting out. She figured it would be easy to find two other people to work for her and charge them space rent or however it went. Either way, it was something she would be looking into.

Kieran sat on one of the bleachers drinking his water. They had just finished another game of two on two, and they were all taking a breather. He watched another group playing on the far side of the gym. One of them looked slightly familiar to Kieran, but he couldn't place him. Shrugging it off, he turned his attention to Cruz, who had come and sat one bleacher down from him.

"I saw your grandfather," he stated.

Kieran slowly brought the bottle from his lips, placing the cap back on it before sitting it down. His jaw ticked, and his eyebrow twitched. This must have been why Paetyn had asked him if he'd spoken to Cruz while he was away.

"You saw the man who donated his sperm to my mother's creation. Not my grandfather." Kieran spat out. Anyone else would have taken offense to his tone, but not his friends, and never Cruz on the infrequent occasion that Paetyn and Nik did.

"He wants to get together with you," Cruz informed him.

Kieran scoffed. He knew that there had to be a reason Cruz was telling him he'd run into the old man. However, Kieran had no desire to meet with him. He hadn't wanted anything to do with Kieran when his parents were still alive. So, Kieran didn't want anything to do with him now.

"Why?" Kieran couldn't help but ask. "Is he dying or some shit?"

"I didn't care enough to ask. I just told him I'd relay the message." Cruz told him, standing. "Message relayed." With that, he walked away from the bleachers to retrieve the ball.

Kieran stayed seated as they started shooting the ball around. His mind on the old man. He would be almost eighty now if Kieran remembered correctly. Maybe he was dying, and he wanted to make some sort of amends before his time was up. Kieran didn't know. He did know that in all of his thirty-five years, the man had never once tried to reach out to him. So, why now?

He got up to join his friends and tried to put it out of his head, but he couldn't. It was there, constantly nagging at him. He had never had any intentions of meeting the man. Had never even thought about it, but now the seed had been planted, and he was more than sure that was probably what the old bastard wanted.

Maybe he wanted to leave his legacy to someone. His mother's family had been well off, which was why her father damn near had an aneurysm when she began to date and ultimately married a young man who grew up in foster care and didn't come for money. The thought of how his parents were treated still pissed him off to this day.

However, if that was what the old man wanted, then Kieran wanted and needed no parts of that. He was successful in his own right. He didn't need whatever the older man was trying to sell because he wasn't buying.

Kieran walked into the condo a little after seven. He was finally able to get his mind off the information Cruz had delivered and focus on their final couple of games. After that, he'd gone to the office to pick up some papers he needed to do some work and headed to the condo.

The smell of delicious food hit him as soon as he entered. He placed the papers on the entrance table and made his way to the kitchen to find Alijah dancing around to the music coming from her phone, which was playing softly through the kitchen. He walked up behind her and wrapped his arms around her waist.

"Hey," she stated, stopping her movements. "You're just in time. It'll be ready in another ten to fifteen minutes."

He leaned in and kissed her neck. "Great. I'm going to go shower really fast."

Once he was done with his shower, he dressed in a pair of sweatpants and headed back into the kitchen, where he joined Alijah at the bar for dinner. They made small talk, and she told him how her friend was coming to visit her in a couple of weeks for her birthday. He found himself telling her that his mother's father wanted to get together with him for some reason. She didn't understand his animosity and hate towards the old man until he told her the entire story while he helped her clean the kitchen.

"Well, what could it hurt to give in and meet with him?" She questioned as she started the dishwasher. "Other than your pride which we both know is not fragile." Kieran didn't respond simply blinked at her. "Maybe he is trying to make amends and apologize," she then stated.

"He can keep his apology," Kieran responded, leaning against the counter. "I don't want it."

Sighing, Alijah walked up to him and pressed her body into his. Kieran gazed down at her with a cocked brow as she wrapped her arms around his neck.

"You're not going to seduce me into talking to him," he informed her bluntly.

"I'm not trying to," she stated, rising onto her tiptoes. He leaned down and allowed her to place a soft kiss on his lips. "I'm just suggesting that you think about it." With that, she removed her arms and headed out of the kitchen. "I'm going to take a hot bubble bath. If someone stops by, you might want to put some boxers on. I can see your dick print."

Kieran smirked to himself. "If you'd like, I'll let you just see my dick," he threw back. He could hear her laugh as she entered her bedroom.

Grabbing the papers from the entrance table, Kieran made his way into his office. They had arrived back from China late Thursday night, and even his body was so out of it that neither one had gone to work yesterday. So, he had called Simon and told him he was in charge of things for the day.

Now, he had some things that he needed to catch up on. His marketing department had come up with a new marketing proposal for the self-aware vacuum his researchers had effectively named Easy Breeze because it made cleaning your floors and carpets a breeze.

Kieran hoped for the marketing department's sake this draft was acceptable. Marketing needed to begin in two weeks, and if this weren't up to par, they would be doing it again on a two-week deadline. If they failed, he would find the people responsible and fire their asses.

After about an hour of going over the new proposal, Kieran was frustrated, irritated, and pissed. He didn't know what was wrong with the department. This concept was only slightly better than the last. He made a mental note to speak with Felix, head of the department, first thing Monday morning. For now, however, he needed to work off his frustrations.

Making his way to Alijah's room, he opened the cracked door to find her swaying to some music again. This time, she was in nothing but a towel. He watched as she placed what he assumed was lotion back onto her dresser before stepping behind her. Kieran put one arm around her waist and pulled her back against him. She didn't stop swaying, so he began to sway with her, grinding his growing erection against her.

"I thought you didn't dance," she stated, looking back at him over her shoulder.

"This isn't dancing."

"Then what is it?" She asked with a raised brow.

"A prelude to foreplay."

He turned her around and removed her towel before leading her to the bed. He placed his hands on her waist, leaned in, and kissed her. When he pulled away, he looked into those beautiful green eyes that had darkened with a need for him.

"I know what your challenge is."

"What?" She questioned.

"I challenge you to take everything I'm about to give you, the way I'm about to give it, without running from me."

He watched as she swallowed. He knew this was going to be hard on her but that she would try. She wouldn't back down from his challenge. If Kieran were honest, he would say she took what he dished out better than any woman he'd ever been with had. However, he wanted to torture her with his oral ministrations without her making him stop, and this was going the be the best way.

"Deal," she whispered

Kieran smirked as he picked her up and dropped her on the bed. "This is going to be fun."

15

Alijah looked on as Felix tried to scramble for excuses to defend himself and his department. They were seated in his office. It was a nice size, but with a pissed-off Kieran present, it made it feel far too small. They had ventured down to marketing to see why they couldn't seem to get a marketing plan together for one of Kieran's products.

She had looked over both concepts sent over to Kieran before the meeting this morning, and she had to agree that they were both a bit elementary. As a consumer, she would have thought that the company selling the product felt that she was far from intelligent if either of those were used.

"I can assure you, Mr. Cayman, you will have a marketing plan that will garner the attention of everyone who passes a billboard by Friday," Felix stated. Alijah could see a bead of sweat running slowly down his temple.

"For your sake, I hope so, Felix. If not, I'm going to fire your entire team and find a new Director of Marketing." Kieran informed him, standing.

Alijah saw Felix's eyes widen, and she had to admit she was also a bit shocked. Would he really fire over twenty people for falling short on one project? As she rose to follow him out, she realized that he would. She had learned that he was serious in all aspects of his life, and he wasn't going to let anyone do something to jeopardize his company's credibility.

She could understand that. However, she didn't want to see all of those people lose their jobs. Her mind was already reeling with a plan as they made their way back to their floor. By the time she sat down at her desk, she had, though only minimal, an idea.

Pulling up the marketing directory, she scrolled until she found Trevor's name. She hadn't spoken to him since she bumped into him after that meeting, but she figured he'd be as good a place to start. She sent him an email telling him to meet her at twelve-thirty in front of the building for lunch and that it was important. It only took a few minutes before she received an email back from him agreeing to meet her.

For the next couple of hours, Alijah went about her regular routine, which now included fighting off Kieran's advances. The man was insatiable, and she had to remind him that they were at work continually. Not that it seemed to matter to him. She had slipped up once and allowed him to take her in his office, and they had been lucky no one happened to come down and speak with him, but she didn't want to chance that luck again.

On top of that, she didn't need any of the other employees knowing that she was sleeping with the boss. They also hadn't established what they were doing. She didn't know if they were dating or just having fun between the sheets in private. She needed to sit down and talk to him about it. While she didn't want to seem like she was trying to force him into something, she wanted to have a clear understanding. After all, she was an adult, and she could handle it if what they were doing was just sex.

Five minutes before twelve-thirty, Alijah informed Kieran she was headed to lunch. When she made it to the lobby, she was right on time, and Trevor was there waiting for her.

"To what do I owe the pleasure of you inviting me to lunch?" He questioned while giving her a dazzling smile.

"Unfortunately," Alijah began signaling for him to follow her out of the building. "This isn't a social visit."

"It wouldn't be my luck if it was. So, why did you want to meet?"

"It's about the marketing plan you all are working on," Alijah responded, glancing at him to see him nodding.

They made it to the little cafe she liked to frequent and ordered before finding a seat. Alijah pulled a notebook from her purse and opened it. She was going to attempt to help them. She had come up with an idea while looking at the other proposals.

As she drew, she explained her idea to Trevor, who seemed to be able to follow it entirely and even threw in his thoughts. When their food was ready, they continued to work while they ate, and he continually complimented her on her artistic ability, and each time she would wave him off.

They only had fifteen minutes to get back to the office by the time they finished. Alijah handed the sketch to Trevor as they walked out. It was just a draft, but the concept was there, and she had drawn in as many details as possible. Trevor had even come up with a tagline. All he needed to do now was clean the sketch and make it presentation ready.

"You know, Alijah, your talents are wasted as an assistant. You should be in marketing drawing up concepts," he informed her as they walked back to the office.

"I don't know about marketing, but who knows. I just thought I should help."

"Well, thanks for that. Actually, a few of my co-workers and I were given another project, and it's been a bit challenging. It isn't due until the end of August, but if you were up for it, I would love to get some suggestions from you."

Alijah thought about it for a moment and didn't see the harm in taking a look. "I can do that. Just let me know when a good time is. Lunch, when I'm not working through it, would be the best time. I'm pretty busy otherwise."

"Mr. Cayman keeps you busy."

You have no idea, Alijah thought as she merely nodded.

When they reached the office, they went their separate ways. When Alijah made it back to the top floor, she was surprised to find a dozen white roses sitting on her desk. Making her way over, she deposited her purse into her bottom drawer before removing the card from the flowers. Her first thought was that they were from Kieran. Opening the card, she discovered it merely read, Just because. There was also no signature on it. Deciding that she would ask him later, she sat down and returned to work. She had so much she needed to accomplish before the end of the day.

● ● ●

They would be flying out later that night to head to Paris. There was a product created by two teenagers that Kieran wanted to see in person. Though she was excited about the prospect of going to Paris, she knew she wouldn't get to see most of what it had to offer. Kieran didn't plan on spending any more than a day there, and Alijah knew it would be spent working.

Deciding she would have to plan a trip for another time to site-see, bringing Erin and Chayse along if they wanted to go, she began opening up the business proposals sent in. Her least favorite part of her job. She had been going through them for half an hour when the elevator dinged. She looked up and saw a tall, slender blonde step off.

Alijah didn't consider herself to be too short. She stood five foot, nine inches in heels, and since she wore those more than anything else, she had begun counting them as part of her height, but this woman was at least five foot, nine inches flat-footed. Putting her at about six feet in the heels that adorned her feet.

"Can I help you?" Alijah asked as the woman seemed about to bypass her desk.

"I'm here to see, Kieran. I'm Rebecca Blowe."

For what? Alijah wanted to ask. Instead, she questioned, "Do you have an appointment?"

"You're his assistant, are you not? Wouldn't you know if I had an appointment?"

Alijah gritted her teeth and swallowed. She took a deep breath to keep herself from acting because she was about to snatch Becky With the Good Hair bald.

"I'll check and see if he can spare a moment for you. He's very busy." Alijah stated, doing her damnedest to remain professional. She had just picked up the phone to dial Kieran when Rebecca decided she would barge into his office. "Ma'am, you can't just..." Alijah began following after her. "Mr. Cayman, I'm sorry, I was going to...."

"It's alright, Ms. Douglas."

"Hello, Kieran."

"Rebecca." Kieran then turned his attention to Alijah. "Ms. Douglas, could you give us a minute?"

Alijah's first thought was to tell him hell no. She would not give them a minute. What did she look like leaving her man with some woman who smelled of slutery, but then she realized they were at work, and he wasn't exactly her man. So, as much as she didn't want to, she nodded and backed out of the room.

Kieran stared at the woman in front of him and knew that he was going to have a headache and need several stiff drinks by the end of their conversation. He hadn't seen Rebecca in years. Not since they ended their relationship, and she so kindly told him she hoped his dick fell off. He couldn't fathom what she could have been possibly doing in his office and what made her have the audacity to just barge in.

"Aren't you going to offer me a seat, Kieran? That would be the gentlemanly thing to do."

Kieran raised a brow at her from his chair. "Yes, it would, but as you stated several times the last time we met, I'm no gentleman. So, you can stand."

Scoffing, Rebecca rolled her eyes and sat. It was silent in the office for a beat, and Kieran decided he would much rather get to what she was doing there and get her the hell out.

"What do you want?" He questioned, leaning back in his seat.

"I have a business proposition for you."

"Not interested."

"You don't even know what it is," Rebecca stated exasperatedly.

"Doesn't matter. It involves you. Meaning I would have to see or work with you in some capacity. So, again, not interested."

He watched as Rebecca rose from her seat and started around his desk. He knew what she would try to do, and she should have known it wouldn't work. It hadn't when they were dating, and it definitely wouldn't now. He wondered why women thought they could seduce a man into anything they wanted. She leaned against the desk right beside him.

"All I need, Kieran, is your sperm."

Kieran swiveled his chair around to look at her while lifting an eyebrow. He had to admit that he wasn't expecting that. In the months that he'd dated this woman, he'd gotten used to her wild and outlandish statements, but this probably took the cake. She was madder than the fucking Hatter if she thought he would give her sperm.

"As much as I shot it down your throat, I'm sure you have plenty," he stated coolly.

He watched as she gritted her teeth before pushing off the desk and standing in front of him.

"Don't be difficult, Kieran. All I want is a baby, and with you, as its father, I can guarantee my child will have a wonderful life. My clock is ticking, and I'm not getting any younger."

"Not my problem," Kieran stated, boredom laced his words.

"Come on." She tried, leaning over and placing her hand on his chest. "You know you want to."

At that moment, Alijah chose to enter his office.

"Mr. Cayman, the pilot called and…." He watched as she trailed off and looked between him and Rebecca. "And I see you're busy." And just as fast as she had come, she was gone.

Kieran removed Rebecca's hand from his chest and stood. "My answer is no, and that's final."

She eyed him for a moment before heading towards the door. "I'll give you time to think about it and change your mind." With that, she opened the door, closing it as she left.

Kieran sat back in his seat. He was wholly convinced that the woman was bat shit crazy. After not seeing someone for two years who just popped up and asked for sperm? She had a few screws loose. If he were to give anybody his sperm, she would be dead last on the list. Shaking his head, Kieran reached for his phone and buzzed Alijah.

"Ms. Douglas, please come inform me of what you needed a moment ago." He placed the phone back on the receiver, expecting her to come through the door a few seconds later as she usually did. Instead, her voice rang out over the speaker of his phone.

"The pilot called. He was able to have the departure time moved up. We're flying out at six this evening instead of nine."

Kieran could distinctly hear when she hung up the phone, presumably with more force than necessary. Picking his phone up, he buzzed her again.

"Ms. Douglas, if there are no pressing matters, could you come into my office?" Kieran listened to her sigh as she picked the phone up before she spoke.

"Considering we will not be here tomorrow; I would say everything is pressing at the moment if I don't want to be swamped when we return."

"Alijah..." But he didn't get to finish because she hung up on him.

Kieran stared at the phone for a moment, trying to figure out what the hell was wrong with her. He took a deep breath to calm himself before he stood up and walked out of his office. He stopped in front of her desk, and she didn't even look up at him.

"Go into my office," he stated. His hazel eyes trying to stare a hole through her. She continued to type; eyes still locked to the screen as she spoke lowly.

"If you need to get your rocks off, you have two fully functioning hands, Mr. Cayman."

Okay, Kieran had had enough. Going around her desk, he yanked her chair back and spun it around. He had one hand around her neck in one swift motion, knowing she enjoyed it, and the other up her skirt.

"Kieran, what are you doing? You can't-"

"Shut up," he gritted through clenched teeth. "Because, yes, I can. Now you're going to take your pretty little ass into my office, and I'm not telling you again. Or I will lay you on this desk and fuck you until the glass shatters."

"You wouldn't," Alijah stated with a gasp. "Someone could come up and see."

"Clearly, you still don't know me well enough," Kieran stated, removing his hands.

He placed them on her waist and lifted her onto the desk, hiking her skirt up as he went. He then set about loosening his belt. He'd just unbuttoned his slacks when she jumped down.

"Okay, fine," she stated as she made a hasty retreat into his office while she fixed her skirt.

Kieran followed behind her fixing his pants as well, then closing and locking the door. He walked over to his desk and sat behind it as she occupied one of the chairs in front of it. It was silent for a minute as she sat with her arms folded under her breast and Kieran became sidetracked as he stared at them.

"I have work to do," Alijah stated, breaking him from his haze. "So, what do you want?"

"For you to lose the attitude and tell me what's wrong with you." From the look she threw him, Kieran suspected he should know.

"Who was that woman?" She finally asked after a moment.

"A woman I used to….an acquaintance from my past." He was going to say a woman he used to fuck but figured she was already mad; he didn't want it to get worse. When she was angry, he didn't get laid. "She...had a business proposition she wanted to discuss."

Alijah scoffed. "I'm sure that proposition included your dick."

Kieran leaned back in his chair. "I don't share my women, Alijah. What makes you think you'd have to share me?"

It was silent for a moment before she spoke. "We aren't together anyway. We're just having fun. So, I don't have a right to..."

"Stop talking." Kieran interrupted. "And come here."

He watched as Alijah slowly rose from the seat she occupied and walked around his desk. He slid his chair back and pulled her into his lap. He leaned in and kissed her lips. "So, my public affection and taking you to meet my friends was what?" When she didn't say anything, he continued. "Because I don't do that often."

Alijah narrowed her eyes at him. "What? Am I supposed to feel special?"

He gave her a devilish smile before answering, "Very." He then leaned in to kiss her again as she rolled her eyes. "Now, go finish working before I fire you."

"You wouldn't," she stated as a matter of fact. "But I thought we were..." She trailed off, leaving the sentence open.

"No, I just wanted to see what was wrong with you." He tapped her thigh, then lifted her out of his lap. "Now go."

He watched the sway of her ass as she walked to the door; when she stopped and turned to look at him, he brought his eyes up to meet hers.

"You know. You may say you don't have a soft spot, but you do. I see it often."

"Not a soft spot. Just thinking with my dick."

Alijah lifted an eyebrow at him before opening the door. "If you say so." By the tone of her voice, he knew she was unconvinced.

16

Alijah was in a good mood as she sat at her desk humming to herself. It wasn't just one particular thing. It was a combination of a few. Their business trip to Paris the previous week had been exciting. Since she had never been, even though her aunt used to have a permanent residence there, Kieran decided they would stay two extra days, and he showed her all of the sites and took her shopping, though she protested the whole time that she could pay for her own things. They even had dinner under the Eiffel Tower. On their last night there, he'd taken her to the balcony of their suite and did things to her under the city lights that were probably illegal in most countries.

Then, upon returning to work that Friday, she was excited to see how Trevor and his team had made the concept the two of them created come to life. The entire time Kieran scrutinized it, she waited with bated breath. If he didn't like it, she was afraid several people would lose their jobs. Once he was done looking over it, he stated that at least someone knew what they were doing and clasped Trevor on the shoulder. Alijah watched as he opened his mouth to give her recognition, but she quickly shook her head, causing his mouth to snap shut.

Now she was bouncing with anticipation. It was already Wednesday, and her birthday was in a few days. That wasn't why she was so happy, though. She hadn't seen Erin in a while and was excited that she would be flying in tomorrow night. Alijah had every intention of having Friday off and spending the day with her friend. She just had to find a way to get Kieran to agree.

So, there she was, working double time trying to get the weeks' worth of work done with only a day and a half left. She was determined to get it done, though. She had seen Kieran do it several times, and if he could do it, she knew that she undoubtedly could as well.

The elevator chimed, breaking her concentration, and she didn't have to look up to know that it was the flower delivery man. When she'd gotten back from Paris last week, three bouquets were waiting on her. There was only one word on each of the cards. By Monday, Alijah knew what the sentence would end up being.

She retrieved the flowers from the young man and thanked him before giving a tip and opening the card. It said, *Gorgeous, Wayne Farley*. Alijah took out all of the other cards and placed them in order on her desk. *Just because this month is your birthday, gorgeous Wayne Farley*, now, she knew the flowers were from Wayne. It made Alijah blush a little bit.

After taking in the fragrance of the flowers, she got back to work. She had been working diligently for half an hour when Kieran emerged from his office. He stopped at her desk and stared at the flowers.

"More flowers?" He questioned as if they offended him. "Did you find out who they were from?"

"Well, they aren't from you." She shot back.

"I give you good dick. Why do I need to give you flowers?" He questioned with a smirk.

"Someone could hear you." Alijah hissed back at him lowly.

"Again, I don't care. They can't fire me. What's the worst that could happen?"

"Someone could think that I slept my way into this job," she informed him, eyes locking onto his.

"But you didn't, so that doesn't matter. Besides, I'm the only one that can fire you."

Alijah rolled her eyes. "Did you come out of your office to simply annoy me?"

"I came to take you to lunch."

Alijah stared at him for a minute. "You mean you're actually going to leave the building?"

Kieran glared at her before turning on his heels, stating he would merely go by himself. Alijah quickly saved what she was working on and grabbed her purse, dropping both phones in before going over to the elevator where he stood. She was not passing up an opportunity to have a lunch date with him. Though he hadn't called it that, she figured it was close enough to one.

When they made it to the street, Kieran took her hand, and they began to weave through the sea of people. They weren't far from her favorite little cafe when someone bumped into her sending her stumbling backward. If it hadn't been for Kieran, she would have fallen. He steadied her before turning to the man that bumped into her, and Alijah could see fire in his eyes.

"Watch where the hell you're going," he informed the man, pulling Alijah closer to him.

"Kieran, hey," Alijah stated, turning in his arms and looking up at him. His jaw was clenched, his left side ticking. "I'm okay. I'm sure it was an accident."

"It was, ma'am. I'm sorry if I hurt you." The man stated sincerely.

"No, I'm fine. You enjoy the rest of your day."

The man wished Alijah the same before hurrying off. She looked up at Kieran again and noticed his eyes followed the stranger through the crowd. Alijah reached up and took his chin in her hand, turning him to face her.

"Hey, let it go. I told you I was okay."

"Check your purse and make sure nothing is missing," he stated, pulling his face from her hands.

"You think he was a pickpocket? I think he was just in a hurry, Kieran."

"Humor me," he stated, still standing in the middle of the sidewalk, forcing people to go around them.

"I'll check it when we're in the cafe. We're in people's way."

She retook his hand and pulled him behind her to the cafe with that stated. When they entered, there was no one in line at the counter, so they were able to place their orders quickly. As they sat while they waited, she went about going through her purse, making sure everything was there. When she was satisfied that it was, she told him as much.

● ● ●

"You can never be too careful," he stated as a reply.

They made idle chitchat. Most of it was about work, and Alijah had to refrain from rolling her eyes several times. The man ate, slept, and breathed his job. Alijah admired him for having drive and desire, but there was more to life than working all the time.

They ate in relative silence when their food came, and she didn't like it. She enjoyed the sound of his deep baritone and, at that moment, would have listened to him talk about work just to hear it. She realized she was a contradiction rolled into one.

Lunch finished, and as they walked back, Kieran again held Alijah's hand. It was the first time they had shown any affection in public other than at the club. However, Alijah didn't count that, considering the lighting was dim, and only his friends paid them any attention.

He had stated that he didn't share and that she wouldn't be sharing him, but he hadn't said what they were doing. It clarified that it wasn't just fun, but were they together, dating? She didn't have the answer, and she didn't want to bring it up so soon after her slight jealous fit last week.

When they made it to the office building, Alijah tried to slide her hand out of his, but he gripped it tighter. When he opened the door and began walking in, she halted in her tracks. A slight panic was rising inside of her.

"What's wrong?" Kieran asked.

"We can't walk through the lobby with you holding my hand. People will talk."

"So, let them talk. We aren't kids."

"Kieran."

He raised a brow at her and asked, "Are you ashamed of me, Alijah?"

She looked into his face and knew that he was joking, but the question was still stupid. No woman in her right mind would be ashamed of the sex on legs standing in front of her. Yet here she was trying to conceal whatever they had going on from the people in the office. It was justifiable to her. She worked there and didn't need the gossip mill going. They would call her all kinds of things. Not to her face, obviously, but they would say them.

"People will think I'm getting special treatment because I'm sleeping with the boss."

"Alijah, do you know how many..."

"If you ask me if I know how many employees you've slept with, I will punch you," she told him.

He raised a brow. "I was going to ask if you knew how many of my employees are sleeping together."

"That's different. Those are two employees on the same pay grade. You are the boss, and I am your assistant."

Getting frustrated with her, he threw out a quick fine before releasing her hand and walking into the building. Alijah took a breath before walking in after him. She could tell that he was upset; she could see it all in his shoulders. However, she needed him to see things from her point of view. She was sure things would be different if she was the boss and he was her assistant, but because they were the way they were, she knew people would have something to say. That was just the way it was — a complete double standard.

The ride back up to the top floor was silent. Alijah didn't know what to say to get him to see her point of view, so she decided to remain quiet. When she settled back at her desk, she got back to work. She was halfway through tomorrow's work and knew she wouldn't have difficulty finishing Friday's work tomorrow.

It was going on three-thirty, and Alijah decided it was now or never to ask Kieran for Friday off. She had given him a few hours to calm down, and she was ready to approach, albeit with caution.

She knocked on his door twice before pushing it open and entering. He was seated behind his desk on his cellphone. She could only assume he was speaking to one of his friends. Locking the door behind her, Alijah made her way to his side of the desk. Typically, she would have taken a seat in front of it, but she was here on a mission and figured it would take a little persuading.

So, she walked around his desk and pulled his chair back, lifting the arms before straddling him. His hazel eyes locked with her green ones as she reached down to undo his belt. She then proceeded to unbutton and unzip his pants. Reaching in, she pulled his semi-erect dick from them. She began to stroke it slowly as she looked up at him from under her lashes. He cocked a brow at her.

"Cruz, let me call you back," he stated before ending the call with his friend.

Alijah watched him as he watched her. She stroked him a few more times before reaching into his top drawer, where he now kept a box of condoms, and grabbing one. She opened it slowly and rolled it down his length. The overall objective had been to persuade him, but Alijah was making herself hot. Lifting, she pulled her panties to the side and was just about to slide down when his hands on her waist stopped her.

"What is it that you want?"

"Well, if you hadn't stopped me, you would know."

"Other than that. I'm usually the one that initiates and controls the sex between us. So, what is it that you want?"

"You know my birthday is Sunday."

"I'm aware."

"And I told you my friend Erin is flying in for it." He simply nodded at her. "Well, she's flying in tomorrow evening, and I was wondering if I could have Friday off."

"No."

"What? Why?"

"Because you don't need Friday off."

"Be reasonable. It's my-"

A gasp cut off Alijah's sentence as Kieran impaled her on his dick. He held her there for a moment, moving her hips back and forth, causing her to grind against him. She placed her hands on his shoulders and forced herself to remain still.

"Give me Friday off."

"You don't need it off," Kieran responded.

"Fine, then I'm not going to ride you."

Kieran cocked his head to the side. That devilish look had entered his eyes, and Alijah knew she had fucked up. She didn't know what was coming, but she knew she'd better try to prepare herself.

He lifted her and slammed her back down his dick with lightning speed as he rose his hips to meet her. He bounced her a few times, repeating the action.

"What was that about not riding me?" He questioned as he bounced her continually on his dick.

Alijah couldn't respond. All she could do was lose herself in the pleasure. Her walls were beginning to contract, and she could feel her orgasm building within her waiting to spill free. She leaned in and pressed her lips to his as he slowed his thrust and her bouncing, allowing her to kiss him. At that moment, a knock came on his door.

Alijah panicked and began trying to scramble off him, but he held her firmly in place and continued his slow strokes. Her eyes widened, and she tried to pull away again.

"Don't move," he whispered against her lips. "What?" He then called out to whoever was knocking at his door.

"It's Carlos from accounting. Um...sorry for showing up unannounced, Mr. Cayman. I tried to call your assistant and tell her that I would be coming down, but she didn't answer her phone, and she isn't at her desk."

"That's because she's at mine, riding my dick," Kieran mumbled into Alijah's neck, earning a slap to his chest.

"Shut up, Kieran. He could hear you and let me go."

"What is it that you needed, Carlos?" Kieran raised his voice and asked as he gave Alijah two particularly hard thrusts. She had to bury her face in his shoulder to muffle her moans.

"I was going over some receipts and expenses, and some things aren't adding up. I thought I would bring them to you."

"Thanks, Carlos. Just set them on Ms. Douglas' desk, and she'll bring them to me when she *cums*." Kieran stated, enunciating the word as he began to speed his thrusts again.

"Yes, sir."

When he was sure the other man was gone, he began to pump furiously into Alijah, bringing them both to release. She was breathing heavily as she sat up and looked at him.

"What is the matter with you? He could have heard us."

"You liked it. The moment you thought we were caught, your pussy drenched me."

Alijah rolled her eyes at him. "Whatever, now about Friday."

"You don't have to work Friday, Alijah."

She smiled before leaning in to kiss him. "Thank you."

"Don't thank me. You don't have to work on Friday because I'm not working on Friday. The boys and I are helping Nik with some things at *Mirage*."

"Wait, so then, this was..."

"A well-needed release," he told her with a smirk.

Alijah punched him in the chest before slowly sliding off him and going into his bathroom to clean up. She wasn't actually mad. The quickie had been excellent, and he had been right. The prospect of possibly being caught did excite her a little bit.

Kieran sat at his desk going over the papers Carlos had brought down, and the young man was right. The reports showed different amounts of money going out, but the corresponding invoices and receipts were adding up to be much less than what was paid. He'd gone over the information twice, and he came to the same conclusion each time. So, there was only one outcome. Someone was stealing from him.

Looking over the paperwork again, he memorized the names of the employees that had worked on them. Gathering everything up, he rose from his seat and headed out of his office.

"We're going to accounting," he told Alijah as he headed to the elevator.

"Should I call them and tell them we're coming?"

"No, this is going to be a surprise visit."

He and Alijah stepped onto the elevator, and he could feel her looking at him. He turned his attention to her, and she reached up and ran her finger across his furrowed brow.

"What's wrong, Kieran?"

"Someone's been stealing from me, and I'm about to find out who it is."

"What?"

He gave her the shortened version of what happened on the brief elevator ride. She looked mortified when he was finished, and he mildly wondered if it was because she couldn't believe that someone had stolen from him or that she knew heads were about to roll.

When the elevator opened on the correct floor, they made their way to accounting. Most of the employees seemed to be slacking off, waiting to pass the next ten minutes by until five o'clock rolled around and they could leave. However, when they noticed him on the floor, everyone wanted to scramble and act as if they were busy and hard at work. From the corner of his eye, Kieran could see Simon, his head of accounting, scramble out of his office.

"Mr. Cayman, we weren't expecting you. No one called me to inform me you would be coming," he stated, cutting his eyes at Alijah.

"It's a surprise visit," Kieran responded, simply walking past Simon to the middle of the floor. "I have three questions for all of you. Do you like your jobs?" At that question, heads began to nod simultaneously. "Do you like your pay?" At that, the room became a bit loud with verbal affirmations. "Do you all want to keep your jobs?" Again, nods went around the room vigorously. "Well, all of you won't." Kieran then stated. "Because someone here has been stealing from me."

The room grew deadly silent as he looked around at each employee. He knew people, knew that most people who stole were cowards deep down. So, all he had to do was find the face of a coward.

"Mr. Cayman, that's a bold accusation to come down here and throw at my people," Simon stated, fidgeting.

Kieran shot him a look that all but said, *shut the fuck up*, before actually speaking. "It isn't an allegation. I have the documentation to back it up." Still, no one spoke. "If you know who it is. I suggest you tell me because I have no qualms about firing all of you."

A girl in the back slowly stood up, and Kieran zeroed in on her. He beckoned her forward and could see that she was on the verge of tears. *You should have thought of that before you stole from me.*

"I did it, Mr. Cayman, but I was only doing what I was told. Simon assured me that he had the invoices for the payouts and that he just needed me to pull the expenses. I swear."

Kieran turned around and locked his gaze on Simon. The man had gone ash white as if he had just seen a ghost or come back from the dead. He was going to wish he had that capability after Kieran was done with him because he honestly damn near wanted to kill him.

"Office. Now." Kieran gritted. Making his way into Simon's office.

"Mr. Cayman. That girl-"

"Told nothing but the truth," Kieran stated, cutting him off. It was silent for a moment.

"Look, I can explain." Simon tried.

"I don't care to hear explanations. You're fired. You have ten minutes to pack your shit up and be off my property."

Kieran walked out of Simon's office and into a smaller one beside it, with Alijah on his heels. The blinds to the office were pulled, and he leaned against the desk away from the door. He pulled her to him, and she fought him mildly.

"Kieran people will..."

"I just had to fire one of the people that has damn near been here with me since the beginning. I could give a damn about what people will say."

Alijah nodded slowly and went to him willingly. As tough and hard-assed as Kieran was, she was coming to see that he had his moments of weakness just like everyone else, and this was one of them.

Kieran held Alijah to him until he heard Simon's door open. He released her and walked out to meet the man feeling betrayed. He knew he should probably let the other man explain why he did it, and he would...one day. That day just wasn't today. He watched as Simon walked to the elevator before getting on. When he was gone, Kieran turned to the rest of the accounting department. He turned to the girl that had assisted Simon unknowingly.

"Ninety-day probation with a twenty percent pay cut. Think of it as a gift," he told her. She nodded rapidly, relieved she hadn't lost her job over following devious orders. "Carlos."

Kieran then stated. The young man stood to his feet. He had been with Kieran's company for five years, and it was a wonder why Simon hadn't promoted the boy to assistant manager, considering he worked efficiently and had been there longer than his co-workers. "Everyone, meet your new Head of Accounting. Your office is over there," he told Carlos, pointing.

With that, he turned and waited on the elevator. He planned to get his things from his office and go to the condo. His day had taken a sour turn, and all he wanted was uninterrupted hours of stress-relieving.

17

Alijah stood at the terminal, waiting for Erin's plane to land. It had been almost a year since the last time she saw Erin face to face. She was more than excited to be seeing her friend after so long.

She didn't know how long she had been waiting, but finally, she saw where the plane had landed on the screen, and the passengers were exiting. It took only a few minutes for her to spot Erin coming through the crowd, and right behind her was Chayse. This was an even bigger surprise to Alijah. She had just spoken to Chayse the day before, and she hadn't told her that she was coming to visit for her birthday as well.

"Erin, Chayse!" Alijah called, waving her arm while making her way over to them.

When she made it to the two women, they all greeted each other with hugs. Alijah then led them out to the waiting car as they made small talk about the plane ride. Timothy was waiting for them in the private pick-up area. After taking the luggage from both women, he placed it in the trunk as they climbed into the backseat.

"Someone's moving on up to the east side," Chayse stated with a smirk.

"Being chauffeured around and shit. I'd have to agree with you, Chayse." Erin concurred.

"Shut up. Both of you." Alijah threw out.

"So, where are we going?" Chayse asked when the car began to move.

"Well, it's still pretty early. I thought I'd let you guys drop your bags off, and then I could fix dinner for us all." Alijah informed, looking at her watch. It was only just after seven. She didn't see the harm in a late dinner. Both women nodded in agreement before Alijah turned her attention to Chayse. "So, how's business. Any exciting shoots recently?"

"No, not really. I did just get commissioned to do a shoot for a magazine. They wanted to feature a particular artist." Chayse informed her, smiling.

"Really? That's great! Who's the artist?"

"It's me," Erin spoke up.

"I'm so happy for you!"

"Thanks."

"So, Chayse is going to do your session. It'll be amazing."

"Yeah, she's going to shoot my model and me," Erin stated with a smirk.

"Who did you get to model for you?" Alijah asked. Both women spoke at the same time.

"You."

Alijah was silent for a minute. "No. I don't think..."

"Come on, And. You're the only person I know that hasn't been touched by another tattoo artist. So, your entire body is my work alone."

"But..."

"And you're gorgeous. So, that's a plus." Chayse threw in, trying to help Erin with her claim.

"But..."

"And the shoot is tomorrow. So, suck it up." Erin then finished.

"Nice, Erin. Way to persuade her." Chayse stated while Alijah groaned.

"Fine." Alijah finally conceded. "How did you even get them to let you choose your own photographer, model, and place anyway?"

"I told them I knew one of the best photographers to walk the streets, had one of the hottest models, and an awesome place to have the pictures done. One of the owners at the parlor knows a guy down here that owns a little jazz spot. He spoke to him, and he agreed to let us shoot the pictures there." Erin informed her.

"Well, I guess that works," Alijah responded.

A few minutes later, they pulled up in front of the condo building. Alijah stepped out, and the other two women followed as Timothy retrieved their bags. They thanked him as he told them to have a lovely evening and departed. Alijah began to walk towards the doors as Chayse looked up at the building.

"Alijah, this doesn't look like a hotel."

"That's because it isn't one," she stated, holding the door open for both women. "It's Kieran's building. Well, some of it."

"Look, no offense." Chayse started as she followed Alijah to the elevator. "But if that man likes to put it on you as much as you've said he does. I don't want to stay with you two. I don't want to hear that all through the night."

"I wouldn't mind it too much." Erin threw in with a smirk.

"First, Erin, be quiet, and second, you aren't staying with us. There's a vacant condo on the floor below Kieran's. It's furnished because it's a timeshare or something. Anyway, he said you could stay there." Alijah stated, stepping onto the elevator. She pressed the button for the floor they were going to, and they took the ride in silence.

When the elevator door opened, she led them to the condo Kieran had shown her the day before. It was smaller than his, as she expected all the other ones were, but it was still very nice. She unlocked the door with the key he had given her before she'd taken off to the airport and stepped aside, holding the door open as they entered.

"This is nice," Erin spoke after a moment as she looked around.

"Agreed." Chayse cosigned.

"Well, the bedrooms are down the hall." Alijah pointed. "Hurry and put your luggage away so we can go up to the condo and I can start cooking."

Alijah waited by the front door as they went to do what she'd asked. When they came back, she led the way out of the condo, locking the door and giving the key to Chayse. After all, she was the more responsible of the two. She led them back onto the elevator and placed her keycard in the slot to access the top floor. The elevator doors opened, and she led the way off and into the condo.

"Make yourselves at home. I'm going to start dinner."

Both women followed Alijah to the kitchen and sat at the bar while she went about getting out the ingredients she needed. She decided she'd cook Shrimp Linguine with a Green Salad. She pulled a bottle of wine from the fridge as well. Taking down three glasses, she went to open the wine, only to find it had a cork in it. Alijah was never a fan of corks because they would break into pieces whenever she tried to take them out. Chayse couldn't do it, and Erin had refused ever since she popped out one, and it hit her in the eye.

She placed the bottle on the bar and made her way down the hall. She checked Kieran's office, but surprisingly, she didn't find him there. Alijah then made her way to his bedroom door, which was closed. She knocked and waited for him to open it. She hadn't been in his bedroom before — just a few glances in here and there.

"Come in, Alijah."

She opened the door to find him running a towel over his damp hair in a pair of sweatpants, and, as usual, he wasn't wearing any boxers. She watched as he threw the towel in the hamper before walking over to her. He pulled her in close and leaned down to kiss her.

"I feel as though you have too many clothes on," he stated, trying to unbutton the jeans she'd changed into right after work.

"Stop it. Erin and Chayse are in the kitchen," she told him, removing his hands. "I came to see if you would open a bottle of wine for us."

"Alijah, you know you can have anything in the condo you want. I don't care if you open some wine."

"It has a cork in it, and I always break them into pieces trying to get them out."

"Come on," he stated, taking her hand. "I'll open it for you."

"Wait!" Alijah blurted, pulling him to a stop. "Put some boxers on. I can see your dick print...and a shirt." She added on as an afterthought.

Kieran stared at her for a moment before finally agreeing to put on some boxer. However, he forewent the shirt and pulled her out of his bedroom and down the hall.

"Ladies," he greeted the two women sitting at his bar. "I'm Kieran."

The two introduced themselves and gawked at him while Kieran opened the wine for them. Then he poured them three glasses before grabbing a beer for himself out of the fridge. He made his way into the living room and turned on the television.

Kieran was mildly amused as he ate his dinner and listened to the three women talk. He quickly realized that Erin was blunt and didn't care what she said. She reminded him of a female version of Nik. He enjoyed when she would say something, and Alijah, who he found out Erin referred to as And, and Chayse often referred to as Ali, would cut her eyes at her with a look that clearly said, stop talking. Though he was sure Erin understood, she just ignored them.

"So, Kieran," Erin stated after taking another drink of her wine. "Word around town is that you know how to lay some pretty good pipe."

"Oh, God." He heard Alijah groan before dropping her fork onto her plate and spearing Erin with a look.

"Is that so?" Kieran asked.

"Yep. I heard you have an impressive piece to work with as well." Erin affirmed.

"Erin, go find your chill because clearly, you lost it somewhere," Chayse told her.

Kieran chuckled. "She doesn't complain. So, I must do something right."

He and Erin joked for several more minutes until Alijah pushed her chair back and rose from the table, taking her plate and glass into the kitchen. He could hear her drop them into the sink and was pretty sure at least one of the dishes broke.

"Seriously, Erin. You knew you were going to upset her. She only told you because she needed someone to talk to, and you go and make a joke out of it." Chayse chastised.

"What? I didn't mean anything by it. She knows that. I don't understand why she's so sensitive all of a sudden."

Chayse sighed and pushed her food around on her plate. "Just stop talking about her sex life, and don't act like you don't know why."

Kieran wasn't interested in any more of the women's conversation and rose from his seat with his dishes. He made his way into the kitchen to find Alijah cleaning it. Kieran placed his dishes on the countertop. Going up behind her, he wrapped his arms around her waist and pulled her back into him. Leaning down, he kissed her neck.

He didn't know what this woman was doing to him. She had him doing things he never did in other relationships. What he was about to do now, he didn't often do in general.

"I'm sorry if I upset you," he spoke softly against her ear. "I didn't know you would take our teasing so badly."

"Are you actually sorry?" She questioned, stepping out of his embrace, and turning to look at him. "Or are you just thinking with your dick again?" She concluded, narrowing her eyes at him.

Kieran sighed. "I genuinely apologize."

Alijah exhaled. "I guess I can't be too upset. I know how Erin is, so this shouldn't shock me."

"If you knew there would be a possibility of her teasing you, then why did you tell her?" Kieran questioned as he pulled her back into his arms.

She went quiet, and Kieran began to play with a few of her curls. After a pregnant silence, he figured she had no intention of answering his question and was about to change the subject when she spoke.

"Erin is more experience with men than I am. So, I needed some...advice, I guess. I mean, clearly, I'm not a virgin, but I haven't been with many men, and none of them have done the things you have to my body. I didn't know how to take that or if I satisfied you the way you satisfied me."

"Believe me, baby. I'm always satisfied." Kieran reassured her. "But if you feel as if you need more practice, I'm more than happy to accommodate you."

He watched as she looked up at him and rolled her eyes. Smirking, he leaned down to kiss her softly on the lips. At least, that had been his intention, but they were locked in a heated battle in a matter of seconds. Their tongues were waging war with one another. It wasn't until he was sure they would collapse if they didn't get any air that he pulled away.

"Go, spend more time with your friends. I have some work I need to do. When you get ready for bed, come to my room. Wait on me if I'm not there."

Alijah nodded, and Kieran leaned in to kiss her once more before releasing her and making his way out of the kitchen. He said goodnight to both Erin and Chayse after telling them it was nice to meet them and headed to his office. He had some work he needed to do, considering he was taking an impromptu day off tomorrow. Kieran needed to call the pilot and schedule a flight. He would usually leave that up to Alijah, but he would take care of it since she had company.

Once that was done, he looked over the schematics the two teenagers from Paris had sent him. He had been very impressed with the two boys' work. He had happened upon them by accident one day as he was clicking through junk mail when a news heading from one of their city's publications caught his eye.

The two boys, Pierre and Michelle, ages fifteen and sixteen respectively, had created a fingerprint recognition lock for handheld weapons. It was lightweight and was meant to be embedded in the butt of the gun.

Kieran thought this was a genius idea. There were so many children, teens, and young adults dying every day because one or another of them got hold of their parent's weapons. With the fingerprint lock, only the person whose print was registered as the owner would be able to operate the gun. It would be placed so that they didn't have to search for it and put their print on it in case of emergency. No, it would be strategically placed where you would hold the gun naturally when shooting it.

He had never been one to make weapons, and he wasn't about to start now. No, he merely wanted to find a weapon's company and put something into play for the two boys, backing them to get them started and then becoming a silent partner.

As usual, Kieran had lost track of time. When he looked at his computer clock, he saw that it was almost two in the morning. Saving his work, he shut everything down before leaving his office. The lights in the front of the condo were off, the only light still illuminating being the hall light, so he assumed Alijah had gone to bed.

Making his way into his room, his suspicions were confirmed as he turned on the light. She lay in the middle of his California King bed. Her curls splayed across the pillows beneath her head.

Kieran closed the door behind him, making his way over to the bed. He turned on one of the bedside lamps before removing his sweatpants and throwing them into the hamper. Going back to turn off the overhead light, he then climbed into bed. When he was settled, he turned off the lamp before pulling Alijah to him.

She rolled over in her sleep and lay her head on his chest, throwing her arm over his waist and twining one of her legs through his. Kieran brought his other arm up and wrapped it around her before exhaling and allowing sleep to overcome him.

18

Alijah stood with a smile on her face as she thought back to that morning. She had awakened in Kieran's bed, but she had been by herself. It was the first time she had looked around his bedroom. The furnishings were nice, and she could tell that they were expensive. The bed, as well as his dressers, were done in rich dark wood, with gray marble on the top as well as for the handles on the chest. She had woken up alone, and she had wondered if Kieran had even bothered coming to bed for a moment.

Pushing the covers off her, she'd gone to get out of the bed when something on the nightstand caught her attention. She had picked it up and discovered a note from Kieran informing her that he had to leave early to help Nik and that he would see her later. Beside the letter, she found a small bowl of mixed fruit. It had made Alijah smile to herself. They weren't flowers, but it was still sweet even though he would deny that being the reason for his actions.

"What do you mean, 'No one called you?!'" Erin's angry voice brought Alijah out of her reverie.

They had pulled up to the address that one of Erin's bosses had given her, and from what Alijah could see, there had been some confusion.

"There has to be some mistake. Ford said he spoke with the owner and that they agreed to allow us to do the shoot here." Erin tried to explain.

"Well, I'm the owner, and I don't know anyone by the name of Ford. I'm sorry. There must have been some misunderstanding." The man who had greeted them at the door stated.

"Look, couldn't you just let us do the shoot here anyway?" Chayse tried. "It won't take any more than about two hours."

"I'm sorry, but I have an actual paying group coming in thirty minutes, and they've reserved the place until an hour before we open tonight." With that said, the man backed into the building and closed the door.

Alijah turned to her best friend, and she could see the anger and devastation in her eyes. She was upset right along with her. It was clear that her boss had lied to her, and in Alijah's eyes, that was just downright shady and unacceptable.

"What am I going to do?" Erin questioned, and Alijah could hear the emotion in her voice. "If I don't deliver to the magazine as I promised, they will pass me up for the next person in line."

"It's okay, Erin. We'll think of something." Alijah told her as she began to pace the sidewalk.

"Why would Ford do something like this to you?" Chayse questioned as she began to rub Erin's back.

The other woman scoffed, and fire entered her eyes as both women watched her realize something. "Because if I fail, he's next in line. That son of a bitch!" Erin exclaimed, drawing attention from a few onlookers.

"It's okay, Erin. We'll find you another place." Chayse reassured.

"Any place we find today will be last minute, and whether it's worth having or not, they'll charge us an arm and a leg." Erin sighed, defeated.

At that moment, a light bulb went off in Alijah's head. She looked down at her watch and saw that it was only eleven o'clock. So, they had plenty of time.

"No, it won't," she told Erin. "Ladies, back to the car."

She didn't give them time to question her as she led the way back to Timothy. Thankfully, they hadn't gotten any of the equipment out of the trunk. When they were settled in their seats and Timothy was in the driver's seat, Alijah spoke again.

"Timothy, can you take us to *Mirage*, please?"

Timothy nodded as they pulled off into traffic. On the ride over, Chayse and Erin asked her what *Mirage* was, but she only told them they would see. It took about fifteen minutes for them to pull up in front of the building. Both women stared in awe at how beautiful the outside of the building was. Chayse thought that she could make a photo shoot work outside of the building if she had to.

Getting out of the car, Alijah told them both to wait while she went inside for a minute. She made her way through the front door and stepped inside. The lights were dimmed, and she didn't see the guys anywhere, but their cars were there, and Alijah figured they were upstairs.

Looking around, she found the door that led to the staircase that would lead her upstairs. She took the stairs two at a time and followed the light and the sound of voices to what she discovered was an office. All four men were standing around the desk, looking at something. It was Paetyn who noticed her presence first.

"Alijah?" He stated in a questioning tone, causing the other men to turn to her.

"What are you doing here?" Kieran then asked, "Didn't you have something you were supposed to do with your friends?"

"That's why I'm here," Alijah stated, turning to Nik. "I need your help."

Nik turned and leaned against his desk to face her. "Okay, beautiful. Tell daddy what's wrong." Nik stated with a smirk.

Alijah leveled him with a glare as Kieran threw him a look that could kill. Then, a smirk of her own slid into place on her lips as she decided to shut him down.

"Fine, I will," Alijah stated, turning to Kieran. "Erin's boss set her up, and the place she was supposed to do her photo shoot wasn't a place where she could. We have to find her somewhere else to get it done, or they're going to pass over her for the magazine cover, and her asshole of a boss will get the spread." As she finished, she could hear Cruz chuckling lowly.

"I guess we know what Kieran is in the bedroom," Paetyn murmured.

"And that's why you need my help?" Nik questioned. "You want to do it here?"

"Yes, please. This means so much to Erin."

Nik shrugged. "I don't see why not. We don't open until nine tonight. Just be done by then."

Alijah surged across the room, wrapping her arms around Nik before leaning on her tiptoes and kissing his cheek. She was so excited about being able to save Erin's magazine spread for her that she hadn't noticed that Nik's hands were caressing her waist until Kieran pulled her away from him. Nik's face housed a toothy grin, and Alijah rolled her eyes at him.

"Oh, one more favor," Alijah stated. "If I can get one of you to show me where the light switches are downstairs and help us bring in the equipment, that would be great. Then we'll stay out of your hair."

"I'll help you," Paetyn spoke up. "I left some papers we need in my car.

Alijah nodded and was about to walk off when Kieran turned her around. He pulled her to him and kissed her, instantly possessing, and claiming her lips. His hands snaked down her back to her ass, and he squeezed firmly, causing her to gasp. He pulled back, and his hazel orbs were locked onto her green one. He leaned in once more and gave her several pecks before releasing her altogether.

"Did you get that message, Nik?" Paetyn asked with a smirk in his friend's direction as he waited at the door.

"Loud and fucking clear," Nik responded as he went back around his desk. "I get it. She's yours." He then stated, directing his sentence at Kieran.

Alijah glared at them. "No, I'm mine," she informed before following Paetyn out of the door.

Both women had looked around the space. It was beautiful and one hundred times better than the tiny jazz club would have been. As Paetyn set done the last of their equipment for them, he flashed them a smile before going back upstairs with the others.

"That man is fine," Chayse stated after she was sure he was out of earshot. Alijah and Erin both nodded in agreement.

"Yes, and he's really sweet too," Alijah told them.

Over the next twenty minutes, Chayse scoped out the club to decide where she wanted to do the photo shoot exactly. She was impressed by the way it was divided. Half of it was distinctly club, the other half a lounge. She figured it would be best to do the pictures in several different areas. She had chosen three outfits for Alijah and two for Erin. Alijah watched her cousin, knowing that this was her method.

Once Chayse had chosen the three spots she wanted to shoot, Alijah helped her play with the lighting for them. When Chayse told her she was satisfied, she left them and went over to get dressed in her first outfit. She was a bit nervous as to what Chayse had chosen for her. She knew her cousin had a great eye, but she still worried. Alijah's tattoos were done in places that couldn't be seen when she was wearing regular clothing. That alone let her know that she would be wearing something a bit...risqué.

She watched as Chayse pulled out the first thing she would be wearing. It was a white turtleneck style halter top and a pair of white boy shorts. It wasn't too bad.

"The white will look good against your skin and make the colors of your tattoos pop. Go change, and then I'll do your makeup," she stated while Alijah watched her dig around and pull out an outfit for Erin.

Walking off to the bathroom, Alijah changed and fluffed up her curly mane. Though she knew Chayse would do so as well. When she walked back out, Chayse had her different camera's set out on the table. As well as her makeup kit and a small traveling vanity set.

Alijah sat down and allowed Chayse to do her makeup. It looked as if she had put Erin's hair into a cute up-do while she had been changing. With her hair up, it showcased the tattoo on the back of her neck.

Chayse didn't put much makeup on her. Enough to make her eyes shine and her lips look kissable. When she finished, she began fluffing her hair out slightly. Separating some of the curls as Erin came from changing. She was wearing dark, ripped jeans with a mint-colored bra and a dark, distressed vest that was left open. Alijah thought about asking why Erin wasn't half-naked but contributed to the fact that all of Erin's tattoos were housed on her upper body. Her back, stomach, arms, one above her breast, and the one on the back of her neck.

When Chayse got done fluffing her hair, she moved aside so that she could do Erin's makeup. Once she was done, they followed Chayse over to the bar since that was where she decided they would start.

"So, what type of idea have you come up with, Chayse? What do you want us to do?" Alijah questioned, leaning against the bar.

"Well, I want you to act like you're in love. For the next couple of hours, you are her woman. I want it to be sexy, spicy." Chayse informed them.

Alijah rolled her eyes. She was not surprised, but it didn't bother her any. It wasn't the first time she would do a photo shoot that looked intimate with Erin. The first time was when Chayse was breaking out and needed diversified pictures for her portfolio.

"Let's get started," Chayse stated.

They had been taking pictures for about fifteen minutes when Chayse sighed, lowering her camera. It was too quiet. She liked to have music going in the background when she was doing a session.

"Ali, do you know where the sound system is and how to work it?" Chayse questioned.

"No," she stated, hopping down from the barstool she had been seated on. "But I'll go ask Nik really quick."

Alijah took off for the office and made her way up the stairs. She walked into the office to find the men standing around the desk once again.

"Hey, Nik." She called, gaining his attention. "Where's the sound system for the club, and how do you work it?"

All the men turned to look at her.

"Well damn," Nik stated. While Paetyn let out a low whistle, Cruz seemed to apprise her from head to toe. And the look in Kieran's eyes, she was all too familiar with it.

"Well?" She asked when Nik didn't speak.

She watched him as he reached into one of his drawers and pulled out a remote before holding it out to her. She walked over and grabbed it as he began to talk.

"Just hit the power button. This remote controls the whole sound system. It's fairly easy."

"Thanks. Sorry for interrupting." She turned to leave, but Kieran grabbed her by her arm and pulled her to him. Immediately both of her hands went to his chest. "No," she stated, pushing him back. He pulled her back to him. "Kieran, I'm serious. Chayse will kill me if she has to redo my makeup before the next setup."

Alijah could see that he wanted to ignore her, so she leveled him with a glare. He took hold of her chin with a sigh and kissed her forehead before leaning in and whispering in her ear.

"Keep this. I like it."

Alijah simply stepped away from him as she made her way out of the office and back downstairs. It didn't take them a moment to get the music on and turned down to a level where they could hear it but still hear Chayse instructing them.

"Okay, Erin. Stand in front of Ali while she's on the stool so we can get some pictures of the tattoos on your stomach. Good." Chayse then stated as Alijah situated her legs on either side of Erin. "Ali, hook your right leg over her hip, put your left arm under hers, hook it onto her shoulder, and lay your chin on her right shoulder."

Alijah followed all of her cousin's directions, and Chayse began to snap several pictures of them in that position. She walked around them, taking the pictures from different angles.

"Alright, Erin, turn towards Ali, and Ali, you wrap your legs around her waist." She paused for a minute to let them get into position. "Now, put her hands on her thighs, Erin." When that was done, she continued. "Ali, reach over with your right hand and pull up the back of her vest to expose her tattoos." When that was done, she spoke again. "Now throw your head back, and Erin, you place your lips close to the back of her jaw, below her ear."

Alijah did as her cousin asked and, once again, heard camera clicks going off. After that position, they took pictures in a few more before Chayse had them change into their next outfit. Alijah and Erin walked into the bathroom and changed carefully to not mess up their hair. They weren't sure if Chayse planned on doing it differently.

When they came out this time, Alijah was dressed in a black halter top that fastened around the neck and had no back. It was loose in the front as well, and if she moved wrong, her girls would say peek-a-boo. She had on a pair of dark denim distressed short shorts. Erin had on a shirt identical to Alijah's. The difference was that hers was red. She had on a pair of black ripped skinny jeans as well.

Alijah found Chayse over by the vanity table and made her way over. She fluffed her hair again and then added a dark liner and shadow to her eyes and a bold red lipstick to her lips. Then she gave Erin the same eye makeup, but her lipstick was more of a matte red.

Alijah made her way over to the couches in VIP where Chayse had directed them, preparing for the next section of the shoot.

Kieran followed his friends down the stairs and almost ran directly into Nik when he stopped abruptly. His first instinct was to hit him upside the head; however, he noticed that Cruz and Paetyn had also stopped. As he followed their eyes, he understood why. There was Alijah, one of her legs thrown over one of the armchairs and Erin's shoulder in VIP as Erin's fingers ghosted along her thighs.

"Am I the only one hard right now?" Nik questioned, causing Cruz to slap him in the back of the head and Kieran to push him to get them all moving again.

They made their way over to the bar. Three of them took seats as Nik made his way around it. It was almost one o'clock. Too early for them to be drinking, but as the saying went, it was five o'clock somewhere.

Kieran watched the photo shoot as he listened to Nik rummage around behind the bar. He could honestly say that he was getting turned on watching the two women pose so seductively together. He was a man, after all. He watched as Alijah straddled Erin in the chair, throwing her head back, as he was sure Chayse commanded, in ecstasy.

"Kieran, you know, a good friend would have told us that her friends were delightful to look at as well," Nik stated as he placed four drinks on the bar before joining the other men.

"You have eyes. So, you're perfectly capable of seeing that for yourself." Kieran responded, picking up his glass.

"True, and my eyes are enjoying what they see very much," Nik stated, drinking from his glass. "I have a question for you, Kieran. How serious are you about, Alijah?"

Kieran rolled his eyes. Somehow, he knew Nik's question would have something to do with Alijah. "She slept with me last night," he responded, taking a drink from his glass.

"We all know you're sleeping together," Nik responded blandly. "That's not answering my question."

Kieran leveled Nik with a glare. "I was referring to the fact that she slept in my bed last night, and that's all we did. Sleep."

All three men turned to look at him. Kieran wasn't known to have women in his bed and not sleep with them. If he allowed you in his bed, then he was going to have sex with you. If there was going to be no sex involved, there was no reason for him to allow you into his personal space.

"I would say he's pretty serious, Nik," Paetyn stated.

"Which means you should stop ogling her." Cruz threw in.

For the next hour or so, Kieran watched, along with his friends, the rest of the photo shoot. He would have to admit that the whole thing was provocative, but he could see the idea behind it. Kieran figured Chayse indeed was good at what she was doing. He was interested in seeing the end result once she cleaned the photographs up.

When they were all done with the shoot, the men went over and began helping them pack up. Alijah introduced her cousin and friend to the two men they hadn't met yet.

"So, you're both from Florida?" Paetyn questioned as he helped move the equipment over to the door.

"Yes," Chayse responded.

"We came to town to do this photo shoot and celebrate And's birthday," Erin added. The three men looked at her quizzically. "Alijah," she then stated.

"It's your birthday?" Nik asked.

"Well, Sunday, but yes," Alijah informed

"We're celebrating tomorrow, though." Erin threw out.

"Big plans?" Paetyn questioned.

"Dinner and maybe going to a club," Erin replied. "You guys should come with us. It'll be fun."

"We don't want to intrude on your plans," Cruz responded.

"Nonsense. I'm sure it will make it that much more fun." Erin stated, eyeing Paetyn.

"If Alijah doesn't mind," Paetyn responded.

"Of course not," Alijah told him. "The more, the merrier."

As the conversation drifted off, Kieran grabbed the equipment at the door and began carrying it out and loading it into his car. There was no need to call Timothy back since they were headed in the same direction. Once, he had everything loaded; he waited for the women to finish their conversation with his friends before they all said their goodbyes.

As they headed back to the condo, Kieran could hardly keep his eyes off Alijah. She was still wearing one of the outfits she had modeled in, and he was having a hell of a time concentrating on the road. He couldn't wait to get her alone to take it off of her.

19

Alijah awoke to one of the best sensations. Her eyes slowly fluttered open, but only long enough to see Kieran's head between her legs before closing again. Spreading her legs a bit wider, she reached down and grabbed a fist full of his hair as he began to suck her clit. She loved that. The way it felt like he was slowly sucking her soul from her body. As he went to pull away, Alijah brought her other hand down to join the first and held him in place.

"Don't stop." She moaned lowly as she began to rock her hips.

Complying with her wishes, Kieran began to suck her clit faster, using his teeth to cause pleasurable friction. He inserted a finger into her and started to stroke slowly in and out of her.

Alijah was on the precipice. As she felt her orgasm building up inside her, she began to rock her hips faster, holding him tighter. Finally, her orgasm hit, and Alijah's hips bucked as she held firm, her legs closing around his head.

"Kieran!"

Slowly, as she came down from her high, Alijah loosened her legs and released him, shivering when he gave her one more slow, lingering lick. He kissed his way up her body before placing a soft kiss on her lips as her chest rapidly rose and fell.

"If I didn't know any better, I would say you were trying to drown me, gorgeous."

Alijah let out a breathy laugh. "You can swim, so I'm sure you're fine."

Alijah watched as he rolled his eyes before giving her one more kiss. He got off of his bed and held his hand out for her. She took it, allowing him to help her out of bed and lead her into the bathroom. There, she found his large tub filled with candles burning around it, and the lights dimmed.

"What's all this?" She questioned.

"I figured," Kieran began as he undressed her. "This would be a good way to start your birthday celebration."

Alijah smiled at him as he took her only article of clothing, which was his t-shirt, off. Once she was undressed, he helped her step into the tub, and Alijah sank down slowly.

"Aren't you going to join me?" she questioned when she saw him turn to leave.

"Not this time. Relax and stay in as long as you like."

With that, he exited the bathroom, and Alijah decided to do exactly what he suggested. Though her birthday was technically tomorrow, she was celebrating it today, meaning that it was her day. She sank deeper into the tub and enjoyed the feel of the hot water on her skin. Kieran's tub was massive. Alijah was sure it could fit four people comfortably.

After relaxing for a bit, Alijah looked around and found that Kieran had brought her bath wash into his bathroom.

When she finished her bath, Alijah grabbed a towel after pulling the plug in the tub. After wrapping the towel around her body, she blew out all the candles. She then made her way to her room, where she did the rest of her grooming and dressed in a pair of denim shorts and a sky blue sleeveless, flowing top so as not to irritate the dream catcher tattoo Erin had given her after the shoot yesterday. She tamed her hair a bit before padding barefoot towards the kitchen.

She stopped in her tracks when she saw the dining table. Across it was spread a breakfast feast. There were omelets, sausage, bacon, hash browns, oatmeal, fruit, and orange juice. At the head of the table stood Kieran in a pair of basketball ball shorts and a t-shirt. His hair was still damp, so she figured he had showered in the bathroom in his home office.

"Is this part of my birthday celebration as well?" Alijah questioned, making her way over to him.

Kieran pulled her in close, snaking his hands down to her ass. "Yes, it is." He then leaned down and kissed her.

"Hmm," Alijah responded as they pulled apart. "You're being extremely sweet today."

Kieran rolled his eyes as he pulled a chair out for her. "Don't get used to it."

"I'm assuming you didn't cook all of this."

"You would assume correctly. I had it delivered." Kieran informed her as he fixed her a plate.

They ate in comfortable silence, and Alijah had to admit it was delicious. She didn't know where he had ordered it from, but she would make sure to find out. When she was finished, she checked the time and noticed she had ten minutes before she and the girls were to go to the spa and nail salon, then to find something to wear for later in the night.

Going into her room, Alijah slipped on her shoes before grabbing her purse. Heading back down the hall, she was stopped by Kieran.

"Going out?"

"Yes. The girls and I are going to the spa and then shopping."

"Okay, take this," he stated, holding out one of his credit cards. "And have fun."

"Kieran, I don't need your money," Alijah informed him pushing his hand away.

"I never said you needed it," he responded, pulling her to him with one hand. "But you're going to take it and use it on whatever you want to." He then continued, placing it in her back pocket. "My birthday gift to you. Have fun." With that, he turned and began to walk down the hall.

Rolling her eyes, Alijah took his card from her pocket and placed it in her purse. If he wanted her to use it, she figured she would pay for the spa with it to shut him up.

Alijah walked into the condo with several bags. After being pampered at the spa, she and the girls had gotten a little carried away. So much so that she was afraid of when Kieran got his credit card bill. She had only intended to use it at the spa but ended up using it in the stores as well once Erin saw it. She insisted that Kieran would want her to use it since he'd given it to her and stated it was his present to her, but she was sure that not even her friend realized how much was spent.

She made her way down the hall to her bedroom and placed the bags on her bed. She had found several things to wear for the night but was leaning towards a two-piece black *Dolce and Gabbana* top and skirt and a pair of black platform *Christian Louboutin* pumps.

She pulled the items from the bag hanging up the outfit on her closet door and putting the shoes on the floor below it. She appraised the outfit and decided she would wear it. She chose to pair it with gold accessories to make it pop.

Going into her purse, she pulled Kieran's card from her wallet and headed out of her room to find him. She knew he was more than likely in his office. As she got to the doorway, she discovered she was right. He was sitting at his desk typing away on his computer. As she walked in, he looked up at her.

"Did you have fun?"

"I did," she responded, walking around his desk.

Kieran slid his chair back, and Alijah slid onto his lap. He cupped the side of her face, and Alijah leaned into it as his lips settled on hers in a gentle kiss. When they pulled apart, Alijah held up his card.

"Here's your card back," Alijah stated, handing it to him.

Kieran took it from her and tossed it on the desk. "Did you use it?"

"Yes, but about that. I may have gone a little overboard," she responded, waving her hand in a so-so motion.

Kieran cocked his head, curious to see what she thought was overboard. "Define overboard."

Alijah reached up and pulled one of her curls as she debated whether or not to tell him. She had spent quite a bit of money. Hell, the outfit she planned to wear for her birthday celebration was almost four grand, including the shoes.

"Well, I was only going to use it to pay for the girl's and my spa treatment, but I used it when we went shopping. I may have also got Erin and Chayse an outfit to wear for tonight. Along with several things for myself."

"That doesn't tell me how much you spent," Kieran informed her, as his lips quirked, and he tried not to smirk at her.

"I spent about..." Alijah cleared her throat. "ten thousand dollars," she finished lowly.

"Okay."

"That's it?" Alijah questioned. "I thought you would be a little upset and have one of your mood swings."

"I made that in the two minutes it took you to tell me how much you spent. It's fine, gorgeous." Kieran leaned in and kissed her.

Alijah turned in his lap to see what he had been working on when she walked in. It was a marketing proposal for another product he wanted to release at the end of October. She studied the concept for a moment and saw where it was they were trying to go, but it wasn't quite there. She made a mental note to talk to Trevor at work Monday and give him a few ideas.

"What are you wearing tonight?" Kieran asked as he ran his hands up and down her sides, drawing her attention from the screen.

"You'll have to wait and see."

"That's fine. I'll just have to settle for seeing what you're wearing under these shorts."

Kieran lifted her off his lap, standing her up. He removed her shorts and licked his lips as he took in the sight of her purple boy shorts. He pulled them down as well, and she stepped out of them. Kieran picked her up and sat her on the empty space on his desk. He pushed her, and Alijah rested on her elbow.

She watched as he spread her legs slowly, running his hands up her thighs. He spread her lips with his fingers before leaning in and giving her clit a long, slow lick. Alijah moaned softly. Again, Kieran licked her clit slowly. This went on for a torturous while before she couldn't take it anymore. Alijah laced her finger through his hair and pulled his head back. She looked down, locking eyes with him.

"Stop teasing me," she stated, slowly dipping one of the fingers on her free hand into her pussy. She then ran it across his lower lip, coating it with her juices. "And eat my pussy," she finished as she pulled him back between her legs.

Kieran's lips locked around her clit, and he began to suck on it. Alijah leaned back against the desk as he pleasured her. He released her clit and began to flick his tongue against it quickly. He slid two fingers inside of her and began to pump them steadily.

Alijah arched off the desk and began grinding her pussy against his tongue while holding him in place.

"Fuck, Kieran." Alijah gasped as she felt herself getting closer. "Suck my clit," she ordered.

Kieran did as she asked, furiously sucking. Alijah felt as if he was sucking the energy entirely out of her. She brought her other hand down and grabbed the back of his neck. She was close.

"Eat that fucking pussy," Alijah stated. As she was about to explode, she felt that familiar feeling in her stomach, letting her know this would be more than an ordinary orgasm.

She sat up as it finally hit her, fingers still locked in his hair. Bucking against his face and she began to squirt.

"Kieran!"

Alijah released Kieran and fell back on the desk. She felt him move away from her as she caught her breath.

"I'm now convinced that you're trying to murder me," he informed her. Alijah looked up slightly to see his face covered in her juices before he began to wipe it off with the shirt he was wearing.

Alijah had just caught her breath as Kieran stood in front of her. She was as ready as she was going to be. He always only gave her just enough time to be prepared. Instead of releasing himself, he picked her up and headed toward his room. He laid her on the bed, and Alijah waited with anticipation of his stroke game.

Instead, she watched as he went to the bathroom, and she heard his shower come on. When he came back out, he began to undress her.

"Shower sex. I like it," she told him.

"No, shower sex," Kieran responded. "Just getting you cleaned up. We have to leave for dinner in a few hours."

Alijah glanced at the clock on his bedside table. She hadn't realized how late she had been out. They were supposed to be meeting Kieran's friends at the restaurant at seven-thirty, and it was almost four-thirty. She knew it would take her a little while to get ready and for them to get through the Saturday traffic. Kieran knew that as well.

"Don't worry, gorgeous," Kieran stated as he pulled her into the bathroom. "I promise to dick you down tonight." With that, he smacked her on the ass and walked out.

Alijah rolled her eyes. He could be incredibly crude at times, but she would be lying if she said it didn't turn her on. That man was just sex personified, and she enjoyed everything about it.

Alijah looked up at the restaurant as she stepped out of the car. The four of them had just arrived at *Bliss*. She watched as Kieran tipped the valet before coming around to her side of the vehicle. Erin and Chayse had been taken in by the restaurant's beauty as well. Kieran placed his hand on the small of Alijah's back.

"Shall we, ladies?" he questioned, and he steered Alijah towards the entrance.

Kieran held the door open for the three ladies as they entered the restaurant. They approached the hostess stand, and before Alijah could even say anything, the hostess began to speak.

"Mr. Cayman, it's so good to see you again." She began to gush as soon as she saw Kieran.

Ignoring the young woman, Kieran stepped behind Alijah and placed his hands on her waist, which was bare. He liked the two-piece outfit she was wearing. He'd told her as much when he first saw her in it. The skirt stopped just above her knees, and the top left her midsection exposed. It was classy and sexy all at the same time.

"Um...your table is ready. Right this way, Mr. Cayman." The hostess finally stated when she realized he wouldn't respond to her.

They followed her to the back to a private room. She stepped aside to allow them to enter. Cruz and Nik were already seated at the table. They stood as the others entered the room. Kieran pulled out the chair at the head of the table for Alijah as the other two men pulled out the other chairs.

"I have to say; you ladies look delicious tonight." Nik complimented as he pulled out Chayse's chair.

"Trust me; you men look just as yummy," Erin responded, looking at the three of them.

"Where's Paetyn?" Chayse questioned after thanking Nik.

"He's here." Came Cruz's short response.

As if on cue, Paetyn came through the door at that moment. He took the seat across from Erin after greeting everyone. Everyone picked up their menus and looked over them as they were already on the table. Alijah glanced up from her menu to find that Paetyn was tapping away on his phone. Figuring he already knew what he wanted, she went back to looking over her menu. So many of the items sounded delicious, and she didn't know which one to choose.

"This place is beautiful." She then heard Erin say.

"Thank you." Came Paetyn's response.

Alijah's head snapped back up to find him with a panty-dropping smile on his face. After all, she was a woman, and she wasn't blind. It wasn't as if she didn't notice that Kieran had some overly attractive friends. It was merely that she was more attracted to Kieran. Therefore, she figured it was okay to acknowledge the other three as men.

"You didn't tell me we were coming to one of Paetyn's restaurants." She directed at Kieran.

"We're at one of Paetyn's restaurants," he responded with a slight shrug.

Alijah glared at him before mumbling, "Whatever," then turning her attention to Paetyn. "What would you suggest I order, Paetyn? There are so many delicious-looking choices."

"Order a sample of each item you're interested in." Came Paetyn's response.

"We could do that?" Chayse questioned, trying to find that option on the menu. She had been having a hard time deciding as well. "I don't see that on here."

"It isn't," Paetyn responded. "But if that's what you want, I'll have the chefs make it for you."

All three women smiled at him. "Thank you, Paetyn," Alijah responded for them.

"You're welcome, Birthday Girl."

For the next several minutes, the women spoke to each other, deciding what they wanted to order before concluding that each of them would order a few different things, and they would share them since it was so much they wanted to try on the menu.

They had just finished deciding when the waiter came in pushing a cart. It held a few bottles of champagne in buckets of ice. He popped one open and filled the glasses on the table before going around and getting everyone's order. Once he was gone, the table broke out into a few different conversations.

"So, Alijah, twenty-five is a milestone," Nik stated, drawing her attention. "Kieran, you remember twenty-five, right? All those long years ago."

Kieran cut his eyes at Nik, and Alijah rolled hers. She was aware of the age difference between Kieran and herself. Hell, if she were honest, she would say that it was one of the things that attracted her to him. Leave it to Nik, however, to bring it up in an attempt to piss Kieran off. The man didn't know when to stop.

"I'm assuming his walk down memory lane to those years would travel in equal distance to yours," Chayse stated before taking a sip of her champagne.

Alijah watched as Nik's eyes slid to Chayse, and he quirked an eyebrow. He then gave her a smile that Alijah had to admit would have made her weak in the knees if she were someone else. Chayse simply rolled her eyes and turned back to continue her conversation with Paetyn. Nik opened his mouth to say something, but Erin stopped him.

"I suggest you think hard about that," she stated, drawing the attention of the table. "I can promise you, Nik, you're seriously unarmed in a battle of wits against Chayse. I hate to admit it, but when she gets going, not even my snark can keep up."

Nik contemplated it for a moment before turning his attention to Erin and striking up a conversation as Alijah did the same with Kieran.

When their food arrived, everyone ate while making small talk. The women enjoyed everything they ordered, and at one point, Erin refused to continue to share anymore. It didn't surprise Alijah; the girl could take down food like a garbage disposal.

Once they finished eating, the ladies reached into their purses to pull out money to pay for their meal.

"Don't worry about it," Paetyn stated, stopping them. "It's your birthday, after all. Think of this as your gift."

"Are you sure?" Alijah questioned, hand still in her purse. Paetyn nodded, and Alijah sighed, snapping her purse closed.

"Where to next, ladies?" Nik questioned as he stood.

"Mirage," Erin informed him. "I'm dying to see how it comes alive at night."

They pulled up to *Mirage* half an hour later. Once they stepped out of the vehicles, they followed Nik to the front of the line and straight inside. He led them to the section they had been in the first time Alijah had come with Kieran.

They all took a seat, and Nik immediately flagged down one of his waitresses, requesting a bottle of champagne, his favorite bottle of scotch, and glasses.

"I have to say; this place is pretty amazing at night as well." Erin complimented. Nik smiled at her.

They broke out into several different conversations as the music played, and they waited for the waitress to return with their drinks.

"Have I told you," Kieran started, leaning in and placing his lips to her ear. "how beautiful you look?"

"Yes," Alijah responded. "But it never hurts to hear it again."

"Hmm...too bad, because I'm not going to tell you again," he informed her, causing her to smack him in the chest with the back of her hand. Kieran chuckled. "I will tell you that you look absolutely delicious, and I can't wait to taste you." He licked the shell of her ear for emphasis, making Alijah take in a breath before he moved away.

The waitress returned with the requested bottles and glasses. Drinks went around, and everyone continued to talk and laugh. Alijah hadn't seen Cruz relaxed before, and she wasn't sure if it was the alcohol or just the overall company, but it looked good on him. She was almost done with her second glass of champagne when a song she and the girls liked came on. The three exchanged looks before getting up and heading to the dance floor.

Kieran watched the three women dance to the upbeat song for a second before putting ice into a glass and pouring himself some scotch. He sipped it slowly, keeping his eyes on Alijah while listening to Paetyn's conversation. He was thinking of opening a bistro in the art district.

The women danced to one more song before coming back and sitting down. A waitress passed by, and all of the women ordered a drink while the men continued to drink their scotch. Alijah glanced at Nik and saw him staring at the tattoos on Erin's arms. Which were visible due to the sleeveless crop top she wore with a pair of high waist flared pants — both a wine red.

She then watched as he turned his attention to Chayse, studying the tattoo on her right shoulder and left thigh. Both were made visible by the fact that she was wearing a spaghetti-strapped crop top, and the high waist skirt she wore had quite a high split. It played peek-a-boo with her skin whenever she moved—making her mocha skin tone pop against the lavender fabric.

"Did Erin do your tattoos as well?" He questioned after a moment.

"Yes. I wouldn't trust anyone else to." Chayse informed him.

Kieran was talking to Cruz when Alijah drew his attention. He turned to her, and he knew what was coming by the look on her face. He tuned into the song playing, and it was something slow.

"Dance with me," she told him, standing, and taking his hand.

"I told you, I don't dance."

Alijah leaned down, placing her free hand on his thigh. "Then think of it as a prelude to foreplay," she told him with a smirk.

Rolling his eyes, Kieran knocked back the rest of the scotch in his glass before standing. "Then I better get to play when the song is over."

He allowed her to lead him to the dance floor. When she found a spot she liked, she turned around, placing her ass squarely on Kieran's dick. Her heels gave her just the proper height advantage. He put his hand on her hips as she began a slow wind.

After a minute, Kieran's attention was briefly pulled to Erin and Cruz leaving out of the building. However, it didn't stay there as Alijah began to drag him to an empty dark corner of the dance floor. She positioned them so his back was turned to the crowd before taking one of his hands and slipping it down her skirt.

"In a daring mood, I see," Kieran stated as he dipped his hand into her panties.

"You said you wanted to play."

Smirking to himself, Kieran leaned in and attached his lips to her neck as he began to finger her pussy. He knew he didn't have much time before one of his friends came to get them when Cruz and Erin returned with her gifts. More than likely Nik since he seemed to live for ruining moments.

He began to move his fingers inside her faster, barely hearing her moans over the music. It was only the music that made him remember where they were and stop himself from making her squirt. He removed his finger from her and instead began to rub her clit furiously. All the while, he was still moving to the music with her.

"Are you going to cum for me?" He asked in her ear before biting her neck. She nodded. He threaded the fingers of his free hand into her hair and pulled her head back. "Not if you don't ask me."

"Please," Alijah stated, Kieran just barely heard her over the music. "Please let me cum for you, Daddy."

With that, Kieran snaked his hand around and grabbed her neck. He read the signs of her body, and right as she began to cum, he pinched her clit and tightened his grip on her neck slightly as she moaned her release.

Kieran waited for her to come down from her high before removing his hand from her skit and releasing her. She turned to look at him as Kieran slid the fingers he'd used into his mouth. When he'd cleaned them, he pulled Alijah into him and kissed her — snaking his tongue into her mouth, allowing her to taste herself.

"When we get back to the condo, I'm going to fuck you incoherent," he informed her. He was enjoying watching her chest rise quickly as her breath hitched. Then, taking her hand like he hadn't promised to fuck her incapacitated, he led the way back to their section, but Alijah stopped him. Going to the bathroom to clean herself up first before rejoining their group.

Alijah was more than a little shocked. When they had made it back to their section, she had been handed birthday presents. Even Nik, Paetyn, and Cruz had gotten her something. She insisted to them that they hadn't had to and even tried to give it back, but they wouldn't take it. Paetyn and Cruz had gotten her a matching earring and necklace set, while Nik had gotten her a bracelet that would go with the set as well.

While she was appreciative of their gifts and thanked the three of them earnestly, she was the most excited about Chayse and Erin's gifts. They had gotten her a *Red Sable* brush set that she knew alone could run hundreds of dollars and some high-quality paints in an entire kit that ran pretty close to the paintbrushes.

She had rushed over and hugged them both, falling into Erin's lap, where her friend wrapped her arms around her waist.

"Well, that's sexy. I think I may need to take a picture." Nik spoke. "If I knew I'd get that reaction for some paintbrushes, I would have bought you some too."

"Shut up, Nik." Cruz threw out as he turned his attention from the women sitting beside him.

"So, And, are you getting some birthday dick tonight?" Erin questioned, causing Chayse to roll her eyes and Alijah to quirk an eyebrow at her.

"If you must know, End," Alijah stated, stressing the nickname, making Erin snort. "I just may be."

Erin smirked at her best friend and poked her in her exposed side, causing her to squirm before the three of them began to laugh.

"I feel like I'm watching the beginning of a very steamy porno." Nik once again butted in.

Chayse cut her eyes at him. "You and Erin should be best friends. You both have no chill and no filter," she told him.

"I have a filter. It's just not fun to use, and I only pull my chill out, weather permitting." He smirked at her.

Alijah shook her head as she got up and made her way back over to Kieran, who was drinking, what Alijah would guess, was his fifth glass of scotch. Not to mention the two glasses of champagne he'd had.

"Please tell me you're not tipsy. I refuse to get hit with lazy dick on my birthday."

Stopping the glass that he was bringing up to his lips, Kieran turned to look at her. "When have I ever given you lazy dick?" When she didn't say anything, he spoke again. "I can guarantee you'll be sore tomorrow."

Alijah licked her bottom lip before biting it. She was looking forward to that.

20

Alijah's back was slammed against the front door as soon as it closed. Kieran had her pinned, hands above her head, as he brought his lips down punishingly on hers. From the way he stole her breath, she knew precisely what kind of night she would be in for, and she was looking forward to it.

She kissed him back with just as much reverence as he was kissing her. Her lips moved in sync, trying to keep up, but she knew it was a losing battle. He was dominating her mouth, and she knew that he would dominate her body in much of the same way. His free hand dipped inside her skirt, and he began to stroke her through her panties.

Alijah broke the kiss, leaning her head back against the door as she moaned out in ecstasy. Kieran attached his lips to her neck and began to suck her sweet spot as he teased her through her panties a moment more before moving them to the side and sinking a finger into her. Though his kiss had been frenzied and hurried, he stroked her slowly — his finger entering and retreating at an agonizing pace. However, the grip on her wrists remained firm, and he sucked on her neck punishingly. The two contrasts were enough to get her worked up instantly, and she needed more.

She began to move her hips in hopes of speeding up his ministrations. It had the opposite effect. Kieran bit her neck slightly before withdrawing his finger. Alijah opened her mouth to protest but was cut off as he slowly slid the finger he'd been torturing her with into her mouth. She moaned as she sucked on it.

"I could fuck you against the door," Kieran told her. His deep baritone was husky and filled with lust. "I could slip deep inside of you and pound your pussy until the door cracked." His eyes locked with hers, and she watched as they darkened with desire. "But I won't. Not right now."

Removing his finger from her mouth, he picked her up and headed down the hall to his bedroom. He turned the light on before making his way over to the bed and sitting on it. Alijah straddling him, her skirt bunched above her thighs. He reached up and laced his fingers in her hair, bringing her down to meet his lips once again.

As they kissed, Alijah began to grind on his lap. She could feel the bulge in his pants growing bigger. She brought her hands up and started to undo the buttons on his shirt. After the first two, she decided it was taking too much effort and just pulled the shirt apart, causing buttons to go flying. She knew he might have been pissed about it later, but she didn't care at that moment.

Kieran reached up and pulled her shirt over her head before getting rid of her strapless bra. Switching their position, he pulled out of the kiss before yanking her skirt down her legs and ripping her panties harshly. He shrugged out of his shirt before getting down on his knees and burying his face in her pussy.

Alijah moaned at the feel of his tongue diving into her. There were no teasing licks. Kieran had gone straight in for the kill. His tongue was like absolute sin as he worked it into her.

Bringing two of her fingers to her lips, Alijah placed them in her mouth for a moment before reaching down and rubbing her clit. She had barely begun when Kieran moved her hand away.

"You don't get to touch yourself," Kieran told her after removing his tongue from inside of her. Leaning down, he gave her clit a long, slow lick pulling a moan from her. "Understand?"

Alijah could only nod. Kieran leaned down and flicked his tongue over her clit again. "Use your words, Alijah."

"Yes, Kieran. I understand," she responded, looking down into his desire-filled eyes.

At her words, Kieran lowered his head again. Taking her clit into his mouth, he began to suck on it slowly, and he slid a single finger inside of her. The motion of his finger was measured. His two actions were causing a slow burn to form in the pit of Alijah's stomach.

Kieran's tongue circled her clit at an agonizing pace. It was a complete contrast from how he had initially begun. He slowly slid his finger into her at the same pace as he circled her clit. He then pulled it out, mimicking the same action.

This went on until the pleasure rising within her stomach was about to boil over. Alijah arched her back as she felt her orgasm surfacing. She was about to tumble over the edge when Kieran removed his finger and tongue.

Alijah's eyes flew open. She didn't know precisely when she had closed them, but she didn't care. Her eyes locked with his, and she could see the mischief in them.

"Kieran," she started as she felt her orgasm receding.

He didn't give her time to continue. Leaning down, he slowly swiped his tongue over her clit while looking up at her. Alijah's breath hitched. Taking her clit into his mouth, Kieran sucked it once slowly. He released it and moved down, sliding his tongue into her leisurely, the entire time looking up at her.

Kieran leaned back and slowly pushed his thumb into her. He moved it in a circle inside of her as he leaned down and blew a stream of cold air on her clit.

Pulling his thumb from her, Kieran replaced it with his tongue as he used his thumb to rub her clit back and forth. He was so in tune with her body that he knew the exact moment her orgasm was about to hit her. He removed his tongue from her and stopped the movement of his thumb.

"No, Kieran." Alijah groaned. Half in pleasure, half in frustration. She reached down with her left hand. Her middle finger brushed her clit just barely before Kieran grabbed her hand and moved it.

"What did I say, Alijah?" Kieran questioned. His baritone had deepened and was filled with lust. Alijah didn't answer him, and Kieran leaned down and bit her clit. It was right on the precipice of pain and pleasure. Her breath hitched, and she moaned out. "Answer me," Kieran demanded.

"Not to touch myself," she answered breathily.

Again, Kieran bit her clit, causing her to moan. "Then keep your hands on the bed." With that, Kieran leaned down and resumed his slow torture.

Alijah wasn't sure how long it went on, but he had brought her to the edge several times without pushing her over, and she wasn't sure exactly how much more she could take. Her fist gripped the sheets, and she felt the flame in the pit of her stomach begin to blaze. She was close. Oh, so close, and if he didn't allow her to cum this time, she was going to hurt him.

When she felt herself about to explode, she could feel him begin to release her clit, which he had been sucking slowly. Reaching down, she laced her fingers in his hair and held him in place.

"Please, Kieran. Please let me cum." Alijah pleaded, her legs shaking as he merely held her clit in his mouth.

Reaching up, Kieran removed her fingers from his hair, placing her hands back on the bed. He loved to hear her beg. Voice laced with desire. It turned him on in a way he had never imagined until the first time she'd done it. Each time they'd had sex after that, he had been sure to make her beg. This had been the most he'd tortured her so far.

Looking up at her, he quickly flicked his tongue over her clit. Slipping two fingers inside of her and moving them at the same speed. He watched as her eyes closed and her back arched. It was only a moment later when her release hit her, coating his fingers.

He slowed both of his movements, helping her ride out the orgasm he had denied her for the past half an hour. He took her clit back into his mouth and sucked on it when it had passed. She began to squirm, trying to move away from him. Placing her feet on his shoulders, she pushed herself away.

Kieran growled. Grabbing her ankle, he yanked her back to him. He placed one of her legs over his shoulders and wrapped his arm around her thigh, locking her in place.

"Don't fucking run from me," he bit out. "This is what you wanted, right? For me to let you cum. Then take it."

He leaned down and took her clit back between his lips again. As he sucked on it, she squirmed and continued to try to get away, but he had her locked in place. Kieran slid his finger into her and began to rotate them with each entry. He continued his ministrations and brought her to another orgasm.

"Kieran!" She cried out his name as her release hit, and her legs shook.

Standing up, Kieran went about removing the rest of his clothes. Well, aware that Alijah was watching him. He'd learned that she enjoyed watching him undress. He had gotten his pants off and was about to slide his boxer briefs off when she sat up. When they hit the floor, Kieran stepped out of them.

Alijah reached up and took his dick into her hand. Kieran locked eyes with her as she began to stroke him slowly. He was already rock hard, but he never got tired of feeling her warm hand around his dick. Tonight, however, he had something else planned. It may have been her birthday, but he was going to make it a night neither of them forgot.

Removing her hand from his dick, he watched as she pouted prettily at him. He had to stop himself from smirking. Kieran brought his thumb up and ran it over her bottom lip.

"No hands, baby," he told her, staring into her eyes.

She leaned in and kissed the tip of his dick. He watched as she circled her tongue around it. Kieran knew that she would try to get him back for the torture he had made her endure, but he honestly wasn't too upset about it.

Slowly, she took him into her mouth as far as she could, and Kieran moaned, throwing his head back. She held him in her mouth for a moment before pulling off with a small pop. She looked up at him as she went to slide onto her knees on the floor, but he stopped her and placed her back on the bed.

He might have allowed her to if she had been any other woman. He had always felt that any man in a committed relationship that allowed his woman to kneel on the floor before him needed his ass beat. Especially any man that let the woman in front of him kneel before them. She was a goddess, and while he had no problem kneeling before her and worshiping her. He felt it degrading to let her get on her knees. As ridiculous as that sounded with the act she was performing.

She gave him a confused look, and Kieran leaned down and pecked her lips. "Stay on the bed, baby."

Alijah didn't question him. Instead, she tucked her feet under her on the bed as he grabbed his dick and pointed it at her. Leaning in, she licked him from base to tip, eyes locked onto his.

Opening her mouth, she took him back inside and slowly began to bob her head. She took her right hand and stroked what she couldn't fit into her mouth. Kieran moaned as he continued to watch her.

She slowly pulled off of his dick but continued to stroke him. Leaning down, Alijah swiped her tongue over his balls before taking one into her mouth.

"Fuck." Kieran groaned as he threw his head back.

Alijah switched her attention to the other one as she continued to stroke his dick. It amazed her that Kieran was always well manicured below the belt. The only hair he had was a thin, happy trail leading from the bottom of his navel to the top of his pelvis.

Alijah took him into her mouth again, sucking him slightly faster than she had been previously. Kieran looked down to find her looking up at him. He laced his fingers in her hair as he moved his hips to meet her pace. He would be lying if he said he didn't want to take control and fuck her throat; however, Kieran knew he was too large for that in this position, and he didn't want to hurt her.

"You are so fucking sexy," Kieran told her. Alijah hummed her response, and the vibration sent a shock through his dick.

He slowly pulled it from her mouth, and she released him with a pop. Kieran placed his hands on the bed and leaned in to kiss her. She caught his bottom lip between her teeth when they pulled away from the kiss.

Reaching between her legs, Kieran began to stroke her clit slowly. Alijah moaned and moved back on the bed as he moved forward. When she was at the head of the bed, she laid back, and he settled between her legs. He continued to rub her clit as he latched on to her left nipple. Kieran bit it gently before laving it with his tongue. He massaged her faster, and her legs began to shake. Just as she tipped over the edge, he grabbed his dick and slipped it inside of her.

"Shit." Kieran groaned as Alijah moaned loudly.

It didn't matter how many times he slid between her legs. She always fit him like a glove. Snug and tight. He held himself still for a moment before leaning up on his hands and looking into her eyes. He didn't know why, but he often found himself staring into those hypnotic green orbs when they had sex. It had never turned him on before. He usually preferred for neither of them to look at each other. However, this was Alijah, and it shouldn't have surprised him; everything seemed to be different with her.

Kieran pulled out slowly before pushing back into her. Both of them voiced their pleasure. Kieran kept his strokes slow and even as Alijah wrapped her legs around him, her arms sliding under his and gripping his shoulders. She threw her head back and enjoyed his deep, slow strokes.

He pushed into her and moved his hips in a figure eight, brushing his pelvic bone against her clit. She moaned out and tightened her legs around him.

"You like that?" Kieran whispered in her ear.

"Mm...yes," she moaned out in response.

Kieran pulled out as much as he could with her legs wrapped around him so tightly. He pushed back in and again moved his hips in a figure eight.

Alijah was enjoying it, but she needed something else. "Mm...Kieran...I..."

He pulled out and pushed into her again. "What, baby? Tell me what you need."

"Fuck me," she moaned. "I need you to fuck me."

Grabbing her legs, Kieran released them from around his waist. He leaned up and took one of her legs, putting it over his shoulder. Pulling out, he snapped his hips and slammed into her.

"Fuck!" She screamed.

Kieran continued to fuck into her, groaning at the warmth of her pussy. She always felt good, but it was ten times better tonight. His pace began to increase, and he threw her other leg over his shoulder. It wasn't long before he was moving inside of her with fast, hard strokes.

Alijah placed her hand between them on his stomach and tried to push him away. Kieran grabbed it along with her other one and held them above her head.

"You asked me to fuck you," Kieran stated through a groan. "Stop trying to push me away and take this shit," he growled out.

Transferring both of her hands to one of his, he placed his middle finger in his mouth before putting it between them and frantically began to rub her clit. Leaning back in, his lips ghosted across hers.

"Cum for, Daddy."

At his words, Alijah arched upwards, pressing her breast to his chest and cumming all over his dick.

"Yes!"

Kieran slowed his pace and stroked her, slowly extending her orgasm. When she came down from her release, she kissed him, and he snaked his tongue into her mouth, massaging her tongue with his.

He removed himself from between her legs and moved down, taking a long slow lick of her pussy. Tasting the sweet nectar she had just released. He licked her once more before flipping her onto her stomach. Grabbing her hips, he lifted her ass in the air. Smacking her ass, he took both cheeks in his hands and massaged them.

Kieran took his dick into his hand and guided himself back into her, causing them to moan in pleasure. He began to stroke in and out of her as he continued to massage her ass.

"You feel so good, baby," he told her, trying to avoid slamming into her a bit longer.

"You do too," she moaned out. She pushed up on her hands, and he released her ass cheeks. Grabbing both of her arms, he brought them behind her back before pushing her top half back down to the bed, never missing a stroke.

Placing his hands back on her ass cheeks, he spread them apart, and Alijah felt warm saliva drip between them before she felt his thumb massaging her other entrance. She tensed slightly. The feeling was foreign, but she would be lying if she said it was unpleasant.

"Relax. I'm not going to take you here. Tonight at least, but you'll love it when I do," he told her. "I'll make it so good for you."

Alijah didn't say anything. She didn't disagree because she was sure that he would make good on his statement if he ever took her that way.

Kieran was losing himself. He began to fuck her harder. Grabbing both of her hips and pulling her back to meet his thrusts. Her moans and screams filled the room, and Kieran angled his hips and began assaulting her g-spot.

Reaching down, he grabbed a handful of her hair, pulling her head up as he continued to hammer into her.

"You like that shit, don't you?" Kieran questioned, slamming into her and swiveling his hips. Alijah's only response was a loud moan. Kieran let go of her hip and smacked her ass. "Answer me!" He demanded.

Alijah's pussy clenched around him. She loved it when he was aggressive with her. It made her pussy dripping wet as her orgasm approached. Alijah could feel it.

"Yes, I like it. Damn, I like it," she responded.

Kieran pulled her up by her hair and leaned back on his knees, pulling her with him as he fucked her. He took his free hand and wrapped it around her neck, squeezing. When he did, her pussy tightened around him, and Kieran groaned. He gave her three more deep thrusts, and she was cumming all over his dick.

"Kieran! Fuck!"

He released her hair and neck, and Alijah fell forward, his dick slipping from her folds. Kieran flipped her over and trailed his tongue from the valley of her breast down over her stomach before licking her clit, causing her to shiver. Sitting back on his legs, he used one hand to push hers farther apart as he slowly stroked himself.

"Play with my pussy, Alijah," Kieran instructed.

Tilting her head, she smirked at him. "I thought I wasn't allowed to touch myself."

"Alijah," Kieran stated firmly.

Her smirk remained in place. "I'm just following your instruction, Daddy."

Leaning over her, Kieran grabbed her chin firmly between his thumb and index finger. "Stop testing me and play with my fucking pussy," he demanded with a snarl.

Alijah swallowed as her pussy clenched involuntarily. Damn, he was sexy when he took control. As he sat back on his legs again, she reached down with her right hand and slowly dipped two fingers into her pussy. She began to finger fuck herself slowly. Watching him stroke his dick while he watched her.

She began to move against her fingers. Watching him was turning her on. A few minutes had passed, and Alijah could feel herself building, getting ready to explode. She was almost there when Kieran moved her hand out of the way. She was about to protest, but he leaned in and latched on to her clit, sucking it as he scraped it with his teeth.

Alijah reached down and grabbed his head, bucking against his lips. "Shit! Don't stop! I'm cumming! I'm cumming!"

Kieran plunged his fingers into her and curled them as her orgasm hit. He released her clit and replaced his fingers with his mouth as she began to squirt. Her climax continued, and he slurped her juices up, drinking from her fountain.

When it passed, Kieran sat up, licking his lips with a smirk. He watched as her chest rose and fell rapidly. Kieran lay beside her. He began to play with one of her breasts as he kissed her shoulder. He would give her a minute before he pushed her body more.

His thumb was rubbing against her nipple when she reached over and cupped the side of his face kissing him. Their tongues clashed, and Alijah moved and straddled his waist. His dick lay against his stomach, and she began to slide her wet pussy against it.

Grabbing her by the waist, Kieran pulled her up to straddle his face. He lifted his head and ran his tongue over her pussy. He rested his head back on the pillow.

"Ride my tongue," I instructed before he stuck it out, and she lowered herself onto it.

It slipped into her easily, and Alijah braced herself against the headboard and began to move up and down slowly. She looked down at him as she circled her hips. She had never met a man who enjoyed giving oral pleasure as much as he did, but she was far from complaining.

Kieran placed his hands on her hips and moved her backward. He grabbed his dick and positioned it for her to slide down. He watched as she threw her head back as he bottomed out. Placing a hand on her lower stomach and lower back, he began to rock her steadily. He knew she enjoyed this. After a few minutes, he let her go and placed his hands behind his head.

Smirking at her, he licked his lower lip. "Giddy up."

Alijah rolled her eyes as she placed her hands on his stomach and began to bounce up and down. Kieran groaned, and if it were possible, he got even harder by the look of bliss on her face and the sight of her breast bouncing.

"Shit," Kieran stated as he bit his lip. "That's it, beautiful. Ride your dick. Take it exactly how you want it," he goaded.

Alijah stopped her bouncing and began to move her hips in a circular motion. As she did, Kieran made his dick jump inside of her.

"Do it again," she demanded.

Kieran appeased her and did as she asked. She started bouncing up and down again, and he raised his hips to meet her downward movements. He pulled her down on top of him and grabbed her ass in his hands. He began to bounce her faster as his upward thrust matched his speed.

"Yes, yes, yes….Oh! Fuck!" Alijah screamed. Kieran lifted her at the last minute, and she rained down on him. Her body was shaking, her nails digging into his chest.

She fell to the side of him, releasing shaky breaths. Her legs were still quivering. Kieran rolled over to hover over her, spreading her legs with one of his.

"Baby, wait," Alijah stated, placing her hand on his stomach. "I don't think I can cum anymore tonight."

Kieran smirked. He loved when she told him what it was she couldn't or he couldn't do when they were having sex. He always enjoyed proving her wrong. Grabbing her chin, he looked into those viridian green eyes.

"Yes, you can," he informed her before slamming into her.

"Oh, God!" Alijah screamed, grabbing his back and digging her nails in.

Kieran smirked again as he stroked in and out of her, even though her nails were biting into his back. "Not God. Just me, baby."

He watched as she opened her mouth to say something witty, he was sure, but he began to pound into her, pulling moans from her instead. He reached down to strum her clit, and her pussy started clenching around him.

Kieran had been holding off, and he could feel his release building within him. He sped up his strokes as he felt his balls begin to tighten. He was close, and he knew that she was too.

"Look at me," he demanded. When Alijah opened her eyes, her breath hitched at the primal, raw desire that looked back at her. "I'm going to cum in my pussy," he informed her. She clenched around him. "I'm going to paint the inside of it with my cum while you rain all over your dick."

His words sent her over the edge, and she clenched around him.

"Oh fuck! Alijah." Kieran groaned as they both found release looking into each other's eyes.

Kieran leaned in and kissed her softly before slowly sliding out of her. He went into his bathroom and turned on the shower. He grabbed two large towels and placed them on the counter as it started heating up. Going back into his bedroom, he picked Alijah up and carried her into the bathroom, stepping into the shower with her.

He sat her on her feet, and she began to sway. He steadied her with a sly smile. He had fucked her until she couldn't stand. Grabbing her bath wash, Kieran squirted it in his hand and began to slowly rub it all over her body. He soaped up her breast, and she leaned back against his chest.

Placing his hands under the shower stream, he rinsed the soap off before slipping his hand between her folds and tweaking her clit.

"I can't, Kieran."

Turning her around, he took her hand and placed it on his already hardening dick. She stroked him slowly as he played with her pussy. When he was completely hard, he switched her position, turning her to face the wall. Placing her hands on it, he pulled her hips back before sliding into her.

Reaching up, Kieran grabbed a fist full of her hair. "Hang on, baby."

Pulling out, he snapped his hips and plunged back in. His rhythm was consistent as she pushed herself back to meet him. The water rained down with the sound of skin slapping against skin. Kieran slapped her ass, causing her to moan out loud.

He slammed into her watching her ass jiggle before he started circling his hips. His dick brushing against her g-spot

"Fuck, this pussy is good," he breathed out.

Slowly, Kieran pulled his dick out of her. Alijah looked over her shoulder at him as he slowly stroked himself. He had stepped under the spray of water, and he looked irresistible.

"Kier-"

He cut her off. "I thought you couldn't," he taunted as he continued to stroke himself.

She turned to look at him, disbelief in her eyes. "Ki....I...Wh....?"

He smirked and stepped toward her. "Trouble forming words there, baby?"

She opened her mouth to say something, but he picked her up and impaled her on his dick. He immediately began to thrust into her furiously. Her arms wrapped around his neck, and she held on for the ride as her moans filled the shower. Her pussy began to spasm, and his thrust became erratic.

"I..I..I...I..." Alijah repeated over and over.

"You what? Talk to me, gorgeous."

"Cumming!" Was the only word she could get out as she began to shake and coat his dick.

Kieran slammed into her one last time and flooded her with his cum. "Oh, baby."

Alijah slumped against him, and Kieran turned and placed his back against the shower wall to hold them up. He would be lying if he said his legs weren't a bit unstable at the moment.

After a few moments, he gently lifted her off his dick and placed her on her feet. They began to shower before the water got completely cold when they had both caught their breath.

Once they had stepped out of the shower and dried off, Kieran gave her one of his shirts, and he slipped on a pair of his boxers. They stripped the sheets from the bed, and he went and got more. Taking them back into the bedroom, Kieran placed them on the bed and left Alijah to change them as he walked out again. He walked into the living room to make sure the door was locked before grabbing a few things and heading back to the bedroom.

He placed the items on the bedside table before helping her finish changing the sheets. When they were done, he climbed in beside her. Reaching over onto the bedside table, he grabbed the bottle of water and a small white pill and gave them to her. Alijah raised her eyebrow at him.

"Plan B," he stated. Alijah nodded, taking it with a sip of water even though she was on the pill.

She placed the water on the nightstand and slid down, getting comfortable in bed. Kieran turned the lights off. He laid on his back, and she moved closer and laid her head on his chest.

"So, you planned to give me raw birthday dick. It was premeditated," she stated with a yawn.

Kieran chuckled, the vibration relaxing her. "Absolutely." With that, he leaned down and kissed her forehead. "Good night, Beautiful."

"Good night."

Kieran closed his eyes, slowly drifting off. He figured she was a bit sore, so he would give her a few hours before ravaging her again.

21

Alijah was sore and a bit ticked off. After a night of fantastic birthday sex and then again that morning, Kieran had told her that they needed to fly to Dolores, Colorado, for business. She had not been amused. When she had reminded him that she didn't work weekends, he told her that technically she wasn't. However, their appointment was at six Monday morning, and it made sense to fly out Sunday afternoon.

So, they had packed and gone to the airport with Chayse and Erin in tow since they were flying out that afternoon as well. Now, she was seated on Kieran's private plane, playing cards. Though she knew them flying out today made sense, she just wanted to spend her birthday lazing around.

She had just finished laying out the cards to start another game of Tri-Peaks when she felt Kieran's hand drop to her thigh. She glanced over at him to find him still reading the reports he'd pulled out when they first took off. Turning her attention back to the cards in front of her, she began to play. Alijah was halfway through the game when his finger started to make slow circles on her exposed thigh due to the shorts she wore.

She bit the inside of her cheek and focused on her game. They'd been in the air for thirty minutes, and she'd learned from Kieran that the total flight was a little over an hour and a half. Alijah figured she could play different card games until they landed.

Kieran's hand began circling her thigh, and Alijah shifted slightly. She had pretty much been ignoring him since he told her she wouldn't get to have a lazy, relaxed birthday.

Finishing up her game, Alijah grabbed the cards to reshuffle them. She heard Kieran lay the papers down on the table in front of him. She could feel his eyes on her but continued to shuffle the cards.

"Can I play with you?" Kieran questioned, and by the tone of his voice, she knew he wasn't talking about the cards.

Alijah laid the cards down and turned to look at him. He'd pulled his lower lip between his teeth, and she could see the mischief in his eyes. He slowly released his lip as she shook her head at him, rolling her eyes playfully.

He took her hand and stood up. Alijah allowed him to lead her to the small bedroom on the plane. She stood in front of him as he sat down on the bed.

Kieran released the button on her shorts before pulling down the zipper. He looked up at her as he pulled them, along with her panties, down. She had taken her shoes off when they'd lifted off, so she stepped out of the clothing items.

"If I didn't know any better, I would say you only like me for my vagina," Alijah told him with a raised eyebrow.

Parting her outer lips, Kieran leaned in and gave her clit a quick lick. "It's a good thing you know better." He pulled his shirt over his head before looking up at her. "Though it is a plus." He threw in, smirking.

Alijah hit him playfully on the chest. Kieran caught her hand and fell back onto the bed, pulling her on top of him. She laughed lightly, her hair falling into her face, and Kieran was in awe. She was so beautiful. Her entire face lit up when she laughed, when she smiled.

Kieran wanted to bury himself deep inside of her, but he knew she was sore. He had woken up twice and taken her during the early hours of the morning. While he believed in pushing her body for her pleasure, Kieran didn't believe in hurting her. He had become so in tune with how much she could take, and he knew that having sex with her at that moment would push her too far.

"I want to fuck you, bury my dick so deep you feel it in your stomach," he told her, watching her chest as her breath hitched. "But I'm not going to hurt you. So..." He finished, trailing off as he pulled her up his body to straddle his head.

Kieran leaned up and flicked his tongue over her clit several times. Taking hold of her waist, he latched onto her clit, laying back entirely on the bed, bringing her down with him.

The suction of his lips on her clit was slow. They had about an hour before they landed, and Kieran was in no hurry. He used his teeth to cause friction against her clit. The action was slow and deliberate.

Alijah moaned at the feel of Kieran's lips on her. She threw her head back and slowly began to gyrate her hips. Kieran lifted her slightly, removing his lips from her clit. Sticking his tongue out, he positioned her, pulling her down and sliding his tongue into her.

His hands on her waist, Kieran slowly moved her up and down. Each time he brought her down, he was sure to breathe out slowly through his nose onto her clit.

"Please don't stop." Alijah moaned.

Kieran lifted an eyebrow even though she wasn't looking at him. If he could smirk with his tongue inside of her, he would have. She thought he was going to torture her again. In this position, however, she had control. Yes, he was lifting and lowering her, but she could take over at any time.

Her legs began to shake, and Kieran knew she was close to cumming. She removed his hands from her waist and laced her fingers through his before placing them on the bed. Alijah continued to ride his tongue slowly. Right before she was about to cum, she lifted off his tongue, hovering over him. Alijah looked into his eyes before sliding back and leaning down to kiss him.

The kiss went on for a few moments as her orgasm subsided. When she was sure she wouldn't come immediately from the contact of his tongue, she slid back up. Kieran stuck his tongue back out, and she slowly slid down on it.

She always enjoyed the way he gave her oral pleasure. He would stiffen his tongue and then wiggle it inside of her. It drove her crazy.

Alijah sank onto his tongue and began to rotate her hips. After a moment of that, she began to rock back and forth. He breathed on her clit, and she began to shutter. Just as she was about to release, she rose off his tongue.

• • •

Kieran reached up to pull her back down, but she laced her fingers through his and slid down to kiss him again. Alijah snaked her tongue into his mouth. She took his lower lip between her teeth and tugged it gently when they pulled apart. She then ran her tongue along it before straddling his face again.

This time, Kieran latched onto her clit. He sucked it quickly as Alijah began to rock back and forth. She looked down, locking eyes with his. His mouth was warm around her clit, and she was a moaning mess.

Alijah was close. She could feel it, her orgasm right at the precipice. As it crept up on her, she placed her hands on the bed and lifted herself. His lips released her clit with a small pop.

Kieran raised an eyebrow at her. "Is this supposed to be payback for last night?" He leaned up and took a lick. "Because I'm sure you're torturing yourself more than you are me."

Alijah giggled before lowering herself again. She began to ride his tongue quickly as Kieran reached up and began to rub her clit with his thumb.

"Kieran. Oh, my...you're always so good to my pussy."

At those words, Kieran stopped rubbing her clit. Placing his hands on her waist, he lifted her. He licked his bottom lip as he cocked an eyebrow at her.

"Whose pussy?" He questioned.

"My..."

She didn't get to finish. Kieran flipped them over. Her back against the bed. He leaned in and licked her clit slowly before dipping his tongue inside her a few times.

"Whose pussy?" He questioned a second time, hazel eyes dark.

Alijah opened her mouth to answer but could only release a moan as he dove between her legs, putting his tongue to work. Kieran knew precisely how to quickly bring her to the edge, and Alijah was a moaning mess.

Kieran reached up and placed his hand around her neck, squeezing as he caused quick friction to her clit with his teeth. He watched as she arched her back, rising off of the bed. Her legs began to shake, and Kieran released her clit. He blew on it.

"Whose pussy?" He questioned again, licking her from opening to clit, circling his tongue around it. "Tell me," he demanded, biting her clit gently.

Kieran observed the signs of her body.

"Yours! Baby, it's yours! All yours!" Alijah screamed as he latched onto her clit, sucking it hard as she came.

Kieran continued to lick her languidly through her orgasm. When it completely subsided, he moved up to hover over her. "I want to bury my dick inside of you right now," he informed her before leaning down to peck her lips, hand still around her neck.

Alijah's eyes were hazed in the afterglow. "Do it."

"Your body isn't ready." He released her neck, kissing her again. "I can wait." With that, he rolled to lay beside her.

"Kieran, where are we?" Alijah questioned as she sat up in the front seat of their rented car.

They had landed about half an hour ago, and a car was waiting for them. Kieran had told her she could stay in the car while he got their bags and signed the paperwork for the vehicle. Once they were off, she hadn't been paying attention to their surroundings. Only when he turned off of the main road, and the trees opened up did she notice.

"Wait here. I'll be right back." Kieran informed her as he exited the vehicle, ignoring her question entirely.

Alijah watched him walk into the building he had parked in front of. Bringing her hand up, she hit the button for the locks. The building was rustic, and they seemed to be in the middle of nowhere. She had seen how these things ended for black people in the movies. She was not about to take any chances.

It only took a few minutes for Kieran to come back. Alijah unlocked the doors when he got to the car and turned to look at him as he got in. He put the car in drive and continued down the dirt road.

"Kieran, where are we?"

"I told you we were coming to Dolores, Alijah," he responded, glancing at her before turning his attention back toward the road.

Alijah rolled her eyes. "I know that. I mean, where are we now exact…"

Alijah trailed off as a beautiful cabin came into view. It was gorgeous. There was a fire pit outside, which she was sure was used for colder months. As she looked around her, she spotted another cabin a short distance from the one Kieran was pulling in front of. She took in the entire area, and it was breathtaking.

"We're at the Dutton Hot Springs," Kieran informed her coming to a stop in front of the cabin. "It seemed like the perfect place to end your birthday."

Alijah turned to look at him. She took her seat belt off, lunged over the middle console, and hugged him. She kissed his cheek before opening her door and getting out of the car. She could feel Kieran behind her as she made her way to the door. She stepped aside to allow him to unlock it.

Once they were inside, Alijah could not believe her eyes. The cabin was beautifully decorated. She opened up a door that led to the bathroom and gasped at the shower. It was exceptional. She would almost say it put Kieran's to shame.

Alijah was stunned. Here she had been irritated with him, and he had surprised her, putting the perfect finishing touch to her birthday. Admittedly, however, she was a bit skeptical. He had spent so much money on her already for her birthday, and by the looks of this place, he was spending a pretty penny.

Alijah walked out of the bathroom to find Kieran sitting on the bed.

"Do you like it?" He questioned.

"Yes," Alijah responded, nodding. "You didn't have to do all this. How much is this costing, Kieran?"

He signaled for her to come to him, and Alijah walked over, sitting on his lap. "I know I didn't have to. Don't worry about how much it's costing."

Alijah huffed as Kieran leaned in and pecked her on the lips. She lay her head on his shoulder as he ran his hand up and down her side. It always amazed her that he had this side to him. One that she knew he didn't let anyone see but her. She was grateful that he trusted her enough to let his guard down and be vulnerable with her, even if it was only for a moment.

"So, I thought tonight we could go see a movie and go out to dinner," Kieran spoke.

Alijah removed her head from his shoulder to look at him. "You mean like a date?" She questioned, a little surprised.

While they had gone out on her birthday and to the opening of *Mirage* along with lunch at work, they hadn't *actually* gone out before. It was a bit of a shock to her.

"Yes, Alijah. Unless you want to keep me a secret here as well." He teased her.

Alijah kissed him. She'd spoken with Chayse, and her cousin had pointed out that it didn't matter what anyone else thought of her relationship with Kieran. As long as the two of them knew what it was, who cared. Chayse also pointed out that people had seen them together at *Mirage*, which was definitely not in a business sense. Any of those people could have been people that worked for Kieran. So, she had decided to say fuck what other people would think and live in the moment.

"We can leave at around six-thirty," Kieran told her, lifting her from his lap. He pulled out his phone and looked at it. "That will give us a little over three hours," he responded, throwing his phone on the bed. "I'm going to get the suitcases from the car. Find a movie for us to go see."

"My purse is in the car with my phones in it," Alijah responded as he stepped out of the door.

"Use mine." Kieran threw over his shoulder as he continued.

Alijah picked up Kieran's phone and laid back on the bed, holding it above her head. She tapped the home button for the phone to light up, and of course, it was fingerprint protected. She placed the phone back on the bed and waited for him to return as she looked up at the ceiling. It only took a few minutes for him to come back with both suitcases.

"I need you to unlock your phone," she stated, holding it up.

"Cyclone," Kieran responded, placing the suitcases by the door.

"What?" Alijah questioned, sitting up to look at him.

"It's the backup password," he told her.

Alijah typed it in and started looking up movies and times. She wasn't surprised that Cyclone was his backup password, though she would never have thought of it. Kieran told her the story of the first product he had successfully purchased and sold. It was a handheld vacuum cleaner. It was light and durable but as powerful as a full-size vacuum cleaner. You could see inside the chamber, and as it sucked up dirt, it swirled within it like a tornado, hence how it came to be called Cyclone.

Kieran went about taking out his laptop as Alijah searched for a movie for them to see. While they were celebrating her birthday, he still needed to work. His goal was for them to have at least two uninterrupted days before it became a working trip. He had planned for them to be there until Friday. With Remy back at the office, he didn't mind being away for the week with Alijah.

He placed his laptop on the bedside table before picking up Alijah's suitcase and putting it next to the bed beside her. He knew that she had packed a lot of work attire. However, he hadn't been alone in his plan to surprise her. He had enlisted Chayse to pack her another suitcase with clothes appropriate for their stay. The suitcases were identical except for the handles, so, while Alijah hadn't noticed, it had been easy for him to grab the suitcase Chayse packed from the trunk when they made it to the airport instead of Alijah's.

"What type of movie do you want to see?" Alijah asked him.

Kieran looked over at her as he unzipped his suitcase. "It's your birthday, baby. Pick whatever you want to see."

After a few moments, Kieran grabbed his toiletry bag before walking into the bathroom and starting the shower. When he walked back into the bedroom, Alijah informed him of the movie they were going to see. Kieran simply nodded as he pulled his shirt over his head. He then made his way to where she still lay on her back and hovered above her.

"Come take a shower with me."

Alijah lifted a brow as she stared at him. "You just want to feel on me," she told him.

Kieran smiled at her before leaning in and kissing her softly. "You're damn right."

Alijah smacked his shoulder, and Kieran laughed as he got up, pulling her with him. He had packed all of her bathroom products in his bag since they had been in his bathroom back at the condo. Once in the bathroom, he stripped her slowly before finishing undressing and stepping into the steaming shower.

"Is that a carnival?"

Kieran could see the approaching rides that Alijah was looking at and nodded. It was indeed a carnival. The lights were beginning to shine as the sun disappeared. They had left the cabin later than expected, and it was almost eight-thirty.

"Can we go there?" Alijah questioned him.

"You want to go there instead of the movies and dinner?"

"Yes," Alijah responded, turning to look at him.

Kieran glanced over at her and was surprised that he didn't run them off the road. She was breathtaking. The last rays of the sun shone behind her as she waited for his response. Green eyes shining, brown hair a mass of curls.

"Yeah, baby. We can go there," he answered, committing the image of her to memory.

Kieran found a park after pulling into the carnival space. Turning the car off, he got out before going and opening Alijah's door. He intertwined his fingers with hers and led the way to the entrance.

After paying their entry fee, Kieran gave Alijah free reign and followed her around the carnival doing whatever she wanted. He loved the smile that seemed to be continuously on her face and the joy she was getting from the simple things they were doing.

They had ridden everything twice and had, what he was sure, was an overly unhealthy amount of fatty food. After which, they had played a few games, and he won a stuffed animal and a goldfish for her, which she had then turned and given to a little girl who had been desperately trying to win her own fish, after making sure it was alright with the girl's mother.

It was after midnight when they left the carnival, and Kieran could tell that Alijah was beyond tired. They were halfway to the cabin when he glanced over and saw that she had fallen asleep holding onto the stuffed butterfly she had chosen.

When they made it to the cabin, Kieran got out and unlocked and opened the cabin door before going back to the car and unbuckling Alijah. He picked her up out of the car carefully and carried her inside. Laying her gently on the bed, Kieran removed her shoes, shorts, and the thin cardigan she was wearing. He then undressed and climbed into bed beside her. Kieran pulled the blanket from the bottom of the bed over them before turning the lamp off. He wrapped his arm around her waist and settled into sleep.

22

Alijah rolled over in bed as she heard the bathroom door open, and Kieran walked out with a towel wrapped around his waist. He walked over to the bed, leaned down, and kissed her forehead. She turned onto her back and stretched as she watched him make his way over to his suitcase.

It was their third day in Dolores at the Dutton Hot Springs, and Alijah was enjoying herself. After going to the carnival on their first day, they went on a hike yesterday and had even driven to a nearby vineyard afterward for taste testing.

Sitting up in bed, Alijah yawned before swinging her legs off the side of the bed and standing. She headed into the bathroom and turned on the shower. While she waited for the water to warm up, she washed her face and brushed her teeth before taking a hair tie and pulling together her wild hair.

Stripping out of her clothes, which consisted of a pair of panties and one of Kieran's t-shirts, Alijah stepped into the shower and began to wash. She vaguely thought she heard a knock on the cabin door but didn't dwell on it as she finished her shower.

Once she was done with her shower, she wrapped a towel around herself and made her way back into the bedroom. There, on the table for two housed in the room, she found a tray with two covered dishes and assumed breakfast had been delivered.

Alijah got dressed, slipping into a pair of jean shorts and a red swoop neck t-shirt after pulling on her panties and bra. She sat across from Kieran, who wore a gray V-neck and a pair of dark jeans. It made her wonder if there was anything this man couldn't make look sexy.

She watched him remove the cover from both plates, and Alijah blessed her food before picking up her fork. Reaching over to Kieran's plate, she forked some of his skillet potatoes before tasting them. Kieran raised a brow at her, and she scrunched her nose slightly as she smiled at him after swallowing.

They ate their breakfast in silence, which was fine with her as she spent that time trying to figure out what they were going to do that day. She didn't mind staying in the cabin, but it was her first time in Dolores, and she wanted to see what else the city had to offer.

Alijah was just about to fork the last bit of her eggs when Kieran's fork beat her to it. She watched as he placed the fork in his mouth, his eyes smirking at her. She playfully glared at him for a moment before shaking her head.

Placing her fork down, she headed over to her suitcase to pull out a pair of socks and slip them onto her feet.

"Should I look for something for us to do today, or are we staying in?" She questioned him as he turned to look at her.

"No, and no. There's a Street Market today. I thought we would go and see what it was about."

Alijah nodded. "Okay. That sounds like fun."

It had been a little while since she'd been to a Street Market, and she was curious to see what all it would have to offer and the people that would be out with their crafts.

Pulling on tennis shoes, Alijah stood, grabbing her purse and heading towards the door. It was already eleven o'clock, and she wanted to get there before everything was picked over or some of the craftspeople left. If this market was like the others she had gone to, it had started earlier that morning and would be in full effect by now.

She didn't have to say anything to Kieran as she heard him stand and pick up the keys on the hook by the door. They made their way out of the cabin to the car. Kieran opened the door for her, and she slipped inside.

Because the cabin was on the outskirts of town, it took them about forty minutes to get to the Street Market. They parked in what had been designated a parking lot a couple of blocks away before getting out and making their way to the festivities.

There were so many vendors out. Some were selling crafts, others selling fruits, desserts, and all different kinds of foods. There also looked to have been a few games and some other contests that were being held. She felt like a child at Christmas. Remembering the last time she had been on an outing like this had been a couple of years ago.

Alijah took Kieran's hand in hers and led him to a booth selling hand-blown glass items. They were beautiful. There was everything from vases to ashtrays, chandelier adornments, to drinking glasses. There was even jewelry with beautiful blown glass charms.

One, in particular, caught Alijah's attention. It was a circular pendant on a necklace; the inside of it swirled with blue and white in the center. She reached out and ran her finger over it gently.

"You have good taste."

Alijah looked up to see the booth attendant speaking to her.

"It's stunning," Alijah told the woman. "You made this, correct?"

"No, not that one. That would be my little sister." The woman told her, inclining her head to a young woman who Alijah assumed was no more than about eighteen or nineteen. She was currently engaged in a conversation with another patron about a piece.

"How much for it?" Alijah questioned.

"Forty dollars."

"I'll take it."

She reached for the tiny coin bag that she had clipped to her belt loop. She had decided against carrying her purse with her and opted to lock it in the trunk. Instead, placing some cash in the coin bag and securing it to her person. Alijah was stopped from paying when Kieran placed a hand on hers' to prevent her from retrieving her money and passing the vendor the money over her shoulder.

Alijah looked over her shoulder at him. "Kieran, I can-"

"I don't care." He cut her off. "We're still celebrating your birthday. So, you won't argue with me about it."

She wanted to, just to spite him, but instead, she merely rolled her eyes at him. Her attention went back to the vendor as she heard her laughing softly.

"My husband's the same way. I feel for you, but I find it's easier to appease him," she told her with a smile.

Alijah was about to correct her and tell her that Kieran wasn't her husband when he wrapped his arms around her waist and pulled her back against him.

"Yeah, baby. Appease me."

Alijah scoffed before thanking the other woman as she unclasped the necklace from its place and handed it to her. She then passed it back to Kieran and asked him to put it on her. He did, leaning down to kiss her shoulder once he had clasped it.

She thanked the woman before she and Kieran headed off to another booth.

They checked out several different craft booths over the next several hours before they decided to try some of the cuisine offered at several stalls for lunch. Both of them got a couple of different things and decided to share.

They took a seat at a small, unoccupied table and enjoyed the different dishes they purchased. Alijah liked them all, but there was one she enjoyed above the others and made a mental note to see if they had a card. She didn't know when she would use it, but it could never hurt to have it just in case.

They then got ice cream from a homemade vendor. They offered flavors that she had never thought to put into ice cream, but she was willing to try something new, which was how she ended up getting a small cup of muscadine-flavored ice cream. She enjoyed the fruit and had even had muscadine wine before but never had thought about it being an ice cream flavor. Kieran had gotten sweet potato flavor.

She would have to admit that she didn't think that should have been a flavor offered in ice cream, but who was she to judge. As she ate her ice cream, she found that it indeed tasted like muscadines. Kieran offered her a bite of his, and she took it. It was...different, but it wasn't bad. However, Alijah knew that it wasn't something she would want to order when she craved ice cream.

Once they finished with their dessert, they made their way to a caricature competition. They needed one more person, and Kieran told her she should enter. Alijah didn't think it would be fair considering she was trained, but he pointed out that someone else there could have been as well. So, she decided to go for it.

Alijah assumed that the vendor was an artist since they would be the one judging the competition and was the model for the caricature. They had a specific time limit, and once it had ended, they would show their drawings, and then a winner would be chosen.

Alijah began drawing once they were told they could. They had fifteen minutes to complete their pictures, so she decided to take her time. She honestly didn't care if she won or not.

When the time was up, she placed her pencil down and waited as the woman walked around to look at the pictures. She got to Alijah's and paused before going back to the front. A moment later, she came back with a gift basket and handed it to her before picking up her picture and showing it to the rest of the people that had been competing.

"Ah, man." She heard a little girl state.

As everyone got up to move on to other things, Alijah made her way to the little girl and gave her the basket. She didn't even know what was in it but figured it wouldn't be something the little girl couldn't have, or else she wouldn't have been allowed to join the competition in the first place. The little girl and her father thanked Alijah before they headed off.

"Come on, baby." Kieran stated, "Let's go look at some more booths."

Alijah took the hand he was extending, and they headed to check out more stalls.

Kieran buttoned the last button on his black dress shirt. He was dressed in a pair of black slacks and black shoes as well. It was a little after seven o'clock, and the sun would be setting in a bit.

When they had gotten back from the Street Market, Kieran had gone and taken a shower, while Alijah had taken a nap. Once he'd gotten out, he'd called the main office and made a few arrangements. He allowed her to sleep for about an hour before going into the bathroom to run her a bubble bath and wake her up.

While she was in the bath, he picked out a little black dress for her to wear along with a pair of red pumps that Chayse had packed for her. Writing a note for her, he placed it all on the bed.

When he heard her getting out of the bathtub, he headed out of the door to ensure everything was going as he had planned.

As requested, when he stepped out of the door, there was a trail of large painted stones on either side of the door. He had asked for some sort of path to follow and had left it up to them to come up with something. Following the trail, it led around back to where the carriage was parked.

Kieran made his way to the carriage and greeted Allen, the man driving and one of the owner's sons.

"Mr. Cayman. Everything you requested is being taken care of and will be ready when your carriage ride is over." The younger man then handed Kieran the white rose he had requested.

"Thank you, Allen," Kieran responded, taking the rose.

It was only about fifteen minutes later when Kieran saw Alijah come around the corner. She stopped briefly and took him in along with the horse-drawn carriage before smiling and making her way to him.

She stopped in front of him, and Kieran reached out and wrapped his arm around her waist, pulling her in closer. Leaning down, he kissed her softly on the lips before releasing her and handing her the single rose.

"Is this part of my birthday present?" She questioned, bringing the rose to her nose. "Or are you thinking with your dick?"

Kieran knew she was teasing him but, nonetheless, rolled his eyes at her. He knew she would never let the fact that he told her that go. However, he didn't mind since she didn't seem to be offended by it.

He shrugged at her before smirking. "A bit of both."

Kieran helped her into the carriage before getting in himself. She slid into his side, and he wrapped his arm around her as the carriage took off. He had planned it to where they would be able to watch the sunset as they rode to their destination. It was still on the Dutton property and typically wouldn't have taken long to get to, but he requested they take the long way around.

Thirty minutes later, the last rays of the sun starting to disappear, they pulled up to a canopy-covered area. There was a table in the middle with oil lamps lit around. There were large pillows on one side of the canopy atop the platform everything was set on.

When the carriage stopped, Kieran got out before reaching up and placing his hands on Alijah's waist and picking her up out of the carriage. They walked over to the table, and he pulled her chair out for her as he heard the carriage take off.

There were several covered dishes, and once he took the lids off of them, they each surveyed the choices before he fixed them both a plate.

As they ate, they took in the scenery around them. It was serene, quiet and Kieran was glad he'd decided to have dinner there instead of taking her out into town as he had first planned to do.

Once they finished eating, Kieran helped her down onto the large pillows before pouring them both a glass of champagne and grabbing the strawberries. By this point, the sun had long ago gone away, and the oil lamps lit up the canopy, but Kieran knew that fairy lights staked into the ground would turn on at a specific time.

"Thank you," Alijah spoke before taking a sip of her champagne.

"You don't have to thank me, gorgeous," Kieran responded, leaning in to kiss her as she brought the glass down from her lips.

He had meant for it to be a brief kiss, but that was far from what it was. Kieran placed his glass down, hearing it tip over as he did so, before putting his hands on either side of her neck. He began to dominate the kiss, and she followed his lead.

At some point, he found himself on top of her, his hand under the skirt of her dress that was hiked up as he slowly ran one of his knuckles up and down the apex of her thighs. He heard her glass fall onto the rug behind them as she slowly moved against his knuckle.

After several minutes, he pulled away just in time for the fairy lights to come on. When they did, Kieran stood, helping her to her feet. He had one more thing he wanted to show her.

They followed the trail of fairy lights until they came upon one of the hot springs. They had a small private hot spring in their cabin, but it wasn't big enough for the two of them comfortably. So, Kieran had requested that the faculty close this particular hot spring for the night for the two of them to enjoy as well as chilling some champagne and providing towels and robes.

"This is pretty," Alijah told him.

"It's going to feel even better," he responded to her. He leaned in and whispered in her ear. "Get naked for me, baby."

He felt her body give a slight tremor before she stepped away, turning to face him. Kieran watched as she slowly began to get undressed. His eyes raked over her body the entire time before she stepped into the spring.

"Do you plan on joining me? Or staring at me all night."

"Joining," he told her as he began to unbutton his shirt. "Definitely joining."

And Kieran meant that in more ways than one.

23

Alijah rolled over in bed with an irritated groan. Kieran's phone was ringing again, and she was close to throwing it in his face for not answering it. She reached over to nudge him, only to discover he wasn't there. Sitting up slowly, she stretched and looked at the clock. It was just a little after eight in the morning. She figured he was on the roof in his gym working out.

Removing the covers from her body, she climbed out of bed as his phone stopped ringing. Making her way into the bathroom, she turned on the shower allowing it to heat up while she went about washing her face and brushing her teeth. Stripping out of her clothes, she stepped into the shower.

After showering, Alijah went into her room and got dressed in black denim shorts and an olive-colored V-neck shirt. She threw her hair up into a messy bun before padding barefoot into the kitchen. She took out the bacon, eggs, and pancake mix for breakfast. She had just taken out the pans she needed when she heard Kieran's phone ring again. She was tempted to go up to the roof to get him, thinking that it may have been business, but figured if it were, they would have called her work phone once they couldn't get in touch with him.

She had just put on the bacon when she heard the front door open. Alijah turned as she heard him come into the kitchen. Sweat was glistening off his body as he walked over and kissed her softly on the lips.

"Did you have a good workout?" Alijah asked him as he pulled a bottle of water from the refrigerator.

"It was fine. I enjoy working out more when I'm watching you," he told her with a smirk.

Alijah flipped the bacon before grabbing a bowl for the pancake mix. "Why didn't you wake me? I would have come with you."

"I'm positive you needed your sleep, baby."

Alijah rolled her eyes as she began to mix the batter. "Go take a shower. Breakfast should be ready in a few minutes," she told him. "Oh, and your phone has been ringing almost nonstop." She tacked on watching him nod before leaving the kitchen.

Twenty minutes later, Alijah sat plates on the bar as Kieran walked down the hall. His hair was still wet from his shower. They sat down and ate, making small talk. Kieran reminded her of the party they were going to on Corey Wexler's yacht tomorrow for Labor Day. Alijah had finally been able to get in touch with him and set up a meeting for the two. It had gone well, and the man had invited them to his party.

When they were done with breakfast, Kieran helped her load the dishwasher before going into the living room and turning on the television. Alijah had a lunch date with Lawrence for one o'clock and decided to kill time relaxing until then. She was sitting with her legs over Kieran's lap as he lazily massaged her thigh when his phone rang again.

"Did you check your phone when you went to shower?" She questioned him.

He took his eyes from the television and glanced over at her. "No, I forgot."

Removing her legs from his lap, Alijah got up and headed down the hall to his bedroom. She grabbed his phone off the bedside table and looked at the name that flashed across the screen right before it stopped ringing. When it did, she realized that he had nine missed calls and thirteen text messages from the same person.

Gritting her teeth, Alijah made her way back into the living room with his phone in hand. She walked in front of him, blocking his few of the television. She held his phone up in front of his face.

"Why has this woman been calling and texting you nonstop this morning?" She asked, showing him the missed calls and texts from Rebecca Blow.

Alijah watched as Kieran glanced at the phone before looking up at her. "I don't know," he responded.

Reaching out, he grabbed his phone and dropped it on the couch beside him before taking her hand and pulling her into his lap. Alijah sighed softly as his lips brushed against hers gently. When he pulled away, Alijah stared into his hazel eyes as he reached up and pinched her chin between his thumb and forefinger.

Whatever he was about to say was cut off by his phone ringing again. Removing her chin from his fingers, Alijah looked down and saw that Rebecca was calling yet again. She groaned.

"What does she want?" She questioned.

Alijah watched as Kieran grabbed the phone, answered it, and placed it on speaker. "What do you want, Rebecca?" He questioned, eyes locked onto Alijah's.

"Hello to you too, Kieran," Came the response from the other end, causing Alijah to roll her eyes. "I was calling to discuss our child," she then stated.

At her words, Alijah's eyes went wide before she began to blink rapidly. *Their child?* She went to slide off his lap when he wrapped his free arm around her waist tightly, keeping her in place.

"We don't have a child, Rebecca, and that's not going to change." Alijah listened to Kieran state, her jaw clenched.

"Kieran, this could work for-"

"No." He butted in, cutting her off before hanging up the phone.

Alijah watched as he tossed it back beside him on the couch, resting his hand on her thigh. She took a deep breath before asking the question she wasn't sure she wanted the answer to.

"What was she talking about?"

For the next few minutes, Kieran recapped the conversation he and Rebecca had in his office over a month ago. When he finished, Alijah was still upset.

"Why didn't you tell me?"

"It wasn't important."

"Some woman you used to date asked you for your sperm, and it wasn't important enough for you to tell me? I specifically asked you what she wanted to talk about, and you said it was a 'proposition.'"

"You were already upset. I didn't want to make it worse."

Alijah shook her head. "Were you considering her offer?"

Kieran scoffed, and Alijah didn't miss the look of disbelief in his eyes. "I would rather have my dick fall off than have a child with that woman in any aspect." Alijah nodded as Kieran leaned in and kissed her. "I apologize for not telling you, but I don't tend to dwell on insignificant things and people. Rebecca and her proposal are both."

Alijah shifted so that she was straddling him. She placed her hands over his shoulder and began to play with the hair at the nape of his neck. He started to run his hands up and down her waist before reaching around and grabbing her ass. She rolled her eyes at him as he began to rub it slowly.

"I'm having lunch today with Lawrence," she informed him.

Kieran's hands stopped moving, and he lifted an eyebrow. "Lawrence?"

Alijah smiled at him, leaning in and laying her head on his shoulder. "My friend Lawrence. The one that brought me back when you got mad that I stayed out all night."

Kieran placed his hands on her waist and moved her back to look at him. "The one that kissed you in the elevator," he stated.

"I told you he isn't attracted to me that way."

Kieran scoffed. "He's a man with eyes. Enough said."

Alijah smirked at him. "Are you jealous?"

He rolled his eyes at her. "Says the woman who was just grilling me a minute ago."

"Touché. You can come with us if you're worried."

"No, I trust you. Just remember, I don't share," he told her, kissing her before moving her off his lap. "I have to go meet Cruz at his office. I'll be back in a little while."

With that, Alijah watched as he walked down the hall before turning her attention back to the television.

Kieran glanced around the yacht as he waited for his drink to be made. He wasn't surprised at the number of people that were in attendance. He had expected nothing less from Corey Wexler. Though the party was supposed to be for pleasure, he knew that he would be proposing a few business deals to some of the people in attendance before the day was out.

As he continued to survey the area, his eyes fell on Alijah. She was over in the corner talking to two other women. She wore a high waist pink skirt with a white lace top. Her hair was up in a bun with tendrils framing her face. The outfit was simple, but Kieran thought she looked stunning. He also knew that he wasn't the only one admiring her. Since they'd stepped foot on the boat, several men had stared at her, and he could all but see the envy in a lot of the women's eyes.

Kieran retrieved his scotch on the rocks and a mimosa for Alijah, making his way to where the women were.

"You are hilarious, Alijah." He heard one of the women speak as he stopped beside them. He handed Alijah her drink, and she thanked him before turning back to the women.

"Kieran, this is Layla Martinez and Gale Wexler. Gale is Corey's wife, and Layla is the new COO of Phantom Technologies. She was just telling me how her company was about to start working on new cellphone concepts." She introduced them, and Kieran didn't miss the look she gave him. He had discussed with her his desire to produce and brand a line of cell phones a few weeks back. "Ladies, this is Kieran Cayman."

"Nice to meet both of you." Kieran greeted with a smile.

"You as well," Layla spoke while Gale nodded along.

Kieran saw Nathaniel Golding as the crowd seemed to part a little at that moment.

"If you beautiful women will excuse, I'm going to go catch up with a business associate." He kissed Alijah's temple before nodding at the other two women and making his way toward Nathaniel. He would let Alijah work her magic in peace.

"Kieran."

At the sound of his name, Kieran turned to find their host. He had been standing at the yacht's railing, looking out over the water.

"Corey. Nice party." Kieran stated after shaking the other man's hand.

"Between you and me, it wouldn't be quite as elegant if I had to throw it myself. I have Gale to thank for that. I'd be lost without that woman." Corey told him.

Kieran laughed. "Tell me about it. Alijah keeps up with everything."

"Ah, your assistant. She and my wife have been almost inseparable. Gale seems to have taken a liking to her."

Kieran nodded. "It isn't hard to do. She's a phenomenal person," he stated, looking over to where Alijah was still talking to Gale, but another woman had joined them in Layla's absence. She must have felt him looking at her because she looked up, eyes locking with his, and smiled. Kieran smiled back and winked at her before turning his attention back to Corey.

The slightly older man was staring at Kieran with a contemplative look on his face. After a moment, he nodded to himself, and Kieran was utterly lost as to what had just happened.

The two men spoke about their upcoming joint business venture for the next ten minutes or so. After they finished their conversation, Corey excused himself to mingle with some of his other guests.

After he walked off, Kieran made his way over to where they were serving food. He grabbed a plate and put a few finger sandwiches and fruit on it. He then made his way over to where Alijah was sitting with Gale. He sat beside her and handed her the plate.

"Here, baby."

"Thank you," Alijah stated, taking the plate from him.

"If you two will excuse me, I'm going to find my husband and make sure he hasn't hidden himself off somewhere," Gale stated, smiling at them.

Kieran grabbed a grape off the plate and popped it into his mouth as Gale walked off. He then picked up a strawberry and held it up to Alijah's lips. She bit into it, and Kieran ate the rest.

"So, Layla and I are having lunch next week," she informed him when she'd finished chewing. "I'm going to see if I can schedule a meeting for you with her. I think her company would be the best to have your phones made through."

Kieran smiled at her before taking her face between his hands and kissing her.

"What would I do without you? Hell, what did I do before you got here?" He questioned.

Alijah pretended to think about it. "You'd fail miserably. You were barely making it," she finished with a smile.

When Alijah finished eating her food, Kieran took her hand and led her to one of the rails. He stood behind her and wrapped his arms around her waist as they looked out over the water.

"It's gorgeous," Alijah stated, leaning back into his chest.

"You're gorgeous," Kieran responded, leaning down to kiss her neck.

The two stood in silence for several minutes, just looking out over the water. It was peaceful, and Kieran felt relaxed, but he often did when he had Alijah in his arms. However, that peace was broken after a while.

"Hello, Kieran." Kieran clenched his jaw, he knew that voice, and he wished he could throw her overboard.

Kieran turned to see Rebecca standing there. He felt Alijah tense in his arms as he watched Rebecca's attention slide from him to Alijah.

"What do you want, Rebecca?" Kieran questioned.

"Can't I just come and greet a *close*, old friend?" She questioned.

"You greeted me. Now, bye, Rebecca." With that, Kieran released Alijah, taking her hand and leading her away.

"I don't like that woman," Alijah stated when he pulled her onto a couch beside him.

"She's irrelevant," Kieran told her.

"She better be," Alijah responded before turning to an approaching Gale and smiling.

Alijah was sitting with Gale discussing their mutual love of art. She learned that the older woman had gone to school and minored in fine arts. While Alijah loved to paint, Gale enjoyed sculpting. She was looking at pictures of Gale's sculptures when her intuition began to tingle.

Looking up, she scanned the yacht, and her eyes fell on Kieran, who had gone to speak with a few other men. Except, Rebecca had just sauntered over to them. Alijah excused herself from Gale for a moment. She made her way toward them as the other men began to walk away. It was just Kieran and Rebecca left, and the blonde had just taken a step closer to Kieran when Alijah slid between them with her back to Rebecca. She wrapped her arms around Kieran's neck.

"I've been looking for you, baby," Alijah told him. She could see Kieran biting the inside of his jaw, and she knew he was trying not to smirk.

Kieran placed his hands on her hips. "You found me, gorgeous."

"Come up to the top deck with me. I haven't seen it yet." Alijah told him. She took his hand and led him away without acknowledging the other woman.

There were fewer people on the top deck of the boat. Alijah led them through the people and over to the railing where they could overlook the part of the deck they had just left. From where she stood, she could see Rebecca. Turning her attention to Kieran, she found that his eyes were on her, and his face housed a smirk.

"What?" She questioned.

"It's cute when you get all possessive," he told her.

Alijah rolled her eyes at him. "Oh, be quiet."

For the next half an hour, they stayed on the top deck, mingling with the few people there before they decided to go. They had been there for a few hours, and Kieran had a video conference in an hour and a half. They had just made it to the bottom when Alijah excused herself to the ladies' room before they left.

She had just finished taking care of business and washing her hands when she opened the door and saw Rebecca leaning against the wall.

"I see Kieran has started bringing his playthings out in public." The blonde spoke, a malicious smile on her face. "And you're his secretary, the hired helped. There's no mystery to how you got your job. You're just like the rest of those trashy young things out for his money."

Alijah stared at the woman for a moment. The first thought that popped into her head was to smack the taste out of that bitch's mouth, but a few people were standing around, and Alijah was not about to let this tall hoe bring her out of character. So, instead, she put on a smile and took a step toward her.

"I'm guessing that makes you an old messy hoe out for his money...and sperm," Alijah stated, smile still in place. It turned genuine when Rebecca seemed to be taken aback by the fact that she knew that. "Before you ask, you desperate bitch, yes, he told me about it because we are in a relationship. Unlike you, I see him other than when I'm on my back. Which I'm sure is how you see all of the men you're involved with."

"You little-"

"Careful, Becky." Alijah began cutting her off. "The only reason I haven't put you on your ass is due to these people and the fact that I have more class than to embarrass my man like that. However, make no mistake," Alijah continued taking a step closer to the taller woman. "When I see you out and about, and I'm sure I will see you, I'm going to whoop. Your. Ass." With that, Alijah took a step back and observed as Rebecca swallowed. Turning her back, she threw out, "Have a great day." Before walking back to where she had left Kieran waiting for her.

24

Alijah was seated at her desk, going through business proposals. It was officially her least favorite job duty. It was close to the end of the day, and she was more than ready for the next hour and a half to pass. She had just moved another proposal to her trash when she heard the elevator ding. She stopped typing; eyebrows furrowed. She knew that Kieran didn't have any more meetings for the day, and no one from the other departments had called her to inform her that they would be coming up.

Turning her attention to the elevator doors as they opened, Alijah smiled, preparing to greet the person that stepped off. It took a moment, but then an older gentleman came into view. He was dressed in a tailored suit. Alijah was sure that it cost more than most people's salaries.

"Good afternoon, Sir. How can I help you?"

"I'm Bronson Atworth. I'm here to see Kieran."

Alijah looked at her schedule even though she knew that this man was not one of Kieran's appointments today.

"I'm sorry, Mr. Atworth. I don't have an appointment scheduled for you today. If you would like, I could see if Mr. Cayman has a moment to speak with you, or we can set up an appointment for the first thing he has available."

"I'd like to speak with him today," Bronson stated.

Alijah smiled at him. "Of course. Let me go in and see if he has a moment. Please, have a seat." She gestured to the chairs in the waiting area.

She waited for him to take a seat, ensuring all of the items she had with personal information were secure before heading for Kieran's office. She knocked twice before entering. Alijah closed the door softly behind her as she saw him standing at the window on the phone.

As she made her way to him, he turned to look at her. He smiled before turning his full attention back to his phone call, and Alijah took a seat in his chair and looked at the email he had up. It was an invitation to a vineyard. She saw that the invitation was dated for Halloween in a few weeks, and Alijah raised an eyebrow, wondering if that was what wealthy people did on Halloween. Get together at a vineyard and drink the night away.

"Do you want to go?" Alijah spun the chair around to face Kieran as he placed his phone on his desk.

"It doesn't matter to me," she responded to his question. "There's a gentleman here to see you. He doesn't have an appointment, but I thought I would ask if you could squeeze him in today."

"What's his name?" Kieran questioned.

"Bronson Atworth."

Alijah didn't miss the stiffening of Kieran's muscles, and it was only a second later, that she saw that irritated tick in his jaw start. His hazel eyes that hadn't looked at her with coldness since they became a couple were now freezing her where she sat.

"Kieran," Alijah stated softly as she stood up. With her sitting down and the sudden shift in his attitude, his height was intimidating. "What is it?" She questioned, placing her hands gently on his chest. "Who is he?"

"My mother's sperm donor," he bit out.

Alijah's eyes widen. "He's your grandfather?" She questioned as if she needed clarification.

"Don't call him that, Alijah. That man deserves no title," he snapped.

Alijah clenched her teeth, removing her hands from his chest. "Don't get pissed off at me because he showed up. I'm just the messenger, Kieran," she stated, crossing her arms over her chest. Alijah watched as he took a deep breath before his eyes softened.

"I know," he spoke, reaching for her hand. He brought it to his lips and placed a chaste kiss on it. "Tell him I don't want to see him and never come back."

Alijah rolled her eyes. "I'm not going to tell him that, Kieran. It's insulting."

"Then tell him I'm not here."

She gave him a look of disbelief before shaking her head. "I've been in here five minutes. He's going to know I'm lying."

"I don't care if he knows you're lying or not."

"Kieran," Alijah stated firmly. "You've been ignoring this man your entire life. You had to know that eventually, you would have to face him. Today just happens to be that day."

"Alijah, I don't-"

"It's okay, Kieran," she stated, cutting him off. "I'll be right here with you."

Alijah watched for a moment, wondering if he would give in and meet with his grandfather. She didn't think the man was so bad from first impressions, but what she had heard from Kieran made it seem like these were two separate men. However, it could have been that he had just changed over the years. After all, to her knowledge, Kieran would be the only relative Bronson had.

"Fine." Kieran finally stated, to Alijah's surprise. "I'll give him five minutes."

Alijah nodded before walking past him and back out of his office. She informed Bronson that Kieran would see him and led him into the office.

The tension was so thick that Alijah would swear that she could see it. Kieran stood behind his desk, those hazel eyes glacier cold again as Bronson walked in, stopping beside one of the chairs and placing his hands in his pocket.

"Mr. Atworth, please have a seat. Can I get you anything? Water? Tea?"

"He won't be here that long, Ms. Douglas." Kieran cut in before the older man could answer. Alijah shot him a look.

"Tea, if you will. Three sugars and milk if you have it." Bronson answered with a soft smile. Not at all detoured by Kieran's harshness.

"Of course," Alijah stated, giving him a smile of her own before excusing herself.

Making her way into the kitchen, she grabbed one of the tea pods and went about making Bronson's tea. Once finished, she placed a dark roast in for Kieran. While his coffee brewed, she added the required sugar and milk to the tea. When she was done, she grabbed the small bottle of scotch from the cabinet and put some into Kieran's coffee.

Alijah took both cups by the handle and made her way back down the hall and into Kieran's office. The silence almost knocked her off of her feet when she walked in. It was thick with distaste, and the tension had grown even heavier. She felt as if it was crashing down on her.

She took a silent breath before making her way to both men and handing them their respective drinks. She threw Kieran a look before retreating to the couch against the wall. On the table in front of it were a few preliminary phone concepts. Her lunch with Layla almost a month ago had been a success. She had gotten Kieran a meeting with the woman, and they were now working on the first phone they would release as partners.

Alijah decided to pick up the different concepts to make herself look busy, hoping that when the conversation between the two men did eventually start, it wouldn't be too apparent that she was doing a tiny bit of eavesdropping.

Kieran sat at his desk, staring at the old man in front of him. His blood was boiling. He couldn't believe that he would have to audacity to show up at his place of business. Kieran was sitting in his chair seething because he had shown up to his company like it were perfectly fine to do so, as if things had changed. For Kieran's entire life, he had ignored the man. He wanted nothing to do with him, and he especially didn't want him in his life.

The man before him had all but kicked his mother out. He had disowned her for marrying Kieran's father. A poor young man from what he deemed, the wrong side of the tracks who came from nothing. His mother's sperm donor had the quintessential old money attitude.

While Kieran had been raised with nannies most of his life, it didn't mean that his parents hadn't been around to give him the love and affection a child needed. They both worked hard to ensure that he had a good life. They were rich by no means, but his parents did well, and they worked for everything they had. He admired them for that.

He would have thought the man before him would have to; he would have seen the life his parents had made for their family, but he hadn't. All he had seen was that his daughter was working, which was unacceptable to him.

Kieran wasn't sure why the old man had been so set on his daughter not lifting a finger and being with someone of his social standing. For Kieran, even as a teenager, that had always sounded like a trophy to him. Something to be taken out and shown to others but then put away when you weren't using it. That was not the definition he felt should be placed on a person.

He was all for a woman that wanted to work and could take care of herself. He enjoyed a woman with intellect and recently discovered that he enjoyed a feisty woman; however, that didn't mean he would mind taking care of the right woman.

Bronson clearing his throat, pulled Kieran from his thoughts. He looked at the older man to see that he was staring directly at him.

"How have you been, Kieran?"

"Perfect," Kieran replied in short. At this point, he just wanted him to spit out whatever it was he wanted to say.

For his part, the other man didn't seem affected. "I wanted to know if you would like to have dinner with me tonight at *Aficionado*."

Kieran knew what the man was doing. He had chosen one of Paetyn's restaurants. Probably in the hopes that Kieran would be more inclined to agree. He was, however, very wrong.

"He would love to."

At those words, Kieran snapped his head over to Alijah and pierced her with a glare. As usual, she was unfazed. He went to correct her and tell Bronson that he would in no way be going to dinner with him when the older man stood up.

"Excellent. I will see you at eight." With that, he left the room. Placing his cup on the table as he walked by.

Kieran watched as Alijah got up and went to close his door. He leaned back in his seat when she turned around to face him, jaw clenched.

"Before you get any more upset, I think this is a good idea," she told him, making her way over to his desk and perching on the edge. "He seems to be trying to make amends. He's extending the olive branch. You can't be stubborn all your life."

Kieran cocked his head as he looked at her. "Remember you said that the next time your stubbornness rears its head."

"Yeah, yeah. I'm serious, Kieran. What's the worst that could happen from going to dinner with him?"

Kieran was silent for a moment as he thought. He didn't want to go. There were a million other things he would much rather do, but this seemed to be one of those things that Alijah wasn't going to let up on.

"Well," he started. "I guess we'll be finding that out together because you're coming with me." He finished with a smirk.

Kieran walked into the restaurant with Alijah's hand in his. The hostess greeted them, leading them to their table after Kieran had given her the name on the reservation. He wasn't surprised that they were led to one of the private rooms.

They found Bronson sitting at the table, tapping away on his phone upon entering. Kieran led the way over to the table, and Bronson stood as they approached. Kieran pulled out a chair for Alijah, and she took a seat, followed by both men.

"I hope this isn't an inconvenience, Mr. Atworth," Alijah spoke, turning her attention to the man.

Kieran watched as Bronson smiled at Alijah before answering her. "Not at all. I expected that you would join us, to be honest with you."

At that moment, a waitress walked in to take their drink orders. Bronson deferred the choice to Kieran, who stated he didn't care. He didn't miss the look that Alijah threw his way.

She then turned to the waitress and asked her to bring them the house special white wine.

When the waitress left, the room lapsed into silence. Kieran caught Alijah glancing back and forth between him and the old man, but he was not about to make a move to start a conversation. She gave him a look that clearly said she wanted him to strike one up. However, after realizing he was not about to do that, she sighed heavily and picked up her menu.

Kieran picked his up as well and scanned the options. Though he was pretty sure what he was going to order, he merely wanted to seem busy to delay speaking to or listening to Bronson for as long as possible.

The waitress came back several moments later with the wine Alijah had ordered. Once she had poured some for everyone, she took their orders.

"Can you show me to the ladies' room?" Alijah questioned the waitress before she left.

Kieran knew precisely what she was trying to do and threw her a look as she stood and began to leave. He watched her go in her knee-length midnight blue dress. She was wearing the jewelry she had gotten for her birthday and a pair of silver shoes. Her hair was pulled up off her face. She was gorgeous, and upon seeing her step out of the bedroom, they almost hadn't made it.

They were matching slightly. It hadn't been on purpose, but it had happened. Kieran was dressed in a black Hugo Boss suit with a midnight blue shirt, black bow tie, and handkerchief.

"That young woman is more than just your assistant. Am I right?" Bronson questioned, drawing Kieran's attention.

"Yes," Kieran replied shortly.

"How long have the two of you been dating?"

"A while."

Kieran watched as Bronson sighed before sitting back in his seat. The old man looked at him for a long moment as if he was contemplating something.

"Kieran, I know that I handled things poorly with your mother in the past, but-"

"Poorly?" Kieran questioned, cutting him off. "You disowned her for falling in love."

"I didn't believe that man was worthy of her. That's the way all fathers think."

"No, that's the way you think. You didn't like my father because he didn't come from money."

"That's not-"

"Don't say it isn't true." Kieran cut him off again.

"Kieran, you don't know the entire story. There are some things, some factors that went into my decision."

Kieran was heated. "Factors? It wasn't a business acquisition! It was the love two people had for one another and your inability to accept it; because my father didn't meet your old money standards!" He spat out through clenched teeth.

"Your father was a delinquent, troublemaker who-"

"My father was a hard-working man who took care of his family."

"Kieran, before you were born, that wasn't the case."

"Yet, you still held your dislike for him when that did become the case."

"He didn't deserve my-"

"Stop talking!" Kieran snapped as the door to the room opened. "I knew I shouldn't have come," he stated, standing.

"Is everything alright?" Alijah questioned as she made her way towards the table.

"We're leaving," Kieran informed her, standing and heading towards the door.

"Kieran-" Alijah started as he passed her but was cut off.

"Now, Alijah."

Kieran waited at the door and watched as Alijah gave the old man an apologetic look before heading toward him. He took her hand and led the way out of the restaurant. They were silent as they waited for the valet to bring the car around. He opened the door for her, waiting for her to get in before slipping in on the driver's side.

They rode in silence for a moment until Alijah broke it.

"I'm sorry, Kieran. I thought that the two of you could at least take steps to mend your relationship." Alijah stated.

Kieran turned to her as he stopped at a red light. He reached out and caressed her cheek. "It's fine, beautiful. I know your intention was good, but that man and I will never have any type of relationship."

With that said, Kieran turned his attention back to the road and proceeded to drive them back to the condo. He couldn't believe the things the old man had said as if they were alright to say. However, he shouldn't have been surprised.

Kieran glanced over at Alijah and licked his bottom lip. He would need a little stress relief, and he always enjoyed relieving stress with Alijah.

25

Alijah was seated on one of the lounge chairs beside the pool. She was dressed in a primarily coral two-piece swimsuit, while Layla was sitting beside her in a one-piece. It was purple, and she had on a matching sun hat. Alijah and Layla had become close over the past month since meeting at Corey's party on Labor Day. She had become close with Gale as well.

Layla decided she wanted to throw a small get-together one last time poolside since the weather was getting cooler. Small being about fifty people. It was the middle of October and relatively warm, but a brisk wind would blow every so often.

"I have to admit, Alijah. That Kieran is a fine specimen of a man." Layla stated.

Alijah turned to look at her and found her looking off into the corner. She turned to see what she was looking at and saw that it was Kieran. He was off in the corner talking to two other men. He was clad in a pair of black Burberry swim trunks. He was shirtless, and Alijah definitely agreed with Layla.

"If I were to bat for his team, he would be my type," she stated. She then turned her head and looked over to where her girlfriend was seated, talking to a few of their friends. "But I don't think any person could separate me from that woman. Well, maybe one," she finished, turning her head and winking at Alijah.

Alijah shook her head, laughing. She'd learned over the past month that Layla was a flirt, but she had seen the way she was with Gemma and knew that she was the only woman Layla honestly had eyes for. Alijah continued looking around the pool.

The party had been in full effect for a little over an hour, and she had met a few new people.

After a few more moments, Alijah got up, informing Layla that she was going to get a drink, and asked her if she wanted anything. After taking the other woman's request, Alijah headed over to the bar. She ordered a *Sex on the Beach* for herself and a *Slow Screw* for Layla.

When their drinks were ready, she grabbed them and headed back to where she'd been sitting. She handed Layla's drink to her before retaking her seat.

"Are you and Kieran going to the vineyard party for Halloween?" Layla questioned after they'd been sitting in silence for a few minutes.

"I thought about it, but Kieran's birthday is November first, and I plan on bringing it in the right way with him," Alijah told her after taking a sip of her drink.

"Freaky ass." Layla laughed. "Well, if that's the case, my birthday is in December. You can help me bring it in right."

Alijah shook her head as she began laughing. Layla was just too much. As she took another sip of her drink, she saw Gemma coming their way. She sat down in Layla's lap, turning her attention to Alijah.

"Is my woman over her flirting with you again, Alijah?"

"Shamelessly," Alijah responded with a nod.

"Snitch," Layla stated before sticking her tongue out.

For the next fifteen minutes, the three women talked. Alijah liked Layla and Gemma. Before meeting Layla and Gale, she didn't have any girlfriends in the city. If she was honest, the only friend she had was Lawrence. So, it felt good to have other women to hang out with and talk to.

"Your eye candy is coming over," Layla stated, nodding her head past Alijah.

Alijah turned and saw Kieran was coming her way. He took the seat beside her after speaking to the other two ladies. Kieran took her drink from her hand and took a sip of it, raising his eyebrow at the fruity taste before giving it back to her.

"Swim with me," he stated after a moment.

Alijah looked over at the large pool, where a few others were swimming. Placing her cup down, she nodded before standing and making her way to the pool. She could feel Kieran's eyes on her ass the entire time. Alijah put a little extra sway in her hips, knowing that he would give her some when they got back to the condo.

Shooting off of the couch, Alijah ran into the hall half-bath. Lifting the toilet seat, she emptied the contents of her stomach. She hadn't known that Kieran had followed her into the bathroom until she felt his hands pulling her hair away from her face.

When she finished, she reached up and flushed the toilet. Getting up, she headed to the bedroom and into the bathroom. Grabbing her toothbrush, she went about brushing her teeth. She could see Kieran looking at her through the mirror as he stood leaning against the door frame.

"Are you alright?" He questioned.

Alijah nodded as she continued to brush her teeth. She rinsed her mouth out when she was done and placed the toothbrush away.

"I'm fine," she reassured him. "Let's finish our movie."

Alijah took Kieran's hand and led him back to the living room where they had been watching *Split*. She waited for him to settle down on the couch again before sitting between his legs and laying her head on his shoulder. She started the movie back, placing her hands over his when he wrapped his arms around her.

"That's it," Kieran stated after she'd just jumped off the couch for the third time to empty her stomach. "We're going to the emergency room."

Alijah wasn't a big fan of hospitals, but she felt inclined to agree with him this time. She felt awful after throwing up the first time. The following two came shortly after. Rising to her feet, she went into the bedroom to brush her teeth again before putting on her shoes and meeting Kieran at the door, where he stood with his keys.

When they got into the car, she lay her head against the window as Kieran began to drive them towards the hospital. It didn't take them long to get there, and once inside, they checked in at the emergency room desk.

While waiting, she had gone and emptied her stomach, which at this point had nothing left, two more times. It was almost two hours before she was called back. A nurse took her vitals before placing her in a room, where she waited nearly another half hour before a doctor came in.

"Hello, Ms. Douglas. I'm Doctor Raymond." He came in, introducing himself. "I see here that it says you've been experiencing some nausea."

"Yes," Alijah responded with a nod.

"Any other symptoms?"

"I had a little bit of dizziness in the waiting room and slight abdominal pain, but nothing other than that."

Dr. Raymond nodded as he wrote some notes. "When was the last time you had your menstrual cycle?"

Alijah thought about it for a moment as she tried to remember.

"Almost two months." She heard Kieran answer. She turned to look at him with a raised eyebrow.

She watched Dr. Raymond look between her and Kieran before asking, "Is that true?"

Alijah nodded. "It sounds about right."

The doctor nodded. "I'm going to have a nurse come in and draw some blood. I want to do some labs and a pregnancy test." With that, he left out of the room.

Alijah let out a slow breath as she tried to quell the nausea she was feeling. If the doctor had waited a moment, she could have told him not to bother with a pregnancy test. Due to the type of birth control she took, she only had four periods a year. So, it wasn't unusual that she hadn't had one in almost two months. Speaking of which, she turned her attention to Kieran.

"How did you know when I last had my cycle?"

"Because I'm the man giving you dick." Was his simple reply.

A moment later, a nurse came in and took some blood, informing them that she would take it down to the lab to have the pregnancy test and other labs run. When she left, the room was quiet until Kieran broke it.

"Have you been taking your pill?" He questioned.

Alijah turned to look at him, and for a moment, she wondered if he thought that she had stopped. That maybe she was trying to trap him. Even though they hadn't had sex without a condom since her birthday, they both knew they weren't one hundred percent fail-proof, and that was where her birth control came in. However, Alijah shook the thought from her head.

"Yes."

Kieran didn't say anything for a while as he looked at her. Then finally responded simply with, "Okay." Making Alijah revert back to her previous thought.

After a while, the doctor came in, and Alijah was more than happy. She was ready to leave. They had been there for hours.

"Well, Ms. Douglas, you aren't pregnant. Unfortunately, it looks like you have food poisoning. The best way to treat it is to stay hydrated and let it run its course."

Alijah nodded. "Thank you, Doctor."

He smiled at her. "Not a problem. Head back to the front, and they will get you all taken care of. You two have a good night."

After finishing up at the front desk, they headed towards the door, and Alijah began to feel a little dizzy, causing her to sway. Kieran reached out and steadied her.

"Are you okay?" He questioned.

"Yes. Just a bit dizzy."

Before she knew it, she'd been lifted off of her feet and into Kieran's arms. He carried her to the car and placed her in the passenger side before getting in himself.

Alijah thought about how she could have gotten food poisoning. She hadn't eaten anything at Layla's. So, it had to have been the little Mediterranean spot they stopped at on the way back to the condo.

"I'll have them shut down," Kieran stated, and Alijah turned to look at him.

"What?" She questioned.

"The restaurant we stopped at. That had to be where you got it. I'm going to have them shut down."

"Don't do that," she stated, turning to look back out of her window.

"Who knows how many other people they've poisoned. I'd be doing Denver a favor." Kieran responded.

Alijah didn't say anything. She just kept quiet. A moment later, she felt herself drifting off to sleep.

Kieran parked the car and looked over at Alijah as she slept. Getting out of the car, he went around to her side and picked her up. She mumbled a little in her sleep as he nudged the door closed. Getting on the elevator, Kieran shifted her, releasing her legs, slowly repositioning her to where he could hold her up with one arm under her butt, her head laying on his shoulder. Reaching into his pocket, he pulled out his wallet, removed his access card, and placed it in.

Once the elevator made it to the top floor, he walked into the condo and carried Alijah to his bedroom. Laying her on the bed, he pulled her shoes and shorts off before heading back down the hall and grabbing a couple of bottles of water. When he made it back to the bedroom, he placed them on the bedside table next to her.

It was after two in the morning, but Kieran wasn't tired. Going into the bathroom, he turned on the shower before taking his phone out of his back pocket and setting it on the counter. He then proceeded to strip out of his clothes. Kieran was just about to step into the shower when his phone rang.

Grabbing it, he silenced it before ever looking at the screen. Kieran looked into the bedroom to make sure it hadn't woken Alijah up before looking at the screen to see who it was. *Rebecca.*

Sighing, Kieran put the phone down and stepped into the shower. He allowed the hot water to rain down on him as he stood directly under the spray.

What happened tonight with Alijah had worried him. He'd never been with a woman who had ever been sick around him before. Or if they were, he didn't ever remember caring, worrying how he had when he was taking Alijah to the hospital or when they were waiting on her blood work results.

Then the doctor had told her he would run a pregnancy test. Kieran hadn't known how to take that. He was positive Alijah wasn't pregnant. They were careful, but he'd asked her if she was still taking her pill for some stupid reason. He didn't miss the look in her eyes when she had looked at him. She tried to hide it, but he had still seen it. It was hurt.

His question had hurt her, and he realized that asking it made it sound as if he thought she had stopped taking it, that she was purposely trying to get pregnant. He felt like an ass, but if he were honest at that moment, he thought she might have.

Kieran groaned. There was no need for him to think that way. Alijah wouldn't do that to him. Of all the women that he had dated, she was the least impressed by his money. Hell, she complained every time he bought something for her. No matter how small the amount of money he spent on it.

The other women he dated would have been all for him finding a way to shut down the restaurant that had given them food poisoning if he had cared enough with them to do it. Alijah, however, didn't want him to. She was a contrast in every way compared to them. From the way she held herself to the way she looked.

Most of the women from his past would deal with his mood swings and attitude. They would tiptoe around him just to please him. Not Alijah, she always came at him, and she never walked on eggshells with him.

Again, Kieran groaned. This time, beginning to wash his body. He had to stop comparing her to other women from his past. Even if it was to show how much more superior she was to them in his eyes.

Kieran finished his shower and stepped out, wrapping a towel around his waist. He placed his palms on the countertop. Kieran was about to walk out of the bathroom when his phone rang again. He picked it up, glancing at the screen before answering it quickly.

"Stop calling me, Rebecca," Kieran stated lowly, glancing out of the bedroom door at a sleeping Alijah.

"Well, I wouldn't have to constantly call you if you would just set a date with me for us to go see the insemination doctor. Unless you want to do this the old fashion way," she responded, and Kieran didn't miss the tone in her voice that told him she was smiling.

"Rebecca, we are not having a fucking child together," he told her through gritted teeth.

"Well, not with that attitude, we're not. You need to do better, Kieran."

Taking the phone away from his ear, Kieran looked at it. This bitch was seven types of crazy. She had to be. There was no other explanation for why she couldn't; no *wouldn't* take no for an answer.

"Don't call me anymore, Rebecca. I gave you my answer." Kieran was about to hang up when her following words stopped him.

"So, you would rather that little girl you're sleeping with spring a baby on you? Get pregnant to sink her hooks in, instead of having a planned child with me?"

Kieran shook his head. "You don't know what you're talking about."

"Oh, I know. That's all she wants, for you to get her pregnant so that you'll be paying for it the rest of your life. Supporting a lavish lifestyle for her and a child she had on purpose." Rebecca paused for a moment before continuing. "I mean, think about it, Kieran. She's in her early twenties. You're at least ten years older than her. I mean, of course, you're attractive, but she's going to want someone her age eventually. Someone who can always keep up with her."

"Don't call me again," Kieran stated before hanging up the phone. He then went to her contact and blocked her number.

Tossing the phone back on the counter, it slid slightly before stopping just a few inches from Alijah's birth control container. Kieran stared at it. Rebecca's words were echoing in his ears. He knew he was stupid for believing anything she had to say. The woman would lie to get her way. But damn it, if his curiosity didn't get the better of him.

Picking up the container, Kieran opened it. It was a three-month pack. The first package was empty. Taking a breath, he flipped to the next one and saw that it had about two weeks left in it. Which corresponded with the day of the month they were on.

Closing the container, he placed it back down before scrubbing a hand down his face. Again, he felt like an ass. He had no reason to doubt Alijah and *definitely* shouldn't have let anything Rebecca said affect that. However, with the situation they had gone through at the hospital being fresh on his mind, her words had just drilled it in deeper.

Grabbing his phone, he walked out of the bathroom, turning off the light. Placing the phone on his bedside table, he dressed in a pair of boxers. He turned the lights off and slid into bed, pulling Alijah to him. He felt guilty for having a moment of weakness and not trusting her.

Kieran had been lying there for a while with her in his arms when he looked over at the clock and saw that it was almost five in the morning. It looked like that guilt wasn't going to allow him to sleep.

26

Alijah lay on her side, watching Kieran as he slept. He'd gotten out of the shower almost two hours ago and had gone straight to sleep. They had been working extremely hard the past couple of days with Layla trying to get the prototype for the cell phone ready.

She had taken a nap when they had gotten off, so she wasn't as tired as he was. Alijah knew that she was going to need all of her energy. It was Tuesday night, Halloween, and Kieran's birthday was thirty minutes away.

Sliding out of bed, Alijah made her way to her room and grabbed the bag she'd stashed in her closet. The weekend after her food poisoning epidemic, she had gone with Layla, Gemma, and Gale, to pick out a few things to celebrate Kieran's birthday.

Taking the bag back into his bedroom, she rummaged through it quietly before finding the first thing she was looking for. Alijah placed it to the side before grabbing the other items out and setting them up on the bedside table closest to him. She grabbed the midnight blue silk scarves and carefully tied his hands to the headboard when finished. For a moment, she thought he would wake up and waited for several beats before she continued.

She opened a package of the deep throat mints and began to suck on two as she looked at his boxers. She was more than sure she would wake him up if she tried to take them off. So, instead, she opted on reaching into them gently and pulling his dick free.

After sucking on the mints for a few minutes and feeling her mouth and throat begin to numb, she chewed them and swallowed. Slowly, she straddled Kieran.

Alijah started by leaving soft kisses on his neck before trailing her lips down to his chest, where she began to bite lightly. She made her way down his abdomen before coming to his dick. Starting at the base, she gave the underside one long lick. She heard him begin to stir as he let out a moan. She took the head in her mouth and sucked on it before swirling her tongue around it.

That woke him up, and Alijah could hear him pull at his restraints before she looked up. His eyes were on her. He tugged at the restraints again before looking at them and then turning back to her.

"What is this, Alijah?"

"Well, I decided this was how we would celebrate your birthday." She grabbed the sides of his boxers, staring into his hazel eyes. "Up," she stated.

"Baby, I would love nothing more than to fuck you all night tonight, but we have a long day tomorrow."

Alijah cocked her head to the side. He'd denied her sex lately, and Alijah had understood because of how hard they were working, but she wasn't about to let that happen tonight. Tonight, she was going to cater to him, to his body.

"No, we don't. I talked to Remy, and he is going to cover for you tomorrow," she informed him. "Now. Raise up."

She watched him hesitate for only a second before lifting his hips, and she pulled his boxers off of him and threw them to the floor.

Leaning down, she took his dick in her hand before slowly lowering her mouth onto it. She went down as far as she could, holding it there and breathing out of her nose. She rose just as slowly as she had descended, took a breath, and repeated the action.

Alijah continued this slow torture for ten minutes before she felt him lifting his hips, trying to speed up her pace. Placing her hands on his thighs, she attempted to hold him down. When that didn't work, she grabbed the other set of silk scarves and tied his feet to the end of the bed — making it harder for him to move.

Getting back in her original position, Alijah went back to her slow torture. Her deep throat mints were beginning to wear off. Releasing his dick from her mouth with a soft pop, she grabbed the spray she'd bought and sprayed it in the back of her throat. She used three sprays and waited a few seconds. Unlike the mints, she knew the spray would take effect quickly. She then sprayed the *Wet Head* in her mouth before sliding back down his body — the whole time Kieran watched.

Alijah could feel both sprays taking effect as she grabbed the base of his dick. One spray numbed her throat while the other helped form extra saliva in her mouth.

"Do you plan to keep torturing me?" Kieran questioned.

She didn't answer him; she merely took his dick into her mouth and began to suck at a steady rhythm. She was taking as much as she could down her throat, and Alijah pleasured the few inches she couldn't with one of her hands, the other playing with his testicles.

"Fuck, Alijah. That feels so good, baby. Don't stop." Kieran told her.

At his encouragement, Alijah sped up her pace. The spray had made her mouth so wet that saliva dripped down onto his dick, testicles, and pelvis—the room filled with the sounds of her sucking and his moaning.

"That's it, baby. Suck that dick. Just like that." Kieran stated. She could hear him pulling on his restraints and knew that if his hands were free, they would be buried in her hair.

Alijah continued to suck. His dick poked the back of the throat each time she descended on it. *Eck eck eck* filled the room along with the sound of her wet hand jacking off the base of his dick. She knew Kieran was loving and hating it all at the same time. He was visual. So, she knew this was turning him on. However, he was also physical, and she knew not being able to touch her was torture, and she loved it.

"Shit, baby, you look so fucking sexy with my dick in your mouth, and it sounds even better," he told her.

Alijah came off his dick briefly, only to spit on it and begin sucking it again. Still at a fast pace.

* * *

"You nasty girl," Kieran stated, and she could hear the smile in his voice.

She continued her actions and felt his balls tighten after another ten minutes or so. Alijah immediately let them go, stilled her hand, and removed her mouth from his dick.

"Fuck, baby. Why did you stop? I was almost there."

Alijah wiped the saliva from her chin. "Don't cum yet, Daddy." With that, she moved up his body.

Taking his left nipple into her mouth, she began to suck on it for a few moments before taking it between her teeth and biting it. Kieran groaned, and she took it that he liked it. She had never done this to him before, but her inner tigress was coming out tonight. She was going to let her freak come out and play. Moving her attention to the other nipple, Alijah did the same thing. She was giving his dick time to calm down.

Releasing that nipple, she slowly trailed her tongue along his abs, outlining them. She slid down some more and gave his dick a long lick causing him to groan again.

Alijah grabbed both of the spray bottles, using them again before going back to sucking his dick. She wasted no time and started off fast, stimulating every part of it. The sounds of her sucking again filled the room, along with his moans and occasional cursing.

She was making a big mess, giving a whole other meaning to sloppy top. She had flooded Kieran's pelvis, testicles, thighs, dick, and her chin with saliva. The sound of her jacking off the base of his dick was reminiscent of the sound his balls made, slapping against her as they fucked.

It was about fifteen minutes before she felt his testicles tighten again. Once again, she stopped everything she was doing, and Kieran groaned in frustration. She looked up at him as she wiped the saliva from her chin and saw the look of horror written on his face, and she knew he had figured it out.

"Alijah, do not do this to me," he told her sternly.

She smiled at him before sliding up and straddling his stomach. "I'm just returning the favor given to me on my birthday."

He went to respond, but Alijah grabbed another scarf, placing it over his mouth. She reached behind his head and tied it as she eyed him with a smirk.

"I'm sorry, baby. I can't hear you," she told him as he mumbled through the scarf.

Grabbing the pop rocks from the bedside table, she slid back down his body before opening them and placing them in her mouth. As they began the explode, she placed his dick back in her mouth and felt his body try to jerk from the sensation but was held down by his restraints.

Alijah began to suck him fast, stopping now and then to add more pop rocks to her mouth when the other ones stopped popping and dissolved — adding to the mess she had already made. When he came close to another orgasm, she stopped, and immediately he began to protest from behind his gag.

Smiling at him, Alijah got off the bed and walked to the kitchen. She had bought a small ice tray for tiny ice cubes. She'd placed it in the freezer while Kieran was in the shower and was more than sure they were ready.

Taking them from the freezer, she emptied them into a small black glass before bringing them back into the bedroom. Placing the cup on the table, she reached in and grabbed a piece before starting at Kieran's neck and trailing it down his body. She circled it around both nipples before trailing it down his abdomen, watching as his muscles flexed from the coldness.

Popping that ice cube and another one in her mouth, she got back on the bed, taking his dick back into her mouth. She felt him flinch slightly and looked up into his eyes. She could see the need in them, but she wouldn't give him what he wanted. She hadn't forgotten how he tortured her, and she believed that turnabout was fair play.

As the ice began to melt, she began to suck him faster. When it was, and the liquid was all that remained in her mouth, she removed it from his dick and spat on it. Grabbing two more pieces of ice, Alijah repeated the process. She did this until the glass was empty, keeping him edging but never allowing him release.

After denying him another orgasm, he began to mumble emphatically under his gag. Reaching up, Alijah took it off.

"Baby." Kieran breathed out. "You'll give me blue balls if you don't let me cum."

In all of Alijah's planning, she hadn't thought of that. She had just wanted to please and torture him simultaneously, but she didn't want to give him blue balls. She decided she had tortured him enough. After all, she'd denied him as many if not more releases as he had her.

Alijah sprayed her throat and mouth once more before taking his dick back into her mouth. Her jaw started to get swore in the middle of her cup of ice, but she hadn't expected anything less. Her man was well endowed, and she had been giving him oral pleasure for over an hour.

She sucked him fast—each time taking him down as far as she could. At one point, she went down further than she was ready to and gagged.

"Fuck! That shit feels good!" Kieran exclaimed. So, Alijah did it again.

She continued to suck him, jacking off the base with a twisting motion while massaging his testicles. Ten minutes later, she felt them tighten up.

"Alijah, I'm going to cum," Kieran informed her. "Baby, if you don't move, I'll cum in your mouth," he told her through a groan. Alijah heard him, but she continued to suck.

"Baby, I can't hold it. Seriously, mo..."

He couldn't get the rest of it out as he let go of the first spurt of cum. Alijah stopped sucking and held him in her mouth but continued the other stimulation. She had given him head plenty of times, but he had never cum in her mouth before. She didn't mind, though. Again, she believed in turnabout being fair play, and she was always coming in his mouth. Hell, he was constantly swallowing it.

She felt his body relax as the last rope of cum shot into her mouth. Some of it sliding down his dick. She had to admit it was a lot. Slowly removing her mouth from his dick, Alijah looked him right in the eyes...and swallowed. After all, spitters were quitters.

"Damn, baby. Your freak is out. You're such a nasty girl tonight."

Alijah took his still hard dick in her hand and slowly stroked it. "You like it," she stated as a matter of fact.

"I never said I didn't. What I'd like right now is to slide into that pussy," he informed her.

Alijah got off the bed, removing her panties and her camisole. She stood there for a moment while Kieran looked her over.

"You should just walk around naked all the time." He stopped for a moment before adding. "When we're here alone." Alijah laughed, getting back on the bed. "I bought more condoms, baby. They're in the drawer." Kieran then informed her, motioning to the nightstand.

Alijah got one out and opened it before rolling it down his dick. She straddled him and began to slide down slowly. He pulled at his restraints, and Alijah locked eyes with him.

"You're not going to untie me, are you?" He questioned.

"No, not yet," she stated once he was embedded fully inside of her.

She began to rock her hips back and forth, never taking her eyes away from his. They were dark with lust. Alijah tightened the muscles of her pussy, though she was sure he couldn't be anymore snug inside of her, and began to circle her hips. Her movements were slow. She was aiming to torture him again.

After about ten minutes of riding him tortuously slow, Alijah turned her back to him and began to bounce up and down on his dick. She could hear him pulling his restraints and knew that he desperately wanted to reach out and touch her. She increased the speed of her bouncing slightly but stopped altogether when she heard a ripping noise.

Turning her head, Alijah saw that Kieran had slightly ripped the scarf holding his left-hand prisoner. Her eyes widened.

"I need to touch you, baby. Take them off, or I may rip them and break the damn bed trying to get free."

Alijah believed them. So, she released his legs before turning back to face him. His dick still inside of her, she reached up and untied the scarf that he had ripped some first and then the other.

No sooner than they were off, his hands went to her ass and began to bounce her on his dick furiously. Alijah almost lost her balance when he first started. Thrusting up into her, he met her each time he brought her down. Placing her hands on his chest, she threw her head back as her first orgasm ripped through her.

"Fuck, Kieran!"

However, her release did not stop him. He quickly flipped them over. Nestled between her legs, he began to pound in and out of her. Taking both of her legs, he hooked them in his arms to penetrate her deeper. He was slamming into her, and her moans echoed off the wall, mixed with his groans.

"Baby, wait. Slow down." Alijah managed between thrusts and moans.

"It's my birthday, baby. Which means I get it exactly how I want it," he told her as he continued to slam into her. "And I want to fuck you just..." Stroke. "Like." Stroke. "This." Stroke.

Placing one hand around her neck and squeezing, Kieran brought his other hand down and began to rub her clit. It didn't take but a minute, and she was climaxing all over his dick again.

Kieran could feel his second release building within him, and he quickly pulled his dick from her pussy. He didn't want to cum yet.

Sliding his body down the bed, he buried his face between her legs and immediately latched on to her clit. She squirmed and tried to push him away, and he knew it was sensitive from him playing with it. Yet, he held it between his lips and slid two fingers into her. She was drenching wet, and Kieran loved it.

Removing his fingers, he placed them at her other entrance and felt her tense. Releasing her clit from his lips, he began to tongue it quickly. When he was sure she had forgotten about the fingers he'd placed at her ass, he slowly started to push one in. She tensed, and he stopped, continuing to lap at her clit as he reached down and began to stroke himself.

When she relaxed again, he continued to push the finger into her. He waited a moment and wiggled it around as he sucked her clit. He then slowly added the other finger to it. He moved them in and out of her slowly for several moments as he continued to give her oral pleasure. He then began to spread his fingers apart inside her, scissoring her open.

Kieran heard her grunt, but he applied friction to her clit to get her mind off it. When all he heard were moans, he released her clit and spat on his fingers before taking her clit back into his mouth and adding a third finger to her other entrance.

She tensed only slightly but began to relax as he took his tongue and began to tongue fuck her pussy. He knew she was getting close by the way she began to breathe, and Kieran removed his tongue and fingers.

"Turn over for me, baby," he stated.

He climbed up the bed and retrieved some water-based lube from the nightstand drawer. He got behind Alijah, lifting her ass higher in the air. He opened the lube and applied some to the condom and then to her hole. She jumped slightly, but Kieran placed his hand in the middle of her back after tossing the bottle to the side.

He snaked that hand around to rub her clit, while he took his dick in the other and began to rub it along her ass. He felt her tense, but he needed her to relax. He dipped his finger in her pussy and began to finger fuck her quickly as he pressed the head of his dick into her ass. He heard her make a startled noise, but she didn't sound in pain if her moans were any evidence to go by.

Kieran's actions were contradictory. He finger fucked her fast, and he slid into her back entrance slow. When he felt her clamped down on his fingers, he knew she was about to come. Right as she did, he pushed his remaining length into her.

"Shit!" She exclaimed, and Kieran held himself still but continued to stroke her through her orgasm.

He gave her several minutes as he continued to finger her lazily. He pulled out slowly and pushed back in even slower. He thought her pussy was tight; this was on an entirely new level. He wanted her to get used to it before he began to fuck her.

Leaning over, Kieran whispered in her ear. "I'm going to make this good for you. Just like I promised."

After several slow thrusts, she began to throw it back into him, moaning loudly. Kieran took that as his queue and began to thrust faster. Her ass bounced against his stomach, and he smacked one of her cheeks, pulling a moan from her.

Reaching up with his other hand, Kieran grabbed a fistful of hair and yanked her head back. He then smacked her ass again as he increased his speed. He leaned over her and began to rub her clit. He could feel his release coming and wanted her to cum with him.

Kieran's balls contracted as he felt his orgasm approaching. He tightened his grip on her hair and rubbed her clit even faster.

"Be a good girl and cum for Daddy," he told her before biting into her shoulder.

That kicked her over the edge as she screamed her release.

"Yes!"

Kieran followed right on her trail.

"Shit, baby! Fuck!"

He slumped onto her back as he caught his breath before slowly removing himself. He knew she would be sore tomorrow and wanted to do whatever he could to ease it. Getting out of bed, he walked into the bathroom and turned on the water in the tub.

To be honest, he hadn't expected her to let him go through with it. He had never done it before because every woman he had ever considered trying it with backed out because of his size. Granted, he may not have been as gentle as he was with Alijah. With her, he had built her up to it. He wasn't sure if he had done that with the others.

Going back into the bedroom, he scooped her into his arms and stepped into the tub with her. Since she had gotten Remy to cover for him tomorrow, he planned on filling his birthday with her body. They had been so busy at work lately that he had been beyond tired and hadn't been fulfilling her needs as he should have been. However, once everything with the phone was taken care of, all would go back to normal. For now, however, he would make up for missed opportunities.

27

Alijah didn't know how she had ended up on her parent's doorstep with Kieran beside her for Thanksgiving dinner. Actually, that was a lie. She remembered exactly how it had come about.

Alijah could hear her phone ringing in the living room. Sliding out of Kieran's arms, she picked up one of his shirts, putting it on as she exited the bedroom. She padded down the hall quickly. Picking up the phone, she answered it without looking at that caller-id.

"Hello," she spoke, bringing the phone to her ear.
"Nicolette."

Alijah groaned internally but managed to keep it from escaping her lips. "Hello, mother."

"I hadn't heard from you, Nicolette. I decided to give you a call since you don't believe in calling your parents.

Alijah rolled her eyes. For the oddest reason, her mother had always called her by her middle name. As far as Alijah was concerned, if her mother liked it so much, she should have just named her that. She was also rolling her eyes at the fact that her mother wanted to play the victim in the situation. Without a doubt, Alijah called her parents far more than they called her. Hell, they hadn't bothered to call and wish her a happy birthday a few months ago.

"I've been busy working, mother. You know that."

"I know that's what you say," her mother responded with condescension. Alijah reached up and gripped her hair,

remaining silent. "However, that isn't the reason for my call. We are having Thanksgiving dinner this year at home. Taila and Chayse will be here."

Alijah stopped for a moment to think. She wasn't sure if she could trust her mother. After all, the woman was a habitual liar. She would tell Alijah anything to get her there. She hadn't been home much since she had left for college.

"I'll see, mother. I may have to work."

"What kind of boss would make you work on..."

"I have to go," Alijah stated, cutting her off. "I'll talk to you later." With that, both women hung up the phone.

Heading back down the hall, she laid her phone on the bedside table before sliding back into bed with a sigh. Kieran wrapped an arm around her waist, and he pulled her close to him.

"Everything alright?" He questioned.

"Yeah. It was just my mother." Alijah told him. She thought for a moment. "She wants me to come home for Thanksgiving. Apparently, there will be a family dinner at my parent's house."

"The office will be closed for the holiday. You should go."

"I don't want to go. I've told you that my parents and I don't get along. What's the point in going and being miserable?"

"I recall telling you something along those lines when the old man showed up at my office," he told her. Alijah sighed, knowing he was right. "I'll let you take the company plane." He tacked on.

Then an idea hit her. Turning to face Kieran, Alijah kissed his chin. "Will you come with me?"

"Alijah, I..." He stopped when she gave him that look he found increasingly harder to resist. Leaning in, he kissed her gently. "If you want me to."

She nodded. "Thank you."

After that, she called Chayse and asked if she and her mom were going to dinner at her parents. Her cousin informed her that they were, so Alijah decided to go. She called Erin to see if she wanted to go as well. Figuring as many people as she could have in her corner would help, but Erin informed her that she was flying out to visit her Dad and grandmother for the holiday.

So, Alijah had called her mother back and accepted her invitation, telling her she would be bringing someone with her. Her mother had been a bit shocked at first. Probably because she never brought people home. Not even in high school.

They had flown in the night before and stayed at the hotel. Now, they were waiting for her mother or father to answer the door and let them in. It was eleven in the morning, and the food wasn't due to be served until three, but her mother wanted everyone there before noon.

When the door opened, it was her father standing there. He greeted her, looking past her to Kieran before nodding in greeting to him and letting them in.

"Father, this is Kieran. Kieran, Cornelius." Alijah stated, making the introductions. Her father nodded before going back into the living room.

"Your mother's in the kitchen." He called over his shoulder.

Alijah rolled her eyes. For as long as she'd been alive, that's where her father thought all women should be, in the kitchen. He wasn't that old, so she didn't know where he got that way of thinking. His parents, her paternal grandparents, had not been that way.

She took Kieran's hand and led the way into the kitchen, where she found her mother mixing something in a bowl. She waited until she placed the bowel on the counter. Her mother was dramatic. So, Alijah knew that had she tried to get her attention with the bowl in her hand, she probably would have dropped it...on purpose.

"Mother," she called, gaining her attention. Her mother looked over her shoulder before turning to face her fully. "Kieran, this is my mother, Anya. Mother, this is my boyfriend, Kieran," she introduced again.

The word boyfriend felt weird rolling from her tongue. She had never called him that before. Though she knew it was technically what he was. She watched as he held out his hand, and her mother placed hers' daintily in it.

"A pleasure to meet you," he told her, and her mother gave him a small smile.

"Did you need any help?" Alijah questioned.

"Not in the kitchen, no. If you could go upstairs and check in on Carter for me, that would help."

"Carter?" Alijah questioned.

"Yes, Nicolette." Her mother stated as if she hadn't just thrown out some random name to her. "He's in your old room."

Alijah looked at Kieran before turning and leaving out of the kitchen. She headed up the stairs with him behind her. When she got to her old room, the door was opened, and she noticed that everything had been changed around. It had been transformed into a little boy's room and said little boy was lying in the middle of the floor smashing *Transformers* together as if they were fighting.

She knocked on the door, and he stated for her to come in without looking to see who it was. When she entered the room, she walked around him to stand in front of him.

"Hey, Carter. I'm Alijah. My mo..."

Alijah didn't finish her sentence. The child looked up at her at that point with a massive smile on his face, and she felt she was kicked in the gut.

"You're my new sister!" He exclaimed, jumping up and hugging her.

Her shock had her paralyzed, and she couldn't even hug the little boy back, but he didn't seem to notice as he beamed up at her with that smile again before going back to his *Transformers*. Alijah made her way out of the room and past Kieran.

"Baby, what's wrong?" Kieran questioned.

Alijah didn't answer him. She made her way back into the kitchen, where her mother was checking on something in the oven.

"Mother, who is that little boy?" She questioned.

"I told you. That's Carter."

"Why is he here?" Alijah then inquired.

"Your father and I are adopting him. His biological mother is having a hard time caring for him."

Alijah wanted to call bullshit and flip out and fire off something smart. She even felt it coming. That is until Kieran placed his hand on her back and steered her from the kitchen, telling her mother they would be right back. He led her outside and to the car they had rented. He pushed her against the passenger side door — his hands on her waist.

"What is it? Do you know that little boy?" Kieran questioned.

Alijah shook her head as she crossed her arms over her chest. "No. But I know who his father is," she told him. When Kieran raised an eyebrow, waiting, she continued. "Cornelius. I'm not his new sister. I'm merely his sister. And I can promise you my mother didn't give birth to him.

Kieran stared at Alijah for a moment before blinking slowly. He processed what she had just said to him, and simply put, she believed that her father had cheated on her mother, had another baby, and now he and her mother were going to adopt and raise the boy. That was *Jerry Springer/Maury* type shit if he'd ever heard any.

"Are you sure?" He questioned.

"Yes. He's the spitting image of Cornelius when he was that age."

Kieran nodded. "Do you think your mother knows?"

"Of course, she does. She and my father grew up in the same neighborhood. They've known each other since they were in diapers. She knows, but this is what she does. Spins things so they fit her needs."

Just then, a car pulled behind theirs. He watched as Chayse got out of the driver's seat, and another woman got out of the passenger side. He watched Chayse smile at him before her eyes turned to Alijah, and she rushed over.

"What did your parents do?" She questioned, and Kieran wondered if her parents doing something to her was a regular occurrence.

After Alijah filled the women in and Kieran was introduced to Taila, Chayse's mother, they all headed back inside the house. He watched the two sisters interact, and though they were cordial, he knew that there was some friction between the two older ladies. While Kieran knew they were blood sisters because of their resemblance, Taila housed a slight French accent. He made a mental note to ask Alijah about that later.

At three o'clock, the food was served, and everyone gathered around the table. Kieran watched as Anya doted on Carter, cutting up his food, poking him softly in the side now and then, causing him to laugh, and running her fingers through his hair. He knew it was bothering Alijah by the way she gripped her silverware. He dropped his hand to her knee and massaged it gently.

"So, Kieran, what do you do?" Taila asked him, striking up a conversation.

"I guess you could say I'm in sales."

"Meaning what exactly?" Cornelius inquired. "Because I don't need my daughter with some drug dealer wannabe."

"Father," Alijah stated.

Kieran lifted his brow at the older man. From what he gathered, neither of her parents seemed particularly interested in what she did, so he wondered why the man was putting on a show for him. He was just about to ask him that when he opened his mouth and spoke again.

"A drug dealer can't do anything for her but get her sent to jail."

"I can assure you. I sell many things. Drugs are not one of them." Kieran replied calmly, taking a bite of his food. He figured it wouldn't be wise to get into it with her father.

"So, you sell stolen goods. Hot stuff. That's no better."

"Seriously, father. Kieran doesn't-"

"No, baby." Kieran cut her off. "That's okay."

It was quiet for a moment before Talia spoke up again.

"Well, if you don't mind me asking Kieran, what kind of things do you sell?"

Kieran smiled at her. "It honestly does vary. I own Cayman Industries. We deal in all sorts of products and business ventures. Whether it's investing in a start-up, creating a new product, or buying rights to an invention a creator has an issue with."

He could hear Cornelius choke on his food, and Kieran held back his smirk and a laugh. Taila and Chayse, however, did not and proceeded to.

Kieran knew his reputation preceded him. Everyone may not have known his face, but they knew his business, knew his name. He had his hands in many things. So, there was bound to be something that people associated him with.

Turning back to his food, he began eating like Cornelius had not just almost died from choking on ham. It was quiet for a while until Taila again broke it. He was starting to see she didn't like quiet.

"Alijah, I saw the photo shoot you and Erin did. It was amazing." Taila told her.

"Only because Chayse took the pictures," Alijah responded with a smile.

"My baby girl is talented," Taila stated, pulling gently on Chayse's ear. He watched as Chayse rolled her eyes playfully at her mother and turned to Alijah and saw a look of longing pass over her face. She wanted that with her mother. It wasn't hard to tell.

"Chayse, when will you get a real job and stop running around taking pictures?" Cornelius questioned.

"When you decided to stop cheating on your wife. So, never," she told him in French.

Taila burst into laughter along with Alijah, and Kieran almost spit out his drink. He had conducted enough business in France to pick up on the language, and he knew from their trip there that Alijah understood and spoke it pretty well. Cornelius and Anya seemed confused, and it simply served to piss them both off.

"What's so funny?" Carter questioned, looking around at all the adults.

"Nothing, sweetheart," Anya responded before running her hand over his hair.

After they had eaten, Cornelius had walked back into the living room, and after helping clear the table, Kieran had followed him. They sat in silence, watching the game for a few moments until Cornelius spoke.

"How did you meet my daughter?"

Kieran debated telling the man the truth or lying but decided he didn't care how he felt about it. "I hired her."

"She works for you," Cornelius confirmed as he turned to look at Kieran, who simply nodded. "So, when you're finally through with her, she'll be out of a job." The older man stated as a matter of fact.

Kieran clenched his jaw. "I don't plan on ever being through with her." He gritted out.

Cornelius only snorted. "What could a man like you possibly want with a young, black girl? Other than what's between her legs?"

Kieran knew that he shouldn't say it. Hell, he even tried to swallow it down, but he had never proclaimed he wasn't an asshole, and he didn't care that this was her father. He was about a sentence away from putting the man on his ass.

"There's a lot of things I want with Alijah. Hearing her moan my name every night is just a bonus."

Kieran watched as the older man's jaw clenched and his eyes bore into him. He wasn't fazed, though. He was the master of that look, and nobody pulled it off like he did. For a moment, he thought the older man would lung at him. Hell, he was hoping he would. But he simply sized him up before pushing from his chair and walking out of the living room.

Kieran smirked to himself, but it fell a minute later. If Alijah found out what he had said to her father, he would be in trouble.

A few minutes passed, and Kieran heard hushed voices from down the hall since he was sitting in the seat closest to it. His curiosity got the better of him, and he followed the whispers, making them out as he got closer.

"How could you do that to her?" He heard Alijah ask.

"You don't know what you're talking about, little girl." He then heard her father respond.

"You know exactly what I'm talking about. You cheated and had a baby."

"I deserved at least one. I still don't know if you're mine." He heard her father snap back, and Kieran was pissed off.

They came into view as he rounded the corner. He could see that Alijah was holding back tears. Then those emeralds sparked with fire.

"Fuck you, old man!" She snapped.

Kieran had expected her father to have something to say to her. Probably something else hurtful. What he had not expected was for him to lift his hand and backhand her.

All Kieran saw was red as he surged across the hall and his fist connected with Cornelius' jaw. He stumbled to the floor, and Kieran snatched him up by his collar, hitting him again.

"Kieran!" Alijah called.

Yet, he couldn't stop himself. The man had put his hands on Kieran's woman. Father or not, he was going to be taught a lesson. He hit him again and felt the cracking of cartilage. Only when Alijah stepped in front of him and pushed him backward did he realize the other women had entered the hall, and Anya was yelling.

"Get him out of my house! See what you've done! You should have found a good black man like your father!"

"Like her father?" He heard Taila question as Alijah drug him towards the door. "The only quality he has from that sentence is black."

The door closed behind them, and Alijah walked over to the car. She waited for him to unlock the door before getting in. The ride back to the hotel was quiet. However, when they entered their suite. Alijah turned on him.

"How could you, Kieran?"

Kieran looked at her as if she was slow. How could he? Had her father not put his hands on her, Kieran wouldn't have beaten his ass. However, being who he was. He had to be a smart ass.

"The mechanics are simple, really. I just allowed my fist to collide with his face repeatedly."

She glared at him. "I'm serious. He's my father. You can't just go haul off and-"

Kieran cut her off by crowding her space. "Yes, I can. Any man that decides he's brave enough to put his hands on my woman needs to be brave enough to take the ass whooping I'm going to give him." He placed his hands on her waist and his forehead against hers. "I'm not going to stand by and watch someone disrespect you or put their hands on you. Father or not. If the Grim Reaper came for you right this second, he'd have to fight me to get you, baby."

His words brought Alijah to her tiptoes, and she pressed her lips to his. He moved his lips in sync with hers as he felt her unbutton his shirt before pushing it off of his arms. Her hands then went to his slacks and worked to release the button and zipper.

Kieran broke the kiss momentarily to pull her dress over her head. He undid her bra and pulled it down her arms throwing it to the floor. Kieran stepped away from her to remove his shoes and the rest of his clothing. He watched as she did the same. He grabbed a condom from the nightstand where they'd had them last night, opening it and sliding it on.

Grabbing her waist, he pushed her backward until she hit the bed and sat down. He climbed over her, moving her backward until they were in the middle of the bed. He placed his lips back to her and reached between them to see if she was wet enough. Usually, he would have spent time devouring her, but he felt overly eager to join his body with hers for some reason. Positioning himself, he slid in slowly. His lips still pressed to hers.

Kieran slid in and out of her slowly. Unlike other times, he fought to control himself and not get lost in the moment. His strokes were long and slow, massaging her canal. Each time he entered her, he swiveled his hips—his pelvis brushing against her clitoris.

He continued this way for almost half an hour before he neared release. He had gotten her off twice. He had been giving her soft kisses the entire time, but he sat up slightly and looked into those green eyes when his release hit him.

Removing himself from her slowly, Kieran rolled to his side and discarded the condom before laying on his back and pulling her to him. He held her as she slowly skimmed her fingers over his abdomen.

He had half expected her to ask him to speed up some time doing their sex. However, she hadn't. It was as if she knew he specifically needed it. Something had changed, and he wasn't sure if she had noticed it, but he had. He didn't know when it happened, and he honestly felt like an idiot for just now realizing it, but she had managed to melt the block of ice he had around his heart and situate herself in it.

28

Alijah took the pen from Trevor and erased what he had just sketched. She'd described how he needed to draw it in great detail, and she knew he was talented enough to do it. Therefore, she surmised that he was trying to mess with her. She sent a glare his way before holding the pencil back out to him. He flashed her a smile, and Alijah simply rolled her eyes at him.

They were working on the marketing campaign for the cell phone the company was about to release. The prototype had come out exceptionally well, and Kieran himself had looked over all of the features alongside Layla. Alijah had to admit that it was a nice phone, and it would be affordable. She would wager that it would be one of the new biggest sellers.

Kieran had assigned the project to Trevor personally since he had done so well on the last three campaigns he had worked on. This, of course, meant that Alijah was helping him because she had lent her assistance in those three campaigns. She did not doubt that Trevor would have been able to do it himself.

He was talented, but she suspected that while he could visualize what he wanted, it was hard for him to translate that to paper often. If there was someone on his team or in his department that could pull the images from his mind as Alijah seemed to be able to and help him bring them to life, she suspected that he would ask them instead.

Watching over his shoulder, she gave directions to him. They were putting the final touches on the last piece of it before Trevor went about making it digital and adding color for the presentation he was meant to give to Kieran in a week. She had faith that he would get it all done in time, and it would look amazing, though she would meet with him again in three days to check his progress.

Looking at her watch, she said goodbye to Trevor and left marketing. She was taking a long lunch today because Kieran would be on a video call with Mr. Lao from China. The man still held no tolerance for Alijah, but she didn't care. Kieran, however, had told her she could use the time for lunch or anything else she saw fit since she had put together everything, he would need in the meeting the night before.

She made her way out of the office building and to the small cafe she enjoyed going to. There she met with Layla and Gale for lunch.

"Hello, ladies." Alijah greeted as she made her way over to the selected table. "Have you been waiting long?"

"No," Layla responded, shaking her head. "We just got here a moment ago."

The three of them headed to the front counter and ordered before sitting again and waiting on their food to be ready. They made small talk, and when their number was called, Layla rose and retrieved their food.

"So, Layla, do you have anything special planned for your birthday?" Gale questioned.

"Well, I'm hoping Alijah will give me whatever treatment she gave Kieran last month," Layla responded with a smirk in Alijah's direction.

Gale reached out and swatted her. "Leave her alone. You're always flirting with her. You are too old for her."

Alijah laughed as Layla turned to Gale with a pout. "I'm too old for her? Kieran's older than I am."

Shaking her head Alijah took a bite of her sandwich before speaking. "I like older men. What can I say? On a different note, what are you seriously doing for your birthday?"

"I don't know. Gemma says she has something planned but won't tell me what it is."

"Well, I'm sure you'll love it," Alijah stated.

"Yes, and whatever it is, you better be appreciative and tell her as much," Gale added after swallowing a bite of her salad. Alijah had noticed that she was like an older sister to

Layla. She didn't know exactly how long they had known each other, but she knew it had been many years.

"Oh, before I forget. Alijah, are you and Kieran coming to my art auction Christmas fundraiser?" Gale questioned.

Alijah bit her lip. "That's the same night as the office Christmas party. I have a piece for you, though, and Kieran is planning on donating."

"That's fine. I know it was a little short notice when I called you about it a couple of days ago. Especially since it's in just a couple of weeks."

The three women talked as they finished their lunch. Alijah said her goodbyes and headed back to the office when they were done. When she reached the building, she still had about twenty minutes left. Getting on the elevator, she pushed the button for Remy's floor.

He had buzzed earlier, saying he had some papers he would be bringing down to Kieran. Alijah figured that she would get them from him since she still had a bit of time. Remy was just as busy as Kieran was most days, and she didn't want him making an unnecessary trip. Especially with his secretary on maternity leave.

She stepped off the elevator on his floor; his secretary's desk phone was ringing. Walking over, she picked it up.

"Cayman Industries. This is Alijah. How may I help you?" She greeted.

"Alijah?" The voice on the other end of the phone questioned. "Are you the temp secretary at the moment?"

"No," Alijah answered simply. She didn't know this person, so she wouldn't give him any information. "Is there something I can help you with, Mr..."

"Sorry. Rudy Crow. I have a meeting scheduled with Remy, but I'm running behind. I just wanted to let him know."

"I will let him know, Mr. Crow," Alijah stated.

"Thank you." Was the response she received before they both hung up.

Walking to Remy's office door, she knocked and waited only a moment before he called for her to come in.

"Hey, Alijah. What brings you down here?"

"Hey. I thought I'd come and get those papers you said you had for Kieran. That way, you didn't have to make an unnecessary trip. I'm sure you're a bit swamped since Chloe is out."

"I am. Thank you." Remy responded, grabbing the papers and handing them to her.

"It's not a problem. Mr. Crow called and said that he would be running a little late for the meeting you have scheduled."

"Thank you again. After the fourth ring, I have her phone set up to ring in here. You must have picked it up before then."

"You know, I don't mind having her calls transferred to my phone upstairs and helping you out until you get a temp."

"That's kind of you, Alijah, but I don't want you overworking yourself."

She waved him off. "It's not a problem. I was a secretary at my last job, and I answered calls for the entire office and routed them to where they needed to go."

"If...if you're sure," he responded hesitantly.

"I am."

Making her way out of his office and back to the desk, she set up the phone to automatically forward the calls to lines five and six on her phone upstairs. No one ever called those lines, so she would know that they were for Remy when they rang.

Before leaving, she asked him to email her his schedule that way, she would be able to place appointments accordingly or reschedule them if need be. Remy told her he would and thanked her again before Alijah stepped onto the elevator. She was only in there a short while, considering Kieran's office was on the top floor, and Remy's was right below his. When she stepped off the elevator, she walked over to her desk, putting her belongings and the papers she'd gotten from Remy down.

Alijah could hear voices coming from Kieran's office. At first, she thought that he may have still been on the video call, but the door was open. He never conducted business meetings with the door open. From where her desk was, she could see into the office but couldn't see his desk because of where it was positioned in the room. She figured it was one of his friends. They stopped by sometimes, and he usually left the door open. She decided to speak to whichever one had dropped by.

As she got closer to the door, she could make out the voice. Going back to her desk, Alijah retrieved a ribbon from her purse, putting it around her hair and tying it away from her face. She then took her pumps off and headed back towards his office.

"Kieran, you don't have to pretend like you don't want this. That little girl isn't here. I know it's just fun for you." She heard Rebecca state.

"Rebecca-" She then heard Kieran start, only to be cut off.

"I know you miss me. The way we were together. The way you used to smack my ass when you hit it from the back. Don't you want to do that again?" Alijah heard Rebecca ask. She was sure the older woman was trying to be seductive.

"I'm positive he doesn't," Alijah stated as she stepped into his office. "But I'll smack the shit out of you." Two sets of eyes turned to look at her. "Didn't I tell you last time," Alijah started as she began to take her earrings off. "That the next time I saw you, I would whoop your ass?" She placed them down on Kieran's desk before taking off the rest of her jewelry and her watch, sitting them on his desk as well.

Alijah watched as Rebecca stood from where she sat and folded her arms across her chest. She was taller than Alijah was by at least six inches with her heels on, but Alijah didn't care.

"I'm not scared of you," Rebecca stated.

Alijah lifted a brow and smirked, wondering where all this bravado was the day of the yacht party. She was sure it was because Kieran was there, and Rebecca thought he wouldn't let Alijah do anything to her. Alijah didn't care that Kieran was there. If he got in her way, she would smack the shit out of him too.

She took steps toward Rebecca until she was only about a foot or so away. She had to give it to her. Even though Alijah could see she wanted to dart for the door, she stood her ground.

"I don't want you to be scared, bitch. I want you to be ready."

With that, Alijah let her hand fly and backhanded the shit out of Rebecca. She then caught her with a right to the jaw, and Rebecca stumbled back screaming. Alijah threw a left jab and hit her right in the nose. That sent Rebecca to the floor, and Alijah was instantly on her ass. She didn't believe in kicking people when they were down, but she did believe in letting her hands fly.

"Didn't I tell you I would whoop your ass?" Alijah questioned while still hitting her. "He's mine, you desperate hoe."

It was much like a parent whooping their child for something and scolding them because all the other woman could do was try to block the attack. She wasn't beating Rebecca's ass over Kieran, though. No, she was whooping her ass for the disrespect Rebecca threw her way at the party and the first time she'd come to the office.

A minute later, Alijah felt herself being lifted, but she was able to get in another hit. Even when she was in the air, being moved away from Rebecca, she still swung.

"Let go of me, Kieran," she demanded through gritted teeth trying to get free.

"Rebecca, I suggest you get your stuff and leave because if I let her go, it's just going to be a repeat," Kieran stated.

Alijah watched, pissed, as Rebecca quickly gathered her stuff and ran from the room. She was able to get out of Kieran's hold and was close on her heels when she felt him snatch her back up. He then closed the door that she had almost made it out of. Alijah whirled on him and slapped him when he let her go again.

She watched those hazel eyes turn cold before his hand went around her neck, and he pushed her back into the door none too gently, causing her to groan in pain.

Kieran groaned after getting off his video call with Lao. It had ended early, and for that, he was grateful. Though he had decided to work with the man, he was still intolerable at times. Buzzing Alijah, he waited for her to answer him. He had told her she could take a long lunch, but he wanted to see if she was back. She didn't answer, but that didn't mean anything. When people called her work cell phone, she couldn't always answer him right away.

Getting up from his desk, Kieran walked to his office door and opened it. He looked out to find that she was still gone. Kieran didn't have a problem with that. He had some emails he could respond to before he ordered lunch, and they went over expense reports when she got back.

He had just finished replying to the first email when he heard the elevator ding. He figured it was Alijah and that she would come in once she saw his door was open. Someone did step into his office a moment later, but it wasn't Alijah. When he saw who it was, he gritted his teeth. Apparently, it was destined for him to get a migraine — first Lao and now her.

"Leave, Rebecca," he told her before turning his attention to his computer screen, dismissing her. He watched out of the corner of his eye as she did the exact opposite and stepped farther into the office.

"She isn't here, Kieran. You don't have to pretend."

"I don't have to pretend not to want you around, Rebecca. That comes quite easily."

"Baby," Rebecca stated in the whining voice that used to irritate the hell out of him constantly. "You're letting your plaything come between us. I've allowed you to have your fun, but it will not ruin the family that we're trying to build."

Kieran looked at her. His left eye twitching. This bitch was crazy. There was no other explanation for it. He mildly wondered if she was this bat shit crazy when they dated and decided that she probably was. However, he had been more interested in what was between her legs than anything she ever did or said.

"I've never hit a woman before, Rebecca, but if you say anything else about Alijah...you'll be the first."

"Kieran, you don't have to pretend like you don't want this. That little girl isn't here. I know it's just fun for you." Rebecca stated.

"Rebecca-" He started firmly, but she cut in over him, cutting him off.

"I know you miss me. The way we were together. The way you used to smack my ass when you hit it from the back. Don't you want to do that again?"

Kieran knew she was trying to be seductive, but that was overshadowed at the moment as he tried to recall what ass she was talking about, but that was neither here nor there. He didn't get to muse in his thoughts long.

"I'm positive he doesn't." He heard Alijah state as she came into his office. "But I'll smack the shit out of you." He and Rebecca both turned to look at her. For some reason, her statement made his dick twitch. "Didn't I tell you last time," Alijah started as he watched her take her earrings off. "That the next time I saw you, I would whoop your ass?" She placed them down on his desk before taking off the rest of her jewelry and her watch. Sitting them on his desk as well and he mildly wondered why Rebecca hadn't tried to leave yet.

Kieran watched as Rebecca stood from where she sat and folded her arms across her chest. She was taller than Alijah, but Kieran knew that her height would not help her if it came to blows.

"I'm not scared of you," Rebecca stated.

Kieran wondered precisely how true that statement was. He could see the tense way she held herself, and the fact that she folded her arms across her chest meant that she was trying to guard herself a bit.

He watched as Alijah took steps towards Rebecca until she was only about a foot or so away. He was surprised Rebecca stood her ground. He was even more surprised that he was getting turned on at the prospect of Alijah beating her ass.

"I don't want you to be scared, bitch. I want you to be ready."

With that, Alijah let her hand fly and backhanded the shit out of Rebecca. She then caught her with a right to the jaw, and Rebecca stumbled back screaming. Alijah threw a left jab and hit her right in the nose. That sent Rebecca to the floor, and Alijah was instantly on her. With the way Alijah was beating Rebecca's ass, he mildly wondered if he should yell, *Finish her!* Because he had only seen this sort of ass beating in video games.

"Didn't I tell you I would whoop your ass?" Alijah questioned while still hitting her. "He's mine, you desperate hoe."

It reminded Kieran of the rare times he would get in trouble, and his mother would talk to him between spanking him. He hated that shit. It made the spanking last longer. However, he didn't mind this. His dick had been slowly hardening with each blow she had delivered, but it surged with blood at her declaration of claiming him and calling him hers. Yeah, he was about to bring a stop to this. He needed Alijah for something far more critical at the moment.

So, he lifted her off of Rebecca with an arm around her midsection. He held her off the ground with her back to his chest. She continued to swing and try to struggle, but he held her firm.

"Let go of me, Kieran," she demanded, trying to get free.

"Rebecca, I suggest you get your stuff and leave because if I let her go, it's just going to be a repeat," Kieran stated.

He watched as Rebecca quickly gathered her stuff and ran from the room. Alijah was able to get out of his hold, and he saw her dash after Rebecca. She was close on her heel; however, Kieran was faster and wrapped his arm around her waist again, pulling her backward. He then closed the door that she had almost made it out of. When he let her go again, Alijah whirled on him and slapped him with what felt like the strength of a thousand angry females.

His hazel eyes turned hard, and his hand was going around her throat before he knew what he was doing. He pushed her harder than he meant to back into the office door.

"I'm not, Rebecca." He hissed at her. "Don't put your hands on me."

"Then you shouldn't have tried to play captain save a hoe and let me continue beating her ass," Alijah stated before pushing him away from her. "Why was she in here anyway?"

Kieran stared down at her. Something was seriously wrong with him. When she slapped him, he had gotten pissed, yes, but now his dick was uncomfortably hard, and all he wanted to do was bury it inside of her. At that exact moment, his control broke.

Reaching out, he grabbed her by the neck again, pulling her to him. He molded his lips to hers and began to lead her in a harsh kiss. His other hand went down to hike her skirt up before ripping her panties away. She gasped, but he didn't release her. He then went about freeing himself from his boxers and pants. Kieran checked to see if she was wet enough for him to bypass foreplay. The entire time he punished her lips with his.

Removing his hand from around her neck, he picked her up and held her against the door. He then positioned himself at her entrance. With one hard thrust, he was seated balls deep inside of her. Alijah removed her lips from his, leaning her head back against the door and groaning.

Kieran didn't waste any time as he began to thrust in and out of her swiftly. Her back was hitting against the door, and he knew if anyone came down to see him, they would know exactly what he was doing to his little assistant, but he didn't care. He slid his dick in and out of her as she moaned without abandon.

After a few moments, he moved them away from the door and walked over to his desk. He removed himself from Alijah's pussy and sat her on her feet before turning her around. He bent her over his desk, pushing her skirt up to her hips, before bending his knees to reenter her. As he fucked her from behind, he slapped her ass, causing her to moan. He pounded into her, and she reached back, trying to push him away.

"Baby...wait," she groaned out.

Kieran grabbed the hand she had on him and then the other one, holding them hostage in one of his. He reached up with the other hand and laced his fingers through her hair, pulling her head back.

"You had to put your hands on me, right?" Kieran questioned, slamming into her hard, causing her to release a surprised moan. "I'm never going to put my hands on you in any way you don't like, baby, but I am going to murder this pussy." He then growled out.

He continued to slam into her over and over. Kieran was sure it was right at the precipice of what she could take. He angled his hips and hit a spot that had her trying to jerk her hands free from him. He wouldn't let her go.

"Stop trying to get away from me, baby," he told her, tightening his grip on her hair a bit. "You're going to take this dick," he commanded, but it wasn't exactly as if he gave her a choice.

"Kieran, please. I apologize." Alijah told him with a moan.

He released her hair then and smacked her ass hard. "It's too late for apologies."

He continued to fuck her, and he knew that she wanted to cum, but he was intentionally not letting her. He hadn't decided whether or not he would allow her to since she had hit him. His first thought was to deny her that pleasure. However, he enjoyed the way her walls felt when she came around his dick.

Reaching around with his free hand, he began to stroke her clit. He could feel his balls tightening, and he decided to let her cum.

"Cum for me," he demanded. "Cum all over my dick."

A few seconds later, he felt her walls tighten as her juices flowed from her. Kieran gave her four more strokes before he pulled out. He stroked his dick twice, and ropes of cum began to paint her caramel ass.

"Shit!" Kieran exclaimed as the last spurt of come left him. He released her hands then. "Stay there."

Going into the bathroom, he turned on the warm water before grabbing one of the towels and his shower gel. He then grabbed another towel that he planned on just wetting. Once he had everything ready, he walked back into his office to find, Alijah still lying across his desk, breathing hard. He smirked to himself. He cleaned her up and then himself as he watched her fix her skirt.

"I should punch you for pulling my hair like that," she told him with a glare.

Kieran wrapped his hand around his semi-erect dick and shook it at her. "Go ahead." He watched her stare at him a moment as she bit her lip.

"Put that away," she then stated.

Kieran threw the towels in one of the chairs and did as she asked. When he was done, he could still feel her staring at him.

"You didn't answer my question."

"What question?" Kieran inquired as he picked the towels up and took them back into the bathroom.

"Why was she here?"

He made his way back into this office and over to his desk; he shrugged his shoulders. "I don't know, baby, but she's looney as a fucking toon."

"I don't want her back here, Kieran. That woman irks me, and I may do more damage to her next time."

He beckoned her around the desk, and she came to him. He pulled her down into his lap and kissed her lips. They were a bit swollen from his earlier treatment.

"I'll take care of it," he told her after they had pulled apart. She went to get up, but he pulled her back down and took her chin between his thumb and forefinger. "You know I'd never hit you, baby, but seriously, don't put your hands on me again. Especially when I don't deserve it."

Alijah simply nodded at him, and Kieran leaned in to kiss her forehead before allowing her to get up. He watched her walk out of his office before picking up his phone and calling security. He would have them keep a close eye on everyone who came into the building and turn Rebecca away if she was stupid enough to return.

29

Kieran sat at the bar, sipping his scotch as he looked out over the people in attendance. It was his company's annual Christmas party. Typically, he would have come, made an appearance for about an hour, and then left. However, as his eyes found Alijah playing hostess, he knew that wouldn't be the case tonight. They had already been here for almost two hours.

Some of his employees had even looked at him strangely when they saw he hadn't left at the hour mark. He had merely ignored them. He knew how out of character it was for him. He didn't need their constant staring to remind him. Though they probably would have been doing that anyway.

When he had shown up at the party, it was with Alijah on his arm. Bringing his assistant anywhere with him wouldn't have been out of the norm. It was the fact that before she pulled away to thank the staff that was working the party that night, he had leaned down and kissed her on the lips.

He had done this for two reasons. The first being that he wanted to stake his claim on her for the men that were eye fucking her. For that, he almost couldn't blame them. She wore a long-sleeve, red lace dress with a split up the right side. The second reason was that he wanted to see if she had been serious a couple of months ago when she said she was done hiding their relationship.

Since then, they had gone out several times, but they hadn't been affectionate at work. These were the people she had been afraid of finding out. So, right there, he had put her on the spot.

After he'd kissed her, Alijah had given him that heart-stopping smile. Over the past few months, she had taken to wearing smudge-proof lipstick. She told him it was her way of making sure he didn't mess up her makeup when they were going out.

Kieran ordered another drink and was waiting for it when he heard his name called. Looking over, he found the manager of the hotel coming his way.

"Good evening, Mr. Cayman."

Kieran nodded. "Carmichael."

"I wanted to check-in and make sure everything was going smoothly."

"It is," Kieran responded, retrieving his drink from the bartender.

"Your wife seems to be enjoying herself, and people seem to be gravitating towards her." Carmichael then stated.

Kieran looked at the man and then followed his eyes to Alijah. She was with a small group of people from his technological department. He didn't know what was said, but it seemed as if they were laughing about something.

"Yes. She has that effect." Kieran responded, not correcting the man. Carmichael had seen them walk into the hotel together and knew that the man had simply assumed.

Carmichael stayed and spoke to Kieran for a few more minutes before leaving. He finished his drink and ordered a *White Russian* made with milk. As he waited, he surveyed the room, but his eyes stopped as he saw Alijah in the corner speaking to Trevor. This wasn't the first time he had seen them like this. He'd spotted them several times at the office together. Always as if they were having some secret discussion.

Kieran wasn't a jealous man. He firmly believed that if you were in a relationship with someone, there should be no cause for jealousy because your partner should not have given you one. However, he was sure that Trevor would take any opportunity he perceived, even if there wasn't one. Kieran decided to remind the young man that Alijah was taken.

Taking the drink from the bartender, he headed in their direction. He was within ten feet of them when Alijah looked up and saw him approaching. She smiled at him as he stopped in front of them.

"Here you go, baby. I thought you might want a drink," he told her, handing it to her.

"Thank you."

"Trevor." Kieran then greeted with a nod.

"Mr. Cayman."

It was quiet between the three of them as Kieran looked out over the ballroom for several moments. However, it didn't stay that way as Trevor broke the silence.

"So, about the New Year's party. You are coming. Right, Alijah?" The younger man questioned.

"I don't know, Trevor. I'm not sure how my schedule looks, but I'll let you know if we can make it," she responded.

Kieran looked at her and raised an eyebrow at her word choice. There was no way he was going to a party hosted by one of his employees. He wasn't meant to be their friend; he was their boss.

"W...yeah, okay," Trevor responded, changing course, but Kieran was sure he was going to question Alijah's word choice as well.

As a song that was finally not Christmas music came on, he watched as a few couples took to the dance floor. Turning his attention again to Alijah, he grabbed her drink from her hand and handed it to Trevor.

"Dance with me," he stated before taking her hand and pulling her towards the other dancing couples.

As they began to sway, he looked down into the green eyes looking up at him. Alijah's beautiful face housed a smirk. Kieran raised a brow.

"Were you jealous, Kieran?" She questioned him.

Kieran cocked his head slightly. "Did I need to be?"

She let out a small, soft laugh. "You're funny," she paused for a moment. "Then why did you want to dance? You don't do that, remember?"

It was Kieran's turn to smirk. "We're in a room full of people. It's the only way I can have your body pulled tightly against mine without it seeming inappropriate." That earned him an eye roll.

"Since the office is closed for the next two days, I thought we could make a gingerbread house," Alijah spoke, looking up at him.

Kieran groaned. "The condo already looks like a reindeer threw up in it and Santa Clause shit in it. It doesn't need anything else," he told her, thinking of how it currently looked like it belonged in some cheesy Christmas movie.

Alijah gasped, hitting his chest lightly. "It does not. It looks like it has some holiday cheer. You're just an old Scrooge," she told him.

Kieran leaned in and kissed her lips before whispering against them, "Ba-humbug."

"You're going to have them staring at us again."

He shrugged. "Let them stare. They may get a show," he stated, running a finger down her neck.

"You can't fuck me in public, Kieran," she told him.

He had been prepared for her to tell him that he couldn't feel her up in public. He would have then referred her back to her birthday weekend, where he had fingered her at *Mirage*. However, being as quick as he always was, he still had a comeback for her.

"Can't is subjective. I can fuck you in public, but I won't. At least not here," he told her. "But I will eventually." He tacked on casually. For this, he received another eye roll as they continued to dance.

Kieran felt a light weight settle across his waist. A moment later, he felt kisses on his neck and then a peck on his lips — first one and then another. By the third one, he was fully awake, opening his eyes slowly.

"Merry Christmas, baby," Alijah whispered against his lips.

Kieran flipped them over and buried his face in her neck. Trailing kisses along it. He reached a hand between them, snaking it down her body and dipping into her panties.

"Can I have this for Christmas?" He questioned, slipping a finger between her folds.

"Yes, but later. I'm making breakfast. So, go shower so you can eat."

"That's what I'm trying to do now," he informed her.

"Kieran," she groaned at him, exasperated.

"Fine." He conceded. He kissed her on the lips before removing his hand from her panties and sitting up. He placed his finger into his mouth as he got off the bed and headed into the bathroom.

"Hurry so the food won't get cold," she called from behind him.

After turning on the shower, Kieran went about brushing his teeth. When he finished, he stepped into the shower and washed his body. Getting out, he went into his room and pulled out a pair of sweatpants. Kieran figured they wouldn't be doing anything today since Alijah had been in one of his shirts.

Walking into the kitchen, he found her placing food on the bar. He took his usual seat, and when she came around and took hers, they began to eat in comfortable silence. Yesterday, there had been anything but silence. She had talked him into making not one but two gingerbread houses with her, and she had played Christmas music all day. He was happy that it wasn't the case today.

Once they were done eating, they cleaned the kitchen together before he watched her skip over to the tree that housed a few presents. He was starting to see that Christmas was her favorite time of year. Kieran sat on the couch and watched as she grabbed one and brought it to him. He had told her she didn't have to get him anything, but he couldn't be too upset that she hadn't listened. She had told him not to get her anything, but he'd just told her she was cute and did it anyway.

It was a long, slightly wide box. Kieran removed the wrapping paper from it before taking the lid off the box. Inside he found a slate gray *Hugo Boss* suit. It was nice. He didn't have one in that color and liked it. Sitting the box aside, he leaned over to kiss her.

"Thank you, baby," he told her he'd be right back before heading to his office.

One of the presents he had gotten her was rather large, and it wouldn't fit under the tree. So, he had hidden it in his

• • •
297

office to ensure she didn't stumble upon it. He hadn't bothered to wrap it, just placed a bow on it.

Going back into the living room, he found her sitting in the spot he'd left her in. When her eyes landed on him and then the item he was holding, they widened, and she shot off the couch over to him. She inspected the box at his side before leaping onto him and wrapping her legs around his waist. Placing kisses on his lips in between her chanting "thank you."

Kieran chuckled, propping the easel box against the wall. He had seen her reaction to her birthday gift from her friends and had seen two of her paintings. She was talented. So, he decided to get her a new easel. He had done some research and had concluded that this was one of the better ones. He had his doubts about it at first because it was only four grand, but after extensive research, it was confirmed.

Carrying her back over to the couch, Kieran sat down with her still straddling him. He had two other gifts for her but decided they could wait for now. However, she didn't seem to be in the waiting mood.

Getting off of his lap, she headed back over to the tree and handed him another box. This one was small. Taking it from her, he took the wrapping off of it. He knew exactly what it was before he opened the box. However, he was stunned by the designer.

"Alijah," he stated in a stern tone.

"You don't like it?" She questioned, worrying her bottom lip.

It wasn't that he didn't like it because he did. It was the fact that he knew she spent far too much money on it. He didn't mind spending an obscene amount of money on her because he knew she would appreciate it. He didn't want her doing the same, even though he also appreciated the gift.

"If you don't like it. We can take it back and get you a different one," she informed him, trying to take the *Rolex* from his hand.

"No, baby. It's perfect. I love it. It's just...I wish you hadn't spent so much money."

She rolled her eyes at him. "I'm positive I'm the only personal assistant in Colorado that makes six figures. I don't spend it on anything but canvasses and personal items. I wanted to get you something nice," she told him. Again, he kissed her.

When he got up, he went to the tree to get her other two presents. He gave her the bigger one and watched her open it. It was a display for all of her paints and would hold up to one hundred different ones. He then gave her the smaller box. When she opened it, Kieran watched her eyes widen and listened to her gasp before she pulled the two-carat diamond necklace from the box.

"This is beautiful, Kieran," she told him.

"I wanted to get you something as beautiful as you. I couldn't find anything. So, I settled for this," he told her, causing her to smile.

"How much did you pay for this?"

"I'm not telling you, and even if I did, I'm not taking it back either way." However, he had only spent about twenty-two thousand on it.

She glared at him playfully before leaning in and kissing him. He immediately deepened the kiss and pulled her onto his lap. His hand went under the shirt that she was wearing, and he cupped one of her breasts as she began to grind on him slowly. He was about to remove her shirt when he heard beeping. It was coming from the screen by his front door. Someone was requesting access to his floor. Furrowing his brow, he sat Alijah on the couch and got up.

"What is it?" he questioned after pulling up the camera and seeing a young man standing there.

"I have a delivery for you."

Kieran raised a brow. "On Christmas Day."

The young man nodded. "My boss is a dick."

Kieran snorted. "Sit it down and get out of the elevator. I'll sign for it and send the slip back to you."

While Kieran knew there were indeed some courier services that worked on the holidays, he wasn't going to take any chances. Especially with Alijah here with him.

After getting the package and sending the signed slip back down, he went back into the condo. Alijah was coming out of the kitchen, and he noticed that the wrapping paper had been cleaned up. She looked at the box covered in wrapping paper in his hand.

"Who's it from?"

"It doesn't say," he responded as he headed back over to the couch with her behind him.

Sitting down, he unwrapped it before opening the box. Inside he found a videotape. It was an old one. The label was peeling off, and the writing was starting to fade. It was writing that seemed vaguely familiar to him, but he couldn't place it at the moment. He picked it up from the box, and there was a card under it that read, Watch Me.

Alijah took the tape from his hands, and he watched as she walked over to the DVD/Blu-ray/VHS combo. It was the only reason he had one. He turned the television on with the remote and put it on the right channel as she placed it in.

It took a moment, and he thought it wouldn't play, but then a face he hadn't seen in over a decade popped onto the screen. It was his mother, Kira, seated in a chair. He then heard a voice he hadn't heard in the same amount of time as a masked figure stepped into view. It was his father, Maverick.

"Is it on?" Maverick questioned as he looked at the person behind the video camera. The camera bobbed slightly as they nodded. "Hello, old man Atworth. By now, you've probably noticed that your daughter is missing. However, I'm sure you've only informed your private security and not the police. After all, how bad would it look if Bronson Atworth couldn't keep his daughter safe."

The camera panned over to Kira, seated in a chair, arms tied behind it and a gag in her mouth. She was crying, and it was clear that she was frightened. It was only for a moment before it went back to Maverick.

"So, here's what's going to happen. You will bring one hundred thousand dollars to the address left with this tape on Friday at noon. Come alone. Your daughter's life depends on it. Once we're at a safe distance, we'll tell you where you can pick up your beloved daughter. Don't do anything stupid, Atworth. Her very life depends on it."

The camera panned to Kira again, and the gag was taken out of her mouth.

"Daddy, please! Just do what they say. I don't want to die here!"

With that, the camera cut off, and the video stopped. Kieran was filled with several different emotions. He was confused, hurt, and overall angry. Kieran wanted nothing more than to get answers from his parents, but that was impossible. At the same time, he wanted to track his mother's sperm donor down and strangle the old man. He had been having a lovely Christmas with Alijah, and the old man had ruined it.

Standing up abruptly, Kieran made his way to his bedroom, trying to put the pieces together. His father had kidnapped his mother, but they had ended up together. Was his mother part of the blackmail plot? She had seemed genuinely scared, and Kieran had never thought she was the best actress growing up. Something had happened; he just didn't know what.

Alijah sat in silence with Kieran and watched the video. She was confused about why someone would send him this on Christmas and its relevance. However, when the camera panned to the woman again. This time staying on her a bit longer, she knew why. That was his mother. She had seen the few pictures he had around of her and his father. But why would someone want him to see this? What was the point?

At that moment, Kieran stood suddenly and walked from the living room. Her breath hitched slightly as something came to her, and she hoped it wasn't true. The man in the mask...was it Kieran's dad?

Shaking her head, Alijah stood to go after him, knocking the box the tape had come in down. Looking down, she saw that the note from inside had fallen out and there was something written on the back. She picked it up. *Now, you know all about your father, dear cousin. If you care to discuss it, call me.* There was a number at the bottom. So, she was right. It was his dad.

Alijah studied the note. She knew from Kieran that his mother was an only child, so maybe his grandfather was their uncle. She could only guess it was a child of one of Bronson's siblings. She only hesitated a moment before deciding to take the note to Kieran.

When she walked into the bedroom, she found him pacing. His jaw was clenched, and his eyes screamed murder.

"Baby," she called softly.

His attention snapped to her, and Alijah had to stop herself from taking a step back. She hated when his eyes took on that hard look because it meant he was genuinely pissed off, and she never liked being on the receiving end of it, even when she wasn't the one to cause it.

Reaching out, he grabbed the front of her shirt and yanked her to him. In an instant, Alijah felt his lips on hers. His kiss was harsh, and he held complete dominance, and all she could do was follow his lead. His hand snaked into her panties, and Alijah moaned as he slid one of his fingers between her folds.

Then, before she could truly comprehend what was happening, he had ripped her panties and thrown her on the bed. She bounced slightly, but he covered her instantly with his face in her neck. She could feel the mushroomed head of his dick at her entrance, but she wasn't sure if she was wet enough for him to penetrate.

"Kier-" She was cut off by him slamming his dick balls deep into her. "Ahhh!" She screamed out.

Kieran pulled his face from her neck and looked at her. Alijah could see the exact moment he was broken from his anger.

"Shit." He cursed, slowly pulling from her. "I'm sorry, baby." He apologized as Alijah watched him drop to his knees between her legs.

She felt him spread her lips gently as he inspected to see if he'd torn her. She didn't think he had, but she knew he wouldn't just take her word for it.

"Damn it." She heard him mumble.

She watched as he got up and headed into the bathroom. She could hear the water in the tub begin to run. A few minutes later, she smelled Cherry Blossom. He came back in and took her shirt off of her. Carrying her into the bathroom, he gently placed her in the tub. She felt a slight sting, like when you got a paper cut and concluded that he must have torn her a little. He leaned in and kissed her. His lips gently moved against her.

"I'm going to go to the gym and work out some of this anger," he stated against her lips.

Alijah gave him a peck. "Work it out on me," she responded.

Kieran shook his head. "I'll hurt you, and then I'll hate myself more than I do now for tearing you." He kissed her forehead. "Relax. I'll be back in a little while."

With that, Alijah watched him walk from the bathroom. She slid down further into the water and did what he asked, and relaxed. The hot water soothed her, and the smell of Cherry Blossom relaxed her. She had showered before she started breakfast that morning, so she didn't technically need another bath but figured she would take one either way.

She stayed in the water until it turned to lurk warm. She pulled the stopper and grabbed a fluffy black towel wrapping it around her body when it did. She dried off and went back into the bedroom. Going into one of Kieran's drawers, she grabbed one of his t-shirts before throwing the towel into the hamper.

Alijah was heading towards the door to put up their presents when she saw the note she had come to show him. She must have dropped it when he'd pulled her in for a kiss. Picking it up, she looked at it momentarily before going to the nightstand and grabbing her phone. She didn't hesitate to call the number. Kieran would be mad when he found out, but at the moment, she was more concerned with the person who had just answered the phone.

"This is Charles."

"Charles," Alijah repeated. "Would you happen to be related to Bronson Atworth?" She then questioned. She needed to make sure this was the right person.

"Yes. He's my uncle. Why? Is he alright? Did something happen?"

"No. I'm assuming he's fine. I've called for another reason." She only paused for half a second. "You sent a videotape to Kieran Cayman today." There was silence on the other end of the phone, and Alijah had to look at hers to make sure he hadn't hung up.

"Who is this?" He asked after a moment.

"Who I am is of no concern. Did you, or did you not send a tape to Kieran?"

"If I did?"

Alijah nodded to herself. "Why would you do that?"

"Because he needed to know that his father isn't the saint he makes him out to be. For years my uncle has been trying to have a relationship with that stubborn boy. It hurts him that his only grandchild hates him without even knowing what truly happened. My uncle is an old man, and though he's in peak health right now, he may not always stay that way. He wasn't going to tell the boy the real reason he didn't like the man. So, I did it for him. That arrogant little bastard needed to be knocked off his high horse."

"How. Dare. You." Alijah stated through clenched teeth.

It wasn't that she didn't see that the man was trying to help his uncle's relationship with Kieran or move it in the right direction, because she did. She had tried to do the same thing while pushing dinner on him, knowing that it wasn't her place to interfere. She would have never done something like this. Charles had gone about it the wrong way, and it was far worse than what she had done.

"This was not the time for you to do that. Of all days, you chose Christmas. A day where happiness is supposed to rule. You took that from him today. And for what reason?"

Charles didn't answer, and there was silence for a while. She heard the front door open and knew that Kieran was back from the gym.

"I have to go," she stated into the phone before ending the call and placing the phone back on the bedside table.

A moment later, Kieran walked in. He was covered in sweat and headed straight to the shower, and Alijah slid the note under her pillow. Getting up, she headed into the living room to finish putting things away before starting their Christmas dinner. She didn't plan on cooking anything too fancy, so she hadn't started the night before as her mother often did at home. She was making Cornish Hens with potatoes, asparagus, mac-n-cheese, and a salad.

As she cooked, she rearranged her plans. She was going to take the gifts she'd bought for Lawrence, Gale, Layla, and Gemma and deliver them. However, she didn't want to leave Kieran, so she decided to do it tomorrow. She had already mailed all of the other presents she had bought.

Going about the task at hand, Alijah tried to figure out the best time to tell Kieran about the note and that she had called Charles.

"Kieran," Alijah called later that night as they lay in the bed together.

"Yeah, baby?"

"About the videotape-"

"I don't want to talk about it," he stated, cutting her off. "If that old man wasn't dead to me before, he is now."

Alijah sighed, getting off of his chest; she turned and retrieved the note from under her pillow before handing it to him. She watched as he read it, and his jaw began to tick. She didn't want to make him any more upset, but she wasn't about to keep the fact that she called the number from him either.

"I also called the number."

Kieran sat up and looked at her while she pulled her bottom lip into her mouth. Alijah watched as he reached up and gently pulled it from between her teeth.

"So was it Charles or Alexander. I'm going to go with Charles. Alexander is too much of a pussy." Alijah gave him a shocked look. "I'm well aware of my cousins. I just don't speak to them."

"It was Charles. He-"

"I don't care what he said." He cut her off, tossing the note onto the side table. He lay back down, pulling her back onto his chest.

"Your gran…Bronson didn't want you-"

"We're not talking about this."

She nodded against his chest. "Okay." It was silent for a moment until he called her name.

"Alijah."

"Yeah?" She questioned. She sat up on her elbow to look at him when he didn't say anything. His eyes met hers.

"I lo..." He cut himself off and paused. "I lost control earlier, and I hurt you in my anger. I'm sorry. I should have apologized before now.

Alijah cocked her head at him and studied him for a moment. She couldn't put her finger on it, but he seemed off. Like he was holding back something. She chalked it up to the fact that he was still pretty upset and was trying to hold it in and stop her from seeing it.

"It's okay. I forgive you." She kissed his lips before laying back on his chest.

She felt him move, and the lamp was turned off a moment later. He wrapped both arms around her and held her tightly, and Alijah wondered if he knew what he had done to her. Even with all of his rough exterior, the way he had made her fall.

30

Alijah sat on the couch with Gale as the older woman told her about another charity event she had planned for Valentine's Day the following month and asked if Alijah would participate. They were going to be auctioning dates with a few of the women from her circle, and she wanted Alijah to be one of them. However, Alijah wasn't so sure.

"Come on. It'll be fun. Besides, you know Kieran isn't going to let anyone outbid him," she finished with a small laugh.

Alijah smiled at her. "You have a point there. I suppose it would be alright. I want to run it by Kieran first, though."

Gale nodded, understanding. "Absolutely."

They continued talking about where the event would be held and the number of women Gale was hoping to get to participate. She already had six. Seven if Alijah was able to help her out. She told Alijah she was even planning on asking Layla and Gemma. The money she raised at this event was going to Domestic Violence Prevention.

"Oh, that reminds me. I saw you on the cover of a magazine." Gale stated.

It took Alijah a moment to realize that she must have seen the spread that she'd done with Erin. "Yeah, the tattoo artist on the cover is my best friend. She's done all of my tattoos and asked me to model for her."

"You both looked gorgeous. The cover photo was magnificent. I bought the magazine and flipped through all of the pictures in the spread. The photographer who took them is very talented. I have a job position for one at my magazine. You wouldn't happen to know the photographer or have their contact information, would you?" Gale questioned.

Alijah thought for a moment. This could be an excellent opportunity for Chayse. However, she didn't want to tell Gale that Chayse was her cousin. If Chayse was to get the job, she wanted her to do it on her own merit; because she was talented and not because they were related, and Alijah and Gale had become friends. So, instead of giving Gale Chayse's number, she opted for something else.

"Her name is Chayse Moret. She has a website. I'll write it down for you."

"Just text it to me. I may lose it if you write it down."

"Of course."

Alijah rose from her seat and headed into the kitchen. She and Gale had gone out to lunch and did a bit of shopping before heading back to the condo. It was a little after four, and Alijah decided to pour them a glass of wine. Once she had done so, she headed back into the living room and handed one to Gale. Only to have the older woman sit it on a coaster on the table.

"I'm sorry. I should have asked if you like red wine." Alijah stated, resuming her seat.

"Oh no. I love it. I just won't be drinking it for a while." Gale pulled something from her purse and handed it to Alijah.

Taking it, Alijah looked down and saw that it was a sonogram. She placed her wine glass on the table before moving over to hug Gale with a smile on her face as she congratulated her. She was happy for her. She knew from Layla, who sometimes had trouble holding water, that Gale and Corey had been trying to have a baby for years with no luck and that Gale was very close to giving up. She had told Layla that she would give up and possibly adopt if she weren't pregnant by her fortieth birthday. Considering that she would be turning forty over the summer, Alijah was glad that she'd been blessed.

"Does Corey know?" Alijah questioned, pulling away and handing the sonogram back.

Gale shook her head. "No. His birthday is next week, and I plan on surprising him and telling him then."

"I'm sure he's going to be excited."

For the next hour, Gale talked to Alijah about how excited she was. Alijah was the third person she told. Her parents were the first two. It didn't take much to see how excited Gale was. She had even asked Alijah to do a painting of her and Corey when she started showing. Agreeing to it, Alijah told her that whenever she was ready, she would be available for her.

After talking for a bit longer, Alijah walked Gale to the door before going into her bedroom. She was in the mood to paint. She set up her new easel and took out all her materials before opening the window. The cold January air filtered in, but she didn't mind. The weather was calling for snow in the next few days, and she was more than excited for it to start. She had plans on painting after it had blanketed the city as well.

For the next two hours, Alijah painted before looking over at the clock on the bedside table. She saw it was a little after seven and jumped up. Going into the bathroom, she started the shower. She went back into the bedroom and to her closet as it ran. She had made dinner plans with Lawrence, and since Kieran was working, she wasn't going to cook even though it was a Saturday.

Once she had decided on a pair of cream-colored skinny jeans, a mint light sweater, and her black boots, she took out her underwear and laid it on the bed before going back into the bathroom. Stripping out of her clothes, she stepped into the shower to clean herself and rid her hands of paint.

When she finished her shower, Alijah got dressed before taming her wild curls. She grabbed her coat and headed out of her bedroom. She got on her Uber app and arranged one before ensuring she had everything and going down to the lobby to wait.

It wasn't long before the car pulled up, and she told them where she wanted to go. She paid the young woman, tipped her, and headed inside the restaurant when they arrived. She immediately saw Lawrence sitting by the window and made her way over to him.

"Hey," she greeted, taking the seat across from him.

"Hey, Lioness." Lawrence returned, and Alijah rolled her eyes at him. "I already ordered drinks." He then informed her.

"Thanks. So..." Alijah trailed off.

"So what?"

"Don't play with me. Did you get the promotion?" Alijah questioned.

Lawrence had informed her that he was up for a promotion at the end of December. It was between him and a woman that worked in his department. Alijah had told him she was sure he would get it, but he hadn't been so sure. So, being the good friend that she was, she had given him a pep talk.

"You are looking at the new Assistant Director of Sales for Global Technologies!" He responded with a smile.

"Congratulations!" Alijah stated, genuinely excited for her friend. "I told you, you would get the job."

The waitress came at that moment and delivered their drinks. The two then placed their orders, having visited the restaurant so much that they didn't need to look at the menu.

Once their orders were placed, Alijah inquired about his new job. Lawrence gave her the rundown and told her that he made a nice commission for each patent or product he was personally involved in selling. As she listened to him list a few of the upcoming things they were going to be pushing soon, she made a mental note of a few that she thought Kieran might be interested in.

When the waitress brought out their food, they ordered another round of drinks and continued to talk as they ate. She told him about the event Gale was planning, and he asked her where it was and what time because he wanted to come and bid on a date as well. However, when Alijah told him that no men were being auctioned off, he scrunched his face and retracted his interest.

When they finished their food, they had one more round of drinks as Alijah asked him if he was seeing anybody. The look he gave her said it all.

"We can't all be dicked down by a Greek god every night. Who happens to be rich."

"Aww." Alijah started sympathetically. "Your boyfriend's not rich?" She joked playfully.

"Shut up, Lioness."

After they finished their drinks, they played rock paper scissors to see who would pay. It was something they came up with back in college when they would argue about who was picking up the tab. Lawrence lost, and Alijah watched him put down enough cash to pay the waitress and leave a tip. They then put on their coats and headed for the door.

"Did you drive here?" Lawrence questioned.

Alijah shook her head. "No, I took an Uber."

He nodded. "Come on. I'll drop you off."

When they were in the car headed to the condo, "Children's Story" by Slick Rick came on, and Alijah began rapping along with it.

"Once upon a time, not long ago, when people wore pajamas and lived life slow."

Lawrence joined in. "When laws were stern, and justice stood, and people were behaving like they ought to should."

"There lived a little boy who was misled by another little boy, and this is what he said,"

They continued singing along with the song and then the next three that came on the radio before they pulled up to the condo. Alijah turned to Lawrence and thanked him for the ride.

"You want me to walk you up?" He questioned.

"No, I'll be fine. Text me when you make it home," she told him. "Goodnight."

"Night, Lioness."

Alijah rolled her eyes as she got out of the car closing the door. She walked into the building and waved to the man sitting at the front desk. It was almost eleven, but she knew he would be there until midnight.

She slipped her key card into the slot to access the top floor, getting onto the elevator. She took the ride up, and for some reason, it seemed longer than usual, but she chalked it up to the fact that she'd had a few drinks and was tired.

Once off the elevator, she put her key into the lock and opened the door, walking inside. She turned, closing the door behind her, and when she turned back around, she was met with Kieran's cold hazel eyes. Something was wrong.

"Baby, what's-"

"Don't fucking 'baby' me, Alijah." He snapped at her, and she clenched her jaw, trying her best not to lose it. Both of them pissed wouldn't solve whatever the hell was wrong. She was about to ask him what that was when he threw something at her feet. "What the fuck is that?" He questioned.

Reaching down, she picked it up and saw that it was Gale's sonogram. She must have forgotten it after she had shown it to Alijah. However, she didn't know why Kieran was so mad. Unless...unless he thought it was hers.

Kieran stood in front of the heavy mahogany door staring at it. It was the same thing he had been doing for the past five minutes. He had thought about turning around and leaving several times, but he'd already come this far, and he had never been a quitter in his life. So, he wasn't about to start now. *But you could*, his subconscious told him. Kieran shook his head before raising his hand and ringing the doorbell before he talked himself out of it.

A moment later, he heard footsteps on the other side. The door opened, and a woman who seemed to be a few years older than him stood before him. She looked at him for a moment when what he thought was recognition flashed in her eyes before moving aside and letting him in.

He mildly wondered if this was something she did often. He could be a murderer there to kill everyone for all she knew. Regardless of whether or not she seemed to recognize him, he was sure he had never seen this woman a day in his life. He was about to tell her why he was there when a voice floated over to him.

"Kieran?" They questioned, puzzled.

Looking over to where the voice originated from, he saw him standing at the opening of the hallway. "Bronson," he returned.

The two men stared at each other for a moment, and Kieran was only slightly aware that the woman was leaving the room. Yet, still, when they were utterly alone, neither one of them spoke.

Several minutes had ticked by, and Kieran started to regret coming if all they were going to do was stare at each other. He had come with a purpose. He needed answers, and he knew that Bronson was the only person that could give them to him.

"Come on. We can go to my office and talk." Bronson stated as if reading his mind.

Nodding curtly, Kieran followed him down the hallway and into his office. He took a seat in front of the desk as Bronson closed the door behind them before sitting on the opposite side. Again, they lapsed into silence as they stared at one another.

"Forgive me. It's just that I never thought you would come here." Bronson told him.

"Well, I wouldn't have, but Charles decided there were some things I needed to know, and now I need some answers." Kieran bit out, still pissed by the video he had received almost a month ago now on Christmas Day.

Bronson sighed. "I apologize that you had to find any of that out. Especially the way you did. Charles had no right." Bronson told him. Kieran was silent. "I didn't want you to know. I didn't want to taint your image of your father as deeply as I thought that video would. I just wanted you to know he wasn't the saint you made him out to be. I wanted to get past that to have a relationship with my only grandchild, the only connection I had left to my little girl."

Still, Kieran remained silent. He wasn't sure if he should believe him or not, but when he had calmed down enough about a week later, he'd asked Alijah about her conversation with Charles, and she had told him that he said Bronson didn't want Kieran to know, that he wasn't going to tell him. However, he was going to give him the benefit of the doubt at the moment.

"I have some questions. I want honest answers," he told the older man.

"I'll answer whatever I can."

"Did my dad kidnap my mom?"

"If you're asking if he was the one who grabbed her, I don't know, but yes. He was a part of the group that kidnapped her.

"Why?"

"For money. At the end of the day, that's what it boiled down to."

"If he kidnapped her, then why...how did they fall in love?"

Bronson sighed. "I don't know. All I know is that Kira told me that he was kind to her. She saw something in his eyes that told her he was much more than what he was doing. She felt like there was another person in him."

Kieran took those words in and let them marinate. He could understand what his mother was talking about. It was, essentially, the same thing with him and Alijah. He was an asshole to the entire world, but she saw a different side of him. She got to see him with his guard down, when he was vulnerable. He was sure she had seen it even before he let her in.

"If you knew she loved him and you saw him doing better for her, for them, then..."

"It's hard to accept someone that had a hand in almost harming the most precious thing in the world to you. Yes, I suppose I could have tolerated Maverick, but every time I looked at him, all I saw was one of the men that held my daughter hostage. That's a hard slight to get over."

Though Kieran could understand that his loyalty to his father ran deep. While he knew it was him in the video, he had watched it several times to make sure he was having a hard time accepting it. Just like Bronson couldn't get past what his father had done to his mother, Kieran couldn't get past the fact that he had worked hard to give Kieran the best life he could.

What he needed were more answers. Then he remembered that he often saw his mother write in journals as he was growing up. He had packed their things into storage after they had passed and made a mental note to go and dig out her old journals. He hoped that maybe she would have written anything in there to shed some more light on the situation.

"I know this isn't going to be easy, and many years have passed, but I hope this can be a tipping point for us in the right direction," Bronson spoke, pulling Kieran from his thoughts.

He looked at the old man who had contributed his sperm for his mother's creation — in turn, making it possible for Kieran to be born. Because had it not been for the man sitting in front of him, he may not have had the life he was currently living. He may not have had the woman who captured his heart and held it tightly. However, he was forever the hard-ass.

"Perhaps," he stated, rising from his seat, and leaving out of the office. He needed to process.

Showing himself out, Kieran got in his car and headed back to the condo. It was a little after eight. He had gotten up and went into the office to do some work. Usually, he would have done it from home, but there were a few documents that had been left at the office.

He knew Alijah wouldn't be there when he arrived. She had sent him a text telling him that she would be going out to dinner with her friend Lawrence. He made a mental note to have her introduce him to the man soon. He wanted to know who he was if he would be spending so much time with his woman, regardless of the fact that they had known each other a lot longer than Kieran had been in her life.

Pulling into a Chinese restaurant, Kieran ordered some food. Once he paid for it, he continued on his way. He figured it would be best to pick something up because he was sure there were no leftovers from the baked chicken Alijah had cooked the night before.

Whipping his car into his parking space in the garage, he grabbed his food, got out of the car, and stepped onto the elevator. He accessed his floor and rode it up. When he made it inside, he headed into the kitchen to get a plate. He fixed his food, grabbing a beer before heading down the hall to his office. He had a conference call with some potential clients in Australia at nine his time. Considering they were seventeen hours ahead of him, it was three p.m. Sunday afternoon there.

He waited for the phone to ring. He answered it on speaker and muted himself as he ate and listened to their proposal. It wasn't bad, but he wanted to see the product in person. He told them as much and stated that he would have his assistant call them when they found time in their schedule.

After hanging up, he made a mental note to have Alijah do that, wondering if she had ever been to Australia. If she hadn't, he would carve out an extra two days so she could see some sights since they were going to Sydney.

Taking his plate back into the kitchen along with the empty beer bottle, he placed it in the dishwasher before rinsing the bottle and putting it into the designated recycle bin that Alijah had gotten.

Going over to the couch, Kieran sat down after grabbing the remote from the table. He was about to turn it on when something on the couch caught his attention. It didn't take him but a moment to realize what it was, and he was pissed. *What the fuck!*

Kieran had been pacing back and forth for the last half hour, seething in his anger. He had tried to calm down, but he honestly couldn't. He had never in his life felt so betrayed...so hurt. It was because of that, that his anger seemed to be boiling. However, he was proud of himself because he hadn't destroyed anything around him, but he knew that was subject to change. He heard the sound of the elevator accessing his floor. Clenching his fist, he tried to get it together but knew it was a lost cause.

Going down the hall, he saw Alijah closing the door with her back to him. She stopped dead in her tracks when she turned around, and Kieran knew his eyes were screaming murder. He needed them to because there was no way he would allow them to portray the hurt that he felt.

"Baby, what's-"

But he cut her off. "Don't fucking 'baby' me, Alijah. What the fuck is that?" He questioned after tossing the picture at her feet.

He watched as she reached down and picked it up, examining it before looking back at him. He had expected to see shock in her eyes because he had found out or even remorse, but he saw neither of those. Instead, she placed it on the side table by the door.

"It's a sonogram, Kieran," she informed him calmly.

"I know what the fuck it is, Alijah!" He snapped at her. "Why would you do that to me? You said you were taking your pills. I believed you."

"Kieran, I-"

"Rebecca was right, and I was so stupid." Kieran continued. "I told her you were better than that. I told her you wouldn't trap me like that, wouldn't do that to me."

"Rebecca?!" Alijah questioned, drawing his attention. "What the hell does that crazy bitch have to do with anything?"

"She may be crazy, but at least she didn't get pregnant on purpose to trap me."

"Trap you!" Alijah exclaimed, and Kieran saw the moment those green eyes sparked. They were about to go to war. "I'm not trying to trap you, Kieran. I have no reason to do that. Contrary to what you may believe, you are not the only man in the world, and I can walk into any room and pull one," she told him. Kieran opened his mouth to say something, but she cut him off. "Shut up!" She snapped. "How dare you insinuate that I was only with you to trap you. If I wanted to do that, I had plenty of opportunities. That's not even mine. If you would have calmed down enough to look at it, really look at it, you would have seen Gale's name on it," she finished.

Kieran was still as she stormed off past him, and a minute later, he heard a door slam. He replayed her words in his head before picking up the sonogram and looking at it. Sure enough, it had Gale Wexler's name on it. His heart sank. He was such a fucking idiot. He had been so enraged when he saw it. He hadn't even looked to see whose name was on it. He had just assumed it was Alijah's.

He sat it back on the table and ran his hand down his face. He had tried to let Rebecca's words a few months back leave his mind once he had reassured himself that Alijah wouldn't do that to him. However, it seemed that somewhere, they had lodged themselves there. Just waiting for the moment to spill from his lips as they just had.

Going down the hall into his bedroom, Kieran went straight into his bathroom and started the water in the tub. He added some bubbles before lighting some candles. Kieran placed his phone on the dock by the sink and began to play some soft music. He knew he needed to apologize, and this was the best way for him to start.

Once the tub was filled, he headed out of the bathroom, intending to knock on Alijah's door and coax her out. However, when he got to the opening of his bedroom, he saw her wheeling a suitcase toward the door. His heartbeat escalated as he quickly walked down the hall towards her.

"Baby-"

"Don't 'baby' me, Kieran," she stated, turning his words against him.

"Where are you going?"

"I'm leaving," she stated simply.

Kieran felt as if there was a weight pressing down on his chest. For a second, he forgot how to breathe. He reached out and grabbed her arm, only for her to snatch it away.

"I'm sorr-"

"No!" Alijah snapped, cutting him off. "You don't get to be sorry. This isn't something that can be fixed with an apology. You accused me of trying to trap you. You called my character and my integrity into question, Kieran. It's like you don't know me at all. We've spent all this time together and shared so many things, yet you honestly thought I would do that to you. What makes it worse is that you let that bitch convince you that it was something I would do. You shouldn't have even entertained a conversation about us with her."

"Baby, I didn't-"

"You did, and you allowed her into our relationship when you let her taint your image of me because that's exactly what you did. You allowed her to win. She achieved one of her goals, and that was tearing us apart. I could have almost forgiven you for your assumptions because I understand you may have had to deal with that before, but I'm not going to do this with you. Any misgivings you should have brought to me. You should have talked to me when she planted those seeds of doubt in your mind. The same way I did when she showed up at your office. The same way I did when I told you I had a conversation with Charles. This shows that I was far too trusting and more invested in what we had than you."

Kieran couldn't speak. There were so many things he could have told her. So many things he could have said. One, in particular, he could have confessed, but his throat was thick, and his chest felt as if it was cracking. A feeling he hadn't felt since the day he was informed of his parent's accident. He was unable to move, and all he could do was watch her walk out of the door.

"I'll email you my resignation," she informed him before closing the door.

Kieran stood there looking at the door she had just left out, then it hit him. That final blow felt almost physical, and it sent him stumbling backward. She had gutted him and left him to bleed out on a battlefield he had created with his assumptions. He placed his hand over his heart, but he was sure he wouldn't feel it beating. His chest was void because the woman he loved had ripped it from him and walked out of the door with it.

It was after midnight as Alijah banged on the apartment door. A minute later, it swung open, and Lawrence stood there in a pair of sweatpants.

"Lioness, what's wrong?" He questioned. Then he noticed the suitcase she rolled behind her. Stepping aside, he allowed her to walk in. "What happened?" He asked, closing the door behind her.

"I really don't want to talk about it tonight. I just want to sleep," she told him as she turned to look at him. She could see that he wanted to protest but instead nodded.

Turning, she headed down the hall to the room she occupied when she had first moved in with him. She rolled her suitcase over to the closet placing it inside. She had only grabbed a few things for the week but decided she would go back one day while he was at work and get the rest of her things.

She saw Lawrence standing at the door when she sat down on her bed. He didn't say anything, just stared at her for several seconds before wishing her goodnight and closing her door.

Standing up, Alijah undressed and changed into a tank top and some sleeping shorts. She was hurt, and all she wanted to do was feel numb. She couldn't believe that he would accuse her of something like that. She had never given him any reason to doubt her honesty, yet he'd let that bitch get inside his head. Worst still, he hadn't even talked to her about it. Yes, she would have been hurt at the time, but she would have gotten over it because he had brought it to her to talk it out.

Instead, he'd kept it from her. Let it simmer in the back of his mind, and at the first opportunity, he had accused her. It was like he didn't know her at all. She had no reason to want to trap him. Hell, she already had him, and he wasn't the only man in the world. If she was the type of woman to merely want a man with money, she could date several men from his company who gave her the eye before finding out that she and Kieran were dating. Hell, and those that still did after they knew.

She had wanted to break something and throw things at him, but that had never been her style. She had never let a man push her to the point of doing something like that. Hell, she had even wanted to hit him, but she had remembered what happened when she slapped him after whooping Becky's ass and opted against it.

Slipping into bed, Alijah slid under the covers and curled into a ball, wrapping her arms around herself. Her heart was heavy, and she could have sworn she heard it cracking. Closing her eyes, she took deep, steadying breaths. She wasn't going to let this affect her. She wasn't going to cry over him. *Then why is there liquid streaming down my face?* She questioned herself as her heart snapped in two.

31

Alijah lay completely still in bed when she heard the door open. She knew that Lawrence was coming to check on her, but she was still in no mood to speak about what happened between Kieran and herself. It had been two days, and she hadn't done much except lay in the bed, getting up only to shower or use the bathroom.

Lawrence would bring her food, and she would eat it. After all, she was upset and sad, but she wasn't about to let that interfere with her health. There was no way she wanted the situation to have that much power over her. Even though, at the moment, it did have her hiding out in her best friend's spare bedroom under the duvet.

Kieran had called her several times. So often wondered if he was even sleeping or just alternating between calling the two phones every hour. As bad as it sounded, it made her feel good to know that he was more than likely losing sleep calling her, worrying about where she was and if they could talk.

Though Alijah could admit that she enjoyed the fact that she was having such an effect on him, she had to admit that both phones ringing nonstop had been annoying. So, after two days of calls that she did not answer and text messages that she did not read, she turned the phones off.

Alijah knew that she could have just blocked his number, but she didn't want to speak to anyone, in all honesty. So, turning them off was the simple solution to that.

However, that was not enough to stop Lawrence, considering she was in his house, and sooner or later, he would demand that she spill what was wrong with her. It was often how their friendship had gone since they met, and one of them got upset about something. They would give the other one space, but at a certain point, they would want them to talk and get whatever was bothering them off of their chest to start helping them heal.

"Lioness, I know that you aren't sleeping, and you can't stay in bed for the rest of your life."

Alijah rolled her eyes. Of course, she couldn't stay in bed for the rest of her life, nor was she planning to with his dramatic ass. She just wanted to stay there for a little bit longer. Then she would get up and get on with her life.

"Fine. I'll let you stay in bed," he told her after a moment of her being silent. "But you're going to have to tell me what happened."

The bed dipped, and Alijah knew that he wouldn't leave until she spoke to him and he got some answers. She didn't want to, didn't need his pushing this time, and she mildly wondered if what she was feeling, her wish to be noncompliant, was the same way Kieran had felt when she volunteered him to go to dinner with his grandfather.

Rolling onto her back, she turned her head to glare at him, but Lawrence simply smiled at her and poked her in the side before becoming serious again.

"I'm ready whenever you are," he told her.

Alijah rolled over onto her side to face him with a sigh before beginning to tell him what happened a couple of nights ago.

The entire time she relayed the events, Lawrence sat and remained quiet. However, she hadn't expected him to say much or speak at all. That was how he often was when someone was upset about something.

When she finished telling him what had taken place, she blinked back the few tears that wanted to spill over, but Alijah would not let them. She had never cried over a man before, and the night that he had accused her of trying to trap him was going to be a time she looked back on as a one-and-done because she didn't plan on doing it again.

Silence hung between the two friends, and she assumed that Lawrence was merely taking in everything she had told him. Honestly, Alijah didn't know where his thoughts would sway. Her being his friend would have his sympathy for her, but she wasn't sure if he could understand Kieran's side as well.

After all, she almost understood he might have dealt with women in past relationships or simple past flings who had tried to trap him for his money. Though she almost understood it, she would not accept it as an excuse.

"Well, Alijah, I don't think anything that I say will be what you want to hear or what you need to hear. This is something you'll have to work out on your own."

"I've already worked it out," she responded, sitting up and placing her back against the headboard. "I sent him my resignation, and that's all there is to it."

Lawrence simply nodded his head at her, standing. "Alright then. Get dressed. We're going to get some lunch, and I'm not taking no for an answer since that's all there is to it," he told her before turning and leaving out of the bedroom.

Alijah sighed as she watched him close the door behind him before getting out of the bed. She would admit that she was starting to feel a bit trapped being in the bedroom for the last couple of days.

Going through the suitcase she had brought with her, she chose a pair of jeans with a V-neck purple sweater. Alijah had showered earlier that morning, so she simply needed to do her hair after getting dressed.

Slipping on her shoes once her hair was done, Alijah made her way down the hallway to the living room. She found

Lawrence sitting on the couch, scrolling over something on his tablet. He looked up when she stopped in front of him.

"That didn't take as long as I thought it would," Lawrence spoke as he closed the cover on his tablet and stood. The two of them grabbed their coats, Lawrence grabbed his keys, and Alijah followed him out of the apartment.

Alijah didn't care where they went to eat, so it didn't bother her when Lawrence didn't ask her where she wanted to go as they pulled out of the parking lot.

Leaning back into her seat, she watched the scenery pass them by as they made their way in the direction of downtown. Alijah leaned back in her seat, listening to the sound of the tires on the road and the soft murmur of music swirling through the car.

Kieran sat staring at his computer screen. He'd lost track of how many times he'd read the resignation Alijah had emailed him, but he was sure that he had it memorized at that point. It wasn't that Kieran hadn't thought that she would send it to him because he knew that she was a woman of her word. It was the fact that he kept continuing to torture himself by reading it.

He had told himself that he would not read it when he got it. Reading it would make it too final. It would cause the ache he had felt in his chest since she walked out of the door to be far more painful. However, when he had been alerted to it in his email inbox, he couldn't help but open it.

Kieran had hoped that somewhere in the email, he would be able to find some emotion from her, as hard as that would be to perceive through words on a screen. He almost wished that she would have gone off on him, said anything to him in the way of their argument.

She had not. Ever the consummate professional, the only thing the email said was that it served as her resignation, and she was deciding to end her employment with his company. It also stated that she would turn in all of the company property she possessed in the following days. The entire cadence of the email was flat.

A knock on his office door grabbed his attention, and Kieran looked up to see Cruz standing there. His friend didn't wait for him to say anything; he just walked in and sat down across from him.

Kieran leaned back in his chair, reaching up to loosen his tie. He had asked Cruz to meet him as soon as he had a chance. That had been yesterday, and here his friend was now waltzing into his office. Kieran knew that he was a busy man, hell, they all were, but to his credit, he was sure he made it sound urgent though he should have known that the other man clearly would move at his own pace.

"What is it, Kieran?" Cruz questioned.

"I need you to locate Alijah for me."

"Why? What did you do?"

"That doesn't matter. I know she's staying with someone. Probably her friend Lawrence. I don't know his last name, but there should be footage of him from my elevator."

Kieran watched Cruz stare at him before nodding his head and getting up. Nothing else was said between them as he watched his friend leave his office.

Turning his attention back to the computer screen, he exited the email before trying to focus back on work. Even though he knew he wouldn't be able to. So, instead, Kieran did something he hadn't done in quite some time and decided to leave work early.

Shutting down his computer, Kieran called Remy's office, letting him know he was leaving for the day. Afterward, he grabbed his briefcase and left out of his office, locking the door behind him. On his way to the elevator, he stopped in front of Alijah's desk and took it in for a moment before continuing.

He had no desire to go back to the condo. It was empty and felt extremely too large without Alijah being there. It was a feeling he hadn't had before she had come into his life.

Before, he had felt as if it was his haven. A place he could go and be away from people and keep people out of his space. Now, he just wanted to walk through the door and see Alijah dancing around the kitchen as she cooked or lying across the couch reading whatever book had caught her attention.

So, instead, he decided to drive around. He'd driven himself to work that morning, not wanting to have Timothy's questioning gaze on him as they drove. Or have the older man ask questions he was not prepared to answer.

Kieran spent several hours driving around until he ended up on a shopping and art strip in front of a building for sale. Pulling over, he parked the car before getting out. It seemed to be a nice building, and its location was optimal. He took his phone out, saving the number. He knew that Paetyn wanted to open a bistro and figured it might be a good place for it. So, he stored the number intending to pass it on to the other man.

The sun had set, and he decided to walk around the strip. It was cold out, but it didn't bother him. The temperature outside was a welcome feeling compared to what he felt from pushing Alijah out of the door, but he would rectify that.

Kieran had never been a man to give up on what he wanted, and he would admit, even out loud to other people, that he desperately wanted Alijah. More than that, he needed her.

About an hour later, he found himself back at his vehicle. Getting in, he started the car and made his way to the condo. Though it was one of the last places he wanted to go, he didn't have anything else he could waste his time on to keep him away. So, he resigned himself to heading back to the empty space.

Kieran was sitting on the bed in the room Alijah had first occupied when he hired her, looking over the paintings she'd done while she had been there. Several had been stored in the closet, others were under the bed, and some were leaning against the wall.

He had known she was talented, and though he had seen a couple of her paintings before, now that he had a chance to sit down, to look at them as much as he wanted to without her taking them from him or shooing while she painted, he knew that she should have been doing far more with her art. Selling her paintings to private collectors or even opening her own gallery.

He was pulled from his musings by the sound of the intercom signaling someone was trying to access his elevator. Kieran planned on ignoring it; however, it became more incessant.

Cursing under his breath, he got up, going down the hall. He brought up the image and saw that Paetyn was standing in his elevator, staring at the camera with a raised brow.

"Let me up, Kieran."

Without saying a word back to the older man, Kieran hit the button to start the elevator, unlocked the door, and made his way to the kitchen to grab two beers. He was sure that Cruz had spoken to Paetyn about the fact that he'd asked the other man to find Alijah. He was confident Paetyn being the person he was; he knew that Kieran had undoubtedly done something.

He had just sat down on the couch when his front door opened. Paetyn made his way over to the living room, and Kieran held one of the beers out to him. His friend took it, occupying one of the armchairs.

"What did you do?"

Kieran opened his bottle and took a drink as he contemplated whether or not to answer that question. However, he knew that it was pointless to try to ignore Paetyn. He had this uncanny way of making you want to talk, and that was saying something considering there weren't many people that could make Kieran do anything.

"I was my usual asshole self," he told him sarcastically.

"It had to be more than that. I've met Alijah, and I know that if anyone can handle your bullshit and put you in your place, it's her. So, you did something other than just your normal asshole routine that caused her to leave."

Kieran took another drink from the bottle. It was shit like that, which made him hate that one of his best friends was so perceptive. He had wondered for years how any of them had dealt with it. Because honestly, it was as if they could never keep anything to themselves when Paetyn decided he wanted an answer. Luckily for them, it wasn't often unless he felt he needed to step in.

So, unlike with Cruz, Kieran told Paetyn what happened. He didn't feel the need to downplay it as he would have with anyone else because he knew that his friend would see right through it.

Once he finished, he expected Paetyn to give him some advice. Some words of wisdom regarding what he'd just told him. It was not what he received.

"You fucking idiot," Paetyn spoke. Kieran rolled his eyes. "Of all the things to say. You brought up another woman. A woman you used to sleep with, one that you know was out to get something from you. You knew bad blood stemmed between the two of them. Why would you even do that?"

"It wasn't as if it was on purpose." Kieran countered.

"It may as well have been. Especially since you entertained any kind of conversation with that crazy-ass woman after you were in a relationship with Alijah."

"Did you just come over to lecture me?"

"Yes," Paetyn told him honestly. "Alijah was good to you. Good for you. There wasn't a thing she wanted from you other than you in this world. Not your money, not your status, and not your sperm."

"I get it, Paetyn. I'm aware that I fucked up, and I'm trying to fix it."

Kieran watched as his friend stood up. "Try harder." With that, the older man turned and left the condo.

Kieran downed the rest of his beer, picking up the untouched one that he had given Paetyn. He recycled his bottle, then placed the other one back into the fridge. Making his way back over to the couch, Kieran lay on his back, staring up at the ceiling. He was contemplating whether or not he actually wanted to go to work tomorrow, and he had never had that thought before.

It was proof that his life was entirely out of sync without Alijah, and it had only been two days.

32

Alijah sat in the bedroom with the window open and a cloth tarp on the floor. She'd been painting for the past hour, and she found it as relaxing as ever. She had been at Lawrence's apartment for a little over a week, and she still hadn't gone and gotten any of her belongings from Kieran's condo. Eventually, she knew that she would have to, but she had no issue putting it off for a bit longer.

Therefore, she'd had to go out and buy new paints, canvases, and an easel, but she hadn't minded. Her art supplies were always things she never had an issue splurging on.

The current piece she was working on was for Gale's nursery. She had told her friend that she would paint a portrait for her whenever she was ready, but this would be a baby shower gift. She had chosen not to focus on one color more than another because she wasn't sure what the sex of the child was, and she didn't want the picture to clash with the nursery colors.

A knock at the door drew her attention, but she didn't turn to look at Lawrence. She tilted her head to let him know that she was listening to whatever he had come to tell her.

"Hey, I'm heading out. I'm having drinks with a potential client." She nodded her head at him. "Also, you have a visitor, and he's fine."

That made Alijah pause in the current brush stroke she was making. She sat down her paintbrush and turned to look at him to find that he had a grin on his face. She raised a brow at him, but he didn't say anything else. Just turned and headed out of the bedroom.

Alijah got up from the stool she'd brought from the kitchen and wrung her wrist for a moment. What if it was Kieran? She still wasn't ready to be face to face with him. If it was him and Lawrence hadn't told her, she would kill him when he got back later.

She took a deep breath, made her way out of the bedroom, and started down the hall as she heard the front door close. When the living room came into view, she furrowed her brow at the man standing there.

"Cruz?" She questioned.

"Alijah," he stated, as she walked over to the couch and sat down. He soon followed.

It didn't take her but a moment to put together why he was there. After all, he worked in security, and she was sure that since she had ignored his calls and text before turning off the phones altogether, Kieran had asked him to look for her.

"Kieran sent you," she stated. It was the only reason he would have been there.

"He asked me to find you. Yes."

Alijah sighed. "Look, I know that you and Kieran have been friends for years, and you don't owe me any loyalty, but you can't tell him where I am."

She watched as Cruz studied her for a moment. "If I were going to tell him where you were, I would have told him five days ago when I found you."

That shocked Alijah. She had only been at Lawrence's house for roughly eight days. So, her curiosity got the best of her.

"When…when did he ask you to look for me."

"Five days ago."

So, after she had turned her phones off, and damn, was Cruz good, but she supposed she shouldn't have expected anything else.

"I'm assuming he asked me instead of Vega because he thought I would find you faster."

Alijah didn't know who Vega was but just assumed he was in the same line of work as Cruz or something close to it.

"Thank you, Cruz, and not that I'm complaining, but why are you keeping it from him?"

Cruz shrugged as he stood. "It wouldn't be as meaningful." This caused Alijah's brow to furrow again as she watched him walk towards the door. "See you later, Alijah."

She watched him leave out of the front door, a little puzzled, before she got up and locked it. She went back into the bedroom and sat down to resume her painting.

As she did so, she thought about the fact that Kieran had someone look for her. She didn't know whether or not she should have been a little flattered or a little irritated. The first because he missed her, the latter because she had walked out and left him for a reason. A reason that he had brought upon himself.

Deciding that she wouldn't dwell on it, she concentrated on what she was doing. She had a lunch date with Gale tomorrow, and though she wouldn't tell her about the painting, she did want to be finished with it. She was sure her friend wanted an answer to whether or not she was going to participate in her auction. Though she wasn't sure, she wanted to. She didn't have anyone she needed to run the idea by now. She just wasn't sure she could handle going out on a date with someone shortly after ending a relationship.

It wasn't as if Gale knew that. The only people that knew the specifics of what happened between her and Kieran were Lawrence and Chayse. She had neglected to tell Erin because her friend was the type to hop on a plane and more than likely physically assault Kieran. While Alijah wasn't against him deserving it, she didn't need her friend trying to fight her battles.

From her conversation with Cruz, she wasn't sure if he knew all of the details but surmised that if he did, he wouldn't be the type to let it be known.

After finishing the initial part of the painting, she set it aside. She needed to let it dry before starting on the next part of it.

Making her way into the kitchen, she went through the refrigerator, deciding that the fruit tray would be a tasty snack.

Alijah made her way back into the living room and turned on the television. She decided that sometime next week, she would look for another job. It wasn't that she didn't have money saved up and could wait a while before she needed to, but she didn't want to have a significant employment gap on her resume.

Flipping through the channels, she stopped when she came across *Waiting to Exhale*. Settling in to get more comfortable on the couch, she ate her fruit while watching the movie. As it was something, she wished she could do.

"Where do you want this to go?"

Kieran looked over to where the young man was standing and pointed to the left. He'd been moving things around the past couple of hours, and it was almost time for him to leave. He had a meeting with Wayne Farley that he wanted nothing more than to cancel, but Kieran knew he couldn't.

After several more minutes, Kieran informed everyone that he was leaving and headed out of the door, getting into his car. He was meeting with Wayne at a lounge for business drinks on the other side of town.

Kieran pulled up half an hour later, getting out and handing his keys to the valet as he received a ticket from the young man.

Walking into the lounge, Kieran surveyed the area before deciding on a space in the back. It would allow him to see who was coming and going and give them privacy to conduct business in peace.

He hadn't been sitting there long when he saw Wayne walk in. It didn't take the other man long before he spotted him and made his way over. Kieran stood, and the two of them shook hands.

"Kieran."

"Wayne." They spoke in the way of greeting before both taking a seat.

At that moment, a waitress came over to take their drink orders. Once she left, Kieran noticed that Wayne's brow slightly rose, but he wasn't going to question it. If he had something to say, he was sure that he would just come out and say it, and Kieran didn't have to wait long for it.

"I'm surprised you came out without, Alijah. I was convinced that she actually ran your company." Wayne stated.

He was making a joke. Kieran knew that; however, it still hit him the wrong way; instead of losing his shit, he merely shrugged before responding.

"I didn't see a reason for her to have to come."

That had not been a lie. When the meeting was scheduled several weeks ago, Kieran had no intentions of bringing Alijah along. It wasn't as if he would need her for what they were going to talk about, and he knew that Wayne was attracted to her, and he didn't see the point in supplying him with the privilege of looking at his woman.

"I see. So, you do give her time off. I was beginning to wonder."

"About?" Kieran countered with a raised brow.

"If she ever got personal time to herself."

It was on the tip of Kieran's tongue to tell the other man that it was none of his concern, but the waitress returned with their drinks. So, he bit his tongue and waited for her to leave.

Once she was gone, he thought about saying it anyway but decided the sooner they got down to business, the sooner he could get back to what he had been previously doing.

"Let's get down to business," he stated, and for the next hour, that was precisely what they did.

Kieran placed the weights down as he finished the last set of his workout. It was well after ten at night, but he was far from tired, and while there was work that he could do, he had decided against it. Instead, he'd gone up to his private gym to work off some steam.

He had finished his meeting with Wayne over two and half hours ago, and instead of going back to what he had been doing, he'd decided to head back to the condo and utilize his gym.

After he and Wayne had finished discussing work, the other man had asked Kieran to tell Alijah at the office tomorrow that he said hello before then telling him never mind and that he would text her.

Kieran had to wonder at that moment if Wayne was testing him for a reaction. If he was trying to see if Kieran would be visibly upset that he wanted to contact Alijah. He had been, but he hadn't let the other man see it. Instead, he merely shrugged and responded that he would tell her for him when he got back to the condo that night, granted she was still awake.

It was petty on his part and, of course, a lie, but Wayne didn't have to know that. The look that briefly passed across the other man's face was almost enough to satisfy Kieran.

So, he returned to the condo and decided to work any tension he was holding from the conversation off.

Making his way onto the elevator and going back to his floor, he opened his front door and headed to the master bathroom. Starting the shower, he stripped out of his clothes, throwing them into the clothes hamper.

Stepping into the shower, Kieran placed his head under the spray of water for several seconds before he began to wash. Thinking back to all the times he had used the same shower with Alijah. It was a thought that he soon shook from his head.

It had been over a week, and he still had not been able to contact her, and Cruz had not given him any word on whether he had been able to find out any information or not, though he hadn't spoken to the other man much since he initially asked him to locate her.

Once he had showered, Kieran stepped out and wrapped a towel around his waist, grabbing another to dry his hair. He made his way back into his bedroom, going over to his dresser to grab a pair of boxers.

When he was dressed, or as dressed as he would get at almost eleven o'clock at night, he sat down at the edge of his bed. Even it had started to feel too large since Alijah left.

Being alone in the condo had allowed him time to think. He knew why he had jumped to such an absurd conclusion when

* * *

he had accused Alijah of trying to trap him and why he had even mentioned Rebecca during the argument.

Simply put, it was because he was a coward.

Kieran had been afraid of what he was starting to feel for her, what he knew he felt for her. It was foreign. Something he had never felt before, and it scared him. He could admit it to himself. Now, he just needed to find Alijah so he could admit it to her.

Lying back on the bed, he looked up at the ceiling. He would give Cruz a few more days, and if his friend could not come up with anything, he would give Vega a call. He was a private investigator that was good at what he did. Though it may take him some time, he always seemed to get results.

Sighing, Kieran closed his eyes, hoping to dream of any time that he had been with Alijah. He would even take a time when they were arguing because even that was better than whatever he was feeling now.

33

Kieran sat at his desk looking over a proposal Trevor's marketing team had submitted to him. He didn't like it. It wasn't up to the same standard that he had been receiving from them, and he figured they had begun to get complacent since they had been doing so well on the past few. Sighing, Kieran replied to the email with one simple word, *No*.

After sending it, he sat back in his chair. He had a few meetings and two conference calls, but he was in no mood for them. If he was honest with himself, he wasn't in the mood to even work, which was a first.

It didn't matter what he did; his mind constantly wandered to Alijah. He was losing sleep at night thinking about that night two weeks ago when she had walked out of the condo and out of his life. True to her word, she had emailed him her resignation the next day.

He had tried calling her, had done it nonstop for an entire week with no results. The work phone he had given her was never on, and every time he called her personal cell, it had sent him straight to voice mail. He had even attempted to find out where her friend Lawrence stayed, knowing that was more than likely where he was, but with no last name to go off, there wasn't much he could do.

Kieran had, however, had his image pulled from the elevator camera from the time he'd brought Alijah to the condo so Cruz could find him. That had been a week and a half ago, and still, he hadn't heard anything. Kieran had even informed the front desk to call him as soon as she walked through the door to retrieve her things. However, every day that he returned, they were still there.

He was losing his mind. He knew he had fucked up, and the chances of Alijah wanting anything to do with him were non-existent, but he didn't care. He wasn't one to give up on something he wanted, and he wanted...needed Alijah. He had known that. He just hadn't known how much until she had walked away from him.

Sleep was eluding him at night, but he was grateful for that. He was sure that her walking out on him would play on repeat like a never-ending nightmare. He had lived it once. Kieran didn't need his subconscious reminding him that he had pushed the most important person in his life away.

His accusations had all but packed her bags for her and thrown her out of the door. He wished he could blame it on someone else, put it on Rebecca and the conversation they'd had, but it was no one's fault but his. Plain and simple.

Kieran mildly wondered if he was scared of the way he felt for her because he wasn't sure if she felt the same way. He wondered if he needed a reason to push her away deep down but concluded that he wouldn't feel so broken without her if that had been the case.

The sound of the elevator dinging pulled him from his thoughts. Without Alijah, he worked with his office door open to see who was coming to see him. He waited, and a minute later, Trevor stepped up, knocking on the open door. Kieran motioned him in, and the younger man walked over and took a seat in front of his desk.

"What is it, Trevor?" Kieran questioned. He wasn't in the mood for what he had scheduled to do today. So, he definitely wasn't in the mood for any impromptu visits.

"I wanted to talk to you about the concept you said no to. Is there a particular reason you don't like it?"

"It isn't up to standard for the product, and it feels as if your team has become complacent in doing your jobs," he told him.

Kieran watched as the younger man seemed to have a conversation with himself. He appeared to be indecisive about something, and Kieran intended to tell him to have his mental breakdown somewhere else. He was going through shit of his own and didn't have the patience, less so than usual, to deal with other people's problems.

"Do you know when Alijah will be back?" Trevor questioned just as Kieran was about to tell him to get out.

That made Kieran stiffen. He hadn't told anyone that Alijah had put in her resignation. Only a few people had asked, and he'd told them that she needed some time off. He knew he was lying to them and himself. He felt if he told people, that if he turned in her resignation, it would make it far too real for him.

"Why?" Kieran inquired.

Trevor sighed. "I'm not supposed to be telling you this because she didn't want any credit for it, but Alijah came up with the last three campaigns my team pitched to you. She even helped me sketch them all out and develop the taglines."

Kieran simply stared at him. He should have guessed as much, but he hadn't. It made sense now why they always seemed to be talking in secret or up to something. She had been helping Trevor with his projects and didn't want Kieran to know because she didn't want credit.

Alijah had not only been doing her duties as his assistant, which she went above and beyond for, but she had also been helping his marketing department come up with the best campaigns he had ever seen from them. She was indeed his better half, and he had fucked it entirely up.

"Just work on it, Trevor. Find a way to fix it. Alijah shouldn't have been doing your work for you. I'm hearing that you're incapable and shouldn't be employed here. So, go and prove me wrong." With that, Kieran turned his attention to his computer, dismissing him.

Once Trevor was gone, Kieran looked at the time before bringing up some documents he needed on his computer for a conference call in ten minutes. He wasn't looking forward to it and honestly would probably do what he had been doing with all of the others. Telling them, he would consider it after looking over their paperwork more thoroughly. Though he knew he might not have been doing it anytime soon.

Kieran hung the phone up and groaned. He had not meant to be on the call for two hours, but the other man had continually asked him questions, and he could admit that he hadn't even listened to half of the call. So, the fact that the man kept asking him questions pertaining to what was discussed had done nothing but irked him, especially when Kieran had told him that he needed to review the information more.

Leaning back in his chair, he seriously contemplated shutting everything down for the day and drowning his mind in the bottom of a bottle of scotch, but he had never been one to turn to liquor for comfort. That was how alcoholics were made, and he could flip and get angry by himself. He didn't need the added influence. He was about to say, " fuck it," when he heard the elevator ding.

Looking at the clock, he saw that he didn't have a meeting scheduled for that exact moment and wondered if it was Trevor coming back or one of his other employees. He didn't want to deal with any of them. He was about to start pushing them off on Remy.

However, the person that came into view at his door was Corey. Kieran furrowed his brow in confusion. He didn't have a meeting scheduled with Corey until next week.

"Hey, Kieran." The older man stated, coming in and taking a seat.

"Hey. Did I forget a meeting we had?" He questioned though he knew he hadn't.

"No," Corey responded, shaking his head. "I was in the neighborhood and thought I would stop in."

Kieran nodded slightly. "How's Gale?"

"She's good. We're expecting, but you already knew that."

Kieran didn't respond, but he realized that Cor just in the neighborhood. It seemed that Alijah had be to Gale. Kieran wasn't sure if his wife had forced him speak to him or if he had come on his own accord.

"You made a mess of things, didn't you." It a question, but Kieran knew it wasn't and, therefore require an answer. "I'm curious why you would thi do that to you. I don't know her the way my wife s

● ● ●

340

Alijah doesn't seem like that type of person. I'm also confused as to why you would be so angry if she had been pregnant since you love her."

Kieran was quiet for a moment. "How do you know I love her?" He didn't deny that he did.

Corey chuckled. "I knew you loved her before you did. Just by the way you looked at her at my yacht party. Your eyes couldn't stay away from her."

Kieran thought back to the yacht party, and he remembered the strange look Corey had given him and how he had seemed to have some conversation with himself. The other man had known that he had loved Alijah then, and as Kieran thought about it, he realized he had fallen in love with her even before that.

"You didn't answer my question."

"You didn't ask one." Kieran countered.

Corey smirked at him. "If she were pregnant, would it have mattered? Would you have left her, loved her any less?"

"No," Kieran answered without hesitation. He wouldn't have loved her less, and now that he thought about the possibility of her having his child, he didn't want that with anyone else.

"Then why the hell are you sitting here instead of going and fighting for your woman?"

"It's not like I haven't been trying. I call, but Alijah doesn't answer. I know she's probably staying with a friend, but I don't know where he lives, and I'm trying to find out. Unless..." Kieran trailed off, staring at Corey.

"She isn't staying with us." The older man stated, knowing what Kieran was getting at. "But, who knows, maybe you'll run into her in the next few hours," Corey told him, taking something from inside his suit jacket pocket and placing it on the desk as he stood. "Enjoy your Valentine's Day, Kieran."

Kieran watched as Corey left his office before looking down at the paper folded in thirds. Picking it up, he unfolded it and saw that it was a flier for Domestic Violence Prevention. Kieran read it over, seeing that it was an auction of sorts. He looked at the date and saw it was for that day.

Checking the time, Kieran saw that it would start at six evening. He had a few hours until then. He wanted nothing

• • •

more than to pack it up for the day, but he had pushed his next meeting back twice now and knew he couldn't afford to do that again. Even if he did, he would still have to wait, but he made a mental note to thank Corey.

Kieran's last meeting had run far longer than he wanted it to. He hadn't gotten out of his office until after five. Now he was stuck in traffic on the highway because there had been a wreck. His hands gripped the steering wheel so tightly that his knuckles were turning white. It seemed that every force in the universe was out to get him and stand in the way, but he wasn't having that shit.

Finally, after almost an hour of being at a standstill, traffic began to move. Pulling his car up at the address that had been on the flier, he got out, tossing his keys to the valet, and taking the ticket the young man handed him. Making his way inside, he followed the signs to the room holding the auction, ignoring the people standing outside talking or heading in other directions to other events presumably.

Walking into the room, he saw Alijah standing on the stage, and she was mesmerizing. She wore a long-sleeve black dress that stopped right above her knees. The dress hugged all of her curves. Her makeup was light, while her lips were a deep wine color matching her shoes. Her hair was in her usual curls, and Kieran wanted nothing more than to take her into his arms.

"Fifteen thousand!" Kieran heard called, and it pulled him out of his thoughts.

"Twenty thousand." Another voice called.

"Twenty-five." A different counter.

"Twenty-five thousand going once, twice..."

"Thirty thousand." Kieran heard a voice, which sounded like Corey's call.

Kieran was not about to let anyone else have Alijah, and he had been so caught up in her that someone else had almost gotten her, and he would have missed his opportunity. It looked like he had something else to thank Corey for.

"One hundred thousand dollars." He called, causing Alijah's eyes to snap to him as all the other people in the audience turned to look at him as he still stood in the back.

"Sold to Mr. Cayman!" The auctioneer stated, banging his gavel.

Kieran watched as Alijah quickly walked off the stage and to the back. He knew she was trying to get away from him, but he was not having it. Kieran followed and saw her go into a room. She was about to close the door when he stopped it with his hand.

"Go away," she told him immediately. He ignored her and stepped inside, locking the door behind him. She would listen to him and if she still wanted nothing to do with him. Then, he was going to work harder to change her mind; because giving her up was not an option.

Alijah sat in the dressing room that Gale had led her to. She still had about two hours until she was due on stage. Gale had scheduled everything down to the minute. So, she had time to get ready while she was there.

At first, Alijah wasn't going to do it. She had no desire to go out on a date with anyone. She was still hurting from her split with Kieran, even if she acted like she wasn't, and was in no way in the mood to be in the company of any man at the moment. For all she cared, they could all disappear for a while. However, it was for charity, and Alijah pulled herself together. She had also told Gale she would help her, and she wouldn't back out.

Deciding that she would do something to her hair first, Alijah got down to work. She wasn't going to do anything significant to it. Merely try to tame her usually wild curls. She had thought about straightening it. Thinking a new look would get her out of her slump but knew it was just wishful thinking. She also honestly didn't have the energy it would take for her to accomplish that.

So instead, she decided to make sure her curls were tight and luscious. She used her shea and argon oil products. When she had gotten her hair the way she wanted it, she went about doing her makeup. She kept it light, deciding that she would play up her lips with a deep wine purple lipstick.

Once Alijah had finished, she unzipped the garment bag and pulled out the black bodycon dress she had purchased just for the event. She hadn't been back to the condo to get the rest of her belongings. She was afraid that she would run into Kieran or wouldn't want to leave. Even worse than that, have a breakdown.

Stepping into the dress, she pulled it up her body, sliding her arms in the sleeves. She smoothed it down before grabbing the wine-colored pumps she would wear with it. Pulling her necklace from inside the dress, she lay it flat against her chest.

She sat back down on the couch and waited for someone to come and tell her when it would be her turn. She picked up her phone and began to scroll through her text messages. She had forty-two unread ones from Kieran. While she wasn't going to open them, for some reason, she couldn't delete them; he had continually called her as well. She knew he was probably trying to apologize, but she didn't want to hear it. She was sure he felt as if he hadn't done anything wrong. It was the way he felt about just about everything else.

There was a knock on the door, and Alijah answered it. She had expected to find someone helping with the event on the other side, but instead, she found Corey. He smiled at her as she stepped aside to let him in.

"Well, don't you look beautiful," he complimented.

She gave him a small smile. "Thank you."

"Are you nervous?" He questioned. Alijah nodded.

She felt no reason to lie to him. She was indeed nervous. While Alijah was confident in herself, this was the first time she would willingly be putting herself on display for the satisfaction of men. They would, for the most part, be buying her body. While each woman had filled out a bio sheet, she knew the men wouldn't be listening to that. They would only be bidding according to the way the women looked.

"I've never done anything like this before," she told him.

"I see. I'll be in the first row, right in the middle, where you'll be standing on the stage. Just keep your eyes on me, and everything will be fine," he told her.

"Thank you, Corey."

"You're welcome," he responded, heading towards the door. "Someone will be by to get you in a few minutes. I think there's one person left in front of you, and then it'll be your turn. Remember, when you get out there, eyes on me."

Alijah nodded before watching him leave and closing the door after himself. She sat back down on the couch and took in deep breaths. As Corey had said, a few minutes later, there was a knock at her door.

She found a smiling young girl there who asked her to follow her before leading her to where she would wait. She could see a little out into the crowd from that position, but not much. However, she could hear everything. The auctioneer had just finished reading the bio of the woman on stage and was opening for bids. They started at one thousand, and it got up to twenty thousand before the auctioneer declared her sold. Alijah could only hope she did that well.

Taking a deep breath, Alijah calmed her nerves as she heard her name announced. Walking onto the stage, she listened as he began to read her biography. Getting to the middle of the stage, her attention immediately turned to Corey. He smiled at her, and it helped her relax a bit. She waited for the auctioneer to finish reading her biography and interests.

"Alright. Let's start the bidding at one thousand dollars."

"Five thousand dollars!" She heard someone immediately call.

"Five thousand, do I hear six?"

"Six." A voice called.

"Six, do I hear seven?"

"Ten thousand." The first voice called again.

"Fifteen thousand." Another called.

"Twenty thousand." Some else called.

"Twenty-five thousand." The first voice called again.

"Twenty-five thousand going once, twice...."

"Thirty thousand." Alijah was surprised by that bid because it had come from Corey. She raised an eyebrow at him.

"One hundred thousand dollars."

Alijah's head snapped in the direction of the voice. She would know it anywhere. Sure enough, she found Kieran staring at her. Her heart began to beat fast, and she took deep breaths to calm herself.

"Sold to Mr. Cayman!" Auctioneer yelled, banging his gavel, and Alijah wanted to kick him in the neck with her heel.

Instead, she turned and exited the stage, quickly heading down the hall and back to the room she had been in. She'd just made it inside and was closing the door when it was stopped. She looked up and saw Kieran there.

"Go away," she told him immediately. He ignored her and stepped inside, locking the door behind him.

Alijah backed away from him. She had to put some distance between them. She needed space. A continent may have been enough space, but she knew she couldn't *I Dream of Genie* herself somewhere else, though she was tempted to try for the hell of it.

This man had hurt her, and here he was now, with the audacity to buy her. She was offended. He had accused her of being with him for his money, and now he was throwing it at her as if she was a possession he could simply obtain, though it was for charity.

"You need to leave, Kieran, and retract your bid."

"I'm not going to do that," he told her simply. Alijah's jaw clenched, and she wanted to slap the shit out of him for standing there so casually as if he hadn't taken a sledgehammer to her heart. "We need to talk."

"We have nothing to talk about," Alijah stated.

"We do."

"No, you would rather make assumptions than talk. So, you can turn around and-"

"I love you," he stated, cutting her off. *Say what?* "I am in love with you, Alijah Douglas."

Shaking her head, Alijah took a step back, and he stepped toward her. He took another step, and she countered again, still shaking her head.

"I was wrong, baby. So wrong. I should have never accused you. I know that you would never do that to me. I wish I could make excuses and blame it on anybody else, but it was me. It was my insecurities. I'm not used to feeling this way. I've never loved any woman until I loved you, and it all felt so surreal that somewhere in me, I knew there had to be something wrong. Maybe I needed there to be because I didn't want to be hurt. I didn't want you to wake up one morning and realize that you could do better."

He'd continued toward her, and Alijah backed up until she was out of space and her back came into contact with the wall. She looked up at him as he cupped her cheek.

"You mean the world to me. I would give up everything for you if you asked me to. I would lay my life on the line if it meant you were happy. I know I fucked up, and I regret letting you walk out of that door. I regret not stopping you at the elevator, but most of all, I regret making such an idiotic assumption."

Alijah felt tears welling in her eyes as she looked into his soft hazel ones. She had never seen them in such a state before. Her eyes then widened in shock as he fell to her feet on his knees, his arms wrapping around her waist and his head on her stomach.

"I was foolish to think you would try to trap me. The truth is, you wouldn't have to. I've been trapped since the day you stepped foot into my office, and it was one I willingly walked into. Everything I am belongs to you. You own every piece of me. Mind, body, and soul. I can't live without you, Alijah, and I damn sure don't plan on doing it."

His arms tightened around her as Alijah allowed her tears to begin to fall silently.

"Come home, Alijah."

At that, she gasped. In the time that she had been with Kieran, he had never once called it home; she hadn't either, though, for that matter.

She placed her hand on his head and stroked his hair. This man, who was so strong, so intimidating to others, was bearing his soul as he essentially bowed before her. He looked up at her, and she saw it. Saw the vulnerability in his eyes. At that moment, she knew. This man that sent others scattering with a look had given his entire being over to her; he had given her complete control. She could break him if she wanted, but Alijah loved this man, and breaking him, would shatter her.

Cupping her hands on each side of his face, she leaned down and kissed his lips. It was a soft kiss, but it was all it took to lift the heaviness from her heart as her tears continued to fall. Their lips still connected, she felt him rise to his feet. She pulled away and watched as his eyes went to the necklace he'd bought her for Christmas. She had put it on that day and never taken it off. He reached up and touched it, and Alijah placed her hand over his.

"I love you," she told him as he reached up with his other hand to caress her cheek, to wipe her tears. She leaned into it. "Take me home."

The ride home was silent except for the sound of the tires on the road. The entire way Kieran held her hand, he would bring it to his lips and kiss it. She would feel him staring at her at each stoplight, and Alijah didn't know why.

When they finally made it, he came around and opened her door for her. Picking her up when she got out of the car, they made their way onto the elevator and up to their condo. Where he stared at her the entire time, she unlocked the door for him, and he carried her in, closing the door with his foot.

"Welcome home, baby." He leaned down, whispering against her lips.

Alijah gave him a soft peck as she tightened her arms around his neck slightly before burying her face in his chest. It didn't take a Rocket Scientist to know that he was taking her to his...their bedroom when he began to walk. She felt herself being sat on the bed and removed her arms from around his neck.

She watched as he took both of her shoes off. He put them to the side before taking off her dress. Alijah lifted to help him, and he removed it from her, throwing it onto the floor and leaving her in her pink boy shorts and bra. The latter of which he unhooked and removed.

Alijah watched as he took off his clothes until he was down to only his boxers before going over to his dresser and pulling out one of his V-neck t-shirts. Walking back over, he dressed her in it before going to his side of the bed. He pulled her to him as he lay down.

* * *

"Tonight, I just need to hold you," he informed her, wrapping his arms around her waist.

She shifted so that she was comfortable. It was only a few minutes before she could feel Kieran staring at her again. Looking up, sure enough, those hazel eyes were locked onto her. She pulled back from him slightly, not missing that he was reluctant to release his hold.

"Why do you keep staring at me?"

"Because I'm trying to figure out how I could have been so stupid as to almost lose my entire world because I don't plan on making that mistake again; because I can't seem to figure out what good thing I ever did in my life, to have been blessed with you. Because you're so fucking beautiful," he told her, kissing her lips. "Because I'm amazed at how you make me feel, by the control you have over me, and I don't want it any other way."

Alijah leaned in and kissed him again as his sweet words sank into her heart. He wasn't alone, though. She knew he held some control over her too.

Epilogue

Twelve days later

"Baby, where are we?" Alijah questioned as they pulled up to a beautiful building in the art district. "I thought we were going to go see an art exhibit," she stated, turning to look at him.

"We are, gorgeous," he responded as he got out of the car.

Alijah tracked him as he walked around to her side of the car. It was eight o'clock on a Tuesday night, so the sidewalks weren't crowded with people, and parking was easy.

When he opened her door, Alijah stepped out, and he took her hand in his leading her to the building. She leaned back, looking up at it. It seemed to be two stories. Kieran pulling her, gained her attention.

"Kieran, there isn't an art exhibit here. It's dark," she told him. He didn't respond. "Babe, we...I don't think we can-"

Alijah was cut off by the lights coming on. She gasped, covering her mouth with her free hand. The space was beautiful, but that wasn't what had her attention. There, on the walls of the entryway, were her paintings. She let go of Kieran's hand and walked a few steps ahead of him. She was stunned.

"Since you wouldn't take the head of marketing position at the office, I figured this would be better," he told her, walking up behind her, wrapping his arms around her waist.

"I wasn't about to take Felix's job and let you demote him," she told him, still looking around.

"You're far better than he is, and I wasn't going to demote him...I was going to fire him."

Alijah heard what he'd said, but she was too engulfed in her surroundings to chastise him. This was absolutely amazing. She felt him lean down and kiss her neck before his lips touched her ear.

"Go look around."

When he let her go, Alijah began to walk along the first floor. There was a beautiful white desk that sat right in the line of sight of the front door. Lining the walls around the entrance were her paintings. As she made her way further into the building, she walked around to the left and then to the right, finding even more of her art. Some of which she knew that she had left at Lawrence's house when she moved out.

Making her way to the stairs, she took them to the second floor as Kieran followed her. There were three main walls with paintings: the one behind her and the two on her left and right. There was a half wall in front of her with paintings on it as well. She walked around it to find paintings on the other side and another half wall, also housing paintings.

The fourth side of the second floor was an expanse of windows with a single four-foot-wide wall directly in the middle, and she could see out and look at the building across the street. Turning to the backside of the final half wall, she had expected to see more of her paintings but instead found empty canvases. She figured they had used all of her paintings and needed placeholders so she would get the full effect.

She smiled. This was the sweetest thing anyone had ever done for her. Kieran had put her work on display in her very own gallery. Alijah was already trying to figure out what to paint and put in the empty spaces when the lights went out.

Again, her hand shot to her mouth, and her eyes began to tear up as she looked at the seven canvases, each housing a letter painted in calligraphy with glow in the dark paint. *Marry Me.*

Alijah turned around to find Kieran leaning against the wall between the windows. One foot propped against it as he held an open ring box in his hand. It was one hundred percent

Kieran, and she wasn't the least bit upset that he wasn't on one knee.

"You forgot the question mark," she told him, wiping one of her tears.

Kieran smirked, eliminating the distance between them. "That's because it isn't a question, baby," he informed her, taking the ring from the box and slipping it on her finger. "You're going to be my wife. I'm not stupid enough to let you leave me again. And asking gives you the option of turning me down, and I can't have that," he told her as she looked at the ring.

It was beautiful and so distinctly Kieran. There was a large diamond in the middle surrounded by two layers of smaller diamonds, and their clarity was almost unbelievable. She knew he could have bought a small island for what he probably paid for it.

"Before you ask how much it cost," he started as if reading her thoughts. "I paid four hundred thousand for it."

Alijah's eyes widened. So, he could have bought a few small islands. "Why would you spend that much on a ring, and why would you tell me that?! You know how I feel about you spending astronomical amounts of money on me."

"You're cute," he told her. "Get used to it. I told you because you would have seen it eventually when you checked the accounts," he finished with a shrug.

"Speaking of accounts. Gale still needs you to send her your check from the auction."

"Then write her one," he told her.

Alijah sighed, rolling her eyes. The day after they had made up, he took her to every bank he had accounts at and added her to each one, personal and business. She had told him he was crazy, but he'd just said no, he was in love. However, she wasn't comfortable doing anything with them.

"Kieran-" He cut her off, pulling her to him and kissing her. "I love you," she spoke against his lips.

"I love you too...but I'm about to fuck you like I hate you." He growled, and Alijah watched as his eyes darkened with want.

Kieran slipped his hand down the front of Alijah's skirt into her panties. He slowly began to play with her pussy. Kieran had told her they were going to an exhibit because he knew she would wear something that would give him easy access. He had every intention of fucking her after giving her, her ring.

Wrapping one of his hands around her neck, he began to dominate her lips. As they kissed, he felt her start to move against his fingers. She was soaking wet for him. He wanted to taste her. He wanted to have her writhing in pleasure under him, and he had every intention of getting those things, but right now, he wanted to fuck her.

Pulling his hand from her skirt and releasing her neck, he pulled the bottom of her skirt up over her waist before tearing her panties. He stuffed the torn fabric into his back pocket before undoing and unzipping his pants. He pulled his dick free of the slit in his boxers, pushing her back into the wall he had been leaning against.

Picking her up with one arm, he positioned himself at her entrance, sliding into her. He listened to her moan out as he groaned. He would never get tired of being inside of her.

He began to move as he stared into her eyes. As they began to flutter closed, he thrust hard into her, taking her chin between his hand.

"You know better, Alijah. Keep your eyes on, Daddy," he demanded, punctuating the command with another hard thrust.

"Fuck, Kieran!" She moaned out loudly, her arms tightening around his neck.

Kieran pounded into her as she moaned unabashedly. Her pussy was warm as it squeezed him. He could feel her clenching around him and knew she was about to cum.

"Cum for me, baby. Show me how much you like this dick and cum all over it," he commanded as he sped up his thrust.

"Yes, yes! Shit! I'm cumming! I'm cumming!" She announced.

She didn't need to tell him. Kieran could feel her clench around him. Her pussy held him like vice grips as she shook in his arms. He watched as pleasure consumed her. Fuck it, he thought, and he pulled from her.

Lifting her higher, he put her legs over his shoulder and dove tongue first into her pussy. She let out a surprised squeak as he felt her hands lace in his hair. Kieran fucked her with his tongue. Wiggling it inside of her as she began to rock against it. He knew it wouldn't be long before her second release hit her. It was never hard to pull it from her.

After a few more minutes of eating her pussy, he felt her legs begin to shake. Just as her orgasm hit her, he latched onto her clit and sucked hard.

"Damn, baby!" She exclaimed. "Your tongue game is the best," she stated through a moan as he licked her slit one more time before letting her down.

"My dick game's even better," he told her. "But you already know that." He smirked. "Turn around and bend over."

He watched as she did what he said. Kieran stroked himself for a few seconds as he took her in. After all, this was one of his favorite views. Lining himself up, he slid back into her, not stopping until he was balls deep, making them both moan out.

"Roses or Tulips?" He questioned.

"What?" She responded in a fog.

"Which one do you want in the morning?"

"Why would you be getting me flowers in the morning?"

He leaned over and placed his lips to her ear. "Because I'm about to commit a crime...premeditated. I'm about to murder this pussy."

With that, his hands went to her hips, and he pulled almost entirely out before snapping them forward and slamming into her.

"Fuck!" She yelled.

"Oh, we're going to fuck alright, baby. Brace yourself."

Kieran began to hammer into her. The sound of her ass clapping as he fucked her spurred him on. Releasing one of her hips, he smacked her ass, earning a moan from her.

"Whose pussy is this?"

"Mm... it's yours."

"I can't hear you. Who owns this fucking pussy?"

"You do, Daddy. It's your pussy," she told him. "It's your fucking pussy."

Kieran angled his hips and began to hit that spot deep inside of her. He was going to push them both over the edge so they could continue round two back at home.

"Right there, baby. Don't stop. Please don't stop," she begged, and it was music to his ears.

Kieran laid his chest on her back, and he reached around and rubbed her clit as he continued to fuck her. She began to clench around him, and he felt his balls tighten.

"Yes, yes, yes!" She chanted.

Kieran released her other hip and wrapped that hand around her throat, squeezing with just enough pressure. The action pushed her over the edge, causing her pussy muscles to clamp down on his dick.

"Shit, Daddy!"

A few seconds later, he began to shoot ropes of cum into her.

"Fuck, baby!"

After his last spurt of cum, Kieran remained inside her for a moment. When he pulled out of her, they both moaned. He tucked himself away before helping her fix her skirt. He took her hand and led her back down the stairs and to the bathroom. He waited for her to clean herself up, leaning against the wall. She fell into his side when she came out, wrapping her arms around him.

"Thank you for this. It's amazing," she told him.

After finding the building a few weeks back when he'd been driving around, he'd decided that he wouldn't give it to Paetyn. Instead, he would turn it into a gallery for Alijah and began working on it immediately. Even before he knew where she was, and they'd made up.

He leaned down and kissed her forehead. "You're welcome," he told her. "Now, let's get home so I can fuck you until you can't walk...or talk."

He didn't wait for her to reply. He led her to the front door, turning off the downstairs lights. He locked up and helped her into the car before getting in and heading home, where he planned on fucking her the entire night, causing both of them to lose all...*Control.*

Made in United States
North Haven, CT
28 September 2023